The Dragon Problem

The Paranormals of Ahl Book 1

ML Conklin

THE DRAGON PROBLEM (The Paranormals of Ahl Book 1)

For information contact: MLConklin@MLConklin.com

Sign up for the newsletter for updates and information on new releases: https://www.mlconklin.com

Book and Cover design by Getcovers.com

ISBN E-book: 979-8-9900731-0-4

ISBN Paperback: 979-8-9900731-1-1

First Edition: June 2024

A Note From The Author

Hey! Thank you for choosing this book. Writing the first book of the Paranormals of Ahl series has been a pleasure, and I hope you enjoy it. There are some things you should know about this book:

1. There's a heavy reference to past child abuse.

2. There's violence throughout the book.

3. There is some profanity.

4. There's a slow-burn (sort of) romantic theme between a dragon shifter and a mage, though it's not the focus.

5. The romance has an age gap (I know some people don't like that).

Chapter 1

I leaned forward and studied the crack. There was a distinct point of impact. Delicate lines spread out from the center, forming intricate patterns. At least it only affected the ward responsible for air filtration and weather. I turned to my brother. "What happened here?"

Mat stood with his back to me and scanned the dense forest, his golden, shoulder-length hair blowing in the wind. "Dragon. An Enforcer team called it in early this morning."

"When were the wards last recharged?"

"Two weeks ago."

Creating and maintaining the outer wards required a lot of different magic types. "Was it regular maintenance?"

"No, population increase. Regular maintenance is not required for another year."

"Huh." I leaned closer. Every magical pocket had its own thick layers of wards, allowing the pocket to grow with the population. They also kept the air clean and recycled waste into rich soil, among other things. If the population increased, more magic needed to be poured into them to maintain it all. They would fail if they weren't maintained, and the pocket realm would collapse. Boosting them required similar magic to the spells that created the barriers. Which meant magic from several different species worked to maintain them. "Has this happened in any pocket other than Allure?"

"Not that's been reported. I sent people out to check, but they found nothing," Mat's gravelly voice was laced with concern.

Allure was a gigantic pocket. If the ward came down, a couple of million supernaturals would die. The realization terrified me. I stepped back. "At least the ward protecting against forest fires is intact. So are the ones that keep us hidden and detect magic to allow access. Has there been a change in the air?"

"No. It is minimal damage. The fact that someone attempted to breach it is concerning."

"Yeah." I glanced at Mat to make sure he had his back turned and moved a couple of steps closer to the ward. Fixing the wards required a specific type of magic. There was a risk of me trying to fix them. My magic was the right kind, or at least one of them was the right kind. Unlike everyone else, the magic inside of me didn't blend like they were supposed to, so I had three smaller pools instead of a single large one.

The smallest was healing magic, which allowed me to heal myself and others. It wouldn't help the wards. The medium-sized pool was my inherent magic. It was the magic I was born with. I could tune it to any spell, but I wasn't sure it would help fix the crack. Then, there was the large pool of ruling magic. The ruling magic was supposed to coax others to follow me and allow me to rule over all paranormals, among other things. I couldn't always control it since it didn't mix with my other two magic pools. It kind of had a mind of its own. I didn't know if I could coax it to fix the crack in the wall, but I had to try. I extended my shaky hand and accessed the three magic wells inside me. Before I lost my nerve, I slapped my hand onto the crack.

Magic surged from my hand, gushing forth, and flowed across the ward, coating it in a white gloss. It reversed so fast I couldn't react. My spine snapped straight. My nose filled with the stench of burned wires as electricity coursed through my body. The ward grabbed my core and took greedy slurps from the ruling magic I kept wrapped around me and concealed. Pain surged from my chest, and I screamed. Gritting my teeth, I tried to disconnect as it was ripped from my body. Something salty filled my mouth. Blood, I realized. The wall kept pulling. I kept yanking back. Pain exploded in my head. Unsure what else to do, I unwrapped the three magics from their tight coil within me and let the wall take it.

The wall yanked me forward. I dug in my heels. Suddenly, the healing magic slammed back into me, completely restored. My inherent mage magic was next. I wheezed at the impact. The ward continued to take gulps of the ruling magic.

My thoughts swung between '*This wouldn't have been a problem if all the magics had mixed like they were supposed to*' and, '*If I were as powerful as I needed to be, I could get out of this.*' I gathered my strength and yanked my hand back, using my body weight to try and help. No matter how much I convulsed and jerked, I couldn't manage to break free. I screamed in rage once I realized it wasn't going to work.

My stupid ruling magic was being drained, and there was nothing I could do to stop it. Spots started dancing in front of my eyes. I hoped I wouldn't die when the magic emptied. With a loud *boom*, the wall released its grip, and I slumped to the ground.

Vision blurry, I swiped my sleeve across my eyes, then rested my head in my hands. I ran some healing magic through myself, and the pain in my head eased. Magic took energy, and using that much magic should have put me in a coma. I was tired but okay, so I tried to sit up. Fear shot down my spine when I realized I couldn't move, causing me to lash out.

"Jenella, it's me." Mat's gravelly voice was close to my ear.

I cracked my eyes open and blinked a couple of times. Mat's face came into view, his golden eyes full of concern.

"I'm okay." With some effort, I pushed his hands off my shoulders and stumbled to my feet, only swaying a little. I braced against a pine tree and checked myself over. I wrapped the two remaining pools of magic around me, concealing them. Turning to the ward, I huffed a sigh of relief. "Ha! It worked."

Mat's jaw clenched as he handed me a handkerchief. "It was a stupid thing to do. It could have killed you."

I wiped my nose and chin. "What would happen to all the paranormals in Allure if the ward failed?"

"A catastrophe on a level we have not seen. Same as what will happen to the Coalition if you die."

I flinched. Mat was right, but I still hated it. "It was a necessary risk," I said nonchalantly, hoping to avoid one of his safety lectures. "Do we know which dragon caused the crack?"

"According to the local shifter pack, a turquoise dragon hit the wall."

"That's not normal." Dragons were big and powerful enough to cause damage, but it didn't make sense that one would attack the wards. They loved the freedom of living in the pockets, where they could be themselves, and never caused much trouble. Their queen was old, fair, and wise. She kept the dragons in line. "Do you think he was being chased and miscalculated? Or was it on purpose?"

"I don't know."

A loud *thwap, thwap, thwap* filled the air, and the forest went quiet. I shielded my eyes from the sun and scanned the sky. Bigger than a house and black as night, the dragon circled the clearing three times before landing on the other side. The heir to the dragon throne examined the ward before stretching his neck out and blowing a massive plume of smoke in our direction——likely aiming for me.

I had a love-hate relationship with him. He served as my personal guard from the time I was about eleven until he met his mate when I was twenty-two. He was rude, arrogant, and stoic. On top of that, he always tried to read my thoughts. Luckily, the ruling magic put the beat down on him every time I felt him intrude. At least it did when my ruling magic wasn't drained. I closed my eyes. This was going to suck.

Mat stepped in front of me. "Bastien. It's nice of you to show up."

Bastien melted from a dragon into a man. His black eyes flicked to me before settling on Mat. "Regent. I have other business to attend to, so I can't linger. Show me what you found."

Mat's jaw clenched. "You are too late. My sister already repaired the damage."

"Is that so? Then you are wasting my time."

I rolled my eyes. "It's not a waste of your time, and you know it."

Mat ignored me. "There was a crack in the wards, and witnesses say a dragon was responsible. The question is, why?"

Bastien rubbed his chin. "Our young ones are not infallible and often make mistakes when learning to fly. It could have been a simple mistake. Did you get a description of this mystery dragon?"

"Witnesses said it was a full-grown turquoise dragon," Mat answered.

"I see." Bastien moved to the ward and focused on the exact spot I'd repaired. "Interesting. I will investigate the matter, but I assure you, no dragon would do this intentionally."

"No one said they would, Bas," I said. "But you must admit, it's odd that a dragon just so happened to run into the ward in such a sparsely populated area. It's miles away from the gates and the dragon training grounds. It could have been catastrophic."

Bastien ran a hand through his midnight hair. "I was unaware you could think critically, princess. I happen to agree. It is unusual."

"It is also a serious crime––of which we will not hesitate to prosecute. The lives of the millions of supernaturals in Allure were put in danger.

If the Dragon Queen chooses to be uncooperative, we will find the one responsible," Mat warned.

My eyes grew wide. It was a serious threat. The different paranormal species each had their own leadership system and laws. They were allowed to govern themselves if they didn't break coalition laws or infringe on other types of paranormals. If they did, the crown that ruled over all paranormals settled the dispute. The crown being me. Or Mat, since he was my guardian and regent. I still had a few years to get my magic to mix and become the most powerful paranormal in the world before I took over the throne.

"I assure you dragons would not risk the lives of the capital's population. Nor would we risk the crown getting involved in our affairs," Bastien growled.

Mat didn't get a chance to respond because the ground began to shake. I swung back to the wall, noting that it was still intact.

Bastien's head snapped toward the thick pine trees, and he took off down a game trail.

Mat clutched my arm. "If there is danger, I am getting you out of here. No arguments."

I yanked my arm free. "Whatever. Let's go." I ran after Bastien.

We made our way down a path that ended in a small clearing with a massive mound in the center. Bastien stood a few feet from it, a stern expression on his face.

"What is it?" I whispered. Mat joined Bastien, but I stayed in the tree line. The amount of magic coming from the mound made my already tired head fuzzy. I rubbed my arms, feeling vulnerable without my ruling magic. I didn't have much control over it, but it always protected me.

The ground shook so hard I had to sit to keep from falling. Mat somehow stayed on his feet, his two katanas in his hands, glowing blue from the magic flowing through them. The shaking grew stronger, and the earth in the meadow bucked. A pained howl pierced the air, and the mound exploded, a giant plume of dirt flying in every direction. Mat flew twenty feet, hit a tree, and landed on the ground limp. Bastien switched to his dragon form and bolted into the sky. Heart racing, I darted toward Mat, ignoring the loud battle cry from something in the crater left by the mound exploding.

"Mat!" The thought of losing my brother was unbearable. He raised me and was the only family I had left. I reached the area where I thought he had landed, scrambling to find anything that would point me in his direction. Another pained battle cry came from the mound. I rubbed my ears and added a projection spell to my inherent magic. "Mat!"

I heard coughing and sprinted toward the sound. Mat stumbled out of the forest, caked in dirt, with a big gash across his cheek. He still had his katanas in his hands. His glowing eyes focused on me. "Leave, Jenella!"

The command spiked my adrenaline, and I turned back to the tree line to follow it for once but froze when a filthy, tattered figure emerged in front of me. The man shook like a dog, causing wet dirt to scatter in every direction.

I threw up my arms to shield my face and screamed. It wasn't my finest moment.

Mat didn't hesitate. He charged toward the man, blades blazing, and swung. The man waved his hand, sending Mat tumbling across the clearing.

"No!" I yelled and stumbled toward my brother on shaky legs. Halfway there, I got yanked backward so hard that pain shot through my neck.

"How dare you send me to sleep and then wake me at your discretion!" The man shook me like a rag doll. My nearly healed head pounded again. The man set me down and yanked me toward the crater. "You see that? Does that look like an honorable resting place? How dare you!"

The guy was insane. I yanked my arm free and spun, slapping him across his face. I slapped him again for good measure. "You attacked my brother, you asshole! I am not going to stand here and take this abuse. You sit down until you're calm enough to have a conversation."

I didn't wait for his response but rushed toward Mat, who sat by a tree shaking his head. I kneeled. "Are you okay, Mat?"

"I told you to leave."

"You slapped me," a deep, calm voice came from behind me, sending a shiver up my spine.

"You deserved it," I answered without turning around.

Mat stumbled to his feet and stepped between the man and me. "Who are you?"

I peeked around Mat to examine the stranger. His long, tangled black hair was strung across his face. A tattered tunic and tan pants hung from a tall, lanky frame. His elegant feet were bare. Even tattered, the man still radiated confidence and strong magic. He ignored Mat, examining me while I studied him.

Bastien landed near the crater and melted into his human form. Naked, he strode across the clearing to the new guy and bowed. "Cousin. Welcome back. Mother will be most pleased."

None of us were fazed by the nudity. The whole idea of the pockets was to allow paranormals to be themselves. There were a lot of different species that shifted, so it wasn't unusual to see naked people walking around. There were a few dragons that could glamour clothes, but they rarely bothered inside the pockets because no one cared.

Bastien and the mystery man silently stared at each other. I realized they were having a conversation with their minds. I stepped out from behind Mat and stumbled a few steps closer, ready to pepper the guy with questions.

Without warning, the man morphed into a dragon twice the size of Bastien, his green and black scales glimmering in the sun. Faster than a snake, he extended a giant talon and grabbed me.

My squeal was muffled as his massive talon cocooned me. My stomach flipped as he launched us into the air. I wiggled, trying to get away. I lashed out with my inherent magic, but I knew it wouldn't work against a dragon.

Draining the pool of ruling magic was something I regretted. I was sure it would have protected me from the guy if it wasn't empty. It would have put this guy in his place whether I wanted it to or not. I should have run when Mat told me to. But I didn't, so I was screwed until I could get some food and sleep to replenish both my magic and energy.

The talon released me, and I hit the ground hard, rolled a few feet, and groaned. "What the hell?" I stumbled to my feet. Out of the corner of my eye, I saw a pink dragon launch into the air from the roof of a nearby building. Relief washed over me when I realized we were on top of Dragon Headquarters in downtown Allure. The queen would never let this giant dragon hurt me.

The now naked man stood a few feet away, his tangled hair swept back, his grass-green eyes narrowed. "You are not Anitta."

I shook with rage when my mother's name registered. "Don't you dare talk about my deceased mother! Who the hell do you think you are?"

His eyes crinkled at the corners. "My apologies."

I stomped toward him. "You threw the Regent of Ahl into a tree and attacked the crown princess. If you don't explain yourself, you'll be in a world of hurt."

The man tilted his head. "Regent, did you say?"

My eyebrows drew together. "Yes. The Regent to the throne of Ahl."

"Ah. So, Anitta is gone. And you are her heir?"

I clenched my fists. "That's what I just said. Who the hell are you?"

He gazed at the black dragon darting toward us, sadness in his eyes. "I am one of the lost. A First that had no desire to rule but was punished because he could."

"You're a First?" I was astonished. There were originally twelve Firsts. They were representatives from other realms sent to guide the inhabitants of this planet through a magical revolution thousands of years ago. A magical revolution that never happened because humans weren't capable of wielding the abundant magic that the planet provided. Legend says the portals crashed right after they came through, so they could never return to their original realms. Lucky for us, the Firsts eventually lost their patience and decided to create one or two magical species each. They were considered our founding mothers and fathers.

A few thousand years later, bored and homesick, they passed their core magic along to their heirs and, one by one, went to sleep. The only First that didn't go to sleep lived in the human world and rarely involved himself with supernaturals. I thought about the implications of a First waking up. For example, they were more powerful than most of us and could take over the coalition with a simple wave of a hand. A grin spread across my face. "You want to take over the coalition?"

His eyebrows drew together. "No. Though I worry why you seem so excited at the thought."

Bastien circled the roof we stood on twice before landing in his human form. "Did I not just tell you that you cannot manhandle the crown princess?"

The guy smirked. "You did. However, I chose not to listen, and she didn't even try to flash away."

I almost face-palmed. If I'd thought about it, I could have used my inherent magic to flash back to Mat anytime. I felt like an idiot because it didn't even cross my mind. "Wait. You're Bastien's cousin? What were you doing in the dirt?"

The man's lips twitched. "You're an inquisitive little thing, aren't you?"

"I wouldn't need to be so inquisitive if you answered a question or two. Most likely." He sashayed toward me, so close I could see the thin scar that ran from the corner of his eye to his earlobe. My eyebrows drew together. "You have a scar?" It was unusual for dragons to have scars. They healed too fast.

His eyes danced with humor. "Yes, I am Bastien's cousin. I was forced into a deep sleep against my will and buried. I have more than one scar."

"Okay...um...I'm Jenella, and you are?"

He leaned forward, his face inches from mine. "Dirty."

My face flushed, my mouth opening and closing, trying to form a response.

Bastien laid a hand on his shoulder. "That is not a woman you want to mess with, cousin. Jenella, you can wait for us in my office."

I dragged my eyes from the First. "But he's a First."

"Drop it, Jenella. Come cousin, we will get you cleaned up."

The man snatched my hand and kissed it before I could yank it back. "We shall discuss the slapping later."

Chapter 2

I watched them go, then limped to Bastien's office a few floors below the roof. Having a First active in the coalition could bring about many changes. My grandmother was the most powerful and, therefore, the leader of the Firsts and later formed the coalition that brought all paranormals together. She became the first queen of Ahl, bonded with another First, a healer, and had three children. When two of them died, she was so grief-stricken she handed her core power—the ruling magic—to my mother and went to sleep.

During my mother's reign, the other Firsts followed my grandmother to sleep, some handing their power to their heirs, others keeping it. Only one stayed awake, but he disappeared from supernatural society and mostly kept to himself. Throwing another First into the mix was going to be either a great thing for the coalition or a total disaster. They were more powerful than any of us. Well, I would be more powerful than them if my magic would mix, but that's beside the point.

Bastien's assistant let me into his office, and I plopped down on the leather sofa, ignoring the cloud of dust that plumed the air from my ruined clothes. I pulled out my phone and texted Mat to let him know I was okay, swiped the curls that had come loose from my face, and concentrated on healing my aching body. The adrenaline wore off, and I realized how tired I was from fixing the wall. Magic required energy, which required food and sleep. If my magic had mixed, the ruling magic could have fed me more energy, though maybe not in this case. As it was, I was a little more limited. I leaned my head back and closed my eyes.

The door swung open. "Bas, I swear I can't do this anymore. I—oh uh—hey, Your Grace. Where's Bastien?"

Aside from the swollen left eye and burns down her side, the woman who entered was the most stunning person I'd ever seen. And that's saying a lot, considering most paranormals had above-average looks. Her black hair was swept into an updo, accenting high cheekbones, symmetrical features, and the perfect color of chocolate brown eyes. If I were a smaller woman, I'd be jealous. "He's helping his cousin. And you know I hate formalities."

"Um, er, sure."

Tracy was Bastien's mate, though I was one of the few who knew. They kept it a secret because of a growing dislike for mixed magic couples. I'd met her just before he quit being my personal guard. She was a witch and a talented alchemist. We bought her potions, and I'd become friendly with her over the years. I liked her and always made an effort to see her when she came to the palace. She didn't mind when I asked questions about her other job as a private detective. I was required by law to spend two to five years working a normal job. I had my heart set on being a detective, and she was a good source of information outside of the books and videos I'd studied for the last several years. The job would allow me to travel and meet other paranormals. More than that, it would give me the freedom I craved. Tracy radiated power but was still a good detective, so I found her advice invaluable. My eyes swept over her injuries. "What happened to you?"

Her shoulders slumped. "It's a long story."

Witches and mages healed as slowly as humans, so they compensated with healing potions or relied on mages with healing abilities. Mat and I were lucky to have healing magic we could use on ourselves; It wasn't common. I patted the sofa. "Come sit down, and I'll heal you."

She shuffled over and perched on the edge of the sofa. "Are you sure you want to? I mean, I can make a healing potion. I just ran out of the ones I usually carry."

Extending my hand, I waited. "I got you." She took my hand, and I closed my eyes and concentrated on the white healing magic within me. It tingled as it poured from my hand into Tracy's. All three of my magics had a distinct feeling to them. Where the healing magic tingled, my inherent magic burned. The ruling magic vibrated or pulsed depending on what mood it was in that day.

I checked each limb before looking for internal injuries. Magic caused the burns rather than fire, which was easier to heal. I healed those before moving on to her eye. Her hip also needed some attention, but it wasn't too bad. I felt a tug in my chest, and tingles ran down my arms as I increased the power until the white light surrounded her. A soothing sensation swept over us. I watched as Tracy's burns scabbed over and disappeared, then I retracted my magic and examined the work. I shook myself out of the stupor and blinked when I noticed her coloring was even more perfect.

She checked her arm and gingerly poked at her eye, then a bright smile formed on her face. "Thank you. You don't know how much I appreciate this." Her smile melted, and her eyebrows drew together. "What happened to you?"

I sighed. "Long story."

"Seems to be the theme of the day. Why are you in Bastien's office?"

"Also, a long story. Why are you in Bastien's office?"

Tracy chuckled. "We're going to be here for days not answering each other's questions because the stories are so long."

"Yeah. I got carried here by a First that just woke up. He seemed to have a bone to pick with my mother."

"Wow. I'm here because I have a bone to pick with Bastien."

As if on cue, Bastien slammed into the office, dressed in an expensive business suit. The mystery man trailed behind him. He wore a black hoodie and jeans, his face beardless, and his long, slightly wavy hair cascaded over his shoulders. He wasn't beautiful like Tracy or classically good-looking like Bastien. His face was rugged, as was his posture. I tore my eyes away from him and focused on Bastien. "Hey, Bas, are you going to give me a ride home?"

Anger flashed in Bastien's eyes at the slight. In Bastien's opinion, dragons should never give people rides on their backs unless they had a non-dragon mate, and then it was acceptable. To him, it was not only demeaning and undignified, but a violation of the sanctity of a bond. Because of his unwavering stance, I regularly poked at him about it. His eyes flicked to Tracy and back to me. "You know my thoughts on that."

I waved a hand. "Yeah, yeah. Then let's talk about the crack in the ward."

"It was a dragon," the First said.

"Yes. A turquoise one. Do you think you're the reason the dragon chose that location to attack the wall? And how could you know that? I thought you were sleeping."

"It wasn't a natural sleep, but magically induced. I was mostly conscious."

I scratched my arm. "And you're sure it was a dragon?"

"I am. I tried to connect with his mind. There was a...mental block of some sort. I'm sorry, Your Grace. I can't tell you more than that. You'll have to ask the nearby shifter pack."

I dropped the subject and picked at my ragged nail. I wished I could pop out of my protective bubble the same way the potential First popped out of the dirt mound. Meeting people was great, but I despised the formalities that accompanied my position. I just wanted people to talk to me without thinking about what they were saying and how they were saying it. I craved freedom like a starving woman craved food. My eyes briefly met Tracy's. I wanted to ask her if she'd help me become a detective, but I was afraid to do more than ask an occasional question. I didn't want her to feel obligated or interpret my request as an order.

Bastien eyed Tracy for a long moment, then turned his attention back to the First. "Prince Mathias is canvassing the area with some enforcers. Jenella cannot do that because she is an easily squashable bug."

"Hey!" I protested.

"Be nice, Bas. Geez," Tracy said.

Bastien huffed. "Fine. I'll refrain from speaking the truth."

I rubbed my temples. "Stop, Bas. I don't have the patience for your attitude today. Especially since your cousin kidnapped me, and one of your dragons just tried to kill us all."

Rage flashed in his black eyes. "Are you holding me accountable for those actions?"

I smirked. "I'm stating facts. Other than whatever the hell he is..." I pointed at the First. "Dragons don't act of their own volition. Someone had to order the dragon to try to bring down the pocket, and your mother is suspiciously absent today. That leaves you responsible unless there is another dragon heir?"

Bastien rubbed his chin, unfazed by my words. "I'm rather surprised you are observant enough to come to such a conclusion, but I assure you neither I nor my mother had anything to do with the crack in the ward."

"I'm rather surprised you're still alive, considering your overall disposition. Any theories on how something like this could happen?"

"None. A few dragons are missing. My mother's location isn't your business."

I nodded in understanding. Bastien was rude, arrogant, and brutally honest. He'd say something in the most insulting way possible if he knew anything. For him to give such an unresponsive answer told me he didn't know what was happening.

"Wait, so a dragon hit the wards and cracked them, and no one knows why?" Tracy asked.

"Apparently," I said.

"It is not your concern," Bastien said at the same time.

I turned my attention to Tracy. "Fixing it caused my ruling magic to flare, which supposedly woke that guy." I pointed to the First. "Though I don't know how. If you have any theories about his awakening or the dragon hitting the ward, I'd be glad to hear them."

Tracy's eyes grew as big as saucers. "Um. Well, maybe the dragon was running from someone or something, and it was an accident. Dragons don't go rogue, so if Deva, er...the queen doesn't know about it, it had to be, right?"

The First examined the ends of his long hair with a frown. "I got into his head. His single focus was to break the wards and destroy Allure. And your magic surged from the wards through the ground and latched onto my magic. It broke the spell that kept me in the false sleep. I assumed it was on purpose."

"This is not an appropriate discussion in mixed company." Bastien waved a hand at Tracy.

Tracy's cheeks heated. "Oh, so that's what I am now? Mixed company? Screw you, Bas! Do you know how much I went through to get here today? How many witches attacked me? I can't even take any cases because they won't leave me alone. I can't walk down the street. But big bad Bastien insists I report to him, and here I am. *Mixed company.*"

"Big bad Bastien?" I couldn't hide the amusement in my voice.

She waved a hand. "Whatever."

"Why are the witches attacking one of their own?" I asked. Witches usually stuck together because they believed in the safety of numbers. Their spell weaving was more potent when they worked together. It was unusual to find a lone witch. I'd always assumed that Tracy had a coven. "Where's your coven?"

"I still belong to my dad's coven, but I don't hang around much." She sighed. "It's part of that long story I don't want to tell. I've had to keep a low profile and stay out of Allure because I can't walk down the street without being attacked. The witches in other pockets have gotten the word, so I can't even take a case. My detective's license is useless at this point. Bas doesn't care about that. No, he insists I report to him without a thought about how it will affect me."

"I did not tell you to report to me," Bastien's voice boomed. "All I said was that I wanted to see you. I wanted you here where you're better protected."

"Whatever. Like I'm any safer here."

I wasn't sure what was happening between the two, so I changed the subject. "Right. So, back to the dragon. If you or the queen figure anything out, will you let me know?"

"I will report to Mathias. You will be too busy figuring out how to work a real job. Have you decided what you want to do?"

"Yes, I decided a long time ago, though I doubt Mat's going to be happy about my choice. I'm considering buying a house and living away from the castle for a couple of years. Mat wants me to work in a safe office job. I'll be stuck in an office job for the rest of my life, so I've been studying to do something more...freeing."

"What is this about?" the First asked. "I thought you were a crown princess. Is that not enough of a job?"

"My mother changed the laws of succession. For reasons I can't fathom, I must be coronated at age thirty-five, even though I can't officially take the throne until I'm forty. Between the ages of thirty-five and forty, I'm required to work at least two years at a regular job and spend the rest of my time acclimating to the queen's duties. I can fully take over from Mat any time after I meet the work requirement, though." It was stupid. Not the work requirement but the coronation requirement. Unfortunately, I couldn't change the laws until I was officially queen, and Mat wouldn't.

"Ah, so she was trying to get rid of you, too..." The First murmured.

"*What?* No. It's so I can learn about the people I'm supposed to rule."

"So you say. Your mother was not as concerned about the people as consolidating her power. I would not be surprised if she planned for you to die during your employment."

"That's awful! I mean, I have no room to speak, but why would she kill her own daughter? That's ridiculous," Tracy interjected. "She's right that it's important you get a feel for what's going on out there. If you buy a house, can I stay with you?"

"Mat will not let her buy a house. *You* will stay here," Bastien growled.

Tracy snorted. "I can't in this political climate."

I ignored their argument. "Mat doesn't get to make that decision."

"Maybe not, but he will insist you have a guard live with you."

"Yeah. I'm sure that'll go well." My relationship with the assortment of guards that Mat assigned me was precarious. I hated them all, except Bastien––though he hadn't guarded me in over a decade since he met Tracy.

"I'll do it," Tracy said. "I mean, it's the perfect solution for both of us. If I'm near you, no way the witches will attack me, and then you have a guard who isn't an old killjoy like Bastien."

"I am not a killjoy." Bastien rubbed his chin. "But I like it. Tracy isn't a traditional guard, but she is very powerful and has a keen eye. She also has the patience of a saint, which is a requirement when guarding Jen."

I grinned. "Which is why you worked out so well."

"Exactly. I am a very patient dragon."

The First threw his head back and laughed. It was such a joyful sound that my own laugh escaped. I stood suddenly. "I'm willing to try, Tracy. It would work better than anyone that Mat has appointed because I like you. Plus, the castle guards hate the assignment, so they'll probably welcome you with open arms. Call Mat's office so he can get you credentials, and you can start as early as tomorrow if you want." I tapped my chin, thinking about her detective's license. "I have something else I want to talk to you about in private."

"Really? I'll do that, but I'm not promising to stick around long. I mean, I have an entire business to run, so I'll have to balance the two, and I need to figure out what to do about the witches. Also, I know what you want to talk to me about because you've asked me about it before. I'll be glad to answer your questions."

"No one ever does. Stick around long, that is. It'll be fine." I headed toward the door. "I want the report about that ward breach, Bas. We can't have dragons going rogue and taking down the pockets."

I pulled my hood up and kept my eyes down as I left the building. I kept my magic wrapped tightly around me to create the illusion that I wasn't as powerful. If paranormals read my false magic level, they'd disregard me if they couldn't see my unique hair and eyes. It was one of the many advantages of hiding my magic. I headed two blocks down and took a left toward the main square of the metropolis. The street leading to the square was one of my favorites, so I raised my eyes to admire it but kept my head down. Built long before the current human government existed, the stone buildings were old. Ornate stone facades flanked the cobblestone street containing charming storefronts. Paranormals in all different forms and states of dress bustled about, searching for treasures or heading to and from the square. The scent of freshly baked bread and barbeque filled the air. I took a minute to savor it, then lowered my eyes and picked up the pace before anyone recognized me.

I spilled out onto the square that was lined with equally charming buildings. Stretching about three blocks, the center contained a park with a playground and a tree-lined sitting area with several tables and benches. On each side of the park were massive stone-lined circles. Since human vehicles weren't allowed beyond the gates, everyone walked or used mages to transport them around the city. While some supernaturals, like shifters, preferred to walk, and vampires could go fluid and move at the speed of sound, mages could flash from one place to another in the blink of an eye.

The circles were created because, as the population grew, mages started smashing into each other mid-flash, causing horrific injuries. The solution was to build a highway of several circles where mages could flash from one place to another using specific routes without fear. Several mages made entire careers transporting paranormals around the city. I headed to the outbound circle and activated my inherent magic. With a flash of light, I landed in the family's private landing circle that was hidden amongst a tangle of shrubbery and vines. I stepped out of the circle and emerged behind a four-story Renaissance-style building.

I glanced at the giant building shaped like a capital "E" and made my way to the family entrance. The door swung open, and a stately man with ice-blue eyes and silver hair bowed. "Welcome home, Your Grace."

I sighed. I hated coming home. It felt too much like a luxurious cage. "Hello, George. How are you?"

His feral grin told me he knew my thoughts and didn't like them. George's griffin family took us in when we were vulnerable and decided to nest in the castle, filling out the role of servants. Don't get me wrong, we didn't force them into the servant role. No one would dare try such a thing with a griffin. They *chose* those roles. Griffins weren't subservient in any way. They served who, how, and when they wanted. Ordering them around was out of the question, and people who tried tended to die. I loved them all. "I am well. I assume you enjoyed your outing?"

I chuckled and kissed him on the cheek. "I adore you, George."

He blushed. "Of course you do. I take it your day was fruitful."

"It was." I followed him through a mudroom to the informal dining room. The room was bright and clean, with mint green walls and massive floor-to-ceiling windows overlooking the well-maintained courtyard between the family and guest wings. The rich wooden floors and the antique rugs made it comfortable. Eight people could be seated at the long wooden table, while the high-backed cream-colored chairs provided a simple seating option. "Did you know the Firsts, George?"

George's face screwed up in concentration. "We knew *of* them, but Helen and I were trying to establish our nest when they went to sleep, so we didn't pay them or politics much attention. I believe Helen studied them before our mating."

Helen bustled into the room carrying a tray loaded with iced tea and small sandwiches, Mat trailing behind her. "I knew of what?" She set the tray down and motioned to the chairs. "I heard you used a lot of magic, Jenella. Sit and have a bite to eat."

I was grateful for the food. Although using my magic gave me an energy boost while I used it, I always felt drained when I used too much. The ruling magic being the exception. It stabilized my energy. Sometimes. I didn't have the best control over it, so it sort of decided when it would restore my energy. I'd learned to disregard it as a source of energy and rely on food and sleep. It was more reliable. Since it was drained after restoring the wall, I was exhausted.

Mat and I both sat. Helen patted her silver hair and focused her chocolate brown eyes on my brother. "Did you find what you were looking for today, Mathias?"

"We found a crack in the main ward. Fortunately, Jenella was able to fix it." Mat's eyes shone with pride.

"Of course she did. Our girl is a magical powerhouse." Helen's eyes glittered as she kissed me on the cheek. She chose the role of my nanny and teacher when I was a kid. Or maybe Mat asked her to help with me because he was busy maintaining the throne after our parents died. Don't get me wrong, Mat spent a lot of time with me, but Helen was always there when he wasn't. Helen and George treated us like we were their own hatchlings, and I loved them dearly.

Mat added several small sandwiches to his plate. "George suggested you tell us about the Firsts. It seems Jen's power surge may have woken one of them."

Helen nudged me to eat. "Oh? I never met any of them besides Jonas, but I studied them in school many years ago."

"What about one with a dragon form?" I asked.

Helen poured the tea and sat. "I remember reading about him. According to history books, he was a different type of dragon than those we see today. Other dragons wouldn't have considered him one of their own if he wasn't related to the queen. It had something to do with the order of birth and his gender that made him different. If I remember right, he was the only First who didn't create a magical species."

My eyebrows drew together. "I thought all the Firsts created a magical species."

Helen shook her head. "Not Drake. The other Firsts forbid it because his aunt and her dragons followed him to this realm, which was against the rules. As such, they declared the dragons his magical species. He was quite the rebel in the stories."

That was Helen's way of saying he was an asshole. It explained why Bastien called him "cousin" in such an adoring voice. "Why did the dragons follow him?"

Helen's eyes sparkled. "Rumor has it that the Dragon Queen was appalled at the idea of him being sent to another realm, so a couple hundred of them followed him here before crashing the portals to prevent being sent back. As I said, the other Firsts were livid and blamed him. It was one of the most exciting things about the Firsts." Helen patted my hand. "Now, tell me about your adventure."

I explained my magic surge and kidnapping. I told Mat about Tracy and her theory about the dragon who hit the wall. It was the most exciting day I'd had in my entire adult life. Wasn't that pathetic? Because I'd been so sheltered and coddled my whole life that there wasn't ever any excitement or adventure. I felt very trapped. I jumped up from my chair to keep from hyperventilating. All three of them started to stand, so I held up a shaky hand. "I used a lot of magic today and need to rest. Thanks for the food, Helen." I rushed from the room.

My suite sat on the east corner of the family wing on the fourth floor. It had a generous sitting area, a kitchenette, and two bedrooms, each with a spa-like bathroom and enormous closets. The suite was comfortable and sophisticated, with plush furniture and cream walls with jeweled accents. I usually loved my little apartment. It was my sanctuary and the one place I felt free.

I parked myself in the window seat in my bedroom, closed my eyes, and focused on breathing. I opened my eyes and stared out over the back of the property. No matter how much I hated the castle at that moment, I still loved the view of the forest with the bubbling creek running through it. I could just make out the small waterfall that Mat and I built when he taught me how to use my magic. The panic of being trapped moved to the background, and I drew in one last deep breath and relaxed.

Clang!

I scrambled to the back of my cage and scrunched into a ball to make myself as small as possible. If the man brought one of his friends down here to "play" with the girl prisoners, I didn't want them to see me. Booming voices and loud clangs filled the dungeon. I scuttled behind the chamber pot.

"Where is she, Jacques?"

Another clang. Some thuds.

Was that father's voice? I didn't trust it because I'd been fooled before. I tucked myself tighter into the corner and squeezed my eyes shut as the banging and shouting got louder. Then everything went silent. I worked up the courage to peak. Father lay on the floor right in front of the cage. His eyes were open, blood flowing from his neck.

A sob escaped my throat, and I flung my non-broken arm across my mouth to muffle it. Drawing attention to myself was never good. A woman screamed, and the sounds of clanging and shouting started again. I heard Mother's firm, commanding voice. Hope blossomed in my chest. I didn't think anyone could beat my mother in a fight. She was the most powerful person on the planet, after all. My six-year-old brain was sure she would save me.

I sprung up and shouted, "Mother, I'm here!" Her eyes snapped toward me just as the man brought the axe down on her head.

I jumped and rubbed the front of my blouse. Relief washed over me as I realized it wasn't a blood-soaked white nightgown. I swiped my sweaty hair out of my face, shuffled to the bathroom, and gazed at my chaotic appearance in the mirror. The problem with childhood trauma is that no matter how hard you try to lock it away, compartmentalize it, or forget, it always finds a way back to the surface. For me, it came in the form of panic attacks and dreams. I was the proud owner of the double whammy that day. I showered, swept my curls into a messy ponytail, and then changed into a T-shirt and leggings. As I switched on the TV to distract myself, I felt myself slipping away from the swirling chaos within my mind.

Chapter 3

I FELT RE-ENERGIZED AS I headed to the second floor of the office wing. I realized my ruling magic was replenished. The morning sun pierced through the windows at the end of the hall. The south wing of the E was different than the family wing. My domain included the entire fourth floor. It contained my gigantic office along with several others meant for staff that I didn't have yet. All the administrative offices, along with several conference rooms, were on the second and third floors. The first floor housed Mat's office, the palace guard officers, and the throne room, where disputes between paranormal groups were mediated.

I rounded the corner and crashed into someone with a *thud*. "Sorry."

Tracy took two steps back and offered me a blinding smile. "Oh gosh. I'm so sorry."

I chuckled. "Not your fault. Did you already get cleared to be my guard?"

Her eyes sparkled. "Yep. It was easy. Mat told me to report to conference room 203. Is that where you're headed?"

My face lit up. "As a matter of fact, I am. Welcome aboard!" I motioned for her to follow me.

"This place is a maze. I mean, it looks big outside, but it's huge inside. You must have had so much fun playing here as a kid."

My childhood wasn't what I'd call fun. By the time we got to this palace——what my mother had called her vacation home——I was so traumatized it took Helen and Mat months to coax me out of my shell. After that, my life was filled with studying, observing political meetings, and practicing magic. I wasn't going to ruin Tracy's awe at seeing the entire palace, so I nodded. "And this is only one wing. What parts of the palace have you been in before?"

"Just the first floor where you met with me and the lab. One time, Helen insisted that Bastien and I have a snack in one of the family receiving rooms, but that's it. How many wings are there? I mean, I've read there are three, but it seems so much bigger."

I stopped outside the conference room. "There's a little over three. The entryway and parlors take most of one."

"What's up, chicky-chick?" a grating voice echoed down the hall. My head snapped in Emine's direction as she strutted toward us.

"Hey, Emine," I ground out.

Her crazy blue eyes glanced at Tracy before returning to me. "Whoo whee! We're about to have some fun, hey sis?"

I hated Mat's significant other——or what we call "a match". Tall, around five foot ten inches, with an overly muscular yet perfectly proportioned body, she reminded me of a brunette Barbie doll on steroids. Her insane obsession with pushing my buttons grated on my nerves. I introduced her to Tracy, who eyed her with a carefully blank face. Emine opened the conference room door, wiggling her eyebrows, "Let's get this party started, ladies!"

I motioned for Tracy to go ahead, then slid into the room behind her. Mat sat at the end of a ten-seat table, George and Helen across from him.

Emine strode straight to Mat, gave him a way too heated kiss for a business meeting, and plopped down in the seat to his right. Tracy glanced around the room before darting toward a chair two over from Emine. That left an entire side of the table for me. I slunk over to the center chair.

Mat cleared his throat. "Jenella, we need to review the details for your coronation. Just so we're all on the same page, it's scheduled to take place in three months, followed by a five-year ascension to the throne." When I nodded, he continued. "The coronation ceremony will take place in the pocket of Mahri." He met my eyes, gauging my reaction.

My heart rate kicked up, and I took a deep breath to keep from panicking. It wasn't fresh news. The original pocket of Mahri housed the castle my grandmother, the first Queen of Ahl, built. We lived there until I was six. It held nothing but terrible memories for me––like my parents dying in front of me. Unfortunately, my mother had decreed my ascension, so we were legally required to follow the plan. Mat called it a tradition. I called it control and planned to change it, so if I ever had kids, they'd have options. "Sure. Whatever."

The corner of Mat's lip ticked up. He knew how much I hated the idea of going to Mahri. "Helen is planning the events for the coronation."

Helen's apple-shaped face glowed as she nodded. "Oh, yes. Most of the preparations are going well. It's been fascinating since I've never planned an event this big."

"George will handle travel logistics and moving people around Mahri. He will also keep track of any guests he deems a threat," Mat continued.

George's face formed a feral smile. "One cannot be too careful, after all."

Mat closed his laptop and pulled out a folder. "Thanks to George and Helen's efforts, everything is planned for the entire week. That leaves the five years between the coronation and when you take on the full duties of the throne. You are legally required to work a job outside the palace for at least two of those years." He slid the folder to me.

It was another law I planned to change. I thought it was dumb that I'd spent the last ten years watching someone else rule instead of being out in the world learning about the people. It seemed like a waste of time since my upbringing was also all about learning how to rule. I opened the folder and frowned. It was full of job applications attached to brochures, including SuperReal Real Estate, the Allure branch of the Bank of Mahri, the Vampire Sustenance Institute, and UFO Transportation of Allure. "What is this?" I asked, utterly confused.

Mat sat back and folded his arms. "Employment suggestions."

I glanced at Tracy's placid face. For the past ten years, I'd dedicated my spare time to becoming a detective. Mat didn't know that, but Tracy did. I tapped the folder. "I'm capable of finding my own employment."

He dragged a hand through his hair. "Yes, but you don't understand the implications of choosing the wrong job. My suggestions will provide adequate life experience while keeping you safe. It would be a bonus if your magic gets straightened out."

"And you think I can gain valuable experience by typing transport schedules?"

Emine coughed to hide a laugh.

Mat ignored her. "Jenella, you know nothing about the workforce. Those are excellent suggestions that will give you valuable life lessons."

"Yeah. I can't wait to learn valuable life lessons while telemarketing." I held my phone to my ear. "Good morning. This is Queen Jenella. I wondered if you'd be interested in donating blood to random vampires to help them control themselves. Whaddya say?"

He ignored my snark, motioning to Tracy. "Hiring Tracinia to watch your back was an excellent idea. She will provide adequate protection while working outside the castle."

I gave him a big, fake smile. "How fun it will be for her to watch me balancing ledgers all day. That will certainly keep her on her toes."

Mat pinched the bridge of his nose. "Fine. If you don't like my suggestions, find something else, but working outside the palace for two to three years is mandatory. Helen, please give us a day-by-day recap of the coronation schedule."

An hour later, after reviewing the coronation schedule––most of which seemed unnecessary to me––Mat grabbed his laptop and left the room. Emine shot me a thumbs-up before following.

George cleared his throat as he stood. "Well, I think that went swimmingly well." He kissed me on the cheek and reached for Helen's hand. "Don't you, dear?"

Helen patted me on the shoulder. "I'm pleased the young prince is still alive. Great job practicing restraint."

I watched them leave before turning to my new guard. "Welcome to the Castle Allure family. So, have you come up with more theories on why the dragon hit the ward?"

Tracy opened her mouth, closed it, then opened it again. "Was that a normal conversation between you and the Regent?"

I stood, dragging the folder with me. "Pretty much. Mat raised me and still thinks I'm a kid. He's way too overprotective, considering I'm supposed to be the most powerful supernatural in the world. Let's head to my office and figure out a better plan for getting me some of the experience. Something that will give me more freedom than office work. And I want to hear your thoughts about the dragon."

"Sure. It's just hard to wrap my brain around someone poking fun at the Bloody Prince."

"I wouldn't call him that to his face. And honestly, someone needs to lighten him up."

Her eyes were wide with terror as we entered my office. A massive room with gleaming acacia floors and plush cream rugs. Located on the front corner of the office wing, it had windows on two sides to let in plenty of light. A hefty wooden desk sat in the center against the wall opposite the door, with two plush chairs in front of it. To the left was a twelve-person conference table with state-of-the-art, magically enhanced presentation equipment. A generous sitting area was on the right in front of the windows. It had two cream couches facing each other and two cream chairs on each end, forming an enormous square. A square coffee table that matched the desk sat in the middle. The whole place was accented in jeweled tones, giving the space a regal feel. "Wow. This is enormous." Tracy ran a hand over the surface of my desk.

I set the folder down and plopped into the plush executive chair. "It doesn't feel so big when you're trying to negotiate territory disputes between a bunch of trolls and kelpies. But I get where you're coming from."

Tracy didn't smile like I'd hoped. She timidly lowered herself into the chair across from me and folded her hands on her lap. "Um. When I agreed to be your guard, I didn't expect to watch you work all day. I figured since you're, well, you, this wouldn't be so involved."

I snorted. "It won't."

Tracy blinked. "Yeah. Okay. Umm...so, the dragon. There's something bigger going on. I mean, I get dragons value their hordes, but the Dragon Queen has never gone there for this long. I tried to get the scoop from Bastien, but he won't say a word about it."

Standing up, I motioned her to follow me to the windows. "You, my friend, will get us in trouble spying on Bastien." I pointed out the window where several griffins were perched along the thirty-foot wall, a few castle guards sprinkled between them. "See all those griffins? Bastien could break through them if he's angry enough. We'll give him some room to investigate but hold him accountable. I'm interested in seeing if you have any theories, though. We can't let that happen again."

Tracy leaned forward, eyeing the security. "Yeah, Bas is pretty fierce when he wants to be. But honestly, I don't care if it hurts his feelings. We could have died yesterday."

"You're right. It could have been much worse. But it wasn't, and coalition law says we have to let the paranormal species solve problems within their faction. We can only involve ourselves if they infringe upon another faction, fail to take proper action, or for a few other, less common reasons. So, keep your eyes open, but since you work for me, you have to let Bas and the queen handle it."

She swallowed. "Okay, sure, but I'm not going to stop needling him. It's what I do. Um, I have one theory, but you'll think it's crazy."

"Try me."

"Well, Drake––that's the First––said the dragon was single-minded. Let's say the queen *is* missing. What if someone is using her to give that dragon orders?"

"Okay. Then why aren't the other dragons acting strange?"

"You mean besides Bas?"

I raised an eyebrow.

"What I mean is, he's hiding something. I know him better than anyone, and he's not acting right. What if he knows but is forbidden from talking? I hate to say it, but that could be possible."

I stared out the window and ran her theory through my head. Aside from not talking about the queen's whereabouts, Bas wasn't acting any differently than usual. Dragons were required to follow the queen's orders to the letter no matter who they were. They were mentally and physically incapable of disobeying. So, why did the dragon run into the wall when the queen was absent? "It's a good theory. But Bas wasn't acting that strange. I'm not sure it's that big of a problem right now."

"I hope not," Tracy said. "I hope it never gets worse since Bas is powerful enough to take on that many griffins."

"Yeah. Now, tell me about being a detective."

Her eyebrows drew together. "What do you want to know? I mean, I knew you were thinking about it as a career, so you already know that I think it's a great job. I get to work for myself. It gives me time to build my alchemy business and spend time with friends and family. Well, it would be great if the witches would leave me alone."

I turned toward the window. "Stick around, and I'll make sure you have ample time to do it all. I'm wondering more about what it takes to become one. My childhood friend is the Deputy Director of the Private Investigative Supernatural Division, and he might be able to help me disguise my identity. Emphasis on might. It makes more sense for me to do something like that rather than selling transport tickets or managing real estate. If my goal is to understand how supernaturals operate, I need to be out there meeting people, not sitting behind some desk. Besides, I like to solve puzzles, so it's a natural fit."

"Then you need to learn investigative techniques and understand a bunch of protocols for the different supernatural groups and their laws. I mean, I suppose that part won't be a problem for you.

"Nope. I doubt I even need to study law. And I've been studying investigative techniques for a while now to prepare myself."

"Umm...there's three tests and a final. One is about the protocols and laws, the second covers investigative techniques, and then there is a physical fitness test individualized for your species." She held up a hand. "I have no idea why that section is there. Once you pass those, they give you a case to solve based on a real one. If you solve it, you get your license. I can help you prepare for that."

I tapped the window seal, thinking about my limited time to work before I'd be forced to take the throne. Three years wasn't a long time. Then, I'd have to return to my luxurious cage in the shape of a castle. I liked that the job would allow me to set my own schedule so I could balance the queen's responsibilities with cases. Getting to meet all sorts of supernaturals in the process sounded perfect. "How long does this process take?"

"It depends on how much you need to learn. I mean, if you apply for the test and fail any part, they put you in a class, and then it takes longer."

"What's the average time? If you had to guess, how long would it take me to become licensed?"

"I don't know. It took me about three months because I'm not great with laws, but you don't have that problem. I'd say a couple of months, at least. Less if you pass the tests on the first try and find a mentor."

I froze. "A mentor?" I'd read that a new detective required a mentor for their first few years. I'd never thought about the details, though. It occurred to me I was living in a fantasy, assuming the rules didn't apply to me because they typically didn't. "Can't you be my mentor?"

"I'm not eligible, but I can ask around for you. You need a mentor to help guide you until you are competent. They're not your boss or anything, just someone you can turn to if you have questions or call if you get in trouble. But don't worry, detectives will be tripping over themselves to be your mentor."

I frowned. I didn't want people tripping over themselves for me. There was too much of that in my real life. If I was going to do this, I wanted to be just another mage. That meant I'd have to wear glamour to disguise myself and couldn't live in the castle. Bastien was right to think that Mat would never go for that. My shoulders slumped at the realization that this idea might not work like I wanted. "What do you think my chances are if I hide my magic and use glamour to take on a new identity?"

"Gosh, I don't know. I mean, I could put in a good word with some eligible mentors, but there's no guarantee."

I shook my head. "This won't work unless people don't know it's me."

"Why would you say that?"

I sank into one of the couches. "Because supernaturals are never themselves when I'm around. They either think they need to kiss my ass, lean into heavy protocols, or lie to me. Very few show me their true selves. I need to be someone different, or I don't stand a chance."

Tracy strode across the room, removing a magically enhanced tablet from her bag. "Okay, let's work this through to see if it's doable and develop a step-by-step process. I mean, if we can't figure out how to change your appearance, we could always find another job that doesn't involve a desk."

I couldn't help the smile that spread across my face. "Okay, let's get to work."

Chapter 4

We marched to Mat's office on the first floor the next morning. We were armed with a plan, and I was as optimistic as I was determined. As I crossed the main lobby, people stopped what they were doing and bowed. The front door guards were usually the newer capital guards who showed potential and were always trying to impress in their crisp purple t-shirts and black combat pants. As we approached the two stationed at the entrance to the guard offices, they opened the double doors in unison. I offered them a cheery "good morning" before dragging a wide-eyed Tracy through and turning down the hall toward Mat's office. "Weird, isn't it?"

Tracy shook her head. "When you said no one treats you normally, I thought I understood, but this is excessive. The dragons don't even treat their queen like that. I mean, supernaturals like their formalities, but that's a little much."

I couldn't have agreed more. We stopped outside Mat's office, where his assistant, Pablo, sat glaring at a laptop. "Good morning, Pablo. Is Mat in?"

Pablo tore his eyes from the screen to focus on me. "Of course. Er. Yeah. Yes. Emine's in there right now. Shall I interrupt?"

As a boggart, Pablo could read emotions and anticipate needs, so he knew the answer but asked as a formality. I liked him because he was protective of Mat and was a little mischievous. Mat liked him because he was proficient and could amp up fear in people without them knowing why. Pablo's nature made him hate formalities as much as I did. "I can wait if they're busy. I only need a few minutes of his time."

He examined Tracy before returning his attention to me. "Very well. I'll alert him to your presence."

"Thank you." I moved to the small waiting area, perched on the edge of a chair, and wiped my sweaty hands on my pants. Tracy admired the artwork. We were only there for a few seconds before Mat's office door opened, and he waved us in.

Mat's office wasn't as fancy as mine, but still sizable. It had dark hardwood floors and a big purple rug with our family crest in the center. He had a war room table with several chairs on one side and a serviceable desk with two chairs in front of it. Emine leaned against the corner of his desk, her face blank as she read something on her phone. Mat strode past her and sat as we took the chairs on the other side of the desk. "Pablo says you found a job to pursue, and I won't like it."

Talk about stealing my thunder. "I'm not sure you'll like it, no. But Emine will be thrilled, I think." I pulled out my magically enhanced tablet and activated a 3D projection of the plan we made the day before. A hologram appeared, showing each step of the process. I pointed to phase one. "I want to be a private detective."

Silence.

A moment later, Emine set her phone down. "I like it. It's perfect."

Mat's eyes never left mine. "I do not."

I waved a hand. "It's not dangerous. Tell him, Tracy."

I could smell her fear as Mat's intense expression focused on her. To her credit, she squared her shoulders and met his eyes directly. "Around eighty percent of cases are not dangerous. I mean, there are some you don't think are dangerous, but they become that way, but it's rare. Jen, I mean Her Grace, can take ones that need a lot of puzzle solving and are less physical."

"It's not dangerous at all," I added unnecessarily.

Emine burst out laughing. "Boy, oh boy, you two suck at this. But seriously, when do you start?"

My brother was a giant man with scars running up his hands and tattooed arms. He always looked half unkempt in his cargo pants and black t-shirt. He had a talent for amping up his deadly charisma at will. It automatically ramped up when he was angry, making people want to pee their pants. His deadly reputation made the feeling much worse. That feeling amped up so much at Emine's words that Tracy put her hands under her legs to hide the shaking.

I was used to it, so I continued. "The licensing test is in a month. In that time, I plan to ask the dragons for some glamour and buy a flat or townhouse to help hide my identity. I think it'll give me a chance to get to know supernaturals without all the ass-kissing and political maneuvering. It's a great plan, Mat. And don't scowl at me like that."

Emine's nod was overly animated. "You have my vote."

Mat shot her the stink-eye before returning his attention to me. "Perhaps your guard should step out of the room."

Tracy sprang to her feet. I grabbed her arm and yanked her back down. "Tracy stays." I left my hand on her arm to keep her from bolting. "You said I needed life experience. And detective work will accomplish the life experience goal much better than sitting in some office updating real estate listings on the Magicnet."

"So, you will skirt your duties and abandon your home."

My unpredictable ruling magic exploded into the room, shoving Mat's ominous magic aside. "No. You want me to get that life experience while keeping me in a bubble, which isn't life experience at all. I don't need your permission to do this, considering I'm an adult, which you seem to forget. I'm running it by you as a courtesy."

We glared at each other in silence, our gold eyes glowing in unison. His magic aura ramped up, and the ruling magic pulsed even though I tried to reel it in. He knew he had no say if I didn't want him to. The law was clear. A couple of months shy of thirty-five, I was ten years past the age of consent. I wanted his approval because he rescued me from Mahri, kept me safe for years, and was the first, and maybe only, person to love me. His approval was also important because I loved him like a father. But I knew I needed to break out of his control, or I'd never taste freedom.

I wrangled the ruling magic and let go of my vice grip on Tracy's arm. "I concede that working an office job would provide some great life experience, and I shouldn't have poked fun. But I'm not interested in an office job, Mat. I'll be stuck in one for the rest of my life. I want more freedom than that, and I don't think that's too much to ask. This is my only chance at that."

His threatening magic receded, and the room breathed a sigh of relief. "Aside from choosing a dangerous profession, you cannot change your identity and move out. There's too much at stake."

Emine hopped from the desk. "I could give her a position with the Enforcers."

"No!" we both yelled. Emine shrugged and sauntered over to the windows. As the head of the Enforcers, or paranormal police, she could easily hand me a job. As a powerful mage with war magic, she could conjure any weapon. It made her reckless, and I didn't want to work with her, let alone *for* her. It grated on Mat's nerves that she never took my safety as seriously as him. She used that knowledge to push buttons every chance she could.

Mat tapped his desk before returning his attention to me. "Tell me how you plan to pull this off, Jenella. I want every detail."

Tracy and I went over our plan again, this time answering questions and giving him more detail. When we were done, Mat sat back and rubbed his face. "It's not a bad choice overall, but I'm still concerned about your safety.

You need to protect yourself with more than anonymity. If something goes sideways, you need an escape plan."

A sliver of hope began to bloom, but I squashed it. I glanced at a blank-faced Tracy before answering. We'd discussed safety, but I knew it wouldn't be enough for Mat. "I thought I'd hire Ray so the new place would be renovated and enchanted against fire or destruction. I can flash inside Tracy's wards if it gets dangerous." Ray was Emine's brother and an architectural mage. He could transform any building to the owner's specifications and enchant against things like fire, flooding, and magical attacks.

"My wards are arguably the best in the world. Adding a little of Jen's magic to them would make it so no one except vampires could cross them. I mean, I'm her guard, after all, and I take my job very seriously," Tracy explained.

Mat was silent for a long moment before inclining his head. "Very well, you've got my blessing with a few conditions." He waited for my nod before continuing. "Provided you can figure out how to get undetectable glamour from Bastien, which I still doubt, you will buy a defendable house. You will also allow me to check and adjust your security measures. You will call me should you find yourself in danger."

I didn't like those conditions because they made it seem too much like boxing me in. "I agree to allow you to check security only if I have veto power should you be too...overzealous with your adjustments. And I'll call you only if I can't handle the situation myself or don't have backup."

"That's acceptable."

Emine clapped. "This shit show is going to be so much fun to watch." She turned to Mat. "Should I make some popcorn?"

Mat's expression softened. "My sister's life is not a show, shit or otherwise, love."

She shook her head. "Sure thing."

I waved my hand dismissively and dragged Tracy out of the room, choosing not to engage with my crazy sister-in-law.

Making our way to the hidden family flashing circle, I linked my arm with Tracy's, and––with a white flash––we appeared in the downtown circle. Tracy flipped her hood over her head and took a breath. "That is the fastest anyone has ever flashed me."

I chuckled. "Sorry about that. I'll try to tone it down if it bothers you."

"Oh, it's fine. I'm sure I'll get used to it."

Dragon Headquarters was in the city's heart, in a tall tower that stretched over two city blocks. Dragons usually lived in more rural locations, but the Dragon Queen, Devarkalara or Deva, liked to keep her finger on the supernatural pulse, so she built the tower tall to allow dragons to launch themselves from one of the many balconies. It somewhat compensated for the lack of wilderness, I guessed. In contrast, our castle was in a suburb that housed estates on the city's outskirts with plenty of wilderness. I often wondered why she didn't build there, so the dragons had more freedom.

We made our way through the bustling city to the tower. After approaching the check-in station at the front desk, where a dragon with deep purple hair and eyes sat staring at a hologram screen in front of her. "State your business."

I removed my hood and leaned forward. "We have an appointment with Queen Devarkalara." I had called and made an appointment during our planning session the night before.

She still didn't spare us a glance, so she missed my dramatic reveal. "The queen is unavailable. I suggest you leave."

My stomach sank. The only magical beings that could do glamour were dragons. If I couldn't get permission to hire one, I couldn't live anonymously, which screwed the entire plan. "Not until I speak to the queen. It's important."

The dragon tore her purple eyes from the screen and focused on me. Her face paled. Before she could say anything, a woman wearing a navy blue suit approached, her matching navy heels clicking on the white marble. She put her hand on the guard's shoulder. "Princess Jenella, Tracinia. I'm Karenalla, personal assistant to Her Majesty. If you'll come with me."

Relief washed over me. We followed her through a labyrinth of white marble halls to an elevator that took us to the upper offices of the tower. Instead of leading us left to the queen's office, Karenalla led us right. I frowned. "I was under the impression I was meeting with the queen."

Karenalla didn't falter. "My apologies. The queen is visiting her horde. However, you're lucky today because Prince Bastien has agreed to meet with you."

I didn't feel lucky. While I had a certain rapport with the queen, I was sure that Bastien would laugh at my request. Karenalla led us to the door and gestured for us to go in. As I stepped through the door, my heart stopped. Bastien sat at his desk, his hands folded, his black eyes examining Tracy with more emotion than I'd ever seen from him. As curious as that was, he wasn't who I focused on. Leaning against the wall behind him stood the First. He looked much different from the last time I saw him. Tall, over six feet, his gangly frame and long stringy hair were replaced with a rugged-looking muscular body and collar-length black wavy hair. His olive skin glowed with health, and his eyes were the most beautiful grass-green color I'd ever seen. Eyes that regarded me with disgust.

I jolted back to reality and strode to the chairs in front of Bastien's desk. "Thanks for seeing us, Bas. I hope your mother is well."

Bastien kept his eyes on Tracy as he inclined his head. "She is."

I snorted. "Stop ogling Tracy."

Tracy made a strangled sound, but I got Bastien's attention. "I enjoy ogling her. I'm sorry you got stuck with such an undesirable job, Tracy. Hopefully, you get the witch matter straightened out soon."

I rubbed my eyes. "Enough of this. I need to talk to you about something important?"

He raised an eyebrow.

"Hey, Drake, is it?" I asked the First.

"Yes. Your attitude is as large as your slaps are hard, considering you're a puny mage. We need to discuss that."

I rolled my eyes. "I wouldn't have slapped you if you weren't hysterical."

Tracy's head turned toward me so fast I was surprised she didn't get whiplash. "You slapped him? How am I supposed to protect you from this, Jenella? I mean, I'm good, but I didn't sign up to fight a First...maybe you should stop insulting everyone before you get yourself killed?"

Bastien threw back his head and laughed.

Drake slunk over to a chair and sat without making a sound.

I sighed. "I'm not in danger here, and neither are you, and you know it." My attention shifted to the laughing Bastien. "Stop, Bas."

He held up a finger, trying to stop laughing. "Oh, Jen. What a gift you've given me today. But yes, *guard* Tracy, please have a seat. I assure you the First will not harm you."

Tracy gingerly took her seat. "Can I be honest?"

"Sure," I said.

"I don't get you. You always argue with these super-powerful people when you aren't even magically or physically strong. I mean, no offense, but your title will only get you so far, and I don't think I'll be enough when everything comes crashing down on you."

Bastien laughed so hard he put an arm across his stomach. "Oh, my dear. You think Jen is weak?"

I ignored him as I unwrapped all three magics, letting the full force fill the room. As I did, her eyes grew enormous. "I keep my magic hidden, but

I can defend myself. These guys are physically stronger, but I'm not above fighting dirty, so I'd get some good blows in before Drake killed us. I argue with my brother because he'd never hurt me." I motioned to Bastien. "Bas won't admit it, but he adores me, and he'd never harm his mate, so we're good there." I shot him a toothy grin.

Bastien put his elbows on the table. "Tracy knows that. Jen is a trouble magnet, but I assure you she can defend herself. Drake does not want to harm her, a rarity amongst people who've had more than one conversation with her."

The First shifted in his seat, and Bastien returned his attention to me. "What did you need from us, princess? Unlike you, I'm busy."

Tracy sighed and folded her arms. "Fine, but you need to tell me what's going on before we walk into situations like this."

"Agreed." I turned my attention back to Bastien. "I need undetectable glamour that will last long term. I'm willing to pay for it with currency but not favors."

Bastien blinked. "I see."

The First leaned forward. "What for?"

I laid out the plan. When I was finished, the First rubbed his chin. "What are your plans for the other Firsts?"

"Other Firsts?"

"Do you plan to wake them or leave them in their hell?"

"Um, I'm not sure what you mean."

He considered me for a long time. "No, I suppose you don't. Very well, I'll provide glamour on a couple of conditions."

Bastien shook his head. "No, you won't, cousin. Besides the fact that dragons don't get involved in outside politics without the queen's approval, attempting to hide her identity is stupid and dangerous."

I opened my mouth to protest, but the First cut me off. "Then it's a good thing I'm not accepted as a dragon. Besides, I like a challenge."

Bastien's eyebrow ticked. "I'll set aside the fact that you are indeed a dragon, even if you believe yourself above our laws. I don't think it's a good idea for you to get mixed up in Jen's mess. She's like a vacuum who sucks people into her toxic environment where there's no escape."

"That's a little extreme...."

The First shrugged. "I don't have anything else to do. Besides, I need something from her, and she...intrigues me."

"Nope. No developing an interest in me. I just want the glamour."

The First's lip twitched. "You were too late to avoid my interest when you used your enormous magic to wake me. And then you furthered that interest when you slapped me. Twice."

I stiffened. I found Drake intriguing, and his amusement made my stomach flip, but I wasn't sure I liked catching his attention. "As I said, I just want glamour. I'll pay you, and then we're done."

"Oh, I doubt that," Drake purred.

Bastien ran a hand through his hair. "How do you plan to pull this off, cousin? Aside from the fact that there is no way to make glamour undetectable, it always requires maintenance to be effective."

"Luckily, I have abilities unlike any other." Drake held out his hand. "May I have your earrings, princess?"

I removed the small gold earrings and placed them in his hand. "How much is this going to cost me?"

The bastard winked.

I tamped down the flutter in my stomach and fought not to squirm. "Nope. *Monetarily*, how much is this going to cost?"

"I don't need nor want your money. I only ask that you have a meal with me, provide a history lesson of my choosing, and consider waking the other Firsts."

My eyebrows drew together. "I'll agree to a history lesson provided it doesn't encroach on my personal boundaries, but I'm not having a meal with you. And I don't know how or even *if* I woke you. Besides, waking a supernatural from their resting sleep is forbidden."

"Perhaps you should look more closely at your mother's actions."

"Huh?"

He leaned forward. "A meal where we discuss waking the other Firsts and a history lesson, or no deal."

I glanced at Tracy for help, but she and Bastien were locked in some weird staring contest. "Fine, one meal that is *not* a date and a history lesson that doesn't encroach on personal boundaries where we discuss the Firsts. I mean it. If your questions make me uncomfortable, I won't answer them."

The look of satisfaction that swept across his face made me want to take it back. He pulled a rolling chair into the center of the room and motioned to it. "Have a seat. Please."

I'd barely sat when he leaned over and sniffed me. "What are you doing!" I scrambled back.

"I need to disguise your scent, or every supernatural with a good nose can find you." He motioned me to roll the chair back. As soon as I was back in position, he reached up faster than a snake and removed the tie from my hair. Curly hair tumbled around my shoulders. He stepped back and examined me. "It's almost a shame to hide that gorgeous hair."

I ran my fingers through said hair. "It makes me stand out like a sore thumb."

He pulled out one gold and one red curl with each hand. "The base color is a common light brown. The gold and red chunks and perhaps the curl make you recognizable. We will go a couple of shades darker than your base color and leave a slight wave." He grabbed my chin. "Now, what to do about this unique face."

"I don't care what you do, as long as I look different."

"No? How about I make you resemble a troll or an ogre?"

"Uh, no. I want to look like a mage."

"Then you should answer my questions."

Drake asked a ton of questions about how I wanted to look. He wanted every detail, from the shape of my eyes to how many freckles across my nose. When he was satisfied, he concentrated on the earrings. "If this look is not perfect, I can adjust it."

It was all I could do not to bounce in my chair in excitement. "How long will it take to do that?"

He sighed. "I forgot how impatient royals are."

"It's not all royals, just the ones who were raised to believe they own the world," Bastien said.

"Indeed," the First said, concentrating on the earrings as they lit with green magic. It only took a few minutes before he returned them to me. "You will need to recharge them once per month. Contact me, and I'll do it at no additional charge."

I stared at the enchanted earrings, sensing their magical properties. I couldn't feel the magic, which was surprising, as my senses were better than most. "Are you sure they'll work?"

The First plucked a mirror off the wall. "Try them and see." Something in his voice made me realize I'd insulted him. Probably not a good idea since he was helping me. I put the earrings in my ears. He gave me a nod of approval and raised the mirror. Tracy and Bastien leaned in to get a better look.

I gasped when I saw myself. My hair and eyes were medium brown, and only a slight wave remained in my hair. My eyes were a little smaller, my eyelashes shorter, and my face square rather than long. My nose had a little hook. I smiled. Even my teeth looked different. "Wow. That's amazing! Thank you, First."

He frowned. "Do not thank me for ruining a work of art. And stop calling me First. You know my name is Drake."

Tracy kneeled in front of me, a broad smile spreading across her face. "Wow, Jenella, I mean, this plan might actually work. How should we test it?"

Bastien folded his arms. "What about Tracy? She's not protected by this anonymous person like she is when she's with the queen. And she can't be seen with both, or it will negate the purpose."

"I will do Tracy's for free."

Tracy's glamour turned out fantastic. Her dark skin stayed the same, though it looked less radiant. Shorter in length, her hair was pin-straight. Her face was a little wider and less symmetrical. She looked plain enough that the witches would overlook her. She grinned as she looked in the mirror. "Oh, my fates. We'll be able to fly under the radar like this. The witches won't even know it's me. I might just keep this look when you get yourself killed."

I chuckled. "Your regular look is better, but this will work for our purpose." My attention shifted to the frowning dragon prince. "What have you found out about that dragon that hit the wall, Bas?"

"We're still looking into it. There are only a few turquoise dragons, and we've narrowed down that list. I'll update Mat on what we find, since you are too busy doing whatever this is."

"Has the queen been able to offer any insight?"

"No. Unfortunately, I haven't been able to reach my mother. It's not uncommon when she visits her horde."

"I hope you hear from her soon. We can't have dragons going rogue and trying to take down the pockets."

"I agree. I assure you, I am taking it very seriously."

"What about names?" Drake asked.

I turned my attention to him. "What about them?"

"If you pretend to be someone else, you need a new name."

I waved him off. "I decided on Jen Hendrix because Bas and Mat already call me Jen, so I'll naturally answer to it. Hendrix is a common mage name."

"It's very close to your real name," Bastien said with a frown.

"Just the first name. I suppose I could make it Jennifer, so it's different. I only need to maintain it for a couple of years while I figure out...life and stuff."

Bastien chuckled. "I doubt you will figure life out, but I commend you for trying. Now, I have matters to attend to, so you may leave." He gave a glamoured Tracy one last thoughtful look before sauntering out of the room.

Chapter 5

THE NEXT FEW WEEKS went by in a whirlwind of house hunting, work-outs, and studying. Tracy tutored me on investigative techniques, and I brushed up on the law. I watched as she mixed alchemy and weaved spells for her business. Most witches could either do alchemy or weave spells. I didn't know it was possible to do both until I met her. She allowed me to absorb some complicated defensive spells and one nasty shredding spell. I practiced solving cases and worked out daily.

The day before the licensing exam, we had two things to accomplish. We had to meet with the Deputy Director of the Private Investigative Supernatural Division (PISD) for a short time so he could write up my profile for potential mentors. When we were done, we had to check on the progress of our new house. Butterflies danced in my stomach as we landed in the flashing circle in the main square of Allure. My freedom was so close I could almost taste it. I flittered down the stairs and around the corner toward the PISD offices and shook my hands, trying to calm myself. "I'm so excited and nervous I can hardly contain my magic."

Tracy peered at me from behind her hood. She chose not to wear her glamour until after our meeting at the PISD. She skirted around an ogre sweeping the sidewalk in front of a shop and nearly knocked over a naked woman who trailed behind two bobcat kittens. "I'm excited for you. But you need to calm down before you burn out your glamour. I mean, I don't know about Drake's magic, but witch spells will burn out when exposed to high levels of magic, especially ruling magic."

I took a deep breath as we approached the offices. The Private Investigative Supernatural Division Offices were in a giant warehouse in the business district. It stood two stories tall with letters on the front that read "PISD". Tracy dragged me through the doors and down a wide tan hall, giving me a mini tour of the areas where detectives were allowed.

I gazed around wide-eyed, admiring the industrial feel. Detectives were independent contractors. Most got work from referrals, but there were interactive screens throughout PISD where they posted jobs for anyone to apply. A few detectives were searching for available jobs as we passed through. Tracy said they were great for new detectives trying to establish themselves. The PISD was one of the organizations that existed at the crown of Ahl's discretion, so I knew their primary mission included licensing and governance. Like most things in the coalition, there weren't many rules other than not killing each other for a case.

We went to the second floor, where the executive offices were, and stopped at a reception desk. A short, squat brownie with a cap of bright red hair took my information and directed us to the seating area. A man strolled up to the desk, his predatory gaze scanning the area and settling on me.

"That's the director," Tracy whispered.

I leaned forward and examined the man. I knew Mat had appointed the chimera director because I attended the meeting. It wasn't until I saw him that I remembered what he looked like. He was just over six feet tall with a sleek, muscular build. His rust-colored hair was cut short, and his bangs stood straight up. He oozed charisma.

Tracy inclined her head as he approached. "Director Cafta."

His eyes flipped back and forth between us. "Tracy. If you're here to reinstate your license, don't bother. You lost your license when you contracted with the crown. The decision is final."

"I have no interest in being a detective again. I'm here to support my friend."

The Director examined me. "A weak mage of Ahl. How interesting. Very well, good day." He turned and strode into his office.

I frowned at his retreat. "What was that about?"

Tracy opened her mouth to answer when a man with dark brown hair came striding out of the office next to the Director's. He pasted a fake smile on his face. "Tracy. Great to see you again. I see you've been recruiting without a license." His amber eyes inspected me from head to toe. "Follow me, ladies."

We followed him to his office, where his smile faded as soon as the door shut. He whirled toward me. "What in the hell do you think you're doing, Jenella?"

My good mood deflated. "How did you know it's me?"

"Prince Mathias is concerned and requested I watch out for you. I agreed only because you're too soft for this type of work. If anything happens to you, I lose my career, reputation, and status." Travis lowered himself into his chair. "You're being coronated in a few weeks, for fate's sake. You need to rethink this ridiculous scheme and be what you were born to be."

Travis was the fifth child of the shifter king and queen, which meant he was the least powerful person in his family. He learned at an early age that power didn't always come in the form of magic. As a result, he focused on his career, becoming powerful there to compensate for his lack of shifter power. He'd befriended me as a child, and I sometimes wondered if it wasn't part of his plan to improve his status. Over the years, I tried to distance myself from him, but it never seemed to work. I leaned back and folded my arms. "No."

His jaw clenched. "This is a huge mistake. You need to stop being so selfish and think of the coalition."

"What I do for the coalition is not your business, Travis. Your job is to find me a mentor."

"I'm not saying this to interfere. I care about you and can't imagine what I would do if I lost your friendship. You need to think this through before you fail and make a fool out of both of us." His eyes held fake pity.

I turned to Tracy. "Why does everyone think I will fail miserably and die?"

She choked back a laugh. "Jen can take care of herself, so no need to worry. Now, about the mentors..."

Travis's face turned sour. "I don't like your choice of friends, Jenella. I thought better of you."

"That's an awful thing to say." Though, since he was my friend, I guessed it was true. "Fine. I'll just call Mat and tell him you refuse to help."

Travis squared his shoulders. "Fine. I'll distribute your profile to possible mentors, but I don't like it. It's beneath you."

Tracy had detoured to the bathroom in an abandoned hallway to put on her glamour earrings. She joined me down the street from the PISD, and we flashed to our new neighborhood.

"Well, that went well," I said.

We headed down the street toward our new house. "That guy is a piece of work. I hope he's not lying about finding you a mentor. I can totally see him sabotaging your success. It wouldn't surprise me if he told everyone who you really are. Are you sure he can be trusted?"

"He's scared of Mat, so he won't give my identity away. But yeah, he might sabotage my success."

"If you don't mind, I'll reach out to some eligible mentors. I mean, does he really think this is about him? Sheesh."

"Travis thinks everything is about him." I needed to end our so-called friendship.

We turned the corner, and I stopped in my tracks. The craftsman-style house I'd bought for my detective cover home was in a middle-class, mixed area where supernaturals who didn't have a pack, family, or tribe lived. The house stood two stories tall with a wide, covered front porch supported by gleaming square white columns. At the top, the small square attic gave it a stately and adorable appearance. The light gray paint was perfect, and the large windows with glossy white trim reflected in the sun.

As I headed for the door, the smile on my face grew wider. I stepped inside and admired the living room with a fireplace, built-in bookcases, and comfortable furniture on the left. An office with open glass doors and a small wooden desk were on the right. As we passed the stairs, I ran my hand over the shiny wooden trim and peered into the small dining room with a rustic table and six chairs. "This place is great."

"There you are," a tenor voice came from the kitchen.

"Ray!" I rushed toward his voice. "Thank you for doing this on such short notice."

His eyebrows drew together. "You're family."

I ran a hand over the counter. "The house looks amazing."

"You should have seen what it took to get that huge magichef through the door." He pointed to an appliance that took up a good chunk of the kitchen.

I had no idea what a magichef was or how to use it, but I assumed it had something to do with cooking. Helen or one of her many kids or grandkids always provided my meals for me. I could count on one hand the number of times I'd even been in the main kitchen at the castle, and the kitchenette in my suite was always stocked with ready-to-eat snacks. "This is nice."

Ray's blue eyes sparkled as he turned to Tracy. "She's pretending she knows how to use one of those. I'm Ray, and you must be Tracy. You have your work cut out for you."

"Yep. Jen, get away from that stuff before you blow up our new house."

I moved to the island and sat on one of the bar stools. "So, what do you think of my glamour?"

Ray shrugged. "It's okay, but I still knew it was you by your voice."

"Yeah. I'll have to fix that." Good thing I had an appointment with the First that afternoon to refresh the glamour. Anticipation shot through me. I rubbed my stomach. "How long until the house is ready?"

"It's about done. You two can move in as soon as you have wards."

"Great. Let's get the wards set up and go see Drake." Tracy headed out the back door.

I slid off the stool and followed Tracy. The First...Drake, I reminded myself, hadn't collected on the meal I owed him, but I knew it was coming. I shook off the thought as we got to work on the layered wards around the house and yard. Tracy set them, and I added my inherent magic, making them super strong. "These wards are great. I don't think even Mat will find fault with this level of security."

Tracy added access spells to the front and back gates and wiped the sweat from her brow. "Yeah. With our magic combined, they're solid. I mean, it'd take an entire coven of witches a good month to bring them down, and even then, I'm not sure they could."

We waited for Ray to finish the kitchen by exploring the top floor. It had two identical master suites, painted in muted tones, each with a massive closet and a spa-like bathroom. Tracy called dibs on the one on the right, so I took the left. When Ray was done, we thanked him and headed toward Dragon headquarters.

Drake seemed distracted. He held out his hand for the earrings and spent a few seconds renewing the glamour and adding a voice variation that raised my voice by two tones. He had me test the voice, then reached up and tucked a loose curl behind my ear. "I shall be less distracted next time."

"Stay out of my head, Drake. The ruling magic doesn't like that and will lash out. What have you guys found out about the dragon that hit the wall? Have you heard from the queen?"

He sighed as he took Tracy's earrings and activated his magic. "The dragon has disappeared. Bastien is working on locating him. Don't worry, we will take care of it." Drake handed the earrings back to Tracy, gave me a slight bow, and left the small room near the entrance.

Something he said or the way he said it bothered me. I glanced back as we left the building. "Was something off about that?"

Tracy shook her head. "I don't know. The entire dragon faction seems off to me."

Chapter 6

I DIDN'T SLEEP WELL that night. When I did, I dreamed of green fire chasing me around a classroom while Travis yelled I was going to fail and die. The next morning, my stomach was sour and raw. Mat's special knock came from the door, and I swung it open. I peeked down the hall, then returned my attention to my brother. "Hey, Mat."

"Good morning, Jenella. May I come in?"

"Sure." I stepped back from the door, my raw stomach flip-flopping.

Mat paced over to the kitchenette, his eyes flooding with emotion. "I came to wish you luck on your exams."

My heart thudded in my chest. "You did?"

"I am not your enemy. I'll admit that I don't like this plan and was skeptical that you'd get this far, but you have proven yourself capable." He shrugged. "I only want to keep you safe because when I look at you, I see that scared little girl I dragged from that cage all those years ago. It's hard to reconcile that with the woman before me."

Tears flooded my eyes, and I swiped my sleeve across them. "Thank you, Mat. That means a lot."

"I still don't like that you chose to pursue a dangerous profession. Just...promise me you'll look after yourself. Don't make bargains outside of basic work contracts, don't trade favors, and ask for help when needed."

Unable to speak, I nodded. And found myself in a bear hug.

"I only ever wanted what's best for you. Hopefully, this helps you find what you're looking for. But don't think I won't stop trying to protect you, even from yourself."

"I'd expect nothing less," I said with a watery smile.

Mat moved toward the door. "I mean it, Jenella. You are smart and strong. Don't let anyone tell you different."

He was trying to convince himself of that instead of me. "Wait."

Mat ignored a stunned Tracy as he turned back, blocking the door. I cleared my throat. "I love you. And thank you for believing in me."

"I love you, too. Don't forget what I said." He nodded to Tracy and slipped out of the room.

Tracy watched him go. She didn't ask about it, and I didn't tell her. It was a tremendous relief to have Mat's support. I didn't realize how much I needed that. Shaking off the thought, I slipped on my shoes. "I think I'm ready."

"You are. I mean, you've been preparing for the licensing exam for what, ten years? You'll do fine. I might have a lead on a mentor if the Deputy Director doesn't find you one."

I stepped into the hall and shut the door. "If there's one thing I know about Travis, he's scared of Mat. He'll find a mentor just so he doesn't get on his bad side."

The sick feeling in my stomach grew as we made our way to the classrooms at the PISD office. I took a deep breath, straightened my spine, and went to the check-in desk. The elf behind the desk glanced up at me and held out a long, elegant hand. "ID and consent forms, please." I handed them over. "This is the licensing exam for independent private detectives. You will be spell-monitored for both the written and physical exams, so don't try to cheat. You will take off any charms and remove any potions from your person. Do not access your magic. If you do, you'll fail. Do you understand these rules?"

"Y-yes."

"Good. Now remove your charms and step into the magic detector." He indicated a glowing blue cylinder to his left.

I removed the bracelet holding Tracy's protective charms and the daggers Mat insisted I carry. The daggers weren't spelled, but I didn't want to take any chances. I touched one of the earrings that held the glamour. Drake's glamour was undetectable by most paranormals, so I hoped the spell couldn't detect it. My hands shook as I stepped into the cylinder. It buzzed as it activated, and blue magic swirled around me before it turned green. I gingerly stepped out. The elf glanced back at his tablet. "You are in booth three. Good luck, Ms. Hendrix."

Relief flooded me as I entered the classroom, thankful that Drake's magic was undetectable by even an advanced spell detector. I needed to think about that more later because if he decided he no longer wanted to be my ally, it could become a problem. I shook the thought off and looked around. There were nine chairs arranged in a semicircle, with tablets docked in front of them. Two were already taken, a blue glow of a spell swirling around the occupants. I made my way to number three and took a seat, activating the spell. The classroom faded, and I couldn't see anything beyond my desk.

Tracy wasn't kidding about the test being easy for me, and I returned to the waiting room two hours later, licensed. As soon as our eyes met, I held up the disc containing my license, a grin on my face. "I did it!"

Her lips twitched. "I knew you'd do well. You totally over-studied for a test designed for supernaturals who have a lot less going for them. I mean, you are...a Mage of Ahl, so...."

There were multiple layers to each magical faction. Shifters had different animal types, vampires were ranked by age, and there were several types of dragons. There were two types of mages. Mages of Ahl were more powerful than forte mages. Both had an internal well of magic to draw from, but forte mages had specific types of magic. War magic was Emine's forte. She could conjure any weapon imaginable. Her brother Ray had architectural magic. Forte mages could only use their magic within the bounds of their forte.

Mages of Ahl were different in that we could use our powerful raw magic, what I called my inherent magic, for anything. We could absorb witch spells and tune our internal magic to that spell. Once we learned a spell, we never forgot it. Ahl magic registered to the senses of paranormals differently than Forte magic, or I would have disguised myself as a more common Forte mage. Other mages of Ahl didn't have healing magic. It was a gift passed down from our grandfather, another First, who created all the healing races like griffins, caladrius healing birds, and unicorns, though unicorns and caladrius were very rare.

I'd spent most of my life absorbing spells. It helped compensate for my three magics not properly mixing. If my inherent magic and the ruling magic mixed like they were supposed to, I could absorb and mimic the magic of *any* supernatural species. Mat thought the magics would mix if I spent more time around other supernaturals. I doubted that. The ruling magic seemed to be waiting for something, and I needed to figure out what. I didn't tell him that, though. I didn't want to ruin my one chance of working in the career I wanted and my freedom by trying to figure out what it wanted. "Hopefully. Let's go move into our new house."

On our way out, we ran into Travis and the Director standing by the classroom. They were talking to the elf who had checked me in. The

Director didn't recognize Tracy with her glamour on and barely spared her a glance before he flashed a fake smile at me. "Congratulations, detective. I hear you did well on your tests."

"Uh. Sure. Thank you, Director. I'm looking forward to meeting my mentor and getting started."

"That's what we wanted to talk to you about. Do you have a minute?"

My stomach sank when I saw the smirk on Travis's face. I clasped my hands in front of me to keep myself from strangling him. "Is there a problem?"

The Director's fake smile grew. "No, not necessarily a problem. I just wanted to warn you that mentors usually choose someone of their own magical species. You are, unfortunately, the only Mage of Ahl. The Deputy Director has made extensive efforts to work around that. Still, there may be a delay in finding a seasoned detective willing to take you on as an apprentice."

I glared at Travis. His smug smile said it all. He'd do the minimum Mat asked and no more. I was no longer sure my secret was safe with him. He cleared his throat. "Don't worry. I was able to find three possible mentors, all capable."

"The only issue is that none of them have participated in the mentorship program for a long time, if ever..." the Director added, his voice trailing off.

My shoulders slumped as I saw my chance of freedom slip away. It took all I could muster to keep a neutral face as I thanked them and bolted out the door.

I stomped down the front sidewalk, anger roaring inside of me. The ruling magic vibrated. It was always a struggle to contain it when I was angry because it wanted to put people in their place. "One job. Travis had one job, and he couldn't even do that. He wants all the benefits in this so-called friendship without putting forward any effort. I could throttle him."

Tracy pulled me out of the way as a herd of horse shifters passed. "Don't lose hope. I mean, younger detectives usually mentor, so they have someone loyal to help watch their backs. It's not unheard of for older detectives to mentor someone."

I ducked as a blue fairy flew too low as he came in for a landing. "It doesn't matter. I'm sure Travis chose people who wouldn't even consider giving me a chance."

"I'm sorry, Jen. I'll see what I can do. What's the deal with you two, anyway?"

I tossed my braid over my shoulder. "When I was a kid, Mat decided I needed to hang out with other kids while staying inside his protective bubble. I'd suffered trauma and had a hard time interacting with people. He thought if I had friends, it would help draw me out of my shell. His first advisor at the time was Gabriel, the Shifter Alpha. He hosted kids from a bunch of packs once a month. Mat sent me to a gathering, hoping I'd make friends. What I found were a bunch of bullies, which didn't do much for my mental state.

"Travis stepped in and stood up for me before I killed them all, which, at the time, I would have. After that, we hung out at those events. Everyone else ignored me if I stuck close to him, mostly. They still sucked. Luckily, Bastien ended the torturous visits when he became my guard. Travis would still come around to introduce me to a new friend every now and then. He was basically my only friend."

Tracy's eyes widened as I spoke. "I hate to tell you this, but that's not friendship."

"I'm beginning to figure that out. Bastien never directly told me how toxic Travis was, but I know he thought it. He protected me, and that was good enough for me."

"But it's not good enough now. Travis was using your title to impress people, and he still is. You don't need friends like that."

She was right. I didn't want to think about it too hard because I'd have to admit I had no idea what having and being a friend meant. "The chance to have genuine friends is something I don't think I'll ever get. I can't make friends as Detective Hendrix because I'll have to lie to people about myself. Beyond that, no one sees past my title. I'll never be able to know who I can trust."

Tracy opened her mouth to respond but was interrupted by a loud roar. We both jumped and swung toward the sound. A yellow creature about thirty feet long and twelve feet tall slithered down the street––a wyrm dragon. Glowing yellow eyes locked on a family of wolf shifters, and the dragon roared again. We watched in horror as it stretched its giant head, opened its mouth, revealing two rows of spiked teeth, and ate one of them.

I yanked my phone from my pocket and texted Bastien and Drake. Just as I hit "send", the dragon turned, plucked a banshee from a roof, and ate her, too. Tracy shoved me out of the way and threw a spell. I ricocheted off a stone building and fell on my ass. The spell hit the creature in an explosion of red light. It caused the dragon to wobble from side to side, bouncing off buildings and ruining awnings. Paranormals bolted in a mass panic. Some dragged kids, and others shoved their way through the crowd to escape.

The dragon recovered and lunged for Tracy. I hopped to my feet. She dove to the right, rolled, sprung to her feet, and threw another spell. I absorbed it and tuned my inherent magic to that same spell as she scrambled to escape his snapping crocodile-like jaws. Tracy threw a potion that barely missed my head. It hit the dragon's face, and its jaw froze shut, bands of magic wrapping around it. I ducked under the dragon and touched a toe, hitting it with ruling magic, ordering him to shift to his human form, then darted away.

It didn't work. The dragon's barbed tail swung toward me, and I flashed away, but not fast enough. One barb caught my back. I gritted my teeth against the searing pain. Tracy raced in, throwing spells and potions. I pulled all the anger that I kept buried deep inside me to the surface, hoping to coax the ruling magic into helping. With a wheeze, I mixed that anger with a shredding spell I'd absorbed from Tracy. I didn't bother to get up as I hurled it at the wyrm. At the same time, Tracy threw a spell. Our magic crashed together just before they hit the dragon, bouncing off and hitting the store's front. Bricks crashed to the ground around us. Tracy yanked me around the corner. "What the hell, Jen?"

I didn't get a chance to answer before a black and green dragon sixty feet long and twice the size of the wyrm descended from the sky, plucked it off the street, and slammed it back down. Drake had arrived.

Bastien's midnight dragon form was right behind him. He shot at the wyrm like a rocket and banged its head on the ground. *Hit it with a knockout spell!* boomed through my head.

I didn't hesitate, tuning my inherent magic to the best knockout spell I knew. I flung it toward the wyrm. The ruling magic finally decided to help and laced itself in the spell, making it ten times stronger. Tracy threw a different knockout spell. Our magic clashed again as it streamed toward the wyrm. Bastien launched into the air right before it hit.

The problem with watching too many movies is that you develop wrong ideas about how things should happen. As a human movie lover, I had certain expectations about how a dragon exploded. Like, I thought there'd be a dramatic "*boom*" sound that made me deaf for a few minutes. But that's not how it went. Instead, a high-pitched "*squeeeeeeeeeeeeeee*" assaulted my ears. Yellow and green goo erupted from the wyrm, splashed against the surrounding shops, and sloshed straight toward us. Tracy dove on me, and we crashed down on the cobblestones, covering our heads with both arms. The goo splashed over us, coating us.

When everything settled, I carefully sat up, ran healing magic through myself, and checked Tracy for injuries. "Are you alright?" I wheezed.

She dropped her arms from her head. "What the hell just happened?"

My back ached, and my arm throbbed, but I could feel the healing magic working. I wrapped my sore arm around my waist. "I don't think mixing our magics is such a good idea."

The sound of heavy wings and shoes pounding on the pavement interrupted our conversation, and I staggered to my feet. "Oh, shit. Bastien looks pissed."

"Yeah, no kidding." Tracy took a nervous step toward me.

Bastien melted into his human form, the blotches of goo disappearing from his naked body. "Can you two not understand simple instructions? I said knock him out, not kill him."

"We *were* trying to knock him out, Bas. Our magics accidentally clashed." I didn't mention the ruling magic acted on its own. I didn't think it would help the situation.

"That is no excuse for killing him."

"That dragon ate two paranormals before you got here, and there's a bunch more injured. Buildings are destroyed. Do you want to explain what the hell is going on with the dragons, or will I have to take official action?"

Bastien's eyes flashed with anger before filling with sorrow. "He was a good dragon. He deserved better."

"Wait, what? I hate to tell you this, but good dragons don't eat innocent people on the streets," Tracy said.

"I don't believe he was coherent."

"What do you mean, he wasn't coherent?" I asked.

"He looked pretty coherent to me," Tracy said.

Bastien shook his head. "There was something wrong with his brain. I couldn't reach him. Like the one who hit the ward, he was single-minded."

I frowned. That didn't make any sense. All dragons had some form of mind magic. Bastien could use it and his ruling magic to make people obey. If the dragon was single-minded, it meant something was seriously wrong. "Who could do that to a dragon?"

Bastien shook his head. "I don't think even my mother could make a dragon act like that." He sighed. "You two get out of here. Do not go anywhere but home."

"I'm sorry, Bas. The implications didn't occur to me." I didn't try to keep the sadness out of my voice.

He inclined his head and shot into the air, shifting into his dragon form.

I reached for my glamour earrings when I stepped out of the shower. Finding them missing, I frantically searched my room. My senses registered we had company, and I texted Tracy about my earrings and then threw on some clothes, grabbed a brush, and wrangled my hair into a messy bun. Tracy texted back that Drake had my earrings, so I headed downstairs.

The arguing voices cut off as I padded into the kitchen. Mat sat at the kitchen table with a stern expression and an untouched drink in front of him. Beside him, Emine devoured a sandwich, not even acknowledging my entrance. Tracy sat across from them, her face red with anger as she glared at Bastien. Next to Bastien, Drake gave me a small wave and opened his palm, showing me the earrings. I nodded, then focused on the ancient vampire who sat next to Tracy, his face expressionless as he played with his phone.

Tarquin wasn't just any ancient vampire. His match, or wife, ruled the vampires for over five thousand years, so he was considered the vampire king. Although, he didn't seem to have any interest in ruling and preferred to be referred to as the Queen's Consort. Rumor had it that they'd been matched for nearly six thousand years and were still happy. I wasn't sure I believed that, but I hoped it was true. The guy had a deadly reputation. He'd been around a little here and there throughout my life, but I never expected to see him sitting in my new house. My eyes swept over him, from his professionally styled dark hair to his expensive charcoal suit. But I wasn't interested in any of that. What intrigued me was that he was also a licensed detective.

I swallowed and took the earrings from Drake, putting them in my t-shirt pocket before heading to the magichef to try to find something to drink.

Mat cleared his throat. "How are you feeling, Jenella?"

"A little sore, a little guilty, but otherwise fine."

"Great! Problem solved. I need to get back to work, so let's move this conversation along," Emine interjected. "So, tell me about the wyrm fight."

Mat grunted as I turned my attention to her. As the head of Enforcers, she rarely headed up investigations. Mat probably insisted only because it involved me. I didn't care. I only wanted to get the lecture over and figure out why the vampire was in my house. "What do you want to know?"

Emine leaned forward, her eyebrows wiggling. "Was blowing up a dragon fun?"

"That is highly disrespectful!" Bastien bellowed.

"I know one dragon who'd be fun to blow up," Tracy murmured.

"Says the witch who can't even control her spells," Bastien countered.

"Killing is never fun," Mat added.

"It's an honest question!" Emine protested.

The First was silent, his long legs stretched out and arms folded, his eyes dancing with amusement. The vampire didn't even look up from his phone.

I pulled on the ruling magic. "Enough!" I pointed at Emine. "That question *was* disrespectful." I pointed at Tracy and Bastien. "I don't know what kind of dick-measuring contest you two have going on, but end it now!"

"And...?" Emine said, unfazed by my orders.

I sighed. "We were just walking down the street. The wyrm wasn't even after us. I texted Bas. What were we supposed to do, let it eat a bunch of people?" I wasn't a coward in dangerous situations, though I didn't go looking for them. I'd been that way since I was six, and Mat and I were fleeing for our lives. He had to fight and kill all the people chasing us, and I couldn't stand it. So I did what I could to help. I was only four months past my sixth birthday the first time I killed someone. It was easy because no one expected a child to brutally attack them. Mat was mortified and forbade me from carrying a weapon after that. I still did, though, and he let me.

The shouting started again, and I buried my head in my hands. It was useless to stop Bastien and Emine when they were on a roll. "Princess."

"Gah!" I shouted into the fray. Somehow, the vampire got close enough to whisper in my ear without me sensing him.

Tarquin's lips twitched. "I am here about your apprenticeship."

Hope zipped through me before I realized he not only knew my real identity but witnessed the dysfunctional and argumentative mess that was my friends and family. My shoulders slumped. "I take it your answer is no."

"That is yet to be seen. Considering your unique circumstances, I wish to know how you plan to become a competent detective."

I reached into my pocket and pulled out the earrings. "The First was kind enough to give me undetectable glamour."

There was no change in the vampire's expression. "The Deputy Director did not give you a glowing reference."

A knife stabbed through my heart. Travis sucked. "It figures. We have a history, and he's not a fan of this plan."

"So why are you set on being a detective?"

I had chills running down my spine from the vampire's aura and didn't want to offend the vampire king as I told him about how I wanted to become a detective for a long time and how Tracy and I formed our plan. I didn't mention my desire for freedom. That seemed too personal to share with a potential mentor. When I was done, he was silent for a long moment. "Be at the vampire headquarters tomorrow at eight."

I clasped my hands to avoid throwing my fist in the air in victory. "So you'll mentor me?"

"This alternative identity idea, along with your inclination to kill dragons, intrigues me enough that I shall ignore that you are a little slow."

He disappeared before my eyes. A smile spread across my face. My freedom was almost locked in. I turned back to the crowd in my kitchen. Sometime during our short conversation, they stopped arguing. Five pairs of eyes, with different levels of excitement and condemnation, focused on me. The smile melted off my face. "Woo hoo?"

Tracy stood and gave me a big hug. "I knew it. I knew he'd mentor you if he got to meet you."

"This is hardly the first time Jenella has met the consort." Bastien's voice was as dry as a bone.

Tracy shot him a look and turned back to me. "When do we start?"

Chapter 7

THE VAMPIRE MANSION SAT in a glen surrounded by pine trees three streets away from the castle of Ahl. Like the Castle of Ahl, it sat on several acres and was enclosed by a thirty-foot warded wall and a guard gate. Unlike the Castle of Ahl, several vampires lined the wall. They stared at us with hard eyes as we approached. The vampire at the gate looked at our credentials without speaking and called behind him for an escort.

Heart beating out of my chest, I wrapped my magic tighter around me and pretended I didn't feel the tingles from so many eyes on us as we were led inside. The modern white vampire mansion had a bright foyer and smelled like furniture polish and new carpet. Shutters covered the windows to prevent the sun from shining through, but it wasn't dim because of the clever lighting. Newer vampires suffered severe sunburns with only a few seconds of sun exposure, but as they aged, their tolerance grew. By the time they were a couple hundred years old, the sun didn't bother them as much. They were still creatures of the night, but that didn't mean they couldn't go out during the day. The closed shutters told me the castle housed some new vampires, which didn't surprise me. The vampire queen tended to take in strays.

We were led into a sitting area with cheery floral furniture and golden wood floors. A fireplace with two antique chairs facing it sat at one end of the room. A sitting area with two sofas facing each other at the other. Our guide asked if we wanted something to drink, disappearing when we both declined. I moved to one of the sofas, perched on the edge, took a deep breath, and clasped my hands on my lap. Tracy sat beside me and leaned on the arm to check her phone.

Movement out of the corner of my eye caused me to snap my head toward the door. Tarquin entered the room with a tiny woman on his arm. He led her to the sofa across from us and kissed her hand. "I present you with my wife, Queen Ara of Umbra."

We exchanged polite greetings. The woman tucked her long, silky black hair behind her ear and examined me. "You're right, dear. I would never be able to tell she's Jenella."

I sighed at the thought of another person knowing my true identity. Tarquin brushed off a chair and sat. "Drake has always been good at glamour."

"Of course. So, Jenella, what do we call your alter ego?" Her eyes sparkled with amusement.

I cleared my throat and explained everything, hoping to save time. When I finished, I leaned back and folded my arms. "I don't expect you to understand my reasons, but I feel it down to the core of my soul that I need to do this. I appreciate Consort Tarquin taking the time to consider me as an apprentice."

Vampires freaked me out. Not because they were apex predators. Many paranormals were apex predators. They did this thing where they went completely still when they were in deep thought. Ara and Tarquin did it when I was done explaining, never taking their eyes off me. I fought not to squirm in my chair. Tracy put her phone in her pocket and they both snapped out of their trance. Ara's face lit up in a smile. "I am thrilled you would choose my Quin as your mentor. That is a great honor, and you are his ideal apprentice."

I blinked. "Thank you?"

Tarquin squinted. "Call me Quin, not Tarquin or Consort. As your mentor, I will not tolerate whining or complaining. Do not expect me to do any handholding. You are responsible for your own cases. You will listen to me and not question my judgment. You might be the incoming queen, but I have been alive for a long time and, therefore, know more than you. If you find yourself in trouble, you will contact me. I do not expect you to find yourself in trouble. Do you understand?"

I sat back and folded my arms. "I respect that you're much older and wiser and will gladly take your advice. However, don't expect me to be a meek little mouse that follows your every order without question. I'm not built that way. Believe me when I say people as strong or stronger than you have tried and failed. I agree to be responsible for my own cases and to try to stay out of trouble. As you pointed out, I am young and inexperienced and will make mistakes. I only ask that you help me learn from them."

Quin nodded. "I agree to the stupidity clause, but not the rebellion clause. If you do not follow my instructions, there will be consequences."

"And I agree to the inexperience clause, but not the dictator clause. I'll follow your instructions if they're reasonable. I'll try to listen to you to the best of my ability. You will at least give me a chance to explain myself without going all vampy when I don't."

His lips twitched. "Vampy?"

I waved a hand. "You know what I mean. Don't try to go all creepy on me. Oh. And if you try to influence me with vampire magic, my magic will lash out at you, and the results won't be pretty."

Ara's laugh sounded like a tinkling bell. "Oh, dear. This is so much fun! You two are meant to work together." She patted Quin on the thigh.

Quin rubbed his chin. "I am aware of the consequences of trying to influence a ruler. As I said, I am much older than you. As such, I agree with the stupidity clause and the ignore a reasonable order clause. I also agree to the vampy clause."

I had to rethink the negotiations to figure out what we agreed to. "Agreed." My head tingled as the magic settled over me. Paranormals didn't make written contracts, but instead used magical oaths, which were more binding. The consequences for breaking one were anything from going bald to losing a limb. You never knew what magic would decide. It kept us honest in our dealings.

I frowned, realizing vampires were immune to magic. "Do magical contracts work on vampires?"

Ara's laugh tinkled again. "Of course, dear. No one is immune to magical contracts or the ruling magic of the throne of Ahl."

Quin slid a manilla file to me. "This client will contact you in the next few hours. I've provided basic details, so you don't sound stupid when he calls. Do not expect me to intervene nor provide any future cases."

I couldn't help the grin that spread across my face. "Thank you. I won't let you down."

He sat back and examined me. "We shall see."

I rested on a park bench in the human world near a pocket named Hospa two days later. I made Tracy stay in our rented car. The smell of fresh-cut grass washed over me as I soaked up the sights and sounds of small children who giggled and chased each other on the playground as their parents looked on. Nearby, a group of older kids played baseball, taunting each other with clever insults. Sadness washed over me. I never knew the feeling of freedom that came with playing a carefree game with friends. I doubted

I ever would. Watching the scene in front of me, I decided to work hard to savor every minute of freedom while I had it.

"Good morning, Jen Hendrix," a smooth, arrogant voice said.

I flinched, ripped from my thoughts. Intelligent brown eyes examined me from the other end of the long bench. The guy's thick brown hair blowing in the breeze. My potential client would have looked forgettable without his fangs peeking over his lips. My shoulders slumped at the realization that Quin had set me up to work on a case for his son. I glanced back at the playground, then chuckled.

The man's mean eyes focused on me. "Is something funny?"

"Oh. Uh. You have…" I cleared my throat. "Your fangs are showing." I pointed to my lip.

His fangs snapped back in. "My source said you were a professional."

I'd forgotten the vampire prince didn't have a sense of humor. So I held up my hand in a stop gesture. "I meant no disrespect. It just caught me off guard. You have to admit vampires your age don't often get caught out in the human world with their fangs down." After the words left my mouth, I realized that wasn't the smartest thing to say. I wasn't making a good first impression.

"Ah, yes. Because you don't stand out at all." His eyes swept my business suit. "But it is me who will draw attention. Tell me, detective, are you such an expert on vampires?"

What a self-important dick. A business suit wouldn't reveal paranormals to humans. Fangs would, though. I kept my thoughts to myself because I didn't want to further alienate my potential client. My newfound freedom needed to be solidified. I slipped on a professional mask. "My apologies for laughing. However, you are outside during the day, so you're clearly old enough to know better than to show your fangs. Then, there's the signet ring on your right hand and the tie with the small family crest on it. You're a member of the ruling family of Umbra. To answer your question, no. I'm not an expert, but make up for it by being extra observant."

The man's smile didn't reach his eyes. "Very well. I'm Jedediah, the natural-born son of the Queen of Umbra. You may call me Jedediah or Master."

My heart skipped a beat when the realization that I had no idea what to say next slammed into me. I kept my face blank while trying to figure out what an average person would say. While Quin had the power and a disposition that scared the hell out of me, this guy didn't. I realized that if I were a low-level mage, I'd be peeing my pants. I fought to restrain the ruling magic that begged to put him in his place. "Okay, Jedediah. If your mother is the Queen of Umbra, that means Tarquin is your father, right?" He nodded. "And since he's a detective, I'll have to pass on your case because I'm in no position to offend him." I hopped off the bench and started walking away out of "fear" of Quin. I hoped the reaction would seem natural, but I had no idea.

"Miss Hendrix." Jedediah caught up with me and blocked the narrow path. "My father is busy with another case and suggested you for the job."

Relief washed over me as I stopped in my tracks. "Why?"

"I run the House of Jedediah, the second-largest vampire house in the world. We were recently swindled out of a lot of money. My father suggested you were the best detective for this type of crime."

I raised an eyebrow. "Did he?" I wasn't sure why Quin lied to his son about my credentials, but he took the bait, so I didn't care.

"Yes. He said you are discrete and professional and, although not the brightest crayon in the box, would find a way to get the job done." He held up his hands. "His words, not mine."

"Why would you hire someone who your father said was stupid?"

"My father can be rather sarcastic and difficult. He is the reason my fangs were out. I had just got off the phone with him before our meeting. He thinks most people are stupid." I stepped around him and kept walking, forcing him to catch up to me to appease the ruling magic that still fought to beat the vampire prince down. He caught up and continued, "You are obviously very bright, although you're the weakest Mage of Ahl I have ever met. Your magic barely registers to my senses." He waved his hand as if erasing that statement. "Though I don't think it will take much magic to solve this case, so that is of no concern."

I came to a screeching halt, put my fists on my hips, and glared. Concealing my magic was a skill I excelled at. I didn't know how to relate to people, but I knew that supernaturals got offended when someone called them weak. I figured if I didn't react, it would seem strange. "Okay. I'll hear you out and decide if it's a case I want to take. If it is, I'm not agreeing to a deal until I can confirm Consort Tarquin is okay with it."

"I assure you, he is. Shall we have a seat?" He motioned to a picnic table.

Once we settled on opposite sides, Jedediah pulled his jacket cuffs down and laced his fingers together on the table. "As I said, we were recently swindled out of some money. We can't figure out who did it, so we don't know who to kill. That's where you come in. I want you to find our money and tell me who did this. I will take care of the rest." His eyes flashed red, and he bared his fangless teeth in an attempt to smile.

I rested my elbows on the table. "Just like that, huh?"

He waved a hand. "I will, of course, be offering a substantial payment for this information."

When I made eye contact with him, I realized I felt slimy magic coat my head. I tore my eyes away before the ruling magic lashed out. "Let's get something straight before we go any further, Jedediah. I will decide to take this case based on whether I think I can solve it. Not based on money, and not because you think you can use persuasion magic on me. I suggest you stop playing your games, or I'm walking, and you can find another detective to take your case."

Jedediah blinked, and the slimy magic retreated. "Very well, Ms. Hendrix. We had an account with three million dollars disappear without a trace. We have conducted an internal investigation that turned up nothing.

I would like you to find it. I will provide you with all the details of our internal investigation."

"Was it in the same bank as your other accounts?"

"No. We keep our money in many different banks inside and outside of the coalition."

"Where was this money located?"

"In the Bank of Mahri."

"And no other accounts were touched?"

"No. Just the one."

"And you've checked all your blood bonds?"

While dragons shared some sort of hive mentality, vampires had an extreme monarchy type of magic. The queen had a magical connection to all vampires through blood bonds. House masters were mini-dictators appointed by the queen. She appointed them based on whether they were powerful enough to blood bond and control vampires. Some cared about the vampires that belonged to their house, others didn't. Ara didn't seem to care as long as the vampires in the house didn't go rogue and the housemaster obeyed her commands. Jedediah appeared to be the latter. Those types of house masters thought of lower vampires as expendable and easily replaced. It irritated me, but the rulers of each magical race had the autonomy to run their kingdoms the way they wanted. My job as queen was to rule over the rulers so the coalition stayed strong and to make decisions when the different races had disputes. "So, you want me to find the money and give you the name of the person responsible so you can kill them? Even if it's a member of your own house?"

Jedediah's eyebrows lowered. "I care very much about my vampires. You should remember that."

"Sure. But you'll kill someone without knowing the reason they took your money?"

"I will kill anyone who takes what's mine."

What a dick. I didn't know Jedediah's parents well, but I knew they cared about their people, at least as much as vampires that old could care. This guy would never stick his neck out for someone else, not even one of his own. I took a deep breath. "Okay. So, do you want me to focus on finding the money or the culprit?"

The interrogation went on like that for several minutes. I learned that the money was there at eight in the morning and gone by ten, with no transaction record noted on the account. Jedediah believed that none of his people had anything to do with its disappearance. He had a list of enemies and suggested I start there. Many of them were dragons.

After I ran out of questions, we watched the kids play while I thought it through. Well, I watched the kids. Jedediah's stare bore into the side of my head the whole time. I stared for a few more minutes out of spite. A petty yet satisfying move. "Okay, Prince Jedediah. I'll take your case, but I'll need all the information about the account. Also, a complete record of your internal investigation and access to your people. Oh, and I need to confirm with Tarquin that he referred me and approved this investigation."

Jedediah pulled an envelope from his jacket. "This contains thumb drives with all the information about the internal investigation. It also has the codes to the Magidrop account, where you can access half of your payment. You do have a Magidrop account?"

I nodded. I did only because Tracy said I'd need one and showed me how to use it. She was the most valuable and likable personal guard I ever had. I hoped she'd stick with me long enough to become a friend. I slipped the envelope into my cross-body bag.

Jedediah held up a hand like we were in court. "I swear on the name of the Royal Family of Umbra and House Jedediah that I'll give you full access to the house records and pay you in full when the case is solved."

I didn't hold up my hand. "I swear on my detective's license that I will conduct the investigation to the best of my ability, provided Tarquin approves of my involvement."

The magical contract snapped into place, and the deal was sealed. He nodded toward my bag. "The relevant phone numbers are in the file. I would like the names of the thieves, but focus on finding the money." Butterflies erupted in my stomach at the thought that I had my first case. Tamping it down, I stood and headed toward the car. Jedediah followed close behind me. I gave him a half-hearted wave when he stopped in front of a vehicle.

Jedediah wasn't looking at me. His eyes were glued to the east. He bolted toward his car so fast that my eyes didn't register movement. I whipped around to see if any humans noticed. A few had their mouths open or were pointing. I didn't have time to consider the problem because a tingle of warning ran up my spine. I scanned the eastern sky to see what spooked him. Flying straight toward me were two beasts, each the size of a bus. One brown and one powder blue, they had long necks and a huge wingspan.

Chapter 8

A PIERCING SCREAM TORE through the air, and everyone in the park turned toward the descending dragons.

A woman who stood by her car screamed, "Shiiiiiiiiit."

"Shit is right." I raced toward our rental car.

Tracy stood by the car, waving her hands. "Jen! Dragons! Get in the car!"

I glanced back at the once-happy scene in the park. Parents scooped up their screaming kids, and people ran in every direction. Some dashed toward their vehicles, while others didn't look like they had any direction in mind. A woman with three kids struggled to get them moving. "We need to help them." I changed directions, picking up her screaming daughter. "To the trees!" I shouted to the scattering parents. "Run to the trees!" I grabbed the lady whose daughter I held and dragged her and her kids toward the tree line. Tracy scooped up another kid and followed.

One of the dragons swept down and skimmed the tops of the trees with its talons and made a beeline toward a woman standing by herself beside the picnic shelter. "Keep going," I urged the mother with a toddler in her arms.

Once inside the tree line, I set the little girl down and spun around. The other parents ran toward the trees as the dragons swept back and forth. At least they weren't spitting fire. I wrapped my magic around me tight, trying to appear as human as possible. The dragons were leaving the humans alone. I didn't understand. Dragons had magic to cloak themselves from humans, and their queen insisted they use it when not in the pockets. Some even used it in the pockets. I'd sensed them. The fact they weren't cloaked was a big problem. I'd bet anything that Bastien and Drake knew more than they were letting on. Whenever I asked about the queen or the wall incident, they claimed to have it handled. This incident proved they didn't. That...was not okay. Especially if dragons were terrorizing humans. My shoulders slumped as I realized I needed to spend time in the palace getting answers. So much for my freedom.

I shook off that awful thought as I noticed a few people with their phones raised. I put my hand on Tracy's arm. "Can you take care of that problem?"

Tracy was already on it, weaving a spell. "Sure, but I doubt I'll get them all. What do you think they're doing? I mean, this is dangerous and against the number one law. Don't they know we wouldn't stand a chance if humans came after us?"

"I don't know. I bet you anything Bastien knows more than he's letting on. He and Drake have been withholding information. Treating me like a child. And I let them so I could be free, so this is partially on me."

She let the spell go. I flipped on my magic sight to see it drift through the crowd, settling on the electronics. The humans didn't even notice. "Yeah. There's no way I can get all of them, but that takes care of the majority."

"Thank you."

The brown dragon screeched as they neared the woman standing by the picnic area. I craned my neck to see the smaller dragon turn in the direction Jedediah had gone. "What is that on his back?"

Tracy didn't have time to answer before a flash of brown swept the top of the trees as it swooped down toward the woman, talons extended.

My heart skipped a beat. They were going to take a human. Without a second thought, I hopped behind a tree and flashed, reappearing on the woman's other side behind another tree. I lunged out from behind it and grabbed her around the waist just as she was lifted off the ground. "I've got you. Fight!" I wrapped my legs around the support beam and held on for dear life. Tracy sprinted toward us, screaming my name. I tightened my grip on the woman as the ruling magic vibrated, wanting to take down the dragon. I wasn't sure what it would do to the woman, and killing a dragon in the human world would be catastrophic. With a tight grip, I swung my head back toward Tracy. She fought to get through the crowd to get to us, her face red with anger.

"Let go of me!" the lady above me shouted. My attention snapped back to the situation, and I realized she wasn't talking to me but beating on the talon with her gloved hand.

The dragon yanked, and we both went flying. I tightened my grip on the woman's waist, desperately trying to hold on. I could flash us both before we hit the ground. Just as I uncoiled my magic, a flash of blue caught the corner of my eye as the smaller dragon snatched us out of the air and deposited us onto a cold floor. We landed in a heap, with me on the bottom and the woman on top, her elbow smashing into my face. I tried to flash, but we bounced off a wall and smashed back down on the floor. "Well, that didn't go like I planned," I gurgled.

The woman sat up and brushed her thick brown and silver hair out of her face. Calm gray eyes examined the cage, assessing every detail. "How are we going to get out of this mess? And are these dragons? How screwed are we?"

I turned on my magic sight as I sat up. The woman's bright white aura with blue streaks glowed so brightly it caused me to squint. "You're a juror," I said with awe. Not only because I'd thought she was human, but because there weren't many jurors in the coalition. They were one of the most respected types of mage. "Why do you look middle-aged?" I'd seen only a handful of supernaturals who looked middle-aged. Some could change the age they appeared, like the griffins George and Helen, who always looked old and stately. Most supernaturals looked like a bunch of thirty-somethings because it was where they stopped aging and they didn't bother to change it. This woman looked like she was in her late fifties.

"What do you mean?" she asked, looking down at herself. "What's a juror?"

My mouth dropped open. It wasn't uncommon for supernaturals to discretely live in the human world and even marry and have children with humans. We monitored several witches and mages who were half-human. But this woman was a full-blooded mage. It was rare to find one unaware of their origins and raised by humans, but it did happen. We had entire teams dedicated to tracking them down. I'd never met a supernatural who reached middle age without being found. They always gave themselves away when their magic developed and they couldn't control it. Shifters were born able to shift, and kids shifted back and forth all the time. Mages were born with magic and slowly grew into it. I was the exception, with most of my magic developing overnight when I was three. "Um...it's a..." I trailed off when I noticed she was no longer paying attention to me but examining the dragon flying beside us. Both dragons banked right, throwing us to the other side of the cage. Right. Our predicament took priority. "I'll explain everything later." I pulled out my phone and saw it had no service.

When I looked back up, the woman had removed her gloves and was leaning through the bars with her hand on the dragon. "Got it!" she yelled, then removed her hand.

"Got what?" I peered over the side. We were too far from the ground, so crash landing wasn't an option. The second dragon flew closer as I stood to examine it. Two men were lying on the floor of the cage, strapped to its back. Well, one man and a bear shifter. The un-shifted man was none other than my new client, Prince Jedediah. His pristine suit was ripped and dirty, and there was dried blood caked on the side of his face. The implications ran through my head. What had he gotten me into? My brother was going to be pissed. *Great.* I threw those thoughts out of my head and examined the cage.

"His sins." The woman with me frantically moved from bar to bar, shaking them.

I swept my eyes over the ceiling but couldn't see a door. We'd come through that way when thrown, but it was solid. I reopened my magic sight, and just like I thought, the whole cage was coated in a spell. Even when I tried to use the ruling magic, it bounced off the spell inside the cage. I put my hand on the woman's shoulder. "You're not getting out that way. It's magically sealed."

She flipped around, shoved my hand away, and threw a punch that would have broken my nose if I hadn't seen it coming from a mile away. I ducked out of the way, caught her fist, twisted her arm, and planted her on her face, shoving my knee in her back. "Calm down."

She bucked and kicked. "Don't you tell me to calm down, young lady. Get off me."

I dug my knee further into her back. "You were the one who said we need to figure out how to free ourselves. I'm just trying to help!"

"*I* was figuring it out while *you* were enjoying the view!"

Letting her go, I took a deep breath. "We're too far off the ground to crash, and this cage is coated in a spell. I need you to be quiet and stay away from the bars while I figure out what kind of spell it is."

She kicked me in the chest. Hard. I flew backward, smashed against the bars, and landed on my butt. "So I take it that's a no?" I wheezed.

The woman's hands flew to her mouth. "Oh my. Oh, my, I'm so sorry. I...it...just...."

I kept my left hand on my bruised chest, reminding myself she thought like a human. "Don't worry about it. It's a difficult situation."

She took a couple of ragged breaths and turned her head toward the other dragon. She got to her feet and moved to that side of the cage. "Are you okay?" her voice was shaky, her southern accent thick.

"Sure. I have healing magic." I slumped and took a couple of deep breaths, checking my lungs.

"You believe in all that mumbo-jumbo?" she scoffed.

I couldn't help it. I laughed. "Mumbo-jumbo?"

"You said magic twice. Are you one of those tree-hugger spiritual types?"

The woman made no sense, so I said nothing as I sat up. I was still sore, but my healing magic made it bearable. Her steely stare chilled me to the bone when I raised my head. "What?"

"I asked you a question, young lady."

"I'm not ignoring you. I just don't have any idea what you asked."

She rolled her eyes. "Why do you think 'magic' will save us?" She used air quotes on the word magic.

I sighed in relief as the pain in my chest eased. "Because I'm a mage, and you're a juror. It's a powerful combination."

She reached out and snatched my hand. A zing went up my arm as her magic connected with me, and she gasped. "You're...you're not lying."

"What? No. Look, we need to get these idiots near the ground. But first, we need to break the magic in these cages." I held up a finger. "Not necessarily in that order. Do you know how to use your...abilities?"

The woman sniffed. "I don't know what you're talking about."

I pointed to the dragon. "You touched him and said something about his sins. What did you mean?"

She sniffed and didn't answer.

I decided I was on my own and began to examine the magic holding us in the cage, my back tingling from her eyes boring into it.

The magic was a high-level witch spell with a few intricate knots here and there. Unlike mages, witches didn't have a pool of magic inside them. Instead, they wove the natural magic in the air into intricate weaves to serve their purpose. Because I was a mage of Ahl, I could tune my inherent magic to witch spells, and sometimes the ruling magic chose to help, but I couldn't weave spells. The only thing I could do was blast out a burst of magic that matched the spell, or if I was lucky, I could tune it to the opposite of the spell and break it. I needed to be lucky.

Sweat trickled down my temples by the time I tuned my magic to the initial spell. I swiped my brow and closed my eyes to work through the reversal.

"You napping?"

My eyes snapped open, and I focused on my new cellmate. "No. I'm trying to figure out how to break the spell. Like I said I would."

She shook her head as if trying to erase my words and turned toward the other dragon. "If I could reach that other...thing...I can learn his sins, too."

That could work. Maybe. The entire purpose of a juror was to extract rights and wrongs from people and punish them for their wrongs with only a touch. She could knock them out until we could get to safety if I freed us from the cage. Except the lady was clueless. "Do you know how to knock it out with your magic?"

"I don't believe in magic."

"Okay. Then, can you use its sins to knock it out?"

"Animals are usually immune to sins."

"They're not animals. They're dragons who are not only sentient, but extremely powerful. We'll have to get them angry enough to attack us." She didn't respond, so I decided it was pointless to try to get her to help. I plopped back down on the floor. "Let me figure out this spell first, then we'll work on how to knock them down."

She sank to the floor, her laugh ragged and broken. I watched her to make sure she wouldn't kick me in the head. When her laughing died down, she raised her head. "You're either nuts, or you're serious. I can't decide." She took a deep breath. "I guess I'm going to have to trust you. It's not like I have much of a choice."

"Yeah, you are." I realized how cold that sounded. "But it's a two-way street. If you can punish people for their sins, you'll need to do it fast."

Her eyebrows shot up. "I'm not God. By touching people, I learn things. I do not judge sins."

I smiled as warmly as I could manage. "Oh, you'd be surprised what you can do. Give me a few minutes."

She rubbed her eyes, smearing her mascara so she looked like a raccoon, then she squared her shoulders, "Okay."

A genuine smile spread across my face. My cellmate didn't see it because she had already turned around to stare at the dragon flying beside us.

It took me another ten minutes to figure out a reversal of the spell. When I got it, I jumped to my feet. "Got it. You'll need to get away from the bars. If this backfires, hold on tight and do not fall off this dragon."

"Wait, what? You're going to what?"

I motioned her to the center of the cage. "Just sit there. If this cage breaks, move fast and hold on to whatever you can."

She skittered to where I pointed, watching me with wide eyes. "Okay. I've got this." She sounded like she was trying to convince herself more than me.

I turned back to the bars and raised my arms. My skin warmed, and prickling ran through my hands. I counted to three and blasted the wall. My magic bounced off the cage and flung back in a shower of sparks, barely missing my cellmate. She screamed, and I dove, covering her with my body as my magic zipped overhead. It blew a hole in the cage floor beside us, then embedded in the ceiling. A loud "*boom*" had both of us covering our ears. I hopped to my feet and shook my head to get my bearings. The dragon descended fast, flinging us both against the bars at the back of the cage.

My back hit hard enough to jar part of the cage open. I grabbed a broken bar with one hand, stretched my other hand out, and latched on. I tried to swing my legs sideways to the cage but couldn't. My hands started to slip, and I screamed out in frustration, trying harder to get a better grip. Strange enough, the main thought that ran through my head was how pissed Mat would be if I didn't flash myself to safety and leave her to die. I didn't want to flash to safety without my cellmate, but it started looking like I had no choice.

Just when I became resigned to leaving her, something latched onto my wrist. I flew back into the cage and slid across the floor, only stopping when my head hit the other side with a *"thud"*. I sat up, holding my head with one hand and a bar with the other. "Thank you."

My raccoon-eyed cellmate stared back at me, horror on her face. "You...I...?"

She didn't get to say anything else because the second dragon swooped toward us. I jumped to a crouch. "Hold on!" She didn't argue. I tuned my magic to a strong knockout spell. I begged the ruling magic to help. It vibrated so hard in anticipation that I almost fell over.

I blasted knockout magic toward the other dragon's head. The dragon carrying the two men shifted to his human form and plummeted. The cage from that dragon bounced off the back end of the dragon carrying us, causing our dragon to careen to the right. I lost my balance, and we flew out of the cage and landed on a wing. I flung knockout magic toward our dragon's head, and it disappeared from under us. We screamed as we tumbled to the ground.

Chapter 9

I COULDN'T BELIEVE WE were still alive. My eyes fluttered open, and I saw that I was on my back in a field of grass. I heard a bubbling creek nearby, sighed in relief, and stumbled to my feet. My former cellmate was not far away, tangled in a bed of wildflowers. Relief washed over me when I realized she was alive.

I stayed still, assessing the situation. The air smelled of pollution, indicating we were still in the human world. I couldn't hear any traffic or see anything other than thick woods beyond the clearing we landed in.

"That was what you called magic?" my former cellmate wheezed out between breaths.

"Yep." I examined myself for injuries. The dragon must have been preparing to land because we didn't fall far. My head still hurt, but other than that, I wasn't in too bad of shape. I couldn't say the same for my companion. Her right wrist was bent in an unnatural position. She had a giant gash on her leg, and her left knee was swollen. I kneeled beside her. "You going to make it?"

"I don't know," her voice was a whisper. "I think I need a hospital."

I took her wrist in my hand. "In order to heal you, I need to straighten this wrist. It's going to hurt like hell."

"At this point, I don't have much to lose." She closed her eyes.

I set the bone before either of us could think about it. She screamed a shrill scream and kicked at the ground with her good leg. I broke into a sweat and started shaking, a distant memory trying to force itself into my head. Shoving it aside, I glanced at her face. My shoulders relaxed when I saw she was unconscious.

My healing magic wasn't part of my inherent magic but an unexpected gift and the smallest pool of the three magics. Mat and I were both recipients of that gift. He tried not to use his on others because it created expectations. He encouraged me to do the same, but I had difficulty not helping when someone needed it. I ran the magic through her wrist, then probed deeper, running it through and healing all her injuries. When I was done, I stood and stepped back.

Her intelligent gray eyes were wide open. "What did you just do?"

"I healed you. You should be good now, though you might be a little tired. We need to check on the others." Before she could pepper me with questions, I strode toward the wreckage that stretched from one end of the small valley to the other. I stopped at an unconscious dragon in human form, examining the woman with long brown hair and pale skin. Her chest rose and fell steadily. A strange magic emanated from her left wrist. I examined it, noticing a lump on her wrist. I shivered at the darkness of the magic. It felt so slimy that I wasn't going to touch it. "That is not good."

As I stood back up, my former cellmate shuffled up beside me. "Who is that?"

"One of the dragons. When I knocked them out, it caused them to shift. I'm Jen, by the way."

She eyed the downed woman. "I'm Verity, and I'm obviously clueless about this stuff." She motioned to the dragon. "I'm not sure this isn't some kind of nightmare."

I couldn't help but admire her straightforward manner. "It's not a dream. It's also the absolute worst way to learn about the paranormal world. You're doing well, considering." I put my hand on her shoulder. "Are you going to hold it together?"

Her forehead creased, and for a second, I thought my new pal might kick me again. "I'm fine, I think. Where are we?"

I spun in a slow circle. We were in a meadow. The wild grasses were about a foot tall, with red and yellow wildflowers interlaced. There were hills around us, and I couldn't hear any traffic. We needed the shifter and the vampire for their enhanced hearing and smell to figure out which direction we needed to go to find a road. I spotted their cage on the other side of the meadow. As I stood, I slung the dragon over my shoulder, giving myself a magic boost of strength. "I have no idea. Let's save the others, and we'll figure out how to get help." I lurched toward the cage.

"Wait up, Jen," Verity called as she gingerly picked her way through the field behind me.

I paused until she caught up and began walking again. "It might be a long walk."

Verity bopped me on the back of my sore head. "What's that supposed to mean?"

"You might want to stop worrying about the flowers and just walk. Conserve your energy."

She huffed and started walking like a normal person. "I thought it was a crack at my weight."

"Why would I care about your weight?"

"You skinny girls are always critical of weight."

"I'm not the one who brought it up." I remembered she knew nothing about supernaturals and assumed I had human views. "We don't care about weight in the paranormal world because some of us can change our weight and age. I know a couple of griffins who choose to look like they're in their seventies." I ran a hand up and down myself. "This isn't even my real appearance. I'm wearing glamour, though I'd appreciate it if you didn't mention that to anyone."

She stopped dead in her tracks. "No kidding? I can do that? And griffins are real?"

"Yep. All you need to do is imagine yourself at a different weight and age and believe it, though I'm not sure how long it would take to change. It's not instantaneous for mages. And yes, griffins are real. Nasty if you get on their bad side, but overall, good people from my experience."

Verity was silent for a minute. She shook her head as if trying to wake herself. "Your secret is safe with me. I got your truth when I touched you."

"Thank you." I set the dragon on the ground and stretched my shoulders. The bear was in the center of the cage, sprawled on his back, basking in the sun. He hadn't shifted back to his human form. Jedediah stood at the edge of the cage, glaring at me, his jacket draped over his shoulder. His dress shirt clung to him and looked damp. "Huh."

"What?" Verity's voice came out in a squeak.

"I didn't know vampires could sweat. And I'm pretty sure he's immune to the spell holding them in the cage." I turned to her and raised an eyebrow.

She waved me off. "You better do your thing. That man—or whatever he is––looks pissed."

I examined the cage. "You better step away from the bars, Prince Jedediah." He stepped back about six inches and crossed his arms. I used the barest trace of magic on the spell. I wanted the prince to keep believing I was weak. With a zap and another *"boom"*, the spell broke. It was much smoother than when I broke the spell on our cage. I made a mental note to use less magic to break spells in the future.

Jedediah crashed through the cage with super speed and swung me around, pinning me against the bars. His hand was on my throat before I could blink. "Don't ever do that again."

"Do what rescue you?" I croaked as I fought to restrain the ruling magic.

His eyes narrowed. "You think you're funny. You're not. You set me up." His spine went straight, and his hand released my throat. Verity let out a horrified scream. She and Jedediah both flew in opposite directions, landing on their asses.

I ran to Verity. "Are you insane? You could have killed yourself." I ran a handful of healing magic through her, but she was okay physically. Mentally, I wasn't so sure.

Her wide eyes met mine. "He's a nasty man."

"He's not a man. He's a vampire and an old one. They haven't always been civilized." I glanced at Jedediah, who was in a stare-down with the bear who'd lumbered out of the cage without anyone noticing. "It's best you don't touch either of them. I'm not sure about the shifter, but…" I shrugged. "Vampires aren't known for being saints."

I offered her my hand, pulling her up. She marched over to Jedediah and planted her hands on her hips. "You should be ashamed of yourself. That girl is your daughter. I will end you if you ever put someone in that position again. Done. Finished. Kaput. Got it?"

I didn't hear Jedediah's response, but he got to his feet and eased away from her. We needed to get out of there as fast as possible. I pointed to the bear. "You need to shift so we can figure out how to get out of here."

With a bright orange burst of light, a giant naked man with a long nose, broad face, and muddy brown eyes replaced the bear. Verity screeched and turned her back. The man frowned before focusing on me. "There is a road about two kilometers to the west. They carried us for about forty kilometers——or twenty-five miles, for those who never learned the metric system." He pointed at Verity.

"That's a long way." I pulled out my phone. "Still no service. Let's head that way. When we get closer to civilization, I'll call someone to come get us." I strode over to the second dragon. Like the woman, he had that horrible magic emanating from his wrist. Unlike hers, the magic came from a bracelet. I reached out to touch the clasp, and my arm got jerked back.

"Don't touch that." The naked bear shifter dropped my arm. "I'm Colonel Ballard with the Enforcers. I was undercover tracking a group of black magic users until you and your prudish friend showed up. I've seen this magic a time or two, and it's some nasty stuff. We need to take these guys back to Hospa."

"What the hell is Hospa?"

I jumped at Verity's voice, but Colonel Ballard didn't. He must have known she was there. He raised an eyebrow. "Is the juror green?"

"Yeah. One of the lost ones, apparently." I motioned to Verity. "Hospa is a pocket. A pocket is like a mini realm where most paranormals live. We have several of them all over the world. Hospa's not far from here, but we need to get moving if we're going to make it there by dark."

Colonel Ballard didn't turn his naked self around, trying to be polite. "It's my home base, ma'am. We need to get back there to investigate properly."

In my short time with Verity, I learned that she preferred truth to politeness. "I'm going to level with you."

"Please do."

"Everything you see is going to be strange to you. You cannot, under any circumstances, tell your human friends about any of this. There are severe consequences. They could be anything from imprisonment in an old-school dungeon to death. Also, that vampire you touched is a prince. His mother leads the vampires. That makes him very powerful. If he did something to one of his vampires, you need to let it go now."

Her face turned red, and she started to speak, but I shook my head and continued. "This is Colonel Ballard from the Enforcers. They are the supernatural equivalent of police, sort of. He needs to get his suspects…" I motioned toward the dragons, "to jail and investigate this mess. Inside supernatural pockets, shifters and other supernaturals often run around naked before or after they shift, so you're probably going to see more naked people in Hospa. There will be all kinds of creatures that fly, slither, and walk. People will have skin colors, hair, eye colors, and shapes you've never seen. Some paranormals, like giants, trolls, and ogres, are huge. Some, like fairies and pixies, are extremely small. Try to ignore them and anything else that doesn't mesh with your human views of the world. Also, we have a value system that is different from that of humans. It will seem weird, and some things will go against your moral code. You'll have to keep your head down, and for the love of Pete, don't touch anyone."

Verity grinned. "Pete? Besides, you're——"

"Yeah." I cut her off. I couldn't have her blurting my identity out in the present company. "We'll get you to Hospa, then find someone to return you to your home in the human world."

She took the hint. "Okay. You have my word. When we get to Hospa, I'll behave myself. But I need some questions answered."

"Deal." I agreed without thinking about it. Verity yelped as the contract snapped into place.

Colonel Ballard chuckled. "Did you just let a rookie sucker you into a contract?"

I shot him a dirty look, which was so fearsome he didn't even notice. "How are we going to transport the dragons?"

"I'll shift. Load them on my back." He eyed Verity. "The rookie going to be able to keep up?"

"She's awfully worried about stepping on the flowers, but I think she can."

"She's right here and can hear you," Verity retorted.

Colonel Ballard patted me on the shoulder before abruptly shifting back to a bear.

Verity and I loaded the two dragons across Colonel Ballard's back, careful not to let the foul magic touch him or us. Jedediah sat under a tree in the shade and watched like the asshole he was. "Ready, Prince Jedediah?"

He hopped to his feet and began heading west without a word. I sighed. The walk wasn't going to be fun.

We lumbered along at a pace that Verity could manage. She kept turning around and eyeing Colonel Ballard, who stayed behind us. I explained that he was guarding our rear. That was her queue to start asking a million questions. "So vampires and shifters are real?"

"Yep."

"And they get along?"

"Most of the time."

"You mentioned witches. Is that what you are?"

"No, I'm a mage."

"What does that mean?"

"There're two types of mages, Ahl and Forte. Mages of Ahl are generally more powerful than other supernaturals, can use their powers in more than one way, and are considered the ruling class."

Jedediah scoffed, and Verity shot him a chastising look. "What's the difference between them? Why are they called different things?"

"It's based on the way our magic works. Like your magic, mine's internal, like a well inside me. Witches use natural magic in the air and weave spells, and I can learn those weaves and tune my magic to them. I can only blast the magic at something and hope it sticks like I did to break us out of that cage. You are a type of forte mage. Forte mages have all kinds of different talents, but they have one forte. Yours is justice. That's why I called you a juror."

And on it went. I answered questions about the fae, leprechauns, griffins, bigfoot, aliens, and almost every other supernatural creature humans had myths about––most of which were based on at least some truth. As we crested a hill above the highway, Verity fell silent to process the information. Jedediah, who kept his distance the entire way, appeared a few inches from my face. "Don't forget to find my money, Ms. Hendrix." And he was gone, moving so fast that he was a blur. He hopped in the back of a waiting SUV, and it sped off without us.

"That man is a piece of work," Verity whispered.

Colonel Ballard, still in bear form, huffed in agreement.

We stayed just over the hill so motorists couldn't see the bear, and I pulled my phone out and sighed in relief when I saw I had a signal. I opened a human app to find our exact location and thought about who to call. Since I didn't have the number to Hospa's Enforcers and Colonel Ballard had already used up a bunch of energy shifting, I didn't want to ask him to shift. Calling Mat would result in a safety lecture, and Tracy was probably mad. I didn't want to deal with either of them right away. I decided to take a chance and call Emine. As Mat's match and the head of the Enforcers, she would know what to do and have the authority to do it. I stood. "Stay here. I'm going to call for help." I put on a burst of magic and got out of shifter hearing range.

Emine answered on the first ring. "What the hell? Did you dial the wrong number or something?"

"Hi, Emine. Very funny."

She cackled. "Did someone die? Have you been kidnapped? You never call me."

I sighed. "I know. Believe it or not, I was kidnapped, but we got away. We need someone from the Hospa Enforcer's office to pick us up."

She belly laughed. "Well, that's interesting. Mat's head is gonna explode when he finds out. It'll be a hoot. Where the heck are you?"

"Mat's going to wrap me in bubble wrap and try to drag me back to the castle when he hears this. I'm north of Birmingham, Alabama, near I-65 in the human world."

"This happened in the human world?" The delight drained from her voice. We didn't have many restrictive laws because there were too many species, and they policed themselves well. Keeping ourselves hidden from humans was law number one. Even though she was crazy, Emine took her job seriously.

"Yes. Dragons snatched us and put us in spelled cages they carried on their backs, right in front of a park full of people. Tracy fried some of their phones, but there will still be video evidence."

"This is bad. You should call Bastien. He needs to know when dragon shit is going down."

"Dragon shit?"

I heard a door slam in the background. "He might have questions that only you can answer. You'll have to call him. Are you in any kind of danger right now?"

My shoulders relaxed. "No. The bad guys are passed out on the back of a bear. I'm with an Enforcer named Colonel Ballard and a full-blooded juror who's been in the human world her whole life and doesn't believe in magic. Also, Prince Jedediah ghosted us. Called his people through his blood bonds and took off, leaving us and the prisoners on the side of the road."

"As in the vampire Prince Jedediah? My, my, my. I knew this whole detective thing was going to be fun to watch. What have you gotten yourself into so quickly?"

"I have no idea. But it's not funny. This, along with everything else...we have a dragon problem. I think Drake and Bastien are holding out on us. They've been distracted and evasive." I allowed myself to feel the fear, and my voice was a little wobbly.

She blew out a breath. "Okay. I'll dispatch a team. You be careful and *call me* if anything else happens. And call Mat when you're safe. I'll break it to him to ease the blow, but he's going to lose his shit. You need to deal with him. Know what I mean?"

"I will. Thanks for your help."

"No probs. Take care. Ride will be there soon." The phone disconnected.

I called the Dragon Queen's office to get Bastien out of the way so I could spend the next several hours or weeks dealing with my brother and Tracy. The lady who answered was coldly professional. "Prince Bastien's office."

"Hello, this is Detective Jen Hendrix. I would like to speak to Prince Bastien, please."

"I'm sorry, the Prince is unavailable. May I take a message?" Her tone told me I wasn't getting through, no matter what I said.

"Yes. Please tell your prince I called because I had some critical information for him but couldn't get through."

"Of course. Anything else?" she said without missing a beat.

"Nope. Thank you." I hung up. I'd have to deal with that later, too.

A few minutes before our ride arrived, I realized, per our agreement, that I had to let Quin know what had happened. My stomach churned as I dialed.

He picked up on the second ring. "Quin."

"Hey, Quin. This is Jen, um, your new apprentice."

"I am not stupid. And?"

I decided to get straight to the point. "Your son and I, along with two others, were just plucked off the street by two dragons, and Jedediah took off and left us stranded."

"Oh, yes, I'm sure my two-thousand-year-old son needs his daddy to discipline him. Just like I am positive you can figure out a suitable mode of transportation." The phone went dead.

"What a sarcastic ass," I mumbled as I realized that my internship was going to be an awful experience.

Chapter 10

WE CLIMBED INSIDE A nondescript white van and drove toward Hospa twenty minutes later. Colonel Ballard shifted to his human form and wore black sweatpants and a black t-shirt with the Enforcer's emblem. I found myself crushed between him and Verity in the middle seat. The unconscious dragons took up the entire back compartment.

We turned off on an abandoned dirt road and navigated bumps and holes for a few miles, ending in a deep ravine. Instead of stopping, we drove right off, landing in the pocket of Hospa. Unlike Allure, cars were allowed in Hospa because of the remoteness and lack of mages for transportation. If our car had a human in it, that human would find themselves with some missing memories on the side of a road miles away from the entrance while the rest of us continued.

Verity squealed and grabbed the door handle.

Colonel Ballard laughed. "Bet you didn't expect that."

The scent of vegetation and swamp washed over me, and I took a deep breath, admiring the untamed jungle to the right of the car. "Welcome to Hospa, Verity. Remember to keep your head down and don't stare."

She watched a family of leopards bouncing through the tall grass with wide eyes. "Why don't you guys live in the real world?"

I grinned. "Paranormals used to live amongst humans. We even intermarried. If I remember right, we left in the fifteenth century. The Catholic Church got ahold of a coven of witches and proof that magic was real. It freaked them out, so they hunted witches for the next few centuries. A lot of supernaturals got caught in the crosshairs, so the Second Queen of Ahl, who ruled all paranormals, created the pocket realms."

"Wow." Verity pointed at a group of baboon shifters teaching their kids. "I suppose I can see where this works better."

"It does. We like living outside human rule. The pockets all have different climates that appeal to different types of paranormals. Hospa attracts those who prefer untamed land, like shifters, dragons, griffins, sprites, dryads, and some types of elves because it's mostly jungle." It was my mother's most outstanding achievement. One I doubted I'd ever live up to during my captivity in the palace.

Colonel Ballard nudged me with his shoulder. "You ever been to Hospa?"

"No. This is my first visit."

"This pocket doesn't cater to mages, so steer clear of the jungles and swamps. You'll feel more at home in town. There are a few hotels and restaurants there."

I nodded as excitement bubbled through me. I'd never stayed in a hotel before and couldn't wait for the new experience...provided Mat didn't kill me for getting myself kidnapped. "Can you recommend a hotel?"

"What kind of hotel do you want to stay in?"

I didn't know there were different kinds of hotels, so it took me a second to answer. "Nothing fancy. Just clean and centralized."

He nodded. "The Red Brick Inn is a good choice. It's not too fancy, but mages seem to like it. You'll need to give us a statement before you go." He leaned forward. "Verity, we'll also need your statement. Don't think you need to hide anything, and don't lie." He pointed to his nose. "We can smell it."

"I don't lie. I'm incapable."

I patted her hand. "I'm sorry, Verity. This is kind of an abrupt introduction to the paranormal world. We have recovery teams that specialize in easing people into it. I'll get in touch with someone who will help you." Based on her pale skin and glassy eyes, I worried that it was too late.

Colonel Ballard cleared his throat. "Right. Also, we'll need you to wake the dragons on your way out."

Her eyes widened. "How do I do that?"

"You don't need to do anything." I turned my attention back to Colonel Ballard. "Verity didn't knock them out. I did. The magic will wear off on its own in a couple of hours."

"Perfect." He turned his head to stare out the window.

The parking lot was about a block away from the Enforcer's station, so we had to walk. There was a scent of wet vegetation and something floral in the balmy air. The mixture wasn't unpleasant, but it was definitely new. Buildings of stone and brick stretched for several blocks in every direction, ending abruptly and replaced by thick woods and swamps in lush green and brown colors. It was late afternoon, and the moist heat was suffocating. Verity and I were still dripping in sweat and flushed as we stepped into the cool air inside the building. The front waiting area was painted gray, with long, skinny windows along two walls. It reeked of disinfectants and paperwork.

A wolf ran around in circles behind the counter, a tropical bird perched on a filing cabinet, cawing. We approached the reception desk, where a human-sized green fairy with brilliant pink wings and hair sat in a chair with her back to us. "Quiet, Stevenson." she yelled at the wolf as she swung her pink eyes to us. Her pointed face scrunched. "What's with the girlies, Colonel Ballard?"

Verity latched onto my arm and shuffled behind me.

"Verity and Jen are here to make a statement about their kidnapping."

The fairy tapped on her keyboard. "Sure thing. Have a seat, ladies. Someone will be right with you." She turned and threw a paperweight at the bird on the filing cabinet, rolled up a stack of paper, and smacked the wolf across the nose. "I said quiet!"

I couldn't help but admire the chaos and tried to imagine that kind of chaos at the palace.

Verity's eyes went wide. "That's animal abuse."

"They're shifters and Enforcers. They'll be fine."

She flinched as another office supply went flying. "If you say so."

It didn't take long before a tall blonde vampire and a short, stocky dwarf came out and stopped in front of us. The vampire's eyes flitted over me before landing on Verity. "Good afternoon, ladies. I'm Sergeant Lorcher. This is Sergeant Cortez. Please follow me." We went through the doors and down a hall before he stopped in front of a small room. "Ms. Verity, Sergeant Cortez will take your statement in here."

Verity's shoulders relaxed slightly, probably because the vampire wouldn't be taking her statement. I admired her bravery as she stepped into the room without looking back.

Sergeant Lorcher led me into the room across the hall, and closed the door behind us, activating a privacy spell.

I'd never given a statement to the Enforcers or anyone else. I was excited to have the new experience and meet regular paranormals. With enthusiasm, I explained everything that had happened. Sergeant Lorcher asked me several pointed questions to try to trip me up, and I methodically shut him down. After years of studying their procedures and observing interviews as part of my training to rule, I knew he was just yanking my chain. Besides, vampires were precise lie detectors since they could hear our heartbeat, so he knew I was telling the truth. When he couldn't trip me up, he sat back, folded his arms, and got to the real reason for the badgering. "Why did you call the head of enforcers instead of the local office, Detective Hendrix?"

My eyebrows drew together. I didn't understand why he would ask me that question. Based on his body language, I needed to be careful with my answers. "I have a prior relationship with her and didn't have the phone number for the local station."

"And you didn't think to ask Ballard for the number?"

"Sure. But he was a little busy being a kidnapper-carrying bear at the time, so..." I shrugged.

He leaned forward, his eyes flashing red. "We don't like the boss mixed up in our business, detective. You should remember that when working in the smaller pockets."

I almost managed to keep my mouth shut. Almost. "Absolutely. I'll make a much better judgment call the next time I'm kidnapped by dragons with your colonel."

"Careful, detective," he growled.

A sense of danger washed through the room, making the hairs on my arms stand on end. "Oh shit," I murmured as the door banged open.

The sergeant was on his feet in a heartbeat, facing off with the man who entered. I stayed in my chair and clasped my hands to hide my sudden trembling. I turned my attention toward the giant man with muscles stretching the white dress shirt he wore. His shoulder-length gold hair was swept back, revealing a face set in stone. His intelligent gold eyes examined me before settling on Sergeant Lorcher. "I am here to question the witness."

Sergeant Lorcher bowed. "Of course, Your Majesty." He shot me a dirty look before pulling out the chair next to his. "Please, take a seat."

Mat inclined his head and sat before his eyes settled on me.

My heart started pounding out of my chest, and my mouth was too dry to say anything. I could count on one hand the number of times my brother used his terror magic on me. This was an even worse reaction than I originally thought.

Mat turned his attention to the vampire. "The humans recorded this...encounter and posted it on the internet."

Sergeant Lorcher met Mat's eyes. "I am aware. This...witness, Detective Hendrix, said she and her friend took care of some of their phones but couldn't get them all."

The danger radiating off Mat increased. One side of his mouth quirked up. That was never good. "Is that so?"

I cleared my throat and tried to work up enough spit to speak. "Yep. Yes. Um. Your Majesty."

He leaned forward, resting his forearms on the table. "Sergeant Lorcher, I need to speak to this witness alone."

The vampire jumped to his feet and headed to the door. "Let me know when you're done, Your Majesty. I'll be just outside." He smirked as he swung the door shut. All vampires sucked that day.

We sat silently, me staring at the table, Mat's eyes boring into me. He slapped the table suddenly. "Explain!"

Anger replaced my fear, and I raised my eyes. "Screw you, Mat. I didn't get mixed up in this mess on purpose."

He pointed his finger at me like he was scolding a child. "You never mean to get in trouble, but here you are up to your eyeballs. I knew you would find it when you took this job, and I should have forbidden this charade." He sat back, "There I was, going about my day, when the TV cut to my precious sister, who only a day ago swore to be careful, being dragged off by dragons. You didn't stay out of trouble. You didn't even bother erasing all the footage of your trouble."

"I was a little busy trying to stay alive, so—"

"This is not a joke, Jenella."

"I know."

"You could have been killed. I didn't spend all those years keeping you safe, so you could just throw it away in one day. Besides being one of the two people I love, do you understand the trouble the coalition would be in if anything happened to you?"

I swallowed the lump in my throat. "Yes. But nothing happened, and I'm fine."

"Yet the first minute I let you out of my sight, you land yourself in trouble. I'm assigning you more guards unless you consider a different job."

"No. No guards. I can't gain that valuable life experience or figure out how to fuse my magic from inside a protective bubble." My eyes blurred with tears. No way I was giving up my freedom right after getting it. "I know you'll never believe this, Mat, but I can take care of myself."

He growled and ran his hand through his hair. "I understand that you don't like the responsibility placed on your shoulders, but you need to at least remember it's there. You've spent a lot of time convincing yourself that being someone else is a better option, but it is not. You cannot save everyone. And you cannot sacrifice yourself every time someone is in trouble."

My throat closed, and a warm tear I couldn't stop ran down my face. That was a low blow. Not a minute went by that those responsibilities didn't weigh me down. "Being a detective *is* everything to me right now, Mat. I..." I took a deep breath. "I'm sorry I let those dragons pick me up. It wasn't necessary for me to jump in and try to save Verity. I'm glad I did, but I shouldn't have." I met his golden eyes. "This chance at freedom is something I desperately need. A gilded cage is still a cage."

Mat ran his hands over his face. "Do you not understand I love you and would never put you in a cage? It's why I've gone along with this nonsense. But make no mistake, your safety is more important than what you consider freedom. I don't like you being out in the world without guards."

"That's what you're trying to do," my voice was a whisper. "Those responsibilities and all that protection you talk about are equivalent to a cage to me. Besides, I have Tracy."

"Those responsibilities will come with great freedom if you let them. And Tracy has proven to be unable to protect you." He let out a breath. "You're all I have left, Jen, and I can't lose you."

Pain stabbed through my heart. Mat wasn't an emotional guy, but ever since our parents were killed, he worked so hard to raise me and hold my throne. I couldn't bear his disappointment. "I promise I'll do my best to avoid danger and better listen to Tracy. But, no additional guards and no sending people to follow me." He'd probably still do it, but it was worth a shot.

He was silent for so long I didn't think he'd answer. "Very well. One more chance, but if you screw up again, I am ending this."

Tension drained from my shoulders. "Thank you." He didn't respond, so I shifted in my chair and added, "Are we done? Because I need a shower."

Mat stood and moved toward the door. "You can go. I'll smooth things over here. You will need to stay in town. I've made reservations for you at the Supernatural Suites."

I trailed behind him. "My plan is to stay at the Red Brick Inn. Colonel Ballard recommended it. I also have a contract with Prince Jedediah that I need to fulfill. If the Enforcers want me to work with them, I will. Otherwise, I'll just check into the hotel and get to work."

He rested his hand on my shoulder. "The Red Brick Inn is sparse, but acceptable. Stay out of the dragon issue."

"Not making any promises. I'm a little pissed that Drake and Bastien have been keeping things from me, despite my asking."

"They have. I'll handle them and the disgruntled detective outside. You can pointlessly argue with Bastien all you want, but do not inject yourself into the Enforcers' investigation."

I reached for the door handle. "Agreed. Don't kill the vampire. He's just doing his job." I paused before turning the handle, reminding myself he only wanted me to be safe. "But I'll hang around for a couple of days to make sure they don't need more information, and I'll be careful. I promise."

"I don't believe you," he murmured before gently pushing me out of the way and opening the door. Wise man, my brother.

I made a hasty retreat to the lobby, where Verity waited for me along with a red-faced Tracy. Verity wore gloves that stretched above her elbows, and her face lit up when she saw me. "I gave my statement! And the nice woman who interviewed me gave me new gloves."

I grinned. "Nice." I turned my attention to Tracy, "Hey, Tracy."

Tracy's jaw clenched. "Let's get to the hotel." She slipped out the door before I could answer.

We trudged through the humid air to the hotel. It was getting dark by the time we made it to the entrance. The place was a stone structure built with bright red bricks seven stories high. The red sign out front boasted freshly stocked magichefs and free Magi-Fi in bright white letters. We checked in and then bought clothes and some toiletries in the gift shop before heading to our rooms, conveniently across the hall from each other on the sixth floor.

We stopped at Verity's door. "You have my number and Tracy's, so if you need anything or get freaked out, call one of us."

She waved me away. "I'm exhausted. I'm just going to take a shower and sleep. Wait. Do you guys sleep at night? Because all the books say you don't."

"We do have our share of nocturnal creatures. It's about 50/50, so sleeping at night is fine, especially for mages."

She nodded. "Right. Then I'll see you in the morning."

"Let me show you how to use the magichef. You'll need it if you get hungry." Tracy pushed through the door, motioning Verity to follow.

I quietly followed so I could learn, too. It was embarrassing how little I knew about what went into taking care of myself. Tracy pointed to the front, which looked like a giant tablet. "It's pretty simple. I mean, you just pull up the menu here, and it shows what's offered, then you push the button, and the item will appear there." She pointed to a plate-like thing on the side. "When you're done, slide the dishes in here..." she pointed to a little drawer underneath, "and they'll be washed and returned for the next meal."

Seemed pretty straightforward to me. Verity, however, leaned in, her mouth hanging open. "You guys can cook and clean magically? This is. This is...my dreams have just come true."

Tracy grinned. "Most hotels hire dragons with culinary magic, although some mages have that type of magic, so they sometimes help out. The First, Drake, just loaded up our magichef the other day, and his food is the best I've ever tasted."

"He *what?*"

Tracy smirked. "I would have told you, but you're oblivious, and I didn't think you'd care."

Yeah, she was mad. "I'm sorry about this whole thing, Tracy. I wasn't thinking. In the future, I'll try to make better decisions."

She snorted. "I'll believe that when I see it."

We said goodnight to Verity and headed to my room next door. Tracy's was across the hall to keep an ear out for us. I waited while she put a strong ward on our doors. "If you ever pull a stunt like that again, I will hit you with a cryogenic spell so fast the ruling magic won't have time to act. Do not think I won't." She retreated to her room and slammed the door before I could respond.

Chapter 11

After Tracy's very justified outburst, the excitement of staying in a hotel for the first time evaporated. I showered, dressed, and braided my hair, leaving the glamour earrings in my ears just in case. I eyed the selections in the magichef. The menu covered a bunch of different diets. Before I could decide, a knock sounded on the door. Thinking it was Verity or Tracy, I swung it open without sending out my magic senses. The smile melted off my face.

Drake stood in the hallway behind a cart. His rugged face contradicted the elegant suit he wore. The five o'clock shadow didn't match his new, professional hairstyle. He raked his green eyes over me from head to toe. "Hello, Jenella. I heard you had quite the day."

I crossed my arms, trying to hide my excitement at seeing him with annoyance. "How did you find my room?"

He grinned. "I asked. People tend to fall all over themselves to assist a First."

I raised an eyebrow.

"I got the snarky message you left with Bastien's office."

Two things crossed my mind at once. One, I needed to be careful to remember who the guy was. And two, I had no idea what the protocol to use when mages received visitors at their hotel rooms. I decided it didn't matter since Drake knew my true identity. "Have you talked to Mat or the Enforcers? I already told them everything so they can fill you in."

A lazy smile spread across his face. "I talked to Mat, but I'd like to hear it from you. I thought we could talk over a meal. You must be hungry after your...ordeal."

My stomach growled.

His smile grew. "We will consider this the meal you owe me."

I sighed and waved him in. Watching as he rolled the cart to the tiny table in the corner. My eyes bounced to the food and back to him as I closed the door. He looked out of place, wearing his finery in this cheap hotel room. "This is unnecessary. You could have just called me back."

He pulled the covers off two plates and placed them on the small table. "I could have, but I remembered you owe me a meal. Besides, I could hear your stomach growling as I flew over the hotel."

The vampire Enforcer would flip his lid when the First appeared on his doorstep. Ha! Take that asshole. The smell of perfectly cooked food overtook me, and I wanted to moan at the yummy goodness. With a sigh, I headed to the tiny table. "Okay. Dinner it is, but this might be inappropriate. It can't become a habit."

Drake sat and handed me some silverware wrapped in a cloth napkin. It was also too fancy for my cheap hotel room. "We shall see. Now, tell me about the dragons."

I unrolled my silverware. "What do you want to know?"

"Everything. Please." He added the please as an afterthought.

I told him the story. Unlike the Enforcer and Mat, Drake seemed as concerned about Jedediah ghosting us as he was about the kidnapping. His eyes glowed as I talked, so I tried to avoid looking at him. When I finished, he cleared his throat. "These things have happened from time to time. I'm sure Mathias has implanted supernaturals in the tech industry and government to eliminate any videos or do damage control. Other than conspiracy theory websites, it'll be forgotten in a few weeks."

"How do you know about the tech industry when you've been asleep for so long?"

Drake's jaw clenched. He closed his eyes and took a deep breath. "I wasn't asleep. It was as if my essence or soul were floating. I was aware but not conscious." He shook his head. "It is hard to explain. After a while, I discovered that my mental magic still worked, and I probed for information from anyone who came near. I can tell you everything that happened in the nearby shifter pack over the last couple hundred years, along with what technology and magics they used. It's the only thing that kept me sane, I think."

The thought horrified me. "That's awful. Why did you choose to sleep?"

"Choose." He drew out the word. "That is an interesting way to put it."

Based on his previous comments, I didn't think it was a choice, but I wanted to know more. "You didn't *choose* to go to sleep?"

His eyes filled with sorrow. "That is the history lesson I wanted, but knowing you somewhat, I'm almost positive you won't have the answers I'm seeking."

"Try me."

He took a bite of food. "Perhaps another time. There is too much going on right now."

I let it go, deciding that I'd do some research about how the Firsts went to sleep. I told him about the very intriguing Verity because I thought it might wipe that anger and sadness from his eyes. "I can't believe she thinks she's middle-aged. She kicks like a horse." I smiled, remembering our ordeal. "She wasn't afraid of Jedediah."

Drake's eyes sparkled with amusement. "Sounds like a true adventure."

"It was, but not the kind I'm looking for."

"I suspect not. Have you met Jonas?"

Jonas was the only First not to sleep. We referred to him as the first shifter. He'd created the shifters and led them for years before handing them off to his son, then to his grandson, though he still kept his eye on them. "A couple of times, but only in passing. No one knows where he is now."

Drake's eyebrows drew together. "He's in Boise, Idaho, and not hard to find if you look."

"Really? I heard he lived in the human world. I never understood why, though."

His fork stopped halfway to his mouth. "I thought you were somewhat joking about being clueless."

"Nope. It happens when you're raised in a bubble. What is it I'm clueless about this time?"

He set his fork down. "Apparently, there is a movement within the pockets to exclude hybrids, and anyone bonded to someone outside their magic type. Jonas and his match, Ann Marie, qualify since he's a shifter, and she's a sorceress. He tells me they moved out of the pockets twenty-five years ago to avoid harassment. His exact words were, 'I'm too old for that shit.'"

I chuckled. "I'd like to get to know him someday."

"You should try to do that soon. Jonas thinks you support the anti-hybrid movement."

My mouth dropped open. "Why would he think that?"

"Because parents of hybrid children are dumping them outside the gates of the pockets when they hit puberty, and you have done nothing to stop it. Jonas and Ann Marie have devoted this chapter of their lives to rescuing the rejects. You don't know anything about this?"

I knew there was an anti-hybrid movement, but I didn't pay close enough attention to it to realize it had grown that big. Mat had taken a couple of actions to try to solve the problem, so I was sure he knew. I thought the whole movement was stupid because each paranormal only had one match or mate, so bonding with someone of a different magic type wasn't a choice. "I knew there was an anti-hybrid movement and that Mat has taken measures to put a stop to it. But not that they were abandoning their kids. Holy crap, Drake. That's...that's...are you sure that's what's happening?"

"Yes. According to Jonas, not enough is being done to address the problem. We did not create the supernatural races to be segregated, and very few kids can control their abilities at the age they're being abandoned. If not for Jonas, the humans would already know about us. Interbreeding among different magical types is part of why we formed the coalition. It's why matches are often of different magic types. There are even...incentives built in for them to have children."

I found that fascinating. I thought the coalition was about safety in numbers, but it made sense that the Firsts wanted to make us blend better than we had. Sometimes, it felt like we had a hundred different kingdoms rather than a coalition. "What kind of incentives?"

Drake chuckled as he cleared our plates and set dessert in front of me. "Do you like gelato?"

It was my favorite. "Yes. Thank you."

"To answer your question would mean breaking a magical oath."

I tilted my head in acknowledgment. If we were expelling people from the pockets for any reason, the entire coalition could fall apart. Mat's insistence that I figure things out took on a different meaning with this information. The revelation also meant that I needed to pay more attention to what was going on. "Do you think Verity was part of that, and Jonas never found her?"

Drake didn't answer for a few seconds, focusing on his dessert. "No, but I think you should stay in touch with her. She most likely trusts you after today, and it's a miracle that she hasn't exposed her magic to humans. Mat said he'd send a recovery team to help her, but it won't be the same as a friend."

"Yeah. I planned on staying in touch. I hope the recovery team is good. She's fierce." I rubbed my chest where she had kicked me and sat back. "What do you plan to do besides busting into the hotel rooms with delicious meals?"

His lips twitched. "While I'm here or with my new chance at life?"

"Both."

"Nothing more while I'm here, although being a thorn in the side of the small-town Enforcers is appealing. I only came here with Bastien to make sure you were unharmed. With my life? Who knows. I am figuring it out, same as you." He cleared the dishes. "Although, I'm not sure why you don't stay in a nicer hotel."

I glanced around the room. "It's a nice place. Clean and low-key. I figured it would be hard to keep a low profile if I lived in the lap of luxury."

"I suppose." He didn't sound convinced. He touched my hand, sending a zing of electricity up my arm. "I must say that my glamour is excellent, even if it does destroy a precious masterpiece."

My heart leaped into my throat at those words, my brain not responding. I pulled my hand away and took a deep breath to stop my head from spinning. "Thank you. For the glamour and the compliment. Why did you decide to help me with that for the price of a meal?"

His eyes settled on the window. "Because I know what it's like to try to find a purpose. A place to fit in. I hope you have more luck finding it than I did. I think you will, considering your optimism. It's a character trait I envy."

"You flatter me."

Drake chuckled. "You think I flatter you when I only speak the truth. Call me if you need anything or if anything else crazy happens, especially involving dragons. If they so much as sneeze in a way you don't like, I will crush them for you."

My stomach flipped. "Just so you know, crushing people won't endear you to them. You can ask Mat about that."

He pushed the cart to the middle of the room, his muscles flexing. "I. Don't. Care." His voice was ragged, and he cleared his throat. "Use the number and please avoid pissing off the queen's assistant again."

"Party pooper."

He brushed a piece of stray hair out of my face and placed his hand on my cheek. The scent of wood smoke and spice surrounded me. "Be safe." The cart disappeared, and he strode out of the room.

"Sure, Drake," I murmured to the empty room, rubbing my cheek. I admit his actions mesmerized me, but not how he wanted me to be. He was flirting. Protective, but not in an over-the-top Mat way. I couldn't figure out why. No one flirted with me. Ever. It was considered taboo because of some stupid rule made by my grandmother. Another useless protocol. I knew he did it because he had an agenda. I needed to determine whether it was helping the hybrids, waking the other Firsts, or both.

After an hour of going over the conversation with Drake in my head from every angle, I pulled out my laptop. I emptied the contents of the torn, bloody envelope Jedediah had given me on the desk. Butterflies fluttered in my stomach as I got to work on my first case.

Supernatural banking was a convoluted mess that didn't have many protocols. Independent contractors paid a booth rental fee to a bank to operate there. They represented their supernatural clients by setting up false identities, shell companies, and multiple accounts. They'd take human money, launder it, grow it, or anything else their client wanted. I heard of a mage that could forge human paper currency. Another could set up regular monthly deposits from what humans would see as legitimate employers but didn't exist. One mage got arrested by human authorities a few years back, and Mat made him disappear. He was still alive, which was unusual when my brother got involved. He was in servitude to the crown in some way. I made a note to follow up on that.

With a sigh, I started by reading the investigation done by Jedediah's vampire house, which was nothing more than bragging about how perfect and superior they were. I didn't find much there, so I moved to the account statements. They looked straightforward, but something about them bothered me. No matter how hard I tried, I couldn't figure out what. I emailed their representative at The Bank of Mahri branch in Allure to schedule a meeting. When my eyes started drooping, I stretched and glanced at the time. It was one-thirty, so I turned off my laptop, climbed into bed, and drifted off.

An evil laugh sounded as the bedroom door crashed open. A man strutted in, cloaked in dark clothes and shadows that no one saw but me. My heart began thundering, and I scurried under my bed, the only place I could go. I curled myself into a tight ball, watching the man's boots as he moved through the room, tears streaming down my face. The dust ruffle lifted, replaced by the man's face. "Why are you hiding from me, you worthless child?"

Sweat and tears trickled down my face as I pressed harder into the wall, my heart in my throat and my stomach rolling. He grabbed my ankle and yanked. My head hit the bed frame, and stars danced in my vision. I pressed my lips together. I didn't dare scream. Screaming always made it worse. He threw me out into the hall, and my tiny body rammed into the wall, sharp pain shooting through my ribs. Wheezing and trying to clear my vision, I began slithering down the hall. He yanked me up by my wrists, and in a flash of white, hot pain, they broke. I whimpered, and he slapped me, "I will have no whining from you."

My wrists and ribs throbbed, and a sharp pain shot up my arms. I knew it wasn't the worst pain. The real pain always came when the broken bones reset themselves. I tried to ignore it, tried to kick, tried to wiggle in a desperate attempt to save myself as he dragged me down the stairs. I was so small, and he was a man, so I couldn't fight. I tried to use my budding magic. He slapped me hard across the face. When we reached the dungeons, he slapped me again, harder. Searing pain exploded through my face and head. "That is for trying to fight me. I rule here, and you will do as I say. You're a nobody! A nothing! Do you think anyone loves you? Do you think anyone can? Nobody could love an ugly little cockroach like you." He opened the cage and shoved me in, my already bruised face slamming into the spelled wires. I couldn't see. He slammed the door and strode off as I struggled to sit up. "Little bitch isn't worth my time."

I looked down at my favorite white nightgown. Watched as blood trickled from my face onto it, ruining its beauty. I cried as I used it to wipe the blood from my eyes. It didn't do any good to cry. I had cried, begging my father not to leave me and trying to tell him about the cage. Pleading for my mother to stay. They said they were busy. They didn't have time to listen. They always left, and the man took their place. I always ended up in the cage until just before they came back. I huddled in the corner, the smell of blood and urine overwhelming my senses, and wished that I was big enough or had enough magic to hurt the man and run away. I wanted to get out of the cage. Pain exploded through my body as my bones reset themselves.

I jerked awake in a pool of sweat with my phone ringing. I reached for it with shaky hands and looked at the screen, still trying to shake off the dream as I answered. "Hi, Travis."

"What the hell do you think you're doing? I stuck my neck out for you to get a mentor, and this is how you treat me?" he growled.

I sat up and fanned myself, trying to stop shaking. "You didn't do anything but try to sabotage my chances."

"You have a mentor. I did my job. Are you going to be marked or maimed when I escort you to your coronation?"

I face-palmed. I should never have agreed to take Travis to my coronation. "Why do you even care? Have you forgotten that I have healing magic? Besides, my coronation is not about you. You're just traveling with me."

"Whatever. Just send me the details so I can adjust my schedule accordingly." He hung up.

I stared at my phone, wondering why I hadn't ended that so-called friendship. I didn't even know if breaking up with a friend was possible, because Travis was my only friend. Opening my web browser, I typed the question. Finding nothing about it on the maginet, I switched to the human internet. According to the human internet, I should pick a good time, be straightforward about my reasoning, and let my friend talk. I threw my phone on the bed. Yeah. That would go over well with Travis. Right after he turned into a giant wolf and tore my throat out, I'm sure he would be very understanding.

I stomped into the bathroom, frustrated and fuming. At least I wasn't shaking from that stupid dream.

Chapter 12

I NEEDED TO TALK to Tracy. I'd screwed up and owed her an apology. As I stood outside her door, I took a deep breath to gather my courage. My knock echoed down the hall, and I smiled when Tracy answered. Anger flashed in her eyes before she took a deep breath and stepped back. "Come in, Jen."

She sat on the bed, so I took one of the chairs at the little table. I wrung my hands as I drew the courage to say what I had to say. "I'm sorry for dragging you into my pissing contest with my brother." She opened her mouth to say something, but I held up a hand. "No. I need to get this out." I waited for her to nod. "As you know, Bastien became my guard when I was about twelve. We drove each other crazy but had sort of a mutual respect. He only took the job because his mother insisted on it for diplomacy and to keep an eye on us. He stayed until he met you, though I don't think he ever knew that I knew he left the job for you.

"Since then, I've had more than a dozen guards. All were high ranking in the castle guard." I sighed, realizing she didn't need the lecture. "To make a long story short, I don't know if Mat gave them unrealistic expectations about their job or they decided that my bullshit wasn't worth their time. They never stayed more than a few months."

Tracy's eyebrows drew together. "Why are you telling me this?"

"You are nothing like any of them, and I like you. I get that I haven't been great to guard."

"More like a disaster."

"Right. But you need to know I won't ever treat you like I treated them. I don't want you to quit, so I need to tell you something I've never told anyone."

"Okay?"

I rubbed my face. "I'm no good at this. But here's the deal. I'm supposed to be the most powerful supernatural in the world. I hide it well and haven't often used my full power. Still, I could level this entire pocket if I wanted to. If I had the energy. That seems like bragging, but it's not. It's a huge problem. I'm not even close to being powerful enough to be queen." I swallowed the lump in my throat. "There's something wrong with my magic. I developed my inherent magic and healing magic when I was three. The ruling magic slammed into me when my mother died three years later. It...didn't mix when I hit puberty like it should have. The three different magics work fine independently, but it's like I'm three different mages rather than one super powerful leader like I should be. The pool of ruling magic is a problem. I don't have complete control over it. More like I'm never sure if it will jump in and help me, and I can't make it help. Sometimes, it just jumps in and handles problems on its own. Because of this, Mat's worried that I'm too weak to defend myself. If word about that got out, Mat thinks it would throw the coalition into chaos. He let me do this job because he hopes meeting other supernaturals will fix it.

"The reason I'm telling you this is so you can see why my brother and I are always in a power struggle and why I will act in certain situations." I stopped, gathering my thoughts. "I need you to work with me and have my back, not be my shield. I get that it's unconventional, and I'm a pain in the ass. So, if you don't like that dynamic and want to quit, I understand. I don't want you to, but I understand. Either way, I'm sorry for dragging you into our power struggle and for not listening to you. If you stay, I'll try to listen to you better, but I can't promise to be anything other than myself."

I stared at the floor, holding my breath while waiting for her answer. She cleared her throat. "I mean, that's not anything I didn't already figure out, but thank you for saying it."

My eyes snapped to hers. "You knew?"

She shook her head. "I get that most people aren't honest with you, but I always will be, even when you don't like it. It's my nature. And, yes, I knew. I'm staying. You couldn't pry me away from this job. Not only because it's the most exciting thing I've ever done, but I don't have to hide the fact that I can both weave spells and do alchemy. Besides, you're kind of amazing. I mean, I want to be there when you get your shit together."

A ragged laugh escaped me. "Thank you. I can't wait to get my shit together."

A loud knock came from the door, and Tracy put on her glamour earrings and gave me the "stay there" look. "Can I help you?" she asked as I craned my neck to try to see around her.

"Yes, ma'am. I'm Titus, and I formerly worked with the recovery team echo. I'm looking for Detective Hendrix."

I stood and went to the door. "I'm Detective Hendrix."

He eyed me. "No, you're not."

I opened my magic ID. "My ID says otherwise." I realized he was a powerful juror, so he probably knew my ID was fake. "Are you here to talk to Verity?"

His eyebrows drew together. "Yes. She wouldn't answer her door, and I wondered if Detective Hendrix would provide an assist."

Tracy elbowed me out of the way. "I've reserved conference room three on the first floor. We'll be there in twenty minutes with Verity."

He inclined his head. "And you are?"

She shot him her award-winning smile. "I'm Tracy, Jen's assistant."

"All due respect, ma'am, but I can sense magic abilities and lies. You are neither a detective nor an assistant. And she is not Jen Hendrix. What's going on here?"

I folded my arms. "We'll bring Verity to the conference room." His skeptical look said he wasn't comfortable with that, so I added, "I swear neither Tracy nor I will harm you without provocation."

He dropped his arms when the contract settled over him. "Very well. I'll be in the conference room."

Twenty minutes later, we entered the conference room with a shaking Verity in tow. I tried to pry her death grip from my arm as I turned my attention to Titus. He had a lean yet muscular body with a face just on the wrong side of beautiful. He disguised his good looks with laugh lines. His chocolate eyes were both intelligent and battle-weary.

Titus glanced at Tracy and me before focusing on Verity. "Are you Verity Wilson?"

She glared at him. "Depends on who's asking and what you want."

His eyes sparkled with humor, and his attention turned to me, holding out his hand. "I don't trust anyone I haven't touched."

I sat across from him and clasped my hands in front of me. "And I don't trust a juror's touch without knowing their intentions."

He pulled his hand back at Verity's sharp intake of breath. "I get that, but I'm not continuing until I'm sure of your character. Because everyone here knows that neither of you is who you say you are." He held out his hand again, wiggling his fingers.

Verity huffed. "Listen, mister. You called us here, not the other way around. Jen and Tracy are here as my moral support, and I decide whether they are trustworthy, not you."

His lips twitched, and he focused on her. "You also don't know how to use your magic or about paranormals. Regent Mathias put you under my care, and I take my job seriously."

Her face flushed with anger, so I put a hand on her arm. "Like most people, I have things I need to keep confidential, so I will need an oath before I allow you to read me."

His eyes bore into me. "Is there something you've done that you shouldn't have?"

"No, nothing like that."

"Fair enough. Then I swear to you any information I learn by touching you will never be told to anyone in any form unless you have committed crimes against the crown or the coalition." Energy zipped over my entire body as the contract snapped into place.

I gingerly reached over and touched his hand, allowing him to read me. He pulled back and met my eyes. "Mathias is brilliant for sending me here without telling me much. I wouldn't have come if I knew what I was getting into." He sat back and eyed me. "I could have used that glamour a time or two in certain situations."

I didn't know what strategy Mat used, but I slumped my shoulders in response. "Thank you, I guess."

He touched Tracy, and a tiny smile formed on his lips. He didn't comment, though, instead focusing on Verity. "I'm Titus, a recently retired recovery agent. Recovery teams go into the human world and look for people like you. I've been assigned to teach you your magic and help you transition. I thought it was an odd request, but it intrigued me enough to show up. So, tell me about yourself."

Verity frowned. "Not much to tell. I was raised by nice, middle-class parents, went to trade school, then worked. I've never been married, have no kids, and live in an apartment. I've already told the nice lady at the police station all this."

Titus rubbed his chin. "I've got all that. How much do you know about your magic?"

She wrung her hands. "I didn't believe in magic until yesterday. I started realizing I could read people in high school. One of my teachers got accidentally knocked out when he put his hand on my shoulder. I just thought I had psychic abilities. The poor teacher thought he was dehydrated. It terrified me because it wasn't like he had any real sins. He was a good man who was biased about grading papers. I started wearing gloves in social situations or pretending to be a germaphobe to avoid shaking hands. I always wore clothes that covered my skin and quit using the ability entirely. As I grew older, I increased my focus on practicing the psychic aspects. I used my touch one time to knock out a man who deserved it until the police could arrive, but I was careful not to let anyone know. Until yesterday."

Titus's eyes twinkled. "So, you kind of know how to use your magic."

Verity glanced at me. "Jen said I have human values and should avoid other...I don't know much about magic or any of this." She waved her hand around. "I'm not sure I want to know more."

Titus nodded. "You shouldn't use what you think are psychic abilities until you understand our morals and values. And it's a good policy not to touch anyone when you don't know what you're doing. I'm going to level with you, Verity."

"Please do."

"I've been assigned to assist you in transitioning. Whether that means I stay with you in the human world to teach you supernatural morals or you move to a pocket and immerse yourself is up to you. But we cannot have a self-trained, powerful juror running around on her own. If you want to move to a pocket, I can help you find a job. If you choose to stay in the human world, I can coach you on using your abilities without causing any damage. I would prefer you at least become familiar with the pockets, though."

"I can also help with that," I interjected.

Verity tried to smile, but it was weak. "That's a lot to think about. I don't know what I want to do right now. It's all so much I think my brain might explode."

I didn't like the sadness in her eyes. "Verity, you don't have to give up your life. Like Titus said, you can stay in the human world, and he will stay and help you."

She shook her head. "It's not that. I don't have any money to move, and I lost my job yesterday. I was in that park trying to decide what to do. My psychic abilities forced me to distance myself from people. I don't have any friends or anything, and my parents are deceased. Y'all showing up drives that point home."

Titus leaned forward. "The crown will pay for your relocation to a pocket and provide you with a stipend until you get on your feet. It's standard protocol with a recovery."

Verity shook her head vigorously. "No. Nope. I'm not taking handouts. Either I'll work for what I have or go without."

I loved this woman and her human values. Most paranormals took whatever they could get. "What did you do in the human world?"

She didn't hesitate. "I was an administrative assistant for three insurance company executives who fired me two days after my fifty-fifth birthday. Not because of my performance, mind you. But because one of them wanted to give his twenty-five-year-old mistress a job."

My eyebrows drew together. "A mistress? So, he was bonded and broke the sacred covenant? Is that even possible?"

Tracy chuckled. "Humans rarely develop bonds because they don't have magic. They claim to be monogamous, but not everyone stays loyal and committed."

"Oh." I didn't know much about humans other than their political systems and what I learned from watching television and movies. Most of what I watched implied there was always a happily ever after. I turned my attention back to an amused Verity. "If you want to work, I need a chief aid to handle office coordination at the castle. It's the equivalent of an administrative assistant, I think." I glanced at Tracy for confirmation, and she nodded.

Verity tapped the table. "So, like, I'd be the secretary to the president?"

"You would be chief aid to the crown princess, soon to be queen. That means the office manager, personal assistant, and advisor all rolled into one. A fitting position for a juror without training." Titus explained.

"I like it. Especially because I'll get to see Jen regularly." Her face fell. "It's a huge change, though. I'll need to think about it if that's okay. What's the pay?"

"The pay's negotiable if you take the job, but somewhere around five hundred thousand dollars per year, I think. And take all the time you need to decide. You can either let Titus know, and he'll get you moved to Allure and settled in, or you can contact me anytime," I answered.

Verity's eyes grew wide as I spoke, and she let out a little squeak, but I didn't know why. "Thank you, Jen. I'll give it some serious thought. But right now, I want to go home and think."

Titus stood. "I've rented the apartment next to yours and will see you home."

I gave her a hug. "If you decide not to work with me, keep in touch. And no kicking Titus, okay?"

"Ha! You can count on it." She turned to Titus. "Alright. Let's go."

Tracy watched them leave. "I really like that woman."

Chapter 13

Colonel Ballard cleared me to leave later that morning. We took a large silver disk that flew at a supersonic speed between pockets, called transports, back to Allure. They ran on magic and were silent and camouflaged from humans. I spent the trip watching for human planes. Once in a while, a transport's cloaking spell malfunctioned, and the humans would see them. They thought we were aliens. Some even described the experience as terrifying. It was good entertainment for us, and I wanted to witness it myself. Unfortunately, it didn't happen on that trip.

We dragged ourselves to our house, exhausted. A raccoon shifter and a bunch of children stood in her fenced front yard a couple of houses down and waved. "Are you the new neighbors?"

I headed in her direction. "We are. I'm Jen, and this is Tracy. Nice to meet you."

Her eyes bounced between us. "Matched?"

"Friends and roommates."

"Ah, I see. I'm Penelope. It's nice to meet you ladies. Please forgive the noise. The children are a little rambunctious. Also, mind your trash. They can make quite a mess if it isn't magically incinerated right away."

My smile grew. "We'll be careful."

Tracy leaned forward. "If you want better wards, let me know. I mean, I'm pretty good with them and could fix you right up."

"Thank you, but we're fine with the ones we have. We haven't had any trouble in this neighborhood."

"That's good to hear, but if you do, let me know, and I'll gladly help."

"We certainly will. Well, I better get lunch started. It was nice to meet you ladies."

We said our goodbyes, and I dragged myself to my bedroom and set my travel bag down on the long bench at the end of the bed. I looked around in disgust. My bed was unmade, two pairs of shoes were beside the door, and clothes were scattered about. I sighed and picked up the shoes. I started gathering dirty clothes. It dawned on me that I didn't know what to do with them, so I threw them in a pile before moving to the bed. I planted my hands on my hips and tried to remember what the made bed at the castle looked like.

"Jen, did you want to..." Tracy stopped in her tracks. "What are you doing?"

I dropped my arms. "I'm trying to clean my room."

She glanced around and burst out laughing. "You've never cleaned a thing in your life, have you?"

I shrugged and went back to studying the bed. "We have a family of griffins that take care of the cleaning at the castle. I'm just working out what it should look like."

Tracy stepped further into the room, peering into the bathroom before stopping in front of the pile of dirty clothes. "What about these?"

"I have no idea. I usually threw clothes in a basket as I undressed and never thought of them again."

Her shoulders shook with laughter. "I mean, most people learn this stuff as kids. Get your clothes, and I'll give you a little cleaning class."

We moved to the closet, and she pointed to a tall cylinder with a hanging bar and an empty shelf attached. "Put the clothes in there and press the button." I did, and after a few seconds, the clothes appeared folded and hung. I beamed as I watched them put themselves away.

Once the clutter had dissipated, she opened a cabinet in the bathroom. She pointed to several potions, all with typewritten labels. "These are potions that I made. I mean, you can buy these from potion shops, but like most alchemy witches, I prefer my own potions, because then I know what's in them."

I read the labels, noting there was one for everything. Three on the left were bigger and marked wood floors, rugs, and tile. "So, I just dump these on the floor?"

Tracy laughed. "One drop is all it takes. It's spelled to clean everything within the wards of your room. One drop of the shower/tub potion cleans your shower and tub, one drop of the toilet cleaner, etc."

I chose floor solutions and moved into the bedroom, dropping a drop on the wood floor. With a poof, a fine mist spread throughout the room, ending with gleaming floors and a subtle lemon scent. I beamed, "And I just do this every day like the bed?"

She stifled a laugh. "No! Once a week is fine for cleaning. I mean, most people only make their bed and pick up their clothes every day."

"Right." I felt like such an idiot, but I tried not to let it show as I put a drop of potion in the shower. "I have an appointment with the vampire rep at the Allure branch of The Bank of Mahri tomorrow. You don't have to come if you need a day off."

"You're not getting rid of me that easily, but I'll wait outside or in the waiting room and let you do your job."

"Thank you. For all of this. I don't know what I'd do without you."

Her smile melted. "I want to dig around and see if I can figure out what's going on with the dragons if you don't mind. Bastien is hiding something, and the First is trying too hard to get close to you."

"The First is definitely up to something. He brought me dinner last night and kind of flirted with me, something about his glamour ruining a work of art."

"Do you think it's insincere?" she asked carefully.

I watched the potion clean the bathroom sink. "I don't know. But, from experience, if someone is nice to me like that, they usually have an ulterior motive. Happens more often than you think."

"I'm sorry you're forced to think about people like that, Jen. I mean, I can see why you would have to be careful. It never occurred to me the different ways people would try to use you. It's got to be exhausting."

I waved a hand. "It wasn't so bad when Bastien was around because everyone was scared he'd eat them. But yeah. You saw how Travis treated me with the mentor thing. He didn't want to help because there was no payoff for him. I've found that most paranormals only want to know me to boost their social status or because I can do something for them. Mat's tried to protect me from it, but it's inevitable. I'm hoping that between the glamour and keeping my magic hidden, I'll be able to make real connections with people. The problem is, I'll be lying to them about who I am, so I doubt it." I shrugged. "Maybe using each other is just the way of the world."

Surprise and horror flashed across Tracy's face. "I guess I better make sure people become afraid of me because that is unacceptable."

I could have kissed her.

The rest of the day and into the evening, I went over Jedediah's files and searched supernatural social media sites and message boards to find out if anyone else had the same problem. I needed to know if his house was specifically targeted. I found a few people who ranted about being robbed, but nothing solid.

Like all vampires, Jedediah owned human businesses, so I used human search engines to see what information I could find there. With Jedediah's shell companies and false identities, finding anything was impossible, even with the information he provided. I paused when I came across a fuzzy video of my kidnapping and read some of the comments. I sighed in relief when most of them said it was fake. Mat covered it up well. I rubbed my eyes, realizing I'd hit a dead end and was wasting time. I closed my laptop and went to bed. I was so exhausted that I fell into a dreamless sleep.

Tracy and I flashed from the small flashing circle at the end of our street to the massive circle in the original town square in downtown Allure. Two gargoyles stood on one side, their rough gray skin blending into the stone building. I took a second to wonder why they were there. It was unusual for gargoyles to be on the ground. I decided it was none of my business and headed in the opposite direction toward the Allure branch of the Bank of Mahri.

The building was about three stories tall, but took up a city block. A stone building typical to downtown, it was lackluster. I wouldn't have known it was a bank except for a sign above the door that seemed too small for such a gigantic building. As we headed toward the main entrance, I watched several dragons launch off the top of dragon headquarters a few blocks over. They separated and swept over different parts of the city. Patrols, I decided. "There's definitely something up."

Tracy hummed in agreement. "I'll wait out here. I want to see if I can figure out what they're looking for."

"Sure." I found total chaos inside the bank. The first floor's layout looked like a maze. An empty security station was to the left, and a crowded waiting area was to the right. The teal carpet was well-worn but not dirty. The lobby stopped about thirty feet from the door, and clusters of open cubicles dotted the rest of the space in no discernable pattern. Several small rooms that reminded me of the interrogation room in Hospa dotted the back wall. A fire elemental stood in a puddle of water near a cluster of cubicles, arguing with a water elemental. Flames shot up her arms. The water elemental doused them, and then the flames started again. Two shifter security guards stood a few feet away, snarling something I couldn't hear because the volume in the place was almost unbearable. There were too many people talking in the open room.

I rubbed my ears and tried not to look surprised. I'd never been inside the bank because, surprise, surprise, I didn't handle my own finances. There was so much to learn that other people automatically knew that I felt like I was drowning. Shoving that thought aside, I focused on a group of leprechauns arguing in the waiting area. One of them clutched a packet to his chest, his face red. I wondered what everyone was so upset about. I slunk over and took a chair not far from them to find out, but they had a privacy spell around them.

A few minutes later, a tall, elegant blonde vampire approached. She plastered a professional smile on her face and assessed me. "Detective Hendrix. I'm Dora Reese, representative of the vampires." We exchanged empty pleasantries as she led me to one of the sparse back rooms. As soon as the door closed, her professional demeanor melted away. "Make this quick, Detective, as I have no time to suffer fools."

"Yet you work for Prince Jedediah," I blurted without thinking.

Her face went blank, and a tiny spark of humor danced in her eyes. "Since I need this meeting to be brief, I'll overlook your insult of a client."

I sucked at relating to people. I kept a tight rein on the ruling magic that begged to lash out and pulled out my notes. "You've managed the accounts for House Jedediah for a hundred years, is that correct?" At her slight nod, I continued. "And how closely do you monitor the accounts?"

She sat back with an irritated sigh. "As you know, House Jedediah has very complicated finances. They prefer to monitor their money on their own, so my role is to move funds around. Will that be all?"

"Do you ever make mistakes when moving those funds?" I asked, ignoring her question.

Her face flushed with anger. "I am the third of the house of Reese. I do not make mistakes."

Magic always favored the number three. It was a fundamental principle. Supernaturals born third always inherited the magic to rule their family, species, or, in my case, the coalition. There were exceptions, like the shifters who took tests to determine leadership. But they were still governed by the magical rule that the third-born was the strongest.

Vampires were made from humans infected by the venom of powerful vampires. They weren't born into magic. One of the Firsts, Lilith, created the original vampires from a hand-picked group of humans. When she realized her magic made them infertile, she gave them venom that allowed vampires to turn other humans as a way to reproduce. The side effect is that they almost die in the process of changing. The only natural-born vampires I knew of were the vampire queen, Ara, who was more than a vampire, and her two kids, Jedediah and his sister, Vesna. I'm not sure how Quin remained fertile, and I wasn't about to ask. My point is that turning humans into vampires is their form of reproduction, so the third vampire made was always the strongest. That didn't make them perfect. "You don't make any mistakes *ever*? I find that hard to believe."

"If you are here to accuse me of breaking the confidence of a client that I've had for over a hundred years, this interview is over."

"I'm not accusing you of anything. I only want to find Prince Jedediah's money. To do that, I need the whole picture. I was told you would cooperate."

Her shoulders slumped. "I don't know anything. I've looked and can't figure out how the account was breached or where it went. It's like it just disappeared. There are no transfer records, no deductions noted, nothing. Look, Detective, I would help if I could, but I can't."

I closed my notebook. "Alright. Can I get hard copies of everything related to that account going back a year?"

She pulled an envelope out of her bag. "This goes back two years. Let me know if you find anything."

I took the envelope. "You, as well."

She reluctantly agreed, though I doubted she was sincere. I wasn't sure if I was frustrated or relieved as I left the tiny room.

I re-entered the war zone.

The fire elemental stood in the lobby's center, surrounded by a fire tornado. The two security guards were unconscious on the floor. One shifter looked like he had severe burns. Cubicles were torn up, and papers were everywhere. An elf attempted to grow vines around the fire elemental while two witches worked together to weave a containment spell. The water elemental infused a constant stream of water into the tornado. The leprechauns were huddled in the corner of the waiting room, eyes wide.

I stuffed the envelope in my cross-body bag and raced through the cubical maze toward the lobby, avoiding the fight. "What's going on?" I asked no one as I hurried past the waiting area.

A male vampire grabbed my arm. "There seems to be an influx of anger here. We should all exit the building before it explodes."

For once, I listened, heading toward the door. We were a couple of steps away when a spell hit the fire tornado, wrapped around the elemental, and exploded. The vampire yanked me and a leprechaun through the door as a torrent of fire and water flew straight into the air and splashed back down. The fire elemental stumbled two steps and fell face-first on the floor, unconscious. A tsunami of water rolled out in every direction. I slammed the door shut just before it hit and ran down the block toward Tracy, who stood in front of a hotel talking to a man with long white hair. For some reason, the vampire followed. I slowed to a walk, keeping pace with him. "Why are you following me?"

The vampire examined me from head to toe. "Sorry. I thought you were someone else. I'm Roman, by the way."

I frowned, "Jen. Who do you think I am?"

"It doesn't matter. I apologize, but I must be on my way." He disappeared.

Tracy turned from the dragon and watched as soaking-wet people poured out of the bank. "What did you do, Jen?"

I held up a hand. "Not my fault this time. It was a fire elemental that lost control. I left before anything happened."

She turned to the dragon. "Good to see you, Glac. Let's go." She didn't bother introducing me to the dragon.

We headed down the street at a fast pace. "Who was that dragon?"

"He runs the Dragon Hotel. He's an old friend, so I asked about the rogue dragons. I mean, he didn't know much, but he said a red dragon tried to take down the pocket of Pyron. Glac thinks it's mind-control."

I stopped in my tracks. "Mind control? On a dragon? No way. Who would be responsible?" Dragons, mental mages, and vampires were the only ones who could mind-control people. And vampires could only suggest. Even mental mages couldn't pierce a dragon's defenses. "Do you think it's infighting?"

"Glac doesn't think so. He thinks it's some kind of outside influence."

"But mind control doesn't work on dragons."

"Nope. He was scared, Jen. And, if you knew Glac, you'd know he doesn't get scared. I think we're in deep shit."

"Yeah." I needed to talk to Mat. The dragon information was too much for a text. I had so many questions. I pointed to a diner about a block down. "Let's grab something to eat." I'd never eaten at a diner before and was excited to see if it was like how it was in the human movies I'd watched.

"Sure, I could eat."

I took in every detail of the diner with wide eyes. A nymph with yellow hair and honey-colored skin sauntered up with a menu in her hand, looked us up and down, and thrust her very impressive cleavage toward Tracy. "You matched, honey?"

Nymphs matched like everyone else, though they weren't sexually monogamous. Their sexual appetites were vast, and one person couldn't satisfy them. They understood that other types of paranormals only slept with their match, so she was being polite, I thought.

"Leave her alone, Lexa," a voice I didn't recognize came from behind us.

I spun to find one of the leprechauns from the bank. He was soaking wet. "Who are you?"

He held up his hands. "I mean you no harm."

Tracy offered him a drying spell and ran it over him when he agreed. "What do you need?"

The leprechaun nodded thanks at Tracy without taking his eyes off me. "Name's Thaddeus Conner, ma'am. I heard the lady at the bank call you detective. I require your services."

Tracy turned to the nymph. "A table for three, please." The nymph's face transformed to a pout at Tracy's lack of interest as she led us to a table and set our menus down before sauntering away.

Tracy and I slid into one side of the booth while the Leprechaun took the other. "Order some food, ladies. I don't bite."

Thaddeus waited until our coffee was poured before he spoke. "I apologize for approaching you like this, Detective. I had me whole life savings taken, and the leprechaun council told me they don't interfere in financial matters. My bank representative won't help because he thinks I'm bad luck. I don't know what else to do, so I took a chance."

Leprechauns were great at making and hoarding money and exceptional at finding things and people. They usually stayed in European pockets. I tried to tune into his magic like I always did when meeting a new supernatural, but it didn't work. It's too bad because I could have used some of his luck. I tapped the table. "I'm a new detective working on my first case, so I don't know if I'm your best choice."

He rubbed his beard. "You're the right choice. I'm sure of it. I can't deny I'm in a bit of a pickle. It's my business account, and me livelihood is at stake."

I took a sip of coffee and glanced at Tracy, but she watched something outside the window. As my mentor, Quin should be available for advice, but I didn't want to ask him after our last conversation. Thaddeus's problem sounded like Jedediah's. My conscience wouldn't let me turn the guy away. "I guess I could try. However, I'll need to divide my time. I've already agreed to the other contract, so it needs to take priority. I'll offer you a discount for the inconvenience."

He shook his head and pulled a bag of gold from his hat. "No need for a discount. Me brother gave me this. It should be enough."

I refused the payment, only asking him for half, but he insisted I take it. He presented the details by sliding a hand-written notebook with receipts hanging out the sides. Some ancient supernaturals refused to use technology, which I'd never understand because it made life much easier. I took the book and met his gaze. "Do you have any enemies? Or any idea who might have stolen from you?"

"I don't know much. The money was there Monday but gone yesterday. The bank doesn't have a record of where it went, nor do I."

Exactly what happened to Jedediah. I was suddenly much more interested. "How much money was it, Lord Conner?"

"Call me Thaddeus. I had half a million dollars. Now I have none."

"It was in the Bank of Mahri?"

"It was."

Of course it was. For the first time, I was glad I was going to Mahri in a couple of weeks. I needed to visit the bank's main branch, where the records were tracked better. "It's my understanding that leprechauns are good at finding things. Why is this different?"

His face flushed. "I can only find objects and people. Bank money is only electronic numbers. It's why we like our gold."

I had a feeling Thaddeus Conner would never put his money in the bank again. We finished our breakfast, exchanged contact information, and discussed the case. I placed the gold and the messy notebook in my bag and hefted it on my shoulder, a little sad that I didn't get to savor my first meal in a diner. As we headed home, I had to switch my bag to a different arm every minute or so because the gold was so heavy. Then I had to listen to Tracy snickering about it.

"What did you do to the bank?"

"Gah!" I jumped and almost dropped my bag as Quin appeared at my side. "Where the hell did you come from?"

"The bank," He scoffed like I was an idiot.

I hefted my bag. "I didn't do anything to the bank other than ask some questions. And what were you doing there?"

"I am your mentor."

Tracy shifted from foot to foot. "Hey, Quin. Are you sticking around for a while? I mean, I need to take care of some stuff and don't want to leave Jen alone. So, if you're gonna stick around...."

"Of course. I live to babysit a perfectly capable adult." His voice dripped with sarcasm.

"Just go take care of your business, Tracy. I'll be fine." I moved my bag to my right arm and continued toward the flashing circle.

"Be careful, Jen," Tracy warned as I waved my hand in acknowledgment.

I could tell when Quin caught up to me because his jump scare reminded me to open my senses, and a chill ran down my spine from his creepy vampire vibe. "There is trouble everywhere you go. I'm beginning to regret my decision to mentor you."

"There's *not* trouble everywhere I go. And it's not like you've been around to be much of a mentor."

"Murder in broad daylight, kidnapped by dragons, bank explosions. Oh, yes. Let's not forget the awakening of a First who peacefully rested for two hundred years."

"He wasn't peacefully resting," I protested. It was all I had because the rest was true. I was beginning to see why Mat worried so much about my safety. "Besides, none of that has anything to do with my detective work. What do you want, Quin?"

"An intelligent, well-behaved apprentice that makes sound decisions. However, I have you, so one must make compromises." He pulled me away from the other pedestrian traffic. "What do you know about the dragon situation?"

My eyebrows drew together at the quick change of subject. "Not much. Why do you want to know?"

"I have been hired by the Regent of Ahl to investigate the case. He was not very forthcoming." Quin's eyes scanned the area. "I will meet you at your tiny house." He disappeared.

I headed to the flashing circle and thought about the Dragon situation while waiting in line. Mat hired a private investigator rather than relying on the Enforcers, which meant he didn't trust them to conduct an honest investigation. Quin only took dangerous cases that most other people wouldn't, although I doubted he'd deny Mat's request for political reasons. And Mat didn't give him any information, which didn't make sense. I balanced the heavy bag on my hip and texted Mat, flashed into my neighborhood's landing circle, and headed toward the alley behind our house. Tracy had it spelled so no one could see who was coming or going from the flashing circle. It made it easier for people like Mat to visit without blowing my cover.

Chapter 14

QUIN STOOD OUTSIDE THE wards on the concealed path behind the house. He poked at the ward. "These are some very impressive wards."

"Yeah, Tracy has some mad skills." I dragged him through them, even though he was probably immune to the magic. One of the many gifts of the vampires.

I set my bag on the table and sighed in relief. "Do you want something to drink?"

Despite human folklore, vampires ate food and drank beverages. They needed to eat just like the rest of us to survive. They also needed blood, but most didn't care what type they got. There were several blood delivery services throughout the pockets. Some vampires had willing paranormal donors because we couldn't be enslaved or turned into vampires by accident. Either option was safer for the coalition than allowing them to prey on humans.

Luckily, most vampires hated enslaving humans, which could happen if their pheromones got out of control during a feeding. Don't get me wrong, vampires weren't good, responsible people who cared about the plight of humans. They didn't in any aspect. They did things this way because they preferred to live their lives without being shackled to a bunch of slaves who depended on them for everything.

"Water is fine." Quin slid into a chair at the kitchen island, examining our smallish house.

I went to the magichef and searched for water. "Aha!" I pushed the button. When nothing happened, I pressed it again. Then again. Three glass bottles of water appeared. I pretended like I meant to do that, grabbed two, and joined Quin at the kitchen island. "So, what do you need to know?"

"The First has been in your home today. Why?" Vampires had super hearing, sight, and smell, and although their smell wasn't as good as the shifters', it was much better than mine. Having a vampire around was like having a mixture of a bloodhound and an electronic listening device. Like all nocturnal apex predators, they could also see in the dark. I wasn't sure what their eyesight was like during the day and didn't want to ask Quin.

"We've been gone all day, so if he was here, it wasn't with permission."

"Yet you are not surprised."

"Nope. I'm pretty sure he's as immune to magic as you are. He and I will have words, though."

"So, you are on speaking terms with him. Tell me about the dragon issues."

I told him about the crack in the wall and the wyrm attacking people on the street, along with the kidnapping. I suggested he talk to Tracy about her friend at the hotel. "They had this weird magic on them that I'm having difficulty placing."

"Weird magic?"

"The male dragon that kidnapped us had this bracelet that radiated a strange and creepy magic. It's not quite black magic. The other had an implant in her left wrist."

"And you recognized it?"

"Yes, and no. It seemed vaguely familiar, but I can't place it."

He asked me a few more questions, warned me to use my brain in all situations, and disappeared.

Relieved to have some time alone, I got to work on my two intertwined cases. I tried to make sense of the notebook Mr. Conner provided. He kept a hand-written ledger that showed steady deposits and withdrawals over the last few months, aligning with starting a business. The receipts were printed bank records to back up his handwritten ledger. The most recent receipts were from Monday when his money was still in the bank, and then yesterday, when it was gone with no transactions listed to show where it went. I opened the electronic files Jedediah had given me. I hoped it wasn't very clever supernatural hackers because I doubted I'd ever find them. The main office of the Bank of Mahri was the only one capable of tracking the complex supernatural accounts, so I had to reach out to them.

I called the bank and made an appointment with the manager for the week of my coronation. I hoped I could wear my glamour and get more information there without drawing attention to myself. My stomach went sour at the thought of going back to our family home and facing my horrific past. It was going to suck, and I'd probably embarrass myself in front of other leaders when I had a panic attack or threw up. There were just too many bad memories. Pushing that aside, I checked my phone, expecting to see a response from Mat, but he hadn't read my message yet. I rubbed my eyes.

I pulled up the pictures and screenshots taken from Jedediah's internal investigation and examined them. I magnified the fine print of the documents. It was my first case, and I wanted to be thorough. I gasped when I came to the human copyright symbol halfway through the third paragraph.

A small circle with a squiggly arrow-like thing replaced the 'C' with a circle around it. I took a screenshot and a picture with my phone. I gasped as a realization hit me. The symbol was precisely the same as the one on the dragon bracelet.

I grabbed Thaddeus's statement and pulled out a magnifying glass. Sure enough, there was the same symbol. I pulled up my account and examined an electronic statement. A copyright symbol stared back at me.

"I need to find out what that symbol means," I said to the empty room.

I planned to drag Tracy to the Allure library to do some research the following day. That changed when Mat called and demanded I report to the castle immediately. Figuring that it was related to my text, I followed his orders willingly for once. Tracy and I flashed to the landing circle near the public entrance at the palace. I should have used the hidden family entrance, but I wanted to see what regular visitors went through to get in.

I could hardly contain my grin when not a spark of recognition flashed in the rhinoceros shifter's eyes. His stony expression didn't change as he focused on us. "State your business."

"I'm Detective Jen Hendrix. I'd like to see House Manager Helen, please."

He turned to Tracy. "And you?"

"Oh, um. I'm with her." She jerked a thumb in my direction.

"Identification," He demanded.

Tracy and I showed our IDs, and we moved to the posh waiting area with four or five other paranormals. It wasn't long before Helen came out, planted her hands on her hips, and said, "For fate's sake, Jen, it's about time you showed up."

I grinned, unexpectedly happy to see the griffin who helped raise me. We followed her to the family elevators, and as soon as the doors closed, she whacked me on the back of the head. "What were you thinking entering the nest like a stranger?"

I rubbed the back of my head. "Sorry, Helen. I wanted to see what regular people go through when they come in. I didn't mean any disrespect."

"Well, I suppose since you were satisfying a curiosity, it was okay, but you better not do it again. It's a grievous insult for a member of the nest to not feel at home." Griffins were touchy about making those they considered family feel welcome. I was glad she didn't take it personally. We entered my suite, and Helen spun around. "I almost forgot. Tracy, your suite has been prepared across the hall. Feel free to come and go from the family entrance any time."

Tracy's eyes grew as big as saucers, and I tried to warn her not to decline with hand signals. "Oh. Uh. Thank you, Helen. I'm honored."

Helen nodded once and gave me a big hug. "You don't be a stranger. And for fate's sake, stop getting into so much trouble."

"Yes, ma'am," I mumbled as she left the room, gently shutting the door.

We entered my office twenty minutes later, and I called Mat from the office phone. When he answered, I said, "Yes, this is Princess Jenella Lissandra Andreas Ahl reporting to his majesty, the Regent of Ahl, as ordered."

"We'll be right up."

Five minutes later, Mat marched in with Titus and a shaking Verity in tow. Titus's eyes swept the room, resting on the corner where Tracy was perched. I jumped out of my chair and yelled, "Verity!"

She stiffened when I pulled her into a hug and then relaxed. "Oh, geez, Jen. You look way different. I take it this is the real you?"

"In the flesh. Please have a seat. Do you guys want something to drink?" I motioned to the plush sitting area by the windows.

They declined drinks, so we arranged ourselves in the seating area, with Verity and Titus on one couch and Mat and I on the other. Tracy stayed in her corner. "So, are you taking the job?"

Verity looked better than she did the last time I saw her. Gone were her raccoon eyes and wild hair, replaced by natural human makeup, her hair scooped back in a neat bun. She wore spelled gloves that allowed her hands full movement but contained her magic. The gloves were normally worn by children with touch magic to help them with control. She adjusted one when she saw me looking at them. "Yes. I've decided to take you up on your offer."

I wanted to dance a jig. Not only would I no longer have to hear Mat nag me about finding an assistant, but Verity would have a safe place to learn about the paranormal world. It took everything I had to stay poised. "Are you sure about this, Verity?"

She nodded in her no-nonsense way. "Titus and I discovered we are what he calls a match and wants to date. I think living and working here is a valid solution while we figure out our relationship. It will also help with my learning."

I blinked. "Wait. You what?"

A small smile broke her professional demeanor. "You're right, Titus. It is the fates that brought us together." She waited for his mumbled acknowledgment and turned her attention back to me. "I am already overwhelmed with all of this, so I don't want to rush into anything. However, I want the job and can start tomorrow if the position is still open."

I glanced at Mat's furrowed brow before turning back to Verity. "The job is yours. Having someone help keep me organized will be a relief." I turned to Titus. "What do you plan to do?"

"He has agreed to work as a crown juror," Mat answered.

The crown juror worked directly for me and helped solve criminal cases and civil disputes when the subject's stories didn't match. I congratulated him. We talked for a few minutes before Mat and Titus left. I then showed Verity around the office area. Mat's assistant, who agreed to train her, joined us, and I handed her off. She was in good hands, so I returned to my desk. I figured I might as well get some work done while I was there.

Two hours later, the pressure of the crown had settled fully back on my shoulders, or head, or whatever. I rubbed my temples and approved the request of the woodland fairies, cutting out a two-acre chunk of land in the pocket of Farine that was maintained exclusively by elves. After signing the deal, I packed up and texted Tracy that I was ready to return to the house.

When she appeared in the doorway, I slipped my glamour earrings into my ears, and we headed through the family quarters and out the back to our private flashing circle. I would have liked to use the front exit to see what happened, but insulting Helen twice in one day wasn't advisable. Griffins were fantastic creatures, but not the most even-tempered. "Wait, Jenella," Mat's voice boomed as we reached the back door.

I sighed and turned around, not wanting to deal with my brother. "Hey, Mat."

Humor danced in his eyes. "Is talking to me for a minute all that bad?"

"Not unless I sense a lecture."

"How about praise?"

I raised an eyebrow.

He chuckled, an unusual thing for him. "I just wanted you to know I find your hiring of the new juror brilliant. Not only will she detect disingenuous people, but she will be a very competent assistant."

"I probably shouldn't tell you I only offered her the job because I like her."

"I know. You should know that Colonel Ballard is leading a raid on the Hospa Dragon Complex and may contact you to assist. You shouldn't go."

I threw my braid over my shoulder, trying to figure out how to respond. On one hand, I wanted to figure out what was going on with the dragons. On the other hand, it wasn't Detective Hendrix's business and would eat away more of my freedom. "What type of assistance?"

"The magical type. He's gathering supernaturals that can handle dragons. Your performance during the kidnapping impressed him, and he mentioned you might be a good person to include. He and Emine are strategizing right now. I cannot make you say no, but I want you to think about it before you commit."

"Tell me about the dragon problem. What do you know, and why did you hire Quin?"

"I hired Quin because Bastien is being evasive, and I want my own intelligence."

My eyebrows drew together. "Bastien's told me multiple times that he has it under control. But he's hiding something. Quin's a good choice to figure out what that is." He wouldn't even talk to Tracy about it, and it bothered her.

"My thoughts, exactly. Bastien's in over his head, and his mother is still absent. Dragons are not stable without their queen, and he knows it. I think this issue goes deeper than we can imagine, and I want to know more. Quin is the obvious choice."

"The dragons are scared." I rubbed my temples. "Something about the whole thing is familiar, but I can't figure out what."

"Let it go, and let me handle it. I assure you I am doing all I can."

"Okay, I'll stay out of it for now, but I might need to get involved if the problem gets worse."

"Understood. Though you need to think carefully before you do."

I gave him a quick hug. "Thank you."

As Tracy and I left the castle and headed to the family flashing circle, I noticed a few castle guards watching us. I had an idea. "Hey, Tracy, do you think if we combined our power, we could create a way to flash directly into my suite?"

Tracy shook her head. "These wards are old, and hundreds of people have added their power to them. I mean, working around them would take months, if not years."

"Even though our magic mixed together is powerful enough to take down a dragon?"

"I don't know. I'll think about it, but don't get your hopes up."

When we returned to our house, I headed to the magichef, excited to have control over what I ate. Helen took care of the menus at the castle, and I ate whatever she served without a fuss. Her food was great, but having control over my choices for the first time made me feel like a baby bird who finally discovered how to fly. I perused the electronic menu and found a tantalizing shrimp stir-fry. "Do you want some shrimp stir-fry?" I called up to Tracy, who'd gone straight to her room when we got home.

"Sure. I'll be down in a sec."

Turning back to the magichef, I froze. The ruling magic vibrated around me in a way I'd never felt. I always wrapped it tightly around myself to keep from being a beacon, and it sometimes protested, but not like that. I learned at an early age that if I didn't hide it, anyone could pinpoint my exact location. The ruling magic was intended to let people know their leader was near and to reassure them. For me, it had always been a way for people who wanted to kill me to find my location.

It constantly swirled around me like a tiny vortex and kind of had a mind of its own. This was different. The vibrations were making my teeth rattle. Swallowing the feeling, I reached out and pushed the button on the magichef twice and stepped back. The magical vibrations increased, and I tried to reel it in and calm it. That didn't work, so I ran to the sink and splashed cold water on my face. It helped a little, but the vibration wouldn't stop. I decided to ignore it, blaming it on being tired.

I realized the magichef wasn't working. As I leaned over to see what I did wrong, food exploded, hitting me in the face. I ducked just in time to avoid getting smacked in the face by two plates. They bounced off the ceiling and shattered as they hit the floor.

Tracy came rushing into the kitchen. "What the hell, Jen? What happened?"

I couldn't answer because the ruling magic vibration had increased to the point it took every ounce of my energy to contain it. My teeth clacked together hard as the magic lifted me from my crouch on the floor. I started spinning with the sheer force of the magic swirling around me. A scream escaped from my throat. I heard voices yelling, but I couldn't listen to what they were saying. Two sets of hands grabbed me, one hard enough to pierce my skin. Their grip stopped the spin so abruptly that it felt like my skull split.

I got two deep breaths in before I was overcome with a mass of swirling colors, and my body stretched. As a kid, Mat took me to the Oregon coast on a brief trip to the human world. I remember being mesmerized as I watched the humans stretch taffy. They folded it over and put it on a machine that spun, pulling it to its limit while turning it over and over until it became stringy and gooey. The best way I could describe what happened is that I was that taffy. The two sets of hands still held me tightly, and another scream joined my own.

The stretching caused the ruling magic to increase its vibration, making my head feel like it was stuffed with cotton. My hair came loose and swirled around me, sticking to my sweaty face. Just when I thought I couldn't take it anymore, I got dumped onto a white marble floor, face down.

Chapter 15

THE PAIN BECAME SO intense that I couldn't hold on to the ruling magic anymore. As soon as I let it loose, I shot into the air and began spinning. My stomach lurched, and I heard several voices shouting as I tried to keep control of both the magic and my bodily functions. A spell hit the magic. I lost control of my other two pools of magic. They unraveled, blasting out in all directions in an explosion big enough to level a building. I hit the floor.

I was breathing so hard I had to lay on the hard floor for a minute with my cheek pressed to the cool marble. When I felt a little better, I tried to sit up. I managed to drag myself to my knees before the dry heaves started. I shoved the curls out of my face and almost face-planted. The realization hit that my full power was displayed for everyone to feel. My heart raced, and I tried to shake off the dizziness. They were going to find us and kill us, and it was all my fault. Sweat trickled down my face, a single drop hitting the white marble floor. I reverted to a helpless six-year-old who had inherited too much power and became a target. I curled into a ball. "They're going to kill us. It's all my fault."

Strong arms wrapped around me and dragged me to a warm side. I kicked and screamed, trying to break loose from the tight grip.

"It's me."

Mat's scent washed over me. "No, Mat! They'll find us. It's all my fault!"

"No, they won't. They can't hurt us anymore. I killed them all."

I kicked out and punched until I broke free of the grip as I once again tried to catch my breath. Somewhere in my sheer panic, the thought that I was no longer a child broke through, and I grabbed onto it with everything I had. The panic began to ease. I took a deep breath and squeezed my eyes tight, unable to face the embarrassment of what had just happened.

I swiped my multi-colored hair out of my face. Somewhere in the emotional, magical mess, my glamour had disappeared. A handkerchief appeared in front of my face. Startled, I took it and wiped my eyes. I took a deep breath to gather courage and raised my head. I was in a huge round room with white marble walls, floors, and a heavy metal door. The arched ceiling was white and made of what looked like plastic, though I could feel some kind of magic emanating from it. Quin stood against the wall, one hand crossed over his chest, the other rubbing his chin. Bastien sat on the floor slightly to my left with a very disheveled Tracy on his lap, both with wide eyes. Mat's face was scratched up. Drake kneeled next to him, concern in his eyes. I cleared my throat. "Sorry."

Drake laughed. Mat shot him a look before moving to Tracy and healing her. "I need to talk to Jenella in private."

"Not until I get an explanation," Bastien growled.

Quin dropped his hand from his chin. "What was that?" Somehow, he still looked pristine, although I was pretty sure he was the second pair of hands that tried to stop me from spinning, based on the claw marks on my sides.

I ignored them and concentrated on trying to wrap my magic around me. My inherent magic and the healing magic were still the same. I re-wrapped them with little effort. I tried not to let my disappointment show. Despite my hopes, the three pools of magic didn't mix. I realized I had a hundred times more ruling magic and struggled to wrap it around myself. I looked for differences. With a glance at Mat, I realized I could see his aura without turning on my magic sight. I also knew the magic type and level of every supernatural in the building without trying. Pain shot through my head, and I groaned. I reeled it in but kept it to a radius a little bigger than the room. A realization struck. "It's my thirty-fifth birthday."

Paranormals didn't celebrate birthdays because we had too many of them, but most of us did keep track of our age. At Mat's raised eyebrow, I continued, "Today's my thirty-fifth birthday, and the year designated for my coronation. My ruling magic just expanded. It must be why I needed to be coronated this year." I glanced around at the white room. "Where are we?"

Drake sat beside me. "Your Mother's path was much the same, although I don't know if this happened."

Mat glanced at Quin before returning his attention to me. "We don't have any information about your ascension other than the laws and decree Mother made about how and when the coronation will take place. Do you think your magic is...different?" He meant fixed.

"Different, yes, but not in the way you're thinking."

"Different how?" Quin's expression held an unusual hint of interest. He moved to stand beside Mat. "Your grandmother had a certain power about her that made everyone want to follow her. She could make an entire room fall in line with a look. Your mother was not nearly as powerful, so she ruled ruthlessly. I want to know if your power is growing because I fear if it does not, we are all doomed."

Drake and Bastien nodded in agreement.

"Explain." Mat's rough voice was low and dangerous.

"Your mother wasn't exactly a wise and just leader, and you know it, Mathias. She wasn't even powerful enough to contain you." Quin's explanation was news to me.

"She wasn't even a quarter as powerful as the Firsts. To compensate, she ruled by fear and...eliminated the competition." Bitterness rang through Drake's voice. "Tarquin is asking if Jenella will grow into her power or if the coalition will go down in flames because she isn't powerful enough to hold it together."

The room fell silent. My education focused on my mother's accomplishments, not her dark side. I knew it existed because why else would you allow someone to beat and cage your heir? When I was younger, I'd told myself my parents didn't know, but that didn't make sense as I got older. I started feeling a block on my inherent magic, like a giant lump in my chest, when I turned twenty-five and knew no one else could have done that. "My mother put you to sleep. That's why you attacked me when you woke up."

Drake's only reaction was a slight incline of his head.

"As touching as this is, I do not care. I want to know if you can end the rebellion before the coalition falls," Quin interjected.

"Rebellion?"

"We will talk about that later," Mat growled.

Drake snorted. "You haven't told her. You realize you're not doing Jenella any favors by keeping things from her?"

"What I do and do not tell my sister is not your concern, First."

I rubbed my face. "Right. Because keeping me in a bubble has worked so well. Hey, I have an idea. Why don't I move into this room? Then nothing can get to me, and I'll never have to face reality. You know, realities like I suck at everything and am not powerful enough. Because fates forbid, I get the information I need to take the throne." I stood and headed toward the metal door. "I'm going home so I can pretend I know how to clean up the mess in our kitchen. You coming, Tracy?"

"Jenella, wait!" Mat said as I reached the door. I stopped, folding my arms over my chest. His face flashed with remorse. "I was only trying to protect you."

"I get that, Mat. But instead, you've put both blinders and rose-colored glasses on me." I pointed to Drake. "I had no idea our mother was a tyrant. A rebellion is something I'm not aware of. No one will tell me what's going on with the dragons. I have no clue how to make my bed or clean a damn kitchen! How exactly is that helping me?"

He looked down at his feet. "You're going to ask me this after the episode you just had?"

"Yes. I'm absolutely going to ask you to stop coddling me and tell me the truth. Because being clueless and useless is not working for me." I yanked on the door, but it didn't budge, so I turned to Bastien. "Where the hell am I, and how do I get out of here?"

He growled, and I realized I was using the new ruling magic to force the truth, which I couldn't do before. I pulled it back as he jumped to his feet. "You do not recognize your own summoning room?"

"Did you not hear that entire conversation? I don't know anything. Just answer the damn question!" My temper was getting out of control, so I took a deep breath. "Please, Prince Bastien of the Dragons," I added bitterly.

Bastien's face flushed. "Your mother was not powerful enough to use the summoning room, so your grandmother put it in my mother's care. It has not been used in years because it takes a lot of power. However, it is yours, should you become powerful enough to use it."

Tracy wrapped her arm around my waist. "Wait, how did we get here? I mean, if Jen didn't know about it at all. Why did we end up here?"

We all turned to Drake, who pointedly tried not to take part in the conversation. He cleared his throat. "I pulled you here when I felt the magic surge."

I ran a hand through my hair. It got caught in the rat's nest of curls, so I jerked it free, taking a few hairs with it. I held them out to Tracy. "Can you use these to make me a charm that protects me from brothers, dragon princes, and Firsts?"

She giggled and waved my hand away. "So you mean this place is safe for Jen to let out her magic?"

Drake's green eyes met mine. "Yes. It is the only place that can contain such magic." He held his hand out. "You eliminated the glamour. I will fix it for you if you'd like."

I spent the next few days pouting while pretending to trace financial transactions through tangled webs of offshore accounts, shell companies, and leprechaun gold transfers. Unable to avoid reality anymore, Tracy and I landed on the family landing pad at the castle early Monday morning. I removed my glamour with a sigh and headed through the door to the palace. "I do not want to go to Mahri."

Before I could whine more, Verity rushed toward us. "Thank God you're here. I have a bunch of stuff for you. Where have you been?"

"She's been avoiding outside contact, mostly," Tracy answered.

Verity stopped in her tracks. "And why would you waste time avoiding reality?"

I sighed as we entered the elevators leading to my office. "Habit. I'm used to having a lot of time alone. What do you have?"

Verity followed me toward my office. "I need to go over the plans for your coronation. Helen is handling most of the event planning, but I'm arranging your travel and meet-and-greet parties. I've heard you've requested your childhood friend travel with you, even though no one knows why you still bother with him. Will he be your date or are you just appeasing him?"

I sat at my desk. "My *date*?"

Verity waved her hand dismissively. "I get supernaturals don't date like humans, but I don't know what else to call it. So, he will travel with you and stay in the castle?"

I stared out the window at the flying supernaturals soaring over the city. "Can I take him on human transportation? I understand that it's much slower than ours. It would be fun to make him suffer."

"As passive-aggressively fun as that sounds, no. Several honored guests will be traveling with you on the transport. I need you to approve the guest list and seating chart. Also, Helen has a list of people staying at the castle in Mahri that you need to approve." She set a packet of papers on my desk. "And we need you to sign off on the ceremony plans. You have a final dress fitting at ten this morning."

I eyed the paperwork. "And this is why I never hired an assistant."

Verity snorted. "I told you I was good at this."

She was. "Thanks, Verity. I'll take a look and return it to you before my dress fitting."

The rest of the day was spent reviewing the plans for something I didn't want to do. My phone rang around four. My head pounded out of my skull, and my eyes were dry and scratchy. I saw it was Travis and rejected the call. "Are you ready to go?" I asked Tracy, who'd spent the day in the palace lab making potions for her clients and sat at the conference table labeling packages.

Before she could answer, Verity appeared at the door. "Prince Mathias is here to see you, Your Grace."

I rubbed my eyes. "Thanks, Verity."

Mat strode in and perched on one of the chairs in front of my desk. "We need to talk about the other day."

"You mean you need to talk about the other day. I'm over it."

"You know that's a lie. What happened to your magic?"

"The ruling magic grew. We already went over this. Now, let's talk about this rebellion I knew nothing about."

Mat's flat stare and increased aura of danger made me want to squirm, but I kept my face neutral and my hands clasped on the desk. My brother was a scary guy.

Tracy gathered her things and rushed toward the door. "I'll wait outside."

Mat leaned forward. "What happened with your magic to cause your panic attack, Jenella?"

Recognizing he wouldn't let it go, I said, "When I realized my magic had unraveled, I panicked." I shrugged like it was no big deal, but we both knew better.

He shook his head. "We think the dragon incidents are related to a long-standing rebellion. They are ramping up their attacks as you near the age of power." Relief flooded me when I thought he'd let the panic issue go. "And you need to talk to a therapy mage to deal with your trauma before you become too powerful, lose control, and kill us all."

I ignored that comment and pulled out the pictures of the symbol I found on the financial documents. "Do you recognize this?"

"Where did you get this?"

I explained the research on my case. He rubbed his chin.

"That symbol was found on the implant and the bracelet extracted from the dragons that kidnapped you. I hired Quin to find out where it came from and why some dragons are going rogue."

"So, how did a clan of dragons get their hands on that sort of magic? It didn't feel right. It felt like...something I know but can't quite place. Do you think the missing queen is leading the rebellion?"

"I don't know who the leaders are or if she's missing. As I said, Quin is tasked with finding those answers."

I studied the symbols. "It looks like my cases intersect with his. Is he researching the symbol?"

"Both the dragons and Enforcers are looking into it. The First says it looks familiar, but he cannot remember where he's seen it. Right now, the best thing you can do is let them work and focus on your upcoming coronation. I'll be sure to let you know if they find anything."

The sit-down and shut-up vibe rubbed me the wrong way. "I'll let Quin do his job, but I'm not going to let it go. Nor am I going to take a back seat." I leaned forward. "Stop trying to put me in a cage, Mat."

His jaw clenched. "I am *not* trying to put you in a cage. I am trying to express the importance of delegating responsibilities and using caution."

"Alright, but I'm still working on my case." I realized how mean the cage statement was but couldn't bring myself to care. I was sick of being coddled and protected. My brother trailed behind me as I stood and headed toward the door. "If you find out anything else, let me know."

The conversation was still on my mind the next day as I headed back to the Bank of Mahri to try to talk to the leprechaun representative. I hoped to get more answers from him than I did from the vampire. Tracy came with me but made it clear we were leaving if anyone started what she called "a magic fit". I agreed only because I didn't want to be caught up in any more trouble.

The effort was wasted. We waited an hour, only to be dismissed. In the short time since the flooding incident, the bank changed its policy to not give out any information to third parties unless approved by executive management and the account owner. Even more reason for me to meet with the bank manager when we went to Mahri, since I already had my clients' approval.

As we left the bank, a shadow fell across the narrow cobblestone street, causing people to gasp and point. Tracy shoved me against a wall and prepared to fight, only to deflate when a royal blue dragon landed in the middle of the road and morphed into a naked woman with blue hair and eyes. "Detective Hendrix, the First has summoned you. You will present yourself to him no later than midnight tonight or face the consequences." She morphed back into a dragon and launched into the air.

I pulled my phone out to text him what I thought of his summons. "Is it normal for me to have a visceral reaction to that order, or is it my title that makes me want to tell him what he can do with it?"

Tracy chuckled. "It's normal. That's why those summonses are so effective. I mean, imagine how people felt when your grandmother used that summoning room. My guess is that most people were confused, angry, and devalued, but couldn't protest without getting themselves in more trouble."

It was a perspective I wouldn't have considered. "Yeah. I think I'll use summoning people both sparingly and strategically, if at all." I texted Drake that I had too much work to bend to his whims and would be there the next day. In addition, I suggested his posterior was an excellent place for him to store the summons while he waited. Tracy and I laughed about it all the way to the flashing circle.

As we flashed to the castle for yet another coronation meeting, pain exploded across my face as we bounced off something. We landed in a heap outside the wall on the family side. "What the hell," I muttered, reaching out and feeling the wards. They were still the same, except a new, potent magic coated them. A magic I recognized. "That jerk changed the castle wards."

Tracy's face screwed up in concentration. "I wish I could create wards like this. Do you know how they were done?"

"They were created by a sorceress, the one matched to the First Shifter, Jonas. Her magic is ancient and powerful." We trudged toward the front entrance. "It became a tradition for everyone who passed through the gates to add a bit of magic, so it's reinforced by hundreds, if not thousands, of different powers. Mat, Helen, George, and I are the only ones who can allow access beyond the front entrance and office areas."

Tracy grabbed my arm and pulled me down the street toward the front entrance. "I know this is going to sound like a stupid question, but who locked you out?"

"Drake. Probably in response to my text. Nobody knows the full extent of what any of the Firsts can do, but this is unacceptable."

We entered the public entrance and were greeted by a waiting and angry Helen. I texted her during our walk to let her know what happened. We headed to my office, where Emine, Mat, Verity, and George waited. Verity shut the door as we took our seats at the conference table. Tracy tried to slink into a corner, but I yanked her into the chair beside me. Mat examined her, then me. "Why are your faces bruised?"

I raised an eyebrow. "You don't know?"

His eyes flashed with anger. "No, Jenella. I don't know. That's why I asked the question."

"No reason to get snotty. Apparently, I can no longer flash through the wards to the family's flashing circle. We bounced off and had to get Helen to bring us through."

He stood abruptly. "What?"

I waved a hand. "The magic signature is Drake's. I plan on handling it when I meet with him."

Mat sat and picked up his phone. "I will handle it today. He was only supposed to reinforce them against dragons, not you. There will be consequences."

"Consequences? You're not going to kill him, are you?" Verity squeaked.

Emine's face lit with a mischievous grin. "Oh, yes. We brutally punish violations against the crown in the supernatural world, Verity. This type of violation is punishable by death."

"You can't just go around killing people!" Verity screeched.

"We can and we will." I kept my voice serious. "We'll probably have to kill four or five people for insulting me during coronation week."

Tracy cough-laughed, and Verity's head whipped to her, her eyes narrowing. "You're screwing with me."

Emine cackled. "Yeah. Because it's too easy!"

My shoulders shook with laughter. "You think we just go around killing people for something as silly as closing a gap in the wards?"

Verity shook her head. "I know every single one of you can and do kill. Your laws are a little loosey-goosey. I don't understand where the lines are or what happens when they're crossed."

Mat set his phone down. "We try not to punish people with death often, but we will. We have dungeons similar to your human jails, but we use them sparingly. Violations are generally handled within the laws of each faction. However, if anyone attacks you, your match, or your children without provocation, death is not only possible but legal no matter the species."

Verity slapped a stack of papers down on the table. "I don't think I could kill anyone."

The realization that Verity was the only one in the room that hadn't killed someone was kind of sad. I hoped being my assistant would keep it that way. "Good. Now, what's this meeting about?"

Verity's shoulders relaxed as she handed each of us a stack of papers. "I have the final transportation schedules worked out. Mat and Emine, along with George and Helen, will take private transport to Mahri on Wednesday to ensure the castle is ready. Jen, Tracy, and I will take the other transport on Thursday morning with a group of dignitaries. This is very different from human events, so I need y'all to make sure I did it right."

"What are the differences, love?" Helen asked.

"Humans don't have to dance around interspecies conflicts. Also, they tend to take their coronations more seriously, or at least make them more formal than throwing a weeklong series of parties. Also, the monarch is the firstborn instead of the thirdborn and takes the throne upon the death of a parent."

I nodded. "Magic favors the number three. We have strict age rules to take the throne. The five-year grace period allows young successors to ease into the position. It only applies to incoming rulers under the age of fifty."

"And the parties are to accommodate guest preferences to keep them out of trouble. You do not want several packs of shifters or covens of witches sitting idle. It tends to cause riots and level cities. The people of Mahri deserve better than that," Helen added.

Verity's mouth opened and closed, and she swallowed. "Right. Speaking of witches, the President of Covens refuses to travel on a transport with Tracy and does not want to go a day early."

Tracy's face flushed. I put a hand on her arm. "That's not your problem. Tell her she has four choices. She travels with Tracy, goes a day early with Mat and Emine, arranges her own transportation, or stays in Allure. I'm fine with any of them."

Mat leaned forward. "Tell her she will be banned if she causes the slightest problem. That goes for every dignitary. We do not take chances with Jen's safety."

It took us three hours to go through the details of a coronation I didn't even want to go to. By the time Tracy and I left, I was grumpy. The thought of facing my awful childhood memories while dealing with a bunch of butt-kissing dignitaries who caused drama just for fun made my head throb. The only bright spot was that I'd secured an appointment with the president of the Bank of Mahri. I hoped to solve my first case before I came back to Allure.

We flashed to our neighborhood circle and headed to our house, neither saying much. I followed Tracy through the wards at our property line. She walked right through, but I bounced off. Tracy frowned and yanked me through. "You need to deal with that First."

I needed to deal with a lot of things.

Chapter 16

One thing I needed to deal with dealt with me instead. My phone rang as the sun started peeking through the windows. I looked at it through blurry eyes and recognized the Dragon Queen's official office number. "This is Jen."

There was a pause. "Detective Jen Hendrix?"

Not the queen, I decided. I sat up and brushed my rat's nest of hair out of my eyes. "Yeah."

"Detective Hendrix, you have ignored the summons from the First."

Before I could say anything, I was in a swirly mass of colors. My body stretched like taffy, and my head filled with cotton. I turned in circles so fast my hair whipped my face and got in my mouth. Gross. I couldn't lift my arms to bat it away. Without warning, I got unceremoniously dumped onto the white marble floor in the summoning room.

I hopped to my feet and turned in a slow circle. The room was empty, so I fought with my hair and realized that I'd been summoned to my own summoning room. I checked my hair color to ensure I still wore my glamour and looked down at myself. Yep. Still in my sleep shorts and tank top. No bra. Great.

I stomped toward the door and was only halfway there when a gremlin with silver hair and a portly shape came through. He eyeballed me with watery blue eyes that held utter disgust. "Welcome to the Home of the Dragons. Please follow me and try to keep up." He clapped his hands twice, turned, and strode out.

I squared my shoulders and followed him. "What is this about?"

"The First has summoned you. You will be on your best behavior and show him the respect he deserves. And next time, try to dress appropriately."

I couldn't hide the anger that flashed through my eyes. The ruling magic snapped out, and I reeled it back in before it hit the gremlin. "Yeah. I'll do that should I not be in bed when summoned."

"No need to be rude. I am merely the messenger."

I trailed behind him and tried finger-combing my hair, but my efforts made it worse, so I gave up. The gremlin led me past two desks in the outer office. One was empty, but the other was occupied by the queen's assistant wearing a pale blue suit. Her royal blue hair was swept up into a professional bun. She looked me up and down, a sour expression on her face. The gremlin opened the door and motioned me to enter the Dragon Queen's office.

The office was much bigger than mine, with a desk in the corner nearest the door and two chairs in front of it. In the opposite corner was a table with comfortable chairs and four giant TVs on the wall. To the right were two rich brown leather couches facing each other. I assumed the ceilings were cathedral-tall to accommodate dragons.

Drake sat at the desk and looked up when I padded in, my bare feet slapping the floor. The gremlin bowed and quietly exited, shutting the door with a *"click"*. I felt a privacy spell snap into place. Drake didn't try to hide the interest in his eyes as they swept up and down my body. "Jenella. I'm not complaining, but why are you here so early, dressed like that?"

I crossed my arms over my chest and stepped closer. It was a huge mistake because the scent of fresh rain, wood smoke, and Drake washed over me. I took a step back. "You summoned me to my own summoning room! On top of that, what the hell are you doing, locking me out of my own wards and ordering me around? In case you forget, I don't answer to you, the queen's assistant, or your borrowed dragon throne."

His eyebrows drew together. "I didn't summon you." His eyes swept over me again. "But it's very nice to see you."

"Haha. One minute, I'm asleep, then I'm spinning and stretched, then bam! I'm on a marble floor! In my pajamas! That gremlin perp-marched me to *not* your office like a criminal. And I haven't had my coffee yet."

Drake's eyes sparkled with humor as he slipped off his jacket and held it out to me. "Here, put this on. You mages are so touchy about nudity that I'm surprised you're able to live in a pocket."

I yanked it on, thankful that it went down to my knees. Inhaling his scent, I rolled up the sleeves and plopped down on one of the comfy chairs in front of the queen's desk. "I'm not touchy about nudity. I'm touchy about being summoned out of my sleep. What is so important that's worth this humiliation? And what the hell did you do to my wards?"

He went to a wet bar and poured coffee. "I didn't summon you. I asked my aunt's assistant to set up a meeting so I could check your glamour and talk about the issues with the Hospa dragons."

I yanked off the glamour earrings and tried to sweep the messy curls out of my face by tucking them behind my ears. They sprung back, so I blew at them and exchanged the earrings for the coffee. "Yet here I am. Tracy is going to be pissed."

A devious grin spread across his face. "Yet here you are."

"It's not funny."

"It's kind of funny."

I thought of the ridiculousness of the situation, and yeah, he wasn't wrong. "Okay. It's kind of funny."

He wiggled his eyebrows. "I wouldn't have missed it for the world. I'm glad I came in early for the first time...ever."

"So, I've been reduced to your entertainment."

"And great entertainment it is." His voice was smooth and dark, his green eyes glittering.

"Down, boy. It's just pajamas, un-brushed teeth, and messy hair. Next time, I'll summon you when you're half naked and see how much you like it."

Silence.

I held up a hand. "Forget I said that."

Drake threw his head back and laughed. "If you say so."

I shook my head. "What do you need, almighty summoning First?"

He slid a folder across the desk. "I have some time-sensitive information for you."

I flipped through the folder. "For the record, I was going to swing by today." The papers were the complete Enforcer's report on the dragons that kidnapped us and several other incident reports involving dragons. "How did you get this? Has Mat seen this?"

"I have my ways. And yes, Bastien gave the Regent all this information and more. After your...revelation about how little Mathias tells you, I decided you should see our reports." He picked up my earrings and examined them.

I read through the reports. There was an incident where a dragon kidnapped a shifter kid from his backyard. I bet the parents were devastated. Another incident involved a house being burned down with a local ogre merchant inside. Overall, there were twelve reported incidents. "What do you and Bastien think is going on? Is it even possible to mind control that many dragons?"

Drake raised an eyebrow. "It's a difficult task, but possible, I suppose. My aunt may be able to reach them and bring them back, but Bastien's efforts have been futile."

"When is the queen expected back? We could use her help."

"I do not know. Bastien says she is visiting her horde, and while some dragons stay for months or even years, my aunt's true horde has always been her family."

"You don't believe Bastien."

He set my earrings down and swiveled toward the window. "Bastien is too angry to look at this objectively, so I have stepped in. And I do not trust anything without proof. It is a product of my age and certain...betrayals."

Drake said that my mother forced him to sleep to eliminate people who were more powerful than her. I wondered if that was one of those betrayals, but I didn't want to pry. A thought struck me that had nothing to do with the current situation. "What's the true story behind your family being in this realm?" I blurted it out before my brain engaged.

His lips twitched. "I told you that I was ostracized by the other Firsts?"

"Yeah. Sort of."

His eyes became distant. "My aunt did not like that I was chosen to come here, so she gathered volunteers and followed, crashing the portal as they came through. The other Firsts were livid. I was an outcast for a couple of hundred years. When they realized humans would not magically evolve, and the Firsts were never going home, they began including me more on your grandmother's insistence. Even then, they didn't include me in their scheme to create supernaturals. I was not allowed to create a magical race because they considered the dragons mine. Ensuring the safety of my dragon family was my sole reason for agreeing, but I never found my place among them, either. I'm a different species than my family, and many don't believe I'm one of them. Like the Firsts, they became bitter after a while and blamed me for being stuck here. I've always appreciated my aunt's insistence that I belonged, even though I didn't."

"But you said you're not a dragon."

"I am, and I'm not. I was the third egg to hatch in the third clutch. Born to a queen of a dragon territory. I would have been a wyvern dragon, like Bastien if I had been female. Boys hatched from the third egg in a third clutch are rare. Powerful males are even rarer. I hatched as a multidrake-landarnarian."

My eyebrows drew together. "A what? How is that possible?"

He shrugged. "Different realm, different magical rules. I am a multidrakelandarnarian. It means I am bigger, have more magic than normal dragons, and have three forms, including one of a Drake dragon. Where I come from, we are prized but not eligible to rule, even though we inherit what you call ruling magic. My mother rejected me because she wanted her heir to be anything but...me. My aunt, her twin, and ruler of a different dragon territory, stepped in and raised me. She did not like that my mother chose me to come here and refused to send me alone. She gathered volunteers and brought a couple hundred dragons here. They have thrived by keeping a low profile and respecting the throne of Ahl."

"Until now," I mumbled. I stood and paced. "What are the chances the person behind this knows all of that? Do you think it's a dragon trying to take control of your aunt?"

"No. The magic doesn't feel like dragon magic."

It didn't, but I did recognize the magic coming from the devices. I just couldn't place it. "Do you have one of those devices I can examine?"

He shook his head. "No. The Enforcers took them. They have approximately five in their possession."

I'd have to hit up Emine or call Colonel Ballard. I shook my head, realizing it wasn't my case. Quin probably already knew about all of this. "Why are you making an extra effort to ensure I know this?"

He handed me the earrings. "As I said, I do not trust easily. I don't trust the Regent to act on this information. He has proven less responsive than I hoped."

There was a story there, but I let it go. "And you have no reason to trust me, yet here we are."

He threw his head back and laughed. "Touche. You are a true gift."

I realized I liked watching him laugh. I doubted he did it often. There were some things that needed clarification. "I might be a spoiled, naïve princess, but even I'm not stupid enough to believe that you are that impressed with me. So can we cut the crap?"

He laughed again. "Since you won't believe me, we can say that I am grateful for you and feel I owe you a debt for waking me."

I knew the ruling magic did some weird stuff the day he woke, but I wasn't convinced I was responsible for waking him. "Yeah, not buying that either, but I'll let it go for now if you tell me why you locked me out of my own wards."

His eyebrows drew together. "I did no such thing."

"I healed a few hefty bruises from collisions that say otherwise. I can't get into my house or the castle. Your magic is the only new magic in the wards."

"I...did not mean for that to happen. I'll fix it immediately." He stood. "I'll get you some sweats and see you home."

I poured myself another cup of coffee and waited for Drake to return. I didn't have to wait for long. He came through the back door and handed me a pair of sweatpants, a hoodie, socks, and shoes. I handed his jacket back and dressed. I didn't bother wondering why they fit so well. "Never summon me again. The ruling magic is unpredictable and sometimes has a mind of its own. It doesn't like it when I'm in a subordinate position. It might kill you or your people without me being able to rein it in."

He sniffed his jacket, then slipped it on. "Noted."

I put on my earrings and reached for my phone, which somehow came through the summons with me. "I need to text Tracy so she can let me in the wards when I flash home."

"No. This is my fault, and I will not leave you unprotected and locked out of your wards. I'll let my aunt's assistant know I'm leaving and give you a ride home."

I raised an eyebrow. "The same assistant that used your magic to summon me?"

"The very same. I will also clarify that using the summoning room is forbidden and lock it down so no one else can use it."

The ruling magic pulsed as we left the office and headed toward the elevators, and I wrapped it tighter around me. "I don't like the idea of being suffocated in your talons again."

"You can ride on my back."

"I thought dragons didn't give rides to non-dragons who aren't their mates."

His eyes dilated so fast I would have missed it if I hadn't looked directly at them. "As I explained, I am not a dragon."

"Right," I muttered, wrapping the vibrating ruling magic tighter before it lashed out at him.

A strong wind blew when we reached the top of the building, and I threw my hood on. Drake shifted immediately and lowered his massive body to the roof. He was a beautiful creature. His scales were huge, about the size of dinner plates. They were midnight black at the base, lightening into a vibrant emerald green. He had razor-sharp spikes along his spine and a crown of shorter spikes around his head. Like his scales, the spikes started out black at the base and faded to emerald green at the tips. His wings looked leather, but I realized they were covered with tiny scales. They glittered like crushed emeralds in the sunlight.

Drake turned his massive head and snorted, causing a long plume of smoke to exit his nose and drift into the sky. Taking a ride from him wasn't a good idea. I understood how that would be perceived in the dragon culture. I knew I should have flashed home. But I didn't want to offend him since he'd given me information no one else would and provided my much-needed glamour. I also wanted to know the feeling of riding on the back of such a beautiful beast without being in a cage. I stepped back, saw the optimal place on his back to sit, flashed to it, and wrapped my arms and legs around one of his enormous spikes. The ruling magic, which had been hard to contain the entire way up to the roof, reached out, wrapped around the spike and Drake's belly, and squeezed.

Another thick line of smoke streamed out of his nostrils, caught the wind, and blew back at me. I went into a coughing fit while trying to untangle the ruling magic from Drake. He extended his enormous green and black scaled head and let out another puff of smoke as the cloud around me blew away. "Sorry!" I yelled as I untangled the magic from his belly. It wouldn't budge from the spike.

That was unpleasant. Drake's voice echoed in my head.

"Right. I forgot you can talk to me." I glanced at the ruling magic, noticing a thin line stretching from the coils around the spike to his head. In the past, the ruling magic wouldn't let any mind magic into my head and often reacted violently. This time, it gave Drake a squeeze and established its own connection.

It seems so. Hold on. Drake launched us into the air so fast my stomach flipped.

I relaxed and unwrapped my legs from the spike. We flew high, but not as high as the dragons that kidnapped me. Drake picked up speed, causing my hood to blow off. I giggled as my hair streamed behind me. Excitement surged as I realized what a unique and new experience riding a dragon was. The ruling magic responded to my delight by releasing Drake and dancing happily around us. I swiped my teary eyes with my sleeve and reeled it in as Drake descended toward a park just outside my neighborhood. I flashed to the ground, and he shifted to his human form, still wearing his expensive business suit. He threw cloaking magic around both of us as we headed toward the back alley that ran behind our house. "If you can shift with your clothes, why did you shift naked the day we met?"

"It takes energy I didn't have that day." His neat appearance was far from the disheveled man who had climbed out of the ground not long before. He buttoned his jacket as we turned the corner and headed deeper into the neighborhood. "Why are you looking at me like that, Jenella?"

"It's Jen. And I was just thinking how much different you look than you did when we first met."

"You don't like it." It wasn't a question.

I shook my head. "It doesn't matter what I think. It must be hard for someone your age to constantly change to keep up with the times, especially being disconnected for so long."

He shrugged. "I've never had a problem with keeping up. I understand that a well-groomed appearance is more accepted but not required in modern times, so I went with that. What, exactly, is your opinion on the matter?"

"I have a team of griffins who dress and style me, so I'm not qualified to offer an opinion."

When we entered Tracy's camouflage spell, he released his cloaking magic. As soon as Drake touched our wards, Tracy ran out of the house, a spell in one hand, a gun in the other. I waved at her, and she stopped in her tracks. "Oh my fates, Jen! What are you doing out there with the First?"

Drake took my hand. "I need a sample of your magic."

I pushed a tiny bit of my inherent magic toward him and turned back to Tracy. "Apparently, he thinks the summoning chamber is a weapon to be used against anyone who ignores him, even the chamber's owner."

Tracy's mouth dropped open. "Oh, he. Did. Not."

Drake's shoulders shook as he motioned for me to go through the wards. "I didn't realize that charging the magic reserves allowed anyone to use the chamber. My aunt's assistant summoned Jenella from her bed."

I stepped through the wards. "Yeah, it's a good thing I don't sleep naked."

Tracy planted her hands on her hips. "I don't know what game you're playing, First, but it needs to stop. I mean, first, you mess with the wards, and then you pull this stunt. You are not only disrespecting and devaluing Jen, but you're putting my job on the line. I won't mention how it pisses off the Regent when people disregard her safety. And if you think pissing off Prince Mathias gets violent, I will tell you it is mild compared to what I will do to you when I lose my temper."

I opened my mouth to say something but thought better of it. I'd already caused Tracy so much trouble, I was amazed she still hung around. Drake didn't have that problem, waving a dismissive hand. "I meant no disrespect with the wards. I was trying to get Jenella's attention and didn't realize my magic would keep her out of them. It was not my idea to use the summoning room, and I assure you neither will happen again, Lady Tracinia."

I face-palmed. "Drake, *please* call her Tracy and me Jen when we're glamoured. Also, you might want to lose the formal speech patterns if you don't want to show your age." I strode toward the house to get some breakfast.

I watched them exchange a few more words before Drake shifted and flew off. Tracy stomped through the back door just as I pushed the button for some fresh fruit on our new magichef. "I'm sorry."

Tracy handed me my fruit and ordered a cup of coffee. "It's okay. I doubt that man would let anything happen to you, but both stunts were extremely disrespectful. I mean, he treated you like you work for him."

It wasn't something I'd thought about, but she was right. The way he treated me wasn't the way an incoming queen should be treated. "You're right. Though, to be fair, I thought that he treated me like any other detective."

"Yeah, well, you're not any other detective, and he knows it."

Chapter 17

I FELT QUIN CROSS the wards and heard Tracy race down the stairs to meet him. I got my answer as to if Quin could cross the wards without permission. Padding down the stairs, I stopped short when I saw them. Tracy stood on one side of the kitchen island, and Quin sat on the other, his hand around a drink. They laughed carelessly. I'd never seen Quin so much as smile, let alone laugh. It was...weird.

I tiptoed past Quin and sat on his other side, trying not to disturb their conversation. He instantly sobered and turned to me. "The PISD Director ordered a meeting with us this morning. Do you know anything about this?"

My eyebrows drew together. "I have no idea. What do you think it's about?"

"You, obviously. Until you came along, I never spoke so much as a word to him or the dragons. But lucky me, I get to interact with both in a day."

"I think you mean to say you got a lucrative case working for a powerful coalition leader because you're my mentor."

"No, I mean to say that because I'm your mentor, I am forced to do the bidding of supernaturals best avoided."

I shrugged. "I'll work the case if it's that much of a violation of your delicate sensibilities."

Tracy snorted. "You two are hilarious." She pointed at Quin. "You would have gotten that case even if you didn't choose to mentor Jen." She pointed at me. "And you are not experienced enough to work the dragon case." When neither of us reacted, she waved a hand. "You should get to your meeting."

"You're not coming?" I asked.

She shook her head. "Nope. Quin is on guard duty today. I'm going to work on making potions to restock my store."

"Your store is very successful. Why the heck are you guarding me again?"

"Because you needed someone you could get along with and couldn't scare away. And I needed someone to shield me from the witches. Besides, Quin insisted I take it and would have a fit if I quit."

I glanced at Quin, who stared at his drink. "So, to retaliate, you recommended him as my mentor."

She didn't answer, and my stomach sank at the realization that I was just a pawn in some friendly competition between two people I had come to like and respect. I'd had a lot of guards over the years, and I didn't like any of them other than Bastien. Sort of. I appreciated that he didn't put up with my crap. Tracy was different. I genuinely liked her. I never tried to push her buttons. The realization that she thought being my guard was a punishment stung. "I see."

Tracy realized what she had said. "No, that's not--"

I stood and headed to the door. "Let's get to our meeting, Quin. The faster we get there, the less time you're forced to spend with me. Have a great day off."

I headed to the neighborhood flashing circle, trying to talk myself out of the hurt. Being in my position, I was bound to meet many people who saw me as a forced obligation. I only took a few steps before Quin caught up. "You misunderstood that explanation."

I swallowed back tears and squared my shoulders. "No, I didn't. I got it loud and clear."

Quin scoffed. "I did not take you on as an apprentice out of obligation."

"Didn't say you did."

"Oh, yes. Let's pretend body language is not a thing."

"Sarcasm is your love language, huh?" I didn't care why he took me on as an apprentice. He wasn't much of a mentor thus far, and it didn't change what I just learned. I changed the subject. "What do you suppose the director wants?"

Quin didn't reply until we reached the flashing circle. "I do not know. I will meet you at the doors of the PISD."

The PISD was buzzing with activity, and, true to his word, Quin leaned against the wall next to the door, arms folded and sunglasses covering his eyes. His creepy vampire magic oozed about, causing people to veer away from him. He dropped his arms. "I don't know what the director wants, but I know he never meets with new detectives. Let me do the talking unless he asks you a direct question, and do not lose control of that stifling magic of yours."

I rolled my eyes. "Do you think Travis did or said something to cause this meeting?"

"I am not the foremost expert on what the deputy director does and does not do. He would make a much better director than the current one." I raised an eyebrow, and he continued. "It has been my experience that people who are only concerned about their social standing will go out of their way to excel in their careers. Travis fits that profile. The current director does not."

He had a point. "Okay, I'll let you do the talking. The quicker we get this done, the better."

A sour-faced mage with organization magic greeted us and ushered us into the director's office. The director sat at his desk, wearing a charcoal suit and a smug smile. "Consort Tarquin, Detective Hendrix. Thank you for coming. Please have a seat."

I got a weird feeling from him. I shook it off and kept my face as neutral as I sat. Quin paced around the room, his creepy vampire vibe ramping up to the point where my arms broke out in goosebumps. "You may call me Detective Tarquin."

The Director's chest puffed out. "Surely you don't expect me to break coalition protocol by disregarding your official title. No, I will refer to you as I always have."

Quin touched a chimera figurine on the shelf beside the director's desk. "I have had many titles over the years, as you well know, director. None of them were Shirley."

I couldn't help it. I laughed. "That's not how the joke goes."

He waved a hand. "I didn't understand most of the jokes in that movie. But we are not here to discuss old human movies or titles. What do you want, Director?"

The director looked from me to Quin, rubbing his chin. "There are several reasons I requested to meet. I wanted to see how you are doing under the consort's mentorship."

A frown formed on my face at the lie. I'd never been able to sense lies, but now they were glaring, thanks to my fresh dose of ruling magic. Not only did I dislike the slimy vibe the chimera gave off, but also the lies. I had to be careful how I answered his question because he could smell a lie, too. "As you can see, I'm fine."

He inclined his head. "And what do you think of your mentor?"

"He's both unique and well qualified to mentor me." I was proud of that dodge.

Quin lowered himself into the chair next to me. The Director leaned forward, lacing his hands on his desk. "May I be direct?"

"Please."

His smile didn't reach his mean eyes. "Consort Tarquin has never shown interest in our mentoring program nor cared about the progress of other detectives. He's been quick and efficient in solving cases, taking on only difficult ones. I'm trying to determine his interest in a low-level mage of Ahl."

"Oh yes, because my motivations and decision-making process are now your business." Quin's voice dripped with his usual sarcasm.

The Director was undeterred. "The fact that you took an interest in a weak mage means one of two things. Either you are preying on her or know something about her that the rest of us don't. So, which is it, Detective Hendrix?"

I smirked. "As Detective Tarquin said, it's not your business as long as I have an active mentor and stay out of trouble. Rule 14-563-B of the detective regulations, in case you were wondering."

He straightened the sleeve of his jacket. "No need to get defensive. I am only looking out for your welfare. An ancient and powerful vampire and a weak mage do not make a good mentor match. The crown insists on the PISD operating at the optimum level of integrity. All you need to do is admit he is an unfit mentor, and I will remove him. I will mentor you myself so that you receive the best possible training."

I didn't know whether to laugh at him, schooling me on what the crown wanted, or shudder at the thought of him mentoring me. "Detective Tarquin began this mentorship by handing me my first case. He has made himself available for questions and responded to all my calls and texts. In addition, he drops in regularly to check on my progress. He has not pried into my personal life, nor has he displayed any predatory behavior toward me. So, you can take your offer——" Quin grabbed my hand so hard I thought he might break it. The ruling magic stirred, so I reeled it in. "Nothing is wrong with our mentor-apprentice relationship. You have no grounds to break it up without our consent. I'll request approval from the Regent if you want. We wouldn't want the crown to frown on the PISD."

The Director's face turned red. "I will be your mentor!"

Quin stood and dragged me with him. "She said no, and I will report this inappropriate conversation to the Regent and request formal approval today. If you continue to harass Detective Hendrix, we will find out which one of us is the bigger predator."

Neither of us said a word until we were out of the building. As we headed back toward the main square, I couldn't stand it. "What do you suppose that was about?"

To my surprise, he answered. "I'm not sure. His intentions are not pure. Several low-level supernaturals have disappeared lately, so it's best to avoid anyone who makes you uncomfortable, which he clearly does."

I stopped in my tracks and held up a finger while working out a revelation. "He has an odd vibe." I looked directly into Quin's eyes––or his sunglasses. "Several low-level supernaturals are missing? And you think they're after me because they think I'm weak? That means the Director is involved."

Quin's eyebrows rose. "I cannot tell if you are stating the obvious on purpose or you think you just had a revelation."

"Whatever. I'll steer clear of him. I'm going to visit my client. You can go do...whatever it is you do. I don't need a babysitter." I made a mental note to ask Mat about missing paranormals.

Quin disappeared without a word, and I turned and stalked down the street toward Thaddeus's deli.

The deli was about a block from Dragon Headquarters, on the edge of the ogre district. It had a cheerful sign and a bright and clean appearance, with yellow chairs and white tables. The smell of pickles washed over me when I stepped inside. Thaddeus stood behind the counter. A big smile lit up his face when he saw me. "Jen! Find me money yet?"

I couldn't help but like the guy. "Hello, Thaddeus. Not yet, but I have some good leads. I have a question for you and would like some lunch."

"I know just the sandwich for you. What can I help with?"

I pulled a copy of the symbol out of my bag. "Do you recognize this? Also, do you have any connection to the dragons? Business interests or anything?"

"No. No business interests other than feeding some of them," he said absently as he examined the symbol. "This is the symbol of an old rebellion. Where did ye get it."

"From your bank statements. Any idea what it means?"

He set a plate with a wonderful-smelling sandwich on the counter. "I can't help with that, but the palace library probably has some information."

Lunch was delicious, and I decided to frequent the place and recommend it to people. I headed home and grabbed my laptop from the office. Just as I was about to shut the door to my room, Tracy stopped me. "Jen, I'm sorry for what I said this morning. I didn't mean for it to come out that way."

I put my laptop on the bed. "You did me a favor, so don't worry about it."

"A favor?"

"I made the mistake of forgetting that I'm your job, not your friend. That's on me because I know better. I've never had a guard I liked or spent so much time with and forgot myself for a minute. I realize now that I don't know much about you, and that's also on me. I apologize."

Tracy frowned. "Wait. You're apologizing to me? That's...no." She barged into my room and plopped onto the bed. "Look, Jen. I've been attacked by witches incessantly as part of an ongoing family drama. When I took this job, it was because I liked you, and because Bastien thought it would stop the attacks. I wanted to save myself, you know?"

"Sure."

"As you saw, it was so bad that couldn't go anywhere. I called Quin, told him the situation, and said you offered me the job. I mean, Mat didn't think I could guard you when I contacted him. Quin, who I knew from being a detective, talked him into it because he thought you and I could protect each other. I didn't see how a spoiled rotten princess could help me. I heard...rumors that you were difficult to guard, and you are." She shook her head and picked at the blanket on my bed. "Drake's glamour hides me well enough that I don't have to worry about the witches, so I could work out a deal with him to alter it and move without being attacked without being your guard. But I'm still here guarding you. I genuinely like you, Jen. I always have. Getting to know you better isn't something I regret."

I noticed she didn't say she didn't regret taking the job. When she staggered into Bastien's office, I couldn't resist the urge to take her in because I felt bad for her. I was so desperate to connect with someone outside my small family that I'd become pathetic. Tracy wasn't responsible for my unbalance nor for providing me friendship. I needed to work on that. "Okay, so that comment meant what?"

Tracy rubbed her chin. "I told Quin you needed a mentor and that he needed to step up because he was the only one at the PISD who knew your real identity. He owed me. I mean, any other mentor would have a fit with the messes you've gotten into." Her face transformed into a sparkling smile.

A ragged laugh escaped me. "I admit, there have been a few incidents. How long have you had your own business?" I was an expert at subject change. Everything she just told me confirmed what I'd originally thought. I decided to let it go.

"I've had my business forever. My dad helped me start it as a teenager, so I would always have an income stream. He's an alchemist, but my magic is different because of my mom, so he knew I'd do well. I became a detective to get me out of the lab. It only took a couple of years before the witches started attacking me, and I couldn't take any cases. Oh, speaking of which, what did the director want with you?"

"The director is a piece of work. He wanted me to denounce Quin as my mentor. Said he would personally mentor me." I shuddered.

"No way! What did you say? I mean, did he say he'd revoke your license?"

"He doesn't have a legal standing to do anything without Mat's approval--which I pointed out. I also made it clear that Quin meets all obligations as a mentor, so there are no grounds. The guy gives me the creeps."

Tracy stood and started pacing. "So, what do you suppose that's about? I mean, why would the director be interested in you?"

I plugged in my laptop. "No idea. Quin said something about low-level supernaturals going missing. He said I should avoid paranormals who made me uncomfortable."

Tracy stopped pacing. "I guess we take that advice. So, what's the plan for tomorrow?"

"Mat and Emine are leaving tomorrow for Mahri, and I need to see them off and stick around the palace until we leave the next day." My stomach soured at the thought of going to Mahri. "You can take tomorrow off since I'll stay in the bubble."

"Nice. I think I'll swing by the dragon headquarters and harass Bastien. He's a little jealous that you and I get along so well and he's hiding something. I want to figure out what it is."

"Drake filled me in on some of it. There have been several dragon incidents, and they don't know why. Bastien is kind of an ass, but he means well. He trusts you, so you might be able to get more information than I can."

Tracy waved a dismissive hand and left my room. I wondered what that was about, but didn't want to pry. I got to work researching that symbol.

Chapter 18

I SAID FAREWELL TO Mat, Emine, Helen, and George and then reviewed the transportation and lodging plan with Verity. I'd be taking our private transport and have several supernatural leaders traveling with me, some of whom were staying the night in the guest wing of the castle in Mahri. The next day, I would have to greet them as they boarded the transport, which was something I was dreading. Tracy was gone most of the day but checked in on me when she returned. She hadn't made any progress with Bastien but said it was fun trying.

I didn't sleep well that night, plagued with the usual nightmares and nerves. The morning was even more fun when I fluctuated between panic attacks and puking. I sat on my bathroom floor, head in my hands. I knew I needed to shower, but couldn't drag myself there. Becoming queen and returning to Castle Mahri were both things I wanted to avoid. I wished I was one of those people who could funnel their trauma and fuel themselves with it. Unfortunately, I wasn't. I functioned every day despite my childhood trauma.

I fantasized about running away, maybe living in the human world like Verity, but dismissed it. I didn't know the first thing about caring for myself with magical aids, let alone without them. Besides, I knew very little about the human world. No, I was stuck. The only thing I could do was enjoy my short period of freedom and keep pretending. And wasn't that a depressing thought?

My stomach heaved again, and I crawled back over to the toilet. That's where Tracy found me. "Oh, my fates, Jen! What happened?"

I shook my head once before dry heaving and melted back to the floor. "I may have some unresolved issues from my time living in Mahri."

"Issues?" she screeched.

I didn't have the energy to look at her. "It wasn't a good time."

Tracy kneeled beside me. "Do you want to talk about it? I mean, when my grandmother killed my mom, I felt better after talking about it with my dad."

I cracked an eye open. "Your grandmother killed her own daughter?"

Tracy grabbed a washcloth and wet it. "Yeah. She tried to kill us both by setting up a car accident. I got injured and lived, but my poor mom." She swiped a tear from her eye. 'My mom was the light, ya know. When she walked into a room, she lit it up. She had a wicked sense of humor and was my everything. I was nine and didn't understand what was going on, not really. Anyway, my dad took me away and kept me safe. Like Mat, he did his best to raise a heartbroken child while his own heart was broken. We talked about it a lot, even though it must have devastated him. He was my rock. I owe him everything."

I sat up. "You and I are strangely similar."

Tracy handed me the washcloth. "Not even close. Now spill."

I wiped my face. "You already know I had another brother. Mat is the oldest, then Jaques, then me. Jaques was...cruel, to put it mildly. The last words he said to me were and I quote, 'You're a nobody! A nothing! Do you think they love you? Do you think anyone can? You're wrong. Nobody could love an ugly little cockroach like you.' I was six years old, and he had just beat the hell out of me and thrown me in a cage in the dungeon."

Tracy winced.

"That wasn't the first time or even the worst." My stomach roiled, and I swallowed a few times. "From the time I was around three and developed healing magic, he'd break my bones and beat me up every chance he got." Mat said that Jaques had built a rebellion and had a bunch of followers. That he was trying to break me. That he was power hungry and wanted a puppet on the throne so he could rule. According to Mat, Jaques planned to kill my parents and appoint himself as my guardian and regent so he could rule. I found that ironic, considering how Mat controlled my life. Although, he did it with love instead of using Jaques's methods. "When I think of Mahri, that's what I think about, and I can't *stop* thinking about it. Why in the hell did my parents leave him in charge of me? They had to know. I think I told them about it. For a long time, I thought my memory of telling them was my mind playing tricks on me. I'm not sure anymore after what Drake told me about my mother."

Tracy rubbed her eyes. "That's...I'm sorry you had to go through that."

I didn't want her pity. "Mat killed him. But not before Jaques killed my parents." I pointed at her. "Don't you dare tell anyone that because the official story is that there was a rebellion, and the three of them sacrificed themselves while Mat escaped with me." At her nod of agreement, I continued. "I didn't really know Mat before that because he was never around. But I remember the concern and guilt on his face as he gently removed me from that cage. Just like I remember the rage on it while he fought and slaughtered Jaques's minions and somehow got us out of that nasty place. So, yeah. Going to Mahri brings back some memories."

She put her hand over mine. "Mat loves you, Jen. And you are a strong, grown-ass woman who can fight her way out of anything. And if anyone even sneezes your way, we'll combine our magic and burn the world to the ground."

Tears streamed down my face. "I don't deserve you."

"I know. Now, put on your big girl panties, and let's storm that castle. And for fate's sake, take a shower."

As I got ready, I kept telling myself I was a strong, grown-ass woman. Going back to Mahri still made me feel like a helpless kid again, but Tracy was right that I wasn't little and helpless anymore. It helped to put it into perspective. I didn't dare eat anything, though.

The transport station in Allure was cavernous and crowded with shiny white tile floors and high ceilings. Outside, dozens of small flying transports were lined up, picking up supernaturals from the flashing circle and the bicycle parking. Others soared overhead, depositing people at their desired craft. There were hundreds of flying creatures under them in a designated flying zone. Blurry vampire forms moved through the crowd so fast they were hard to see, while mages lined up near smaller flashing circles to get to their transports. I watched a phoenix shedding a trail of sparks across the ceiling before landing, transforming to human form, and taking a complimentary robe from an attendant. With my head high, I marched into the private transport area. Travis walked to my left, Tracy, Verity, Titus, and three griffins behind me. A host of castle guards fanned out around us.

"Holy hell. How long is this walk?" Verity said a couple of minutes into the journey.

I glanced back and saw that her face was focused on the flying paranormals, her eyes wide.

Tracy chuckled. "Humans don't walk as much as us. This is actually a short walk. I mean, some packs shift and use their animal forms to go clear across the pocket sometimes. We're lucky Jen can flash groups."

"You shouldn't let the help call you by your first name or talk to you like that," Travis scoffed.

I ignored him. "Are you okay, Verity? If you need a break, let me know."

"Just a little sweaty. I'm sure it'll be fine."

"I'll carry her if she gets too huffy," Titus said.

The sound of a slap and a, "You will not! Sheesh."

A laugh burst out of me. "Thank you, Verity. I needed that."

"It's what I'm here for. Oh, by the way, the Dragon Queen is not coming. She sent Bastien instead."

It was customary for the hosting dignitary to greet the visiting dignitaries at the door when traveling together, so I positioned myself outside the transport. Half the castle guard went in, and the other half made a semi-circle around me. Travis stood to my left, signaling he was an honored guest. I suggested he go in and find his seat, but he ignored me. Tracy and Gilbert, a manticore and the head of the castle guard, stood behind us while Verity went to the entrance with a tablet to check off guests as they arrived. Titus stayed with her.

I was glad that I was no longer sick to my stomach. I bumped my power out a little because power was the only thing most of these leaders respected. Movement at the door caught my eye, and Travis straightened next to me. "Don't ruin this for me," he said under his breath.

I snorted, then tried to smile professionally as the first guests appeared. Relief flooded me to see Gabriel and Linda, the shifter king and queen, and Travis's parents. Spending a lot of time with them as a kid, I learned some valuable lessons. Lessons like fights and political maneuvering were required to secure your place in a pack. The most confident usually wins, and my favorite lesson—how to handle bullies. I also learned to never show fear. Shifters could smell fear and considered anyone afraid of them prey. The downside was that spending so much time with them, the griffins, and Mat, I became too desensitized to fear people I should be afraid of, like the vampire queen who came through the door next.

Linda kissed Travis on the cheek while Gabriel's eyes swept over him. He nodded in approval before bowing to me. "Your Grace. Thank you for having us."

My smile became genuine. "Thanks for coming, Alphas. How have you been?"

Linda offered me a warm smile. "Very well, thank you. We're thrilled to watch you grow into your potential."

"Thank you."

I settled into a rhythm of greeting people and felt much better. When the president of witches approached, I nodded. "Madam President. Thank you for coming."

She eyed Travis before stopping before me. "Hello, Your Grace. I hope you don't mind if we take over your transport." She motioned to the group of ten witches behind her. Witches often traveled in covens, so I wouldn't have said anything if she hadn't pointed it out. The fact that she pointed it out made me suspicious. Gilbert, as head of the guards, must have agreed, because he made a hand signal to the castle guard. Three guards, a mental mage, an invisibility mage, and a rattlesnake shifter slipped through the transport door.

I kept my face neutral and waved a hand dismissively. "It's no problem. I understand how ineffective most witches are without a coven."

Her face flushed with anger, and she leaned forward. "You lack sound judgment and do not have much power. You cannot fault me for protecting my own against such inadequacies."

The ruling magic unraveled before I could stop it. Wind swirled around me, and hair came loose from the clip, holding it back. My body glowed gold. I heard Tracy gasp as all the witches in the room slammed against the walls except for the president, who was forced to her knees. My stomach tickled as it started siphoning her magic. I clutched my chest. "No. No. No." I urged the magic to give it back. The last thing the coalition needed was a bunch of leaderless witches.

All but about ten percent of her power flowed back into her. I could tell by her widening eyes when she realized I could take all her magic away, and she couldn't stop me. I concentrated hard, trying to get ahold of the ruling magic. The wind dissipated, and the glow dimmed.

It released the witches, and I craned my neck to see if Tracy was okay. She still stood behind me and gave me a slight nod. I returned my attention back to the still-kneeling president of covens. "I don't know what made you think me weak or that it was acceptable to come to my event and insult my judgment. You have two choices. Either apologize and act civilly or leave." I allowed her to rise. Her face flushed with anger, so I leaned forward and stared into her eyes. "I assure you that if you try anything like that again, the outcome will not be as favorable."

To my surprise, she stormed out, leaving the coven members. I turned to the vice president and raised an eyebrow. His brown eyes glanced at Tracy, and he waved a hand. All but three witches followed the president. "Thank you for having us, Your Grace. I will ensure the witch contingent practices courtesies."

"Well, wasn't that exciting," Verity said as she watched them enter the transport.

I turned to check on my people and the other leaders. The only leaders in the room were two wide-eyed swamp elves, a scowling Bastien, and a smiling Drake.

Travis straightened his jacket. "You could have left me out of that, Jen. It's ridiculous that you treat me poorly after all these years of friendship."

I pointed to the transport. "Go join your parents, Travis."

"Psh. You're clearly angry at the witch and taking it out on me. Really, Jen, you need to learn not to project your dismay onto others."

I waved a still-glowing hand, and the castle guard whisked him through the transport door. I turned to the Elves. "My apologies, Your Majesties." When Bastien stepped up, I frowned. "Where is your queen, Bastien?"

His jaw clenched. "It's not the time nor the place." When I didn't respond, he added, "Later."

I kept eye contact briefly before nodding and motioning him to the transport. A still-smiling Drake winked at me before following.

The rest of the greetings went fast because of my poor attitude and their fear of what I would do if they stepped out of line. Proving just how fast rumors traveled throughout the coalition. When the last guest was aboard and the guards dispersed, I turned and pulled Titus aside. "Keep an eye out for retaliation from the witches and make sure Mat knows what happened here. Stick close to Verity. It's been my experience that she's unpredictable when riled and could accidentally hurt someone. I want Bastien and Drake to sit with me and Tracy."

I stood on the beach and stared at the palace where I was born. The sea breeze and the smell of the salty air swirled around me. I brushed my hair back with a trembling hand and swallowed emotions I didn't want to recognize. The leaders staying at Castle Mahri streamed past me to the door. I couldn't make myself step onto the property because it felt like I'd be swept back to my childhood if I did. Bile rose, and I swallowed.

"Are you just going to stand there?" Travis reached for my elbow.

I jerked my arm away. "No. I was just waiting for you to catch up," I lied, wondering if I could use my magic to blast this house to bits without hurting anyone inside.

Travis ignored my lie and took off his sunglasses to admire the house. "So this is it, huh? Impressive."

I had to admit, it was impressive. The gray stone castle rose to the sky, gleaming in the sunlight. Several turrets rose above the structure, making it appear grand. A purple flag with our family crest adorned the tops of each one, waving in the wind. A double door of thick, dark wood sat in the middle of the primary structure at the top of wide sweeping steps. "Come on. Let's get this done." I squared my shoulders and took that first step down the pristine stone walkway, forcing myself forward with each step. I managed to will myself up the wide staircase leading to the door and tried to keep my stomach from revolting.

As we approached the top of the steps, an older, distinguished-looking man stepped out. "Hello, Your Grace. Welcome to your home in Mahri."

"George!" I ran the rest of the way up the steps and hugged him tight. "How was your trip?"

George returned my hug and stepped back. "Hello, Jenella. It was fine, and yours?"

I stepped into the ornate foyer and took a deep breath, ignoring the quivering in my stomach. "The start was eventful," I said cryptically as I watched people bustle around, no one paying attention to me, just like I liked it.

I turned to see if my entourage was still behind me. They were all accounted for, except for Travis, who stood outside, George blocking his way. I put my hand on George's arm. "George, you remember my friend Travis."

George stepped out of the way. "Oh, I remember him. I wanted to ensure Master Travis remembered me."

Travis visually shivered, and I bit back a smile. "Okay. Sure."

"Is that Jenella I hear?" Helen bustled into the foyer and swept me up in a hug. She wore a black pantsuit and had her silver hair in a loose bun that couldn't have looked more grandmotherly. I always thought she wore it that way to give her victims a false sense of security.

"Good to see you, Helen." I straightened my jacket. "This place is different than I remember."

"Oh, yes. Mathias has changed things to make you feel more at home. I'll show you your new room." She glared at Travis. "And will your friend stay in the family quarters?"

My eyes bounced back and forth between them before shrugging. "The guest wing will be fine. Tracy can stay near me like always."

"Hmmm. George will get him settled." Helen headed toward the stairs. "Well, come on then."

As we followed, I tried to find a sense of familiarity. The chandelier in the center of the foyer was still the same. There were still two sweeping staircases, but the wall colors were different. Once covered in solid white, they were covered in fancy wallpaper and muted colors. The beautiful woodwork and exposed stone interlaced throughout was breathtaking, and the same antique furniture was peppered throughout the many rooms, although not in the same places. Some of the furniture was new. The cold, unwelcoming feeling I remembered was gone, replaced with a sense of warmth and welcome.

The hallway leading to the family suites was smaller than I remembered. Other than a new rug running down the center, it hadn't changed much with its rich wood paneling and antique sconces that threw off a soft yellow light. We passed my old bedroom, which was in the center of the hall, and continued to the last doors.

"Tracy, you will stay in the room on the right. Jenella, you'll stay in the one on the left." She handed us physical keys with a blue magic glow to them. "Verity and Titus are one floor down, and Mathias and Emine are all the way at the other end of the hall."

I thanked her and entered what used to be my mother's office. The cold, regal office was now a bright, airy bedroom decorated in light blue and cream. Like most of the furniture in the house, the sleigh bed was antique. Thick stone framed the old-fashioned windows. They still let in a decent amount of light. I sighed in relief at how different it felt from the bitter cold I remembered. Helen put my bags down, hugged me, and rushed down the hall to attend to our guests.

Tracy stood at the door, her eyes sweeping around the room. "You got this, Jen?"

"Yeah. I'm good. You don't need to stay. Thank you, though."

She gave me one last thoughtful look before closing the door with a soft click.

After I got my stuff settled, I decided to find Mat. I needed to tell him about the witch incident and pry information out of him about the dragon problem. I changed clothes and headed out to find him.

To this day, I'm unsure what came over me. I stopped outside my old room and noticed the door slightly ajar. I don't remember when my hand reached for the doorknob. My stomach flipped, and I shook as I cracked the door open. Every muscle in my body tightened at the sight. The room had been renovated like the rest of the castle, yet it somehow felt the same. A four-poster bed was on the left instead of a small antique bed. A new dresser, matching the bed, took the place of the small white one that used to hold a jewelry box and two dolls. The dresser was still positioned under the window. They replaced the flowered rug and curtains with brightly colored red and gold ones that complimented the new paint job.

I wrapped my arms around myself and stepped into the room, a wave of nausea rolling over me. On the right side of the room was a new wardrobe, and next to it, was a portrait of a little blonde girl about four years old. Her head down, long curly hair flying in the wind as she stood in a field and smiled joyously at the basket of flowers she was carrying. She looked happy. Like she didn't have a care in the world.

It was a painting of me. It was a lie. That scene never happened, and I certainly never smiled. The sick stomach was replaced with red-hot anger that radiated from my core. I clutched my fists so tight my fingernails cut into my palms. That girl knew more pain at four than any child should ever know. Portraying her as happy and carefree somehow insulted me. Red clouded my vision, and I yanked the picture off the wall and threw it across the room. It bounced off the door and landed on the floor without enough damage. I let out a frustrated shriek as I tuned my raw, inherent magic to a shredding spell and blasted it at the painting until it burst into pieces.

I stormed over to the dresser, ripped the drawers open, and threw them across the room. The mirror was next, followed by the wardrobe. I started flashing around the room, destroying everything in my path. Feathers from the pillows and mattress flew, and wood shavings coated the air. Still, it wasn't enough to satisfy my rage. All three magics unraveled with a *"boom"* that shook the room, but I didn't care as I tore apart the bed, only seeing the one I'd hidden under so many times.

The door burst open, and I found myself hugged from behind, arms pinned. "Jen! What the hell are you doing?"

My rage melted away at the sound of Mat's voice. "I...it wasn't her. It was a lie." I burst into tears and turned into him. "It wasn't her."

Mat held me for a long time, not saying anything. When I stepped back, the guilt and hurt on his face made my heart crack into pieces. "I'm sorry, Mat. I shouldn't have come in here."

"Ya think?" came from the corner where Emine brushed feathers off her chestnut brown hair. She usually scared the hell out of me, but the rage in her crystal blue eyes caused me to shake uncontrollably.

Helen and George stood wide-eyed in the doorway with a perplexed Tracy. My cheeks flamed as I realized I'd thrown a tantrum like a child. I wrapped my magic around myself and turned back to Mat. "I'm sorry. I don't know what made me do that."

Emine huffed and strode towards me, laying her hand on my shoulder, and flashed us to the back garden. I didn't have time to orient myself when she shoved me away and I landed on my butt. "What the hell, Jen! Do you have any idea how much work Mat put into this shindig?"

"Shindig?"

"The great lengths he went to ensure everything was handled, so it went off without a hitch?"

"I'm sorry. I——"

"No. Of course, you don't, because Mat has sheltered and spoiled you for the last thirty years. I get it. Your early childhood sucked, and you've got emotional shit. But news flash, we all have shit to deal with, including Mat!" She stomped back and forth before stopping in front of me. "And right now, you're just more shit. Is that what you want to be?"

"No...."

"Then get off your ass and deal with it. If you need to work out that anger, find me. I'll be glad to spar. Find someone to talk to. I don't care how you handle it but stop bottling that shit up before it drags you and everyone that cares about you down. Stop. Being. Shit." She disappeared.

I shuffled around the garden, thinking about what Emine had said. She was right. I hadn't thought about how Mat felt about this trip. I hadn't given a single thought to anyone else, focusing only on my feelings. Mat was here when our lives came crashing down, same as me. But he took care of business and kept going where I...acted like a spoiled brat who couldn't control herself. Where I had a victim mentality, always blaming Mat for my problems just because he was convenient, he jumped into action. He'd got me to safety, taken on the role of a parent and of Regent, cleaned up the mess made during the attack, changed the castle to make it more comfortable for me, and given me everything else in the world. And here I was, throwing it in his face and treating him like a captor instead of a cherished brother. And wasn't that selfish?

I flashed back to the hallway. Mat leaned against the doorway facing the destroyed room. His golden hair was covered in feathers, and his black T-shirt and jeans were covered in sawdust. He turned his head as I started forward, his golden eyes dull. "I'm sorry I made you come here for this. We should have stayed in Allure." His rough voice made me flinch.

I'd never felt so small seeing what I'd done to him. "You did everything you could to make it welcoming and new. It's me that's the problem, not you or the castle. I just have...shit I need to deal with, and none of it is your fault."

His brow creased. "Did Emine say that?"

"She pointed out that I might be the problem in her very Emine way."

He let out a dry laugh. "I can imagine. She thinks I coddle you."

"She does. And you do. Want to take a walk?"

We headed toward the beach until we came to a white gazebo lined with benches. We sat next to each other, facing the sea. Fidgeting, I stared at Mat's scarred hands and arms. "I'm sorry. I'm not sure what came over me. I saw that painting and just lost it."

"You had an episode of PTSD."

"Maybe. That's still no excuse for not controlling myself. The truth is, since...since we left Mahri, I've had a pretty good life. You gave that to me. I've been having such a pity party about coming here." I choked back tears. "You aren't responsible for all that horrid stuff that happened when I was little. You weren't even here, and it's unfair to blame you."

"Isn't that just it? I wasn't there. I should have been there and done something."

"It's not like you had a choice."

"Neither did you. You were just a child, and I wasn't. It was my duty to protect you."

A tear streaked down my face, and I brushed it away. "That doesn't excuse my behavior. I'm not a child anymore. I'm not weak. For some reason, when I'm near you, I play the role of a spoiled child. That needs to stop. I need to take responsibility and stop blaming you for everything. It's immature and selfish."

Mat took my hand. "That may be. But what you really need to do is deal with your emotions. Talk to me, Jen. What happened in this castle?"

My heart picked up pace, and I broke out into a sweat. I moved to the other side of the gazebo and took a deep breath. "I was dragged from under the bed, beaten, and put in that cage. Often. I still have nightmares."

His hand landed on my shoulder. "I'm sorry. Even though I knew some things––I should have had that room sealed years ago."

I reached up and put my hand over his. "Seal it later. It's not something you should be worrying about right now. I'll come back and fix it. It might be helpful to my dealing with...shit."

A thousand emotions flashed through his eyes. He dropped his hand. "Very well. I'll ask George to magically seal it while we're here. You need to get some rest. Dinner is at seven, and our guests will want you at your best."

We started back toward the castle. "Travis will love that. We should sit him between Bastien and Drake and see who shifts and eats him first."

"We're not doing that."

"Please?"

"I thought you said you would grow up and deal with things like an adult."

"You're no fun, Mat."

He reached out and poked me in the ribs. "As much as I hate to ruin your personal entertainment, we are here on business."

"Yeah, yeah."

"Behave yourself."

Chapter 19

Travis sat halfway down the dining room table on the other side of his parents, his face red with anger. Mat and Emine sat to my right, followed by Ara and Quin, while the First Jonas and his match, Ann Marie, sat to my left, followed by Drake and Bastien. The vampires stared at their plates, completely still. I tore my eyes away from them and made small talk, as I was expected to do. Even Emine seemed to be on her best behavior. Boring.

I focused on the First Jonas while we waited for the main course. He appeared as an unremarkable middle-aged guy with brown hair and brown eyes. His unassuming looks contrasted with the enormous power I felt rolling off him in waves. I gave him a polite smile. "I don't know if this is the right time, but I'd like to talk to you about the hybrids."

He peeled his eyes away from Ara and Quin, whom he had been staring at all evening. "I hoped to speak with you and your brother about them."

Ann Marie leaned over him. "What he means is that the way they're treated is a travesty, and something needs to be done."

My attention shifted to the sorceress. She was a petite blonde with kind sky-blue eyes and a delicate face. I liked her immediately. "I agree. My hope is to work with you two to find some solutions."

"Excellent. I have a lot of ideas." She lifted her glass toward me, and I genuinely smiled.

The dinner dragged. The cocktail party afterward was a series of small talk and congratulations that I could have done without. They didn't mean it. It was what they were supposed to say. As soon as possible, I slipped away from the festivities, scrubbed my face, traded the dress for a soft pair of pajamas, and let my hair down.

I pulled out my laptop and sat in one of the plush chairs to get some work done. I decided to start with Jedediah's case because that's where these two cases had begun. Leaning in to get a better look, I pulled up the pictures and screenshots from his house's internal investigation. I enlarged the copyright mark, transferred it to a photo program, sharpened it, and tried to make it a little easier to see.

Mat's special knock sounded on my door. He'd used it for as long as I could remember, so I didn't hesitate. "Come in."

He strode into the room, wearing a pair of black sweatpants and a white T-shirt. His eyes scanned every corner before he quietly shut the door behind him and crossed his arms. "I came to make sure you're okay. Are you working at this hour?"

"Yep. I'm not acclimated to the time change and couldn't sleep."

He took the chair next to me. "That makes two of us."

I showed him the image on the screen. "Have you found any information about this symbol yet?"

The color drained from his face. "You need to drop this case right now."

"Not going to happen. I know it has something to do with the rebellion. Tell me what it means."

He got up and began pacing, the muscles on his scarred arms flexing as he made fists. His golden eyes glowed. "Hand this case off to someone else and walk away. That symbol represents something you don't want to mess with."

I watched him as he continued to pace. His usually deadly aura was absent. I'd never seen anything make him that nervous. It made me nervous because he was nervous, but I didn't give up. "And what does it represent exactly?"

He ran a hand through his hair. "Many years ago, a secret society tried to tear the coalition apart. They infiltrated all levels of the government and killed many people. They almost succeeded in wiping out the coalition leadership. That was their symbol."

If I thought my head was spinning when I found the symbol, it was nothing compared to hearing that. "Do you think they're the ones responsible for what Jaques did?" my voice was a squeak.

"Yes."

"Then shouldn't we pursue this so it doesn't happen again?"

Mat stopped pacing. "We?"

"Well, yeah. Quin's already looking into the dragons. Finding out who stole money from Jedediah and Thaddeus are my cases, so I need to solve them." I tapped my chin. "They're intertwined. You might think I'm crazy for saying this, but I think they have the Dragon Queen, or she's involved somehow."

"Do you really?"

"I don't know. Yes. Drake and Bastien haven't exactly been forthcoming. Drake even gave me some information about the dragon uprising to appease me. My point is I could follow the financial trail and share information with Quin. He might agree to work on this together from two different angles." I doubted it, but it was worth a try.

"No. You will not have anything to do with this."

"I already have something to do with this. As I said, they're my contracted cases, and clients trust me to solve them. I can't just hand them off."

He sat down and leaned forward, his head in his hands. "You can't pursue this, Jen. Let the Enforcers and Tarquin handle it. I can't protect you from these people when you're out running around."

I set my laptop on the table between us. "Mat, I understand you want to protect me, and I appreciate that you care. But I can help. I know I can. I'm not a little girl anymore."

He met my eyes. "You can't help if you're dead. You're the only family I have left, and the coalition depends on your survival. Those people..." he pointed to my laptop, "are dangerous. They could be anywhere waiting to kill you, and you would never know it."

"That would be true if I couldn't sense their magic. Besides, hardly anyone knows my identity. They won't be looking for ordinary Detective Jen Hendrix."

"Getting involved will put her, and therefore you, on their radar."

"Maybe." I tapped the arm of the chair. I suspected I was already on the radar, but Mat didn't need to know that. "What if I did the investigative work and let the Enforcers bring the hammer down on them?"

"You will still catch their notice."

"Not if I play it smart. I can stay behind the scenes. Fly under their radar."

"If they are active again, they could be anywhere. Anyone you encounter could be a member, even one of the Enforcers. Not all of them carry the odd magic."

"I'll be careful, then. I'll call for help if I need it."

He sighed and stood up. "I'm not going to talk you out of this, am I?"

"No. But you've given me a more careful approach to the case."

I hoped it would give him more confidence in me, but he shook his head. "I don't like you involved in this, and I can't stress enough how dangerous these people are."

"I got that."

"Very well. I'll let you do your job for now, but if I get wind of even a minor threat to you, I'm pulling you back home, kicking and screaming if I must."

No, he wasn't. "Thanks, Mat."

He pointed at me. "This goes against my nature and everything I stand for. I promised I wouldn't cage you, and I'm trying to keep that promise. Work with the Enforcers, Tarquin, or anyone better equipped to handle it. Don't try to be a hero. And let Tracy protect you."

"I will. I won't. Er...." No way was I going to be put in the position of being dragged back to the castle to waste my days away in a safety bubble. He waved a hand dismissively and slipped out the door.

I shut my laptop and went to bed. And spent the rest of the night afraid to fall asleep and have more horrifying dreams. I hopped out of bed the second the sun appeared over the horizon.

To get to the breakfast room, I had to pass the back entrance that led to the dungeons. I hoped to avoid that area so I didn't fly into another rage. But I needed coffee, so I had to pass it. I took a deep breath and prepared myself before approaching the turn leading to the dungeon entrance. When I made the turn, I put my head down and counted my steps to avoid thinking. I'd just passed the door and turned left toward the breakfast room when I rammed into what felt like a brick wall.

"Watch where you're going."

I stepped back and looked way up to meet Bastien's eyes. "Sorry about that. I haven't had my coffee yet." I motioned toward the breakfast room.

"Humph," he grunted. "What were you doing?"

"Practicing avoidance for the greater good," I answered. I went to step around him, but he didn't move. "Excuse me."

He still didn't move. "Avoiding what?"

I glanced at the back door. "Nothing."

"Bastien, let Jenella through," Drake's smooth voice came from the room.

Bastien stepped aside. I didn't take my eyes off him until I got to the coffeepot. After pouring my coffee, I gathered enough courage to ask Drake. "What's with Bastien acting like a goon?"

His lips quirked up as he buttered some toast. "Bastien doesn't like being in Mahri without his mother. There's a large dragon population here that wants his attention and asks too many questions. It makes him twitchy."

"I see." I piled some fruit on a plate. "And why is she absent?" I said it loud enough so Bastien could hear.

Drake chuckled. "Leave him be, Jenella. You don't want to push his buttons."

I perched on a chair across from him. "Says you."

He gave me a polite smile. "What do you have planned today?"

"Work, ceremony preparation, parties, the usual. You?"

"I am without a purpose. I thought I might tour Mahri and see what's changed. Do you and Tracy want to go?"

My heart skipped a beat. "I wish. Mat has meticulously planned this week, and unfortunately, that means my presence is required. Tracy might take you up on it, though."

Travis entered the room, and I noted that Bastien didn't stop him, though he came into the room and glowered. Travis eyed my casual appearance. "You should dress better. You look half put together, and it's embarrassing."

"Whatever."

He focused on Drake, searching for camaraderie. "She acts as unprofessional as she looks."

"Jenella is perfection, no matter her attire. Her attitude is...refreshing." His voice made it clear the conversation was final.

Travis sat beside me, unfazed by Drake's tone. "She should always consider the impression she makes on others."

In other words, he worried about what people would think about him. "I dunno. I like to think one of the few perks of being queen is that I get to do what I damn well please."

Drake stood, picked up my coffee cup and his, and refilled them. "I understand where you get your ideas about attire, Travis. However, Jenella should never change who she is for anyone." He set our cups back on the table before he continued. "If living this long has taught me one thing, it is that trying to meet the expectations of others is a waste of time." The haunted look flashed across his face so fast I would have missed it if I hadn't been staring at him in awe.

Travis contemplated his response. "I respectfully disagree, Sir First. A queen's responsibility is to her people, not herself. Since Jenella refuses to show her power, I don't see why she can't be more formal or dress better."

"Jenella is right here and can hear you."

Drake grinned. "That she is." He turned his attention back to Travis. "Although I see the reasoning behind your argument, I still believe she should be herself. Her unpredictable nature is an asset as a leader. It will either solidify her rule or, at the very least, keep everyone guessing. Possibly both. It will be entertaining to watch."

I got up, slammed my dishes into the bin, and headed to the door. "I'll just be on my way so you two can continue to speculate on my entertainment value." Not noticing the door to the dungeon, I hightailed it back to my room. I was sick of Travis and needed to be done with that so-called friendship. I liked Drake's way of handling him. Watching him ruin Travis's selfish plans to tailgate my status would be as entertaining as watching me fumble through being queen. Still, I wondered why Drake engaged in the discussion in the first place. It wasn't his business.

I threw out that train of thought as I put on some leggings and a sports bra and headed out for a run. I was outside stretching when Mat came out and started stretching beside me. "Good morning."

"Morning," he grumbled.

"Do you plan on running with me?"

"Yes. I know a good trail. It's hard, so you might be unable to keep up."

"Bring it on."

The trail was difficult. It covered hills, sand, streams, and some obstacles that had to be jumped over or ducked under. I found myself truly happy for the first time since landing in Mahri. The ocean breeze kept us cool, and spending time with the brother I thought of more like a father was priceless. When we came around the last bend heading back to the castle, Mat slowed to a walk. "What did you think of that?"

I couldn't help but smile. "It was great."

"I thought you'd like it." He rammed his shoulder into mine. "See, Mahri isn't all bad."

I looked around at the lush greenery and glittering ocean. "You're right. It's great, except for the memories."

"The memories are in the past and can either be left there or dealt with and then left there. The castle can be changed if you'd like. Do you want to keep it when the inheritance is settled?"

I contemplated the question. Running from my family had consumed me so much that I never considered the possibility of getting rid of the castle. I should have educated myself better. "How long has it been in the family?"

"For about a thousand years."

That was a long time, even by supernatural standards. "I think it should stay in the family, but I don't want to live here."

"Agreed. The house in Allure better suits us."

"But I want the dungeons eliminated. That entire area razed or filled in or whatever."

Mat didn't answer until we spilled out onto the back gardens. "I took care of that years ago."

My head shot up. "You did?"

"You're not the only one who has bad memories. It was one of the first things I did after we settled in Allure. I had it cleared out, and it stayed that way for a long time. It is now a state-of-the-art gym. It's free for the locals to use when we are not in residence."

Relief washed over me. "You've always been solid. To me, you're larger than life and invincible. It never occurred to me that you had some shit emotions about this place until Emine pointed it out yesterday. I'm sorry."

Mat snorted. "Invincible, I am not. I appreciate the sentiment, though."

We made our way back to the castle and went our separate ways. I took a shower and climbed the winding stone stairs of a tower in search of Verity. When I discovered the door partially open, I pushed my way in. I didn't remember that part of the castle. With it being such a vast building, I doubted I remembered much of it. The spacious room was round, decorated with delicate yet classy dark wood antiques and dark green fabrics. Verity stood at one of the tall windows, looking out. "I called dibs on this room in case you were thinking it's yours."

I grinned. "I did hear a rumor that it's all mine. Good thing you set me straight."

She turned around, a smile lighting her face. "This place is amazing! Never in my life did I think I'd end up at the top of a tower in an ancient castle looking over the plebes in the garden. You, young lady, have a charmed life."

I peered out the window next to hers. "I guess I never thought of it that way. It's just my life."

She shook her head. "You should rethink it. You are truly blessed." She moved to the small desk antique desk. "Let's go over the details for the coronation ceremony so we can continue window gazing."

After our brief meeting, we stared out the windows for a while, then headed to the library to research Mat's information about the rebellion. We found several hefty tomes with small passages that glossed over the uprising, but not much more. Several hours later, Verity excused herself with a yawn.

Eventually, my stomach grumbled, so I headed downstairs to get something to eat. Halfway down the stairs, I noticed the silence and was grateful that everyone had made themselves scarce. Glancing at the clock, I realized the time had gotten away from me, and it was late. I shuffled into the kitchen and approached the magichef, wrapping my magic tightly around me before choosing soup and salad. I stood at the counter and made quick work of the meal. As I headed back to my room, my feet involuntarily stopped in front of the back door next to the dungeon.

I wanted to look at the new gym so I could praise Mat for his efforts. I broke out into a sweat and started trembling. Not wanting to fly into another rage, I headed to the kitchen, ordered a bottle of vodka, and poured a glass. I drained it and took the vodka bottle with me as I returned to the dreaded door. I sat on the floor in the small hallway leading to the dungeons and poured another drink. Mat was so much stronger than me, I realized. He always just dealt with problems while I ran away from them. At that moment, I wanted more than anything to be like Mat. But I wasn't Mat. Where he slayed our enemies and repurposed dungeons without blinking an eye, I couldn't work up the courage to turn a doorknob.

"Having a private party, or can I join?"

I only jumped a little, thanks to the alcohol. "Ha ha."

Drake lowered himself to the floor, his scent washing over me. I didn't want to acknowledge how much it settled my nerves. I turned my attention to him. He wore jeans and a black T-shirt. I eyed his rugged appearance and decided he was right. I preferred the wild First, who jumped out of his resting place and shook me. He eyed the bottle of vodka. "Why are you sitting on the floor in the hallway?"

"See that door?" I motioned to the dungeon door with my glass.

"Yes?"

"That door and I are having a showdown."

The corner of his eyes crinkled. "May I ask why?"

"You can."

He leaned forward. "Why?"

"I'm not telling you, but I'll tell you about our bet if you want." I waited for his acknowledgment before continuing. "The deal is, if I win, I go through the door. If the door wins, I don't. Pretty simple."

He looked the door over. "It looks like a sturdy door. What do you think your chances are?"

"It's 50-50 right now, but I think I can take it after a couple more drinks."

He removed the vodka bottle and glass from my hands and set them on a nearby table. "Well, now it's two against one, and I'm much bigger and fiercer than that door." He tapped his chin. "I think our odds are significantly better. Perhaps 75-25."

I swallowed, trying to avoid noticing how good he smelled. I did what I always did in uncomfortable situations. I changed the subject. "Don't not-dragons need their beauty rest?"

"They normally do, yes. But considering I've been sleeping for a couple hundred years, I think I can skip a few minutes." He held out a hand. "Let me help you."

I extended a shaky hand and touched his. The ruling magic sent a zing down my arm. My eyes snapped to his to see if he felt it, but Drake's stoic face never changed as he pulled me to my feet. I removed my hand before leaning over and eyeing the door handle. "The problem is that the handle doesn't want to be turned."

"Do you want me to try? I'm an excellent negotiator."

"No." I took a small step forward and touched the doorknob. It didn't feel like the doorknob of doom. It just felt like another doorknob, the faker. I put my forehead against the door. "Drake, promise me you'll run if I go into a mad rage and start destroying things. I don't want to hurt you."

He put his hand on my back. "I've got scales, Jenella, and am nearly impossible to kill. I'm not leaving until I'm sure you're okay. If I get maimed along the way, so be it."

I bit back the tears that threatened to spill. "Please don't. I'd never forgive myself if I hurt you." I swallowed. "It's times like this that I wish I was Mat." I swung the door open and stepped inside.

Instead of the narrow stone staircase, there was now a much broader, dark wood staircase that overlooked the entire floor. The stench of suffering was replaced with the smell of the ozone and cleaning magic. The holes that had been called cells were gone. In their place were rows upon rows of shiny exercise equipment. On the far wall were two brightly lit classrooms. On the left wall was an outside entrance with double doors. A short hall led to a room with what looked like an obstacle course. I sauntered to the center and faced the wall next to the stairs. It had floor-to-ceiling screens that showed a mountain range. "This place is fantastic."

Drake eyed me for a few seconds, strode over, and...hugged me? He pulled back. "I'm glad you beat whatever made you fear opening that door."

Unable to say anything without crying, I nodded and stepped back. I ran my fingers over a treadmill that now sat where the entrance to the hall that housed my cage used to be. I glanced in that direction, noting the area looked just like the rest of the gym. Mat was an amazing person.

"He did it as much for himself as you."

Drake must have plucked those thoughts out of my head. I briefly wondered why the ruling magic allowed him to do that, but dismissed it. I was already feeling emotional and having a puzzle overload and I didn't need to add to it. "Yeah." Stomach raw, I took one last look around before heading to the stairs.

Drake put his hand on my lower back and guided me out of the dungeo...er...gym before shutting the door with a click. He picked up my vodka and glass. "So, I assume you don't need these anymore?"

"I'm good." I turned back to the door. "Thanks for uh…" I waved a hand.

He stopped with his back to me. "Sometimes, our mind makes things more difficult than they are. Do not let whatever that was define you, Jenella. You are so much more than that."

"Yeah." I didn't sound very convincing.

He shook his head. "Congratulations on your victory over the door-knob."

"Yeah. Um. Thanks for your help." I felt all kinds of awkward, so I high-tailed it to my room.

Chapter 20

THE FOLLOWING DAY, MAT, Emine, and I met with the legal team and signed all the paperwork for my transition to queen. They made Mat my Regent until I chose to relieve him of his duties and second to the throne until I had children. I hated every minute of it but tried not to let it show.

I had my appointment at the Bank of Mahri that day and scrambled to change clothes so I could make it on time. Tracy was on a mini vacation since I was surrounded by people who would protect me. She said she had to catch up on her business anyway, so the timing was great. Travis had gone off to spend time with his family, so I didn't have to put up with him. I ran down the stairs and out the front door to a hovering cart used for transport in Mahri. They didn't have as many mages, so there weren't many flashing circles. Most paranormals used magic-powered carts that the dragons had invented. They hovered just off the ground. I hopped on the driver's side. "Aaarggh!" I screamed as I realized someone was already in the cart.

"Ha! Gotcha!" Emine lounged in the passenger seat, decked out in her usual leather, her brown hair pulled into a high ponytail, her enforcer's badge hanging around her neck.

"What the hell, Emine! What are you doing in my cart?"

"It's a castle cart. And I'm your official Enforcer partner for this case." She wiggled her eyebrows.

"No. No way. We can't work together. We'll kill each other."

She let out an evil cackle. "Riggght? This will be fun!"

I realized she wasn't going anywhere, so I slammed the cart in reverse and abruptly backed up, hoping she would hit the windshield. No such luck.

We strode into the bank side by side. Like the branch in Allure, it was controlled chaos, with agents running everywhere and a loud mixture of voices in several different languages. Sturdy stone columns were strewn throughout the ground floor. Stone floors stretched for what looked like miles. Just inside the doors, a giant in a security uniform looked us up and down, his eyes landing on Emine's badge. "State your business."

I stepped forward. "I'm Detective Jen Hendrix, and this is Princess Emine of the Enforcers. We have an appointment with Sir Thornton."

His eyes bounced back and forth between us. "I will let him know you're here."

It only took about five minutes for a dragon with orange hair and eyes to approach us. "Hello, I'm Mr. Thornton." He turned to Emine. "I apologize, Princess Emine, but I only expected Detective Hendrix to ask some routine questions. What is your business?"

I held my breath as I waited for Emine to answer, sure her attitude would ruin our chances of getting an interview. Emine linked her hands behind her back. "My apologies for encroaching on Detective Hendrix's appointment, Sir Thornton. We found an intersection between her case and the one we were investigating. I volunteered to attend since I was in town for the Queen's coronation."

My head snapped toward her so fast that I almost got whiplash. I'd never heard Emine in professional mode, and it frightened me more than her usual attitude because it was so...smooth. And normal. I disguised my surprise when I noticed Mr. Thornton looking at me for further explanation. "During my investigation, I found some vital information that both you and the Enforcers needed to have. I've agreed to a mutual investigation. Princess Emine was kind enough to volunteer to assist with this interview." I almost choked on that last part. It wasn't exactly a lie, but it wasn't the truth.

The bank manager eyed her skeptically. "Very well, please follow me."

When he turned his back, Emine shoulder-bumped me hard and winked. I ignored her.

He led us to a corner office on the second floor. The office was decorated in solid gold, which was no surprise considering he was a dragon. Mr. Thornton sat in the gold executive's chair behind his desk. He offered us the visitor's chairs, which, of course, were also gold. He clasped his hands on his desk. "So, what can I help you with?"

I pulled out a file I prepared for him. "I have two clients who are customers at this bank. Their accounts have been emptied with no transaction records. I wondered if you would help track the money and return it if possible." I handed him the folder.

He opened it and examined the documents. "This is disturbing." He stopped at the page I buried in the middle that contained the symbol and ran his hand over it. His eyes flashed, and I gripped the arms of my chair tighter. He slammed the folder closed. "I'm sorry, detective, I can't help you. If your clients would like to inquire, I would gladly help them."

"My clients have inquired and were ignored." I pointed to the folder. "It's on the last page of the report. They signed forms appointing me their representative."

The dragon rubbed his chin. "This is not the first time customers have pulled their money from accounts and accused us of emptying them. Some supernaturals are motivated by greed. I believe Prince Jedediah falls into that category. Leprechauns, in general, fall into that category."

Said the dragon in the golden office. "I assure you my clients have a legitimate claim."

Emine shifted in her chair. "Any thoughts about that symbol you were so gently rubbing?"

"Surely, I don't know what you mean."

She got up, yanked the folder from under his hand, ripped the picture of the symbol out, and threw it on his desk. "That's what I mean. Let's cut the crap, Thornton. If that is even your name. You're an old dragon, and that symbol has been around for a long time. You know what it represents. Why are you pretending you don't?"

"It is an internal matter and none of your concern. The Enforcers have no evidence of this—" he jabbed his finger at the picture. "—symbol having anything to do with my bank or interspecies conflict. You have no business being here."

"You know what I think? I think you thought you could bully my colleague here into dropping the matter, and me showing up threw a wrench into your plans." Emine whipped out her serial killer smile. "Bummer, isn't it?"

"Let's all stop accusing each other." I pointed to the dragon. "You can lie about that symbol all you want. It was only placed there as a test. You failed. What I want is my client's money back, and I want it back today."

He tapped his desk. "What makes you think that symbol has anything to do with your client's money disappearing?"

"It was left as a calling card in both of the empty accounts."

"Oh, please. Why would they do something so obvious?"

"Who cares? They stole money from my clients and left that symbol. I need you to trace where it went and a magical contract ensuring the funds will remain in their accounts when it's returned."

He leaned forward. "Or what?"

"Or you're taking a trip to the Enforcer's station, where we will keep you from your dragon form and use other fun techniques to get our answers," Emine said.

He burst into his dragon form. I flashed to one corner of the room, Emine to the other. Stone and glass rained down from the ceiling as the enormous orange dragon thrashed in an attempt to escape. Emine conjured a thick lasso and began swinging it in loops. She threw it with a "Yeeeeee hawwww," locking it around his neck.

I dove under him and threw shredding magic at his underbelly. It made a few cuts, but it wasn't enough to stop him. I rolled to the right as his foot came down, missing me by inches. I jumped to my feet and ran. Emine tied the lasso to a stone pillar and jammed knives between his scales as she tried to climb him. "Go childhood room on his ass!"

It took me a second to realize she referenced my tantrum at the castle. It was a great idea, but it wasn't easy to fly into a blind rage on cue. I threw the nastiest magic I could think of at this wing as I sprinted under him to get onto his tail. "Emine! Go for the eyes!" I jumped on his swinging tail and grabbed his scales, attempting to climb up his back. I tried to unleash my rage as I climbed. When I got to his wings, my anger was in full swing. The ruling magic slammed against its restraints. White fiery rage filled my belly. I kept climbing, kept letting it build. When I reached his back, I focused on the same wing and let it all go.

Emine emerged on his neck, and her knives disappeared, replaced with some kind of high-caliber rifle. I wasn't sure what it was precisely because most supernaturals didn't use guns, and I was busy raging. I only knew that when she started shooting at his head, the sound was so loud my ears rang. The dragon blew a stream of orange fire that caught the wind and blew to the right, hitting a building across the street. I coughed as smoke filled the air.

Still, I raged and shredded. I managed to destroy the joint of one wing. Just as I went to start on the other, the dragon broke the rope that anchored us to the building and tried to fly away. I saw Emine brace herself with knives. I grasped for something to hold on to. He didn't have spikes down his back like Drake, so I was out of luck. I tried to jam my hand between two scales, but they held tight. I bounced on his back three times before jamming one hand into a broken, sharp scale. The dragon turned, drew in a breath, and let loose a raging inferno on the bank before turning and trying to fly away.

Because his wing was so shredded, his balance was off, and he could only fly in circles. I gripped tighter as we rose to the sky and started spiraling toward the ground. Just when I thought I would lose my grip, Emine yelled, "Fire in the hole!" with so much glee I knew we were screwed. I peered over the side to get a map of the land and flashed to the ground. I hit harder than I intended, rolled, and hopped to my feet.

The dragon thumped off the building beside me. I ducked around the corner as chunks of building rained down. I threw knockout magic at his head when it swung my way. The ground shook as his body crashed into the intersection next to the bank. Emine ran up, her dark hair white from dust, her leather clothes covered in blood. "Woo hoo! That was so fun!" She held up her hand for a high five. "Good cop, bad cop gets them every time."

"That was not good cop, bad cop. That was terrible cop, psycho cop."

Her eyebrows knitted together, "I don't think you're a psycho. Just a little off."

I shook my head and put my hands on my hips. "What do we do now? This was the only good lead I had."

She patted me on the shoulder. "It was a productive day. We know who took the money and that those secret society pukes are active."

"We do?"

"Obviously, it was the dragons."

"It's not obvious to me. We don't have any proof."

"Proof schmoof. Dragons have been doing that kind of thing for centuries. They're usually better at hiding their involvement." She waved a hand. "My point is that it wouldn't take much mind control to get them to steal. It was totally them."

"Let's say you're right. That doesn't help get my client's money back, which is *why we're here!*"

She patted me on the shoulder. "NMP. Not my problem, in case you missed it."

I kicked a rock. "I didn't sense mind control on him. It was most likely the secret society, but there's no proof the dragon was one of them."

"Exactly. That's what I said."

"That is not what you said."

Enforcer vehicles started pouring into the area, and she nudged me toward them. "They had mind control on him. One doesn't simply recruit a dragon to do their bidding without the Dragon Queen knowing, no matter who they are. He wouldn't be a part of the secret society if she didn't authorize it. If you want to retrieve the money, deal with her."

Except the queen was missing, and Bastien was in charge. I couldn't imagine him having anything to do with a secret society.

The rest of the day was spent giving a formal statement and adding magic to help load the dragon on a magical transport. Unlike the kidnapping dragons, this one didn't change to his human form when he got knocked out. Bastien showed up and used his magic to help us load him into the transport and explained that it was because he was badly injured. He agreed to help with the shift when the dragon woke up, then ignored me, and I was okay with that.

Emine slipped away to talk to some bank employees, but she made me stay behind and help the Enforcers. I was exhausted when we climbed back into the cart to leave. "What did the bank employees have to say?"

"That jackass dragon was transferred here from a small branch in Hospa a couple of months ago. The assistant manager was up for the gig, and it pissed her off. When the calls started coming in about missing money, she hoarded the reports out of spite. She's in deep shit."

"Ugh. Office politics."

"Exactly."

"I'll check in with Colonel Ballard in Hospa and see if he found anything. Will the dragon be able to answer some questions for me when he wakes up?"

"Wouldn't hurt to talk to the Colonel. And, yeah, he'll be able to answer questions, but I doubt he will. Let us handle it, and I'll pass on any information we get."

When we pulled up in front of the castle, Mat stood on the front steps with his arms crossed. I took out my glamour earrings. "He looks pissed."

Emine opened her door. "Yep."

I got out and followed her up the walkway. "Hey, Mat."

"I thought you were going to an interview, not dragon hunting."

Emine kissed him on the cheek. "It was a hoot! Jen and I kicked some serious dragon ass. I even got to use a bomb."

Mat raised an eyebrow. "You set off a bomb that could have injured my baby sister?"

She patted him on the chest. "I get it. She acts like a kid, but she's a grown-ass woman. No need to keep coddling her."

"Hey!" Emine ignored me and ducked into the castle.

Mat watched her go inside. "Are you okay?"

"Yeah." I smirked. "That was pretty awesome. Emine is a psycho."

He didn't roll his eyes, but I could tell he wanted to. "Go get yourself cleaned up. We have events to attend, and you need to do something about Travis. He's acting like it's his coronation."

I showered and called Colonel Ballard. He didn't answer, so I left a message on his voicemail asking him to contact me as soon as possible. I texted Quin, so he didn't think I was trying to poach his case and begrudgingly dressed for the next event. I met Travis on the stairs and told him to back off before Mat lost his temper. His face paled, but I doubted he would stop acting important. It was his nature.

The rest of the week was uneventful as I was whisked from one place to another. I didn't hate every minute, so at least I had that going for me. "I'm going to need a week of sleep after this," I told Helen as she slipped me into my coronation gown, the final ceremony of the week. Although Mahri wasn't so bad, I couldn't wait to return to Allure. The people were friendly, and it was steeped in magical traditions we just didn't have in the West.

Helen looked tired, too, which was unusual for a griffin. "I know, sweetie. Just the ceremony and after-party left, and we can go home." She activated a spell to make my gown fit me like a glove.

I turned to the mirror and froze. The floor-length gold gown matched my eyes perfectly. Amethyst stones glittered thick at the waist, then scattered in a random pattern as they went down the A-line skirt and ended in a pattern of crowns around the hem. The bodice was conservative, with a sweetheart neckline and capped sleeves. A gold necklace had a giant amethyst that matched the ones in the crown that sat on my head. My unruly light brown hair was styled in an intricate updo, highlighting the gold streaks that ran through it while allowing the red streaks to peek out. "Wow."

Helen grinned. "You look lovely."

I did. Though it wasn't me staring back in the mirror. It was a fake image designed to present an unrealistic ideal. I kept those thoughts to myself and returned Helen's smile. "Thank you."

Her smile melted into a frown. "You have many people who care about you and want to see you succeed. It's tough to carry the weight of the world on your shoulders when you also have a chip on them. It's been my constant hope you would realize your worth someday. I know what happened to you as a child stole it. I hope you can eventually see what a magnificent person you are." She pointed to the mirror. "The woman there reflects only an ounce of the beauty you have inside you. Believe that." She strode out of the room, leaving me feeling like a fool for my thoughts.

The ceremony went without a hitch. I managed to stay gracious as people streamed into the after-party and congratulated me. I couldn't help but think about what Helen said as I made my way to the front of the ballroom. Did I not want to be queen because of Jaques's abuse? I didn't know. I inclined my head at Mat as I sat. He turned to the crowd. "I present to you the Third Queen of Ahl, Jenella Lissandra Andreas Ahl."

The crowd cheered, and I forced myself not to wince, keeping a neutral expression as I waved my thanks. Music started, and they turned their attention to food, dancing, and drinking, mostly ignoring me. Mat sat on the throne to my right and patted my hand. My eyes flipped to the gold and amethyst circlet on his head. "Nice crown. It almost makes you look approachable."

"I cannot wait to not be approached. It makes me...twitchy."

Meaning he wanted to draw his katanas and kill people. "Yeah." I agreed. It made me want to run away.

I eventually made it through the crowd, looking for the First Jonas or the sorceress, Ann Marie. I saw them talking to the shifter alphas earlier, so I knew they were there. Despite being stopped several times, I managed to spot them having a quiet discussion at a table in the back corner of the ballroom. I slipped around the side so they saw me as I approached. "Sir First, Ancient Ann Marie, thank you for coming."

Jonas didn't respond, but Ann Marie managed a fake smile. "Thank you for having us, your grace. We're thrilled to be here."

I snorted. "You don't have to pretend to be glad to be here, and you can call me Jenella. May I have a seat?"

Jonas motioned to a chair across from them and studied me. "You are not what we expected."

I gathered my gown and sat. "No? How so?"

He tapped the table. "I thought you'd be more..." he didn't finish.

"Powerful?" I waved a hand at his acknowledgment. "Sorry to disappoint. I had to become good at hiding my power at a very young age. It's a habit now." Not wanting to elaborate, I abruptly changed the subject. "I'd like to discuss the hybrid situation if you have the time."

Ann Marie waved her hand, and a privacy spell swept around the table. "I hope you don't mind, but this crowd is not exactly pro-hybrid."

"I appreciate the privacy. Although I thought I understood the hybrid situation, it's come to my attention that we haven't been paying it the attention it deserves. I didn't realize kids were being abandoned. Drake told me you dedicate yourselves to rescuing them and keeping them hidden in the human world."

They exchanged a look, and Jonas sat back. "I thought you were heartless rather than inept."

Ann Marie kicked his foot, but I preferred his honesty. "Not inept, I hope, but sheltered. I've been kept in a bubble most of my life. Unfortunately, the information didn't always get through. I do know that Mat has tried to change the view of hybrids and has ordered the leadership council to take action."

Ann Marie nodded. "He has, but this anti-hybrid sentiment has become ingrained in supernatural society. I suspect it started with an alternate agenda and gathered momentum like a snowball rolling down a hill."

"When did it start?"

"Only about thirty or so years ago. Supernaturals threw away thousands of years of tradition almost overnight. Now, they're not only kicking out mixed-magic couples, but preteen kids." Jonas wagged a finger. "Fates forbid they have a preteen kid with hybrid magic that lowers their parent's societal standing."

"So, they really are throwing kids out of the pockets?" Supernaturals generally cared deeply for their kids and would die before harming them. We weren't as fertile as humans, only able to have kids with our true match, so they were cherished when we had them. Well, mostly. "That's not okay."

"Agreed. We have a network of people who work to round them up, adopt them, and raise them in the human world."

That sounded like a vast, organized network. When I first heard about their efforts, I thought maybe a couple hundred, but now I wasn't so sure. "How many are there?"

Jonas leaned forward. "Thousands. The coalition was set up specifically to prevent this. We can only care for so many before we're exposed to humans. The question is, what are you going to do about it?"

I didn't know. "I'll see what my brother is working on and figure something out. If it's a prejudice that has become ingrained, it won't be easy, but we'll make it a priority."

Ann Marie tapped her champagne glass. "This is a relatively new prejudice that started around the time the second queen was assassinated. Before that, all children were celebrated, and no one batted an eye at mixed magic couples."

"Do you know where it started?" I asked.

"No. But it's suspicious how fast the sentiment grew."

"I'll look into that, too. Do you mind if I contact you if I have questions?"

We exchanged information, and I headed back into the crowd to mingle, thinking about it the whole time. Mat had always said that without a strong queen, the coalition would crumble. I was certain that both the hybrid situation and the problems with the dragons resulted from being without a monarch for years. As much as I hated the idea of being a queen, paranormals needed someone to take control and provide solid leadership. I needed to fix my magic fast if I were to be that person.

I stayed at the coronation party until I couldn't stand the butt-kissing and political posturing anymore and headed back to my room. I was exhausted but knew I wouldn't sleep. The coalition had a lot of problems. Whether I liked it or not, they were my problems.

I threw on a pair of sweats and removed the spells that pinned the crown on my head. As I dissipated the last one, the crown fell, bounced off the dressing table, rolled across the wooden floor, and under the wardrobe. I sighed, got down on the floor, and peered under the wardrobe. A flash of gold told me the crown was against the wall. I lay on the floor, angled my neck weirdly, and jammed my arm under the heavy wardrobe. I added a little glow to my arm so I could see better. A prick to my finger caused me to yank my hand back. I shook out my hand and tried again. I got it that time and yanked it out as fast as I could.

"Click."

I spun back toward the wardrobe at the sound. I questioned my sanity as I pulled on the wardrobe. It moved easier than it should have. I jumped back. "What the hell?" I pulled it harder. A burst of air blew my hair back when it swung open like a door. I peered into the hidden room behind it but couldn't see much, so I backed away.

I grabbed a chair and wedged it between the wardrobe and the wall to keep the secret door open and reached into the room, searching for a light switch. I couldn't find one, so I lit up my hands. The hidden room was small, about a hundred square feet. A table with a wooden chair sat in the center of the room. Heart pounding, I stepped in, ran my fingers over the table's surface, and recognized the spell that kept it from getting dusty. The entire room had bookshelves full of books. I noticed the spine of the closest books, pulled one out, and flipped to the first page.

The book was handwritten in the ancient language of Mahri. Part of my schooling included studying the language, but I was far from fluent. I squinted as I translated a few of the words. I gasped and stepped back when I realized it was a diary. Turning to the inside cover, I fixated on the name. Lissa Andreas Ahl, the first Queen of Ahl. My grandmother. I scrambled to the room's other side, to the newer ones. They were written in Mahri as well, but the handwriting was different. The title page showed it belonged to my mother. With my heart in my throat, I closed the diary and hugged it to my chest. I had accidentally found a connection to my mother and grandmother. A tear slid down my cheek, and I wiped it away. Unable to deal with the complicated emotions, I set the diary down and ran to find Mat.

Mat and I spent most of the night reading the diaries. His face grew hard as he read through our mother's last entry. "Why did she do this? Why put these here?"

I returned a book to the shelf. "I don't know. But this was her office. The question is why no one has found them until now. It wasn't that hard."

Mat stood and rubbed his hand over the book he held. "Because no one else is you. You were meant to find these." He examined the opening. "It was probably magically hidden and sealed."

I looked at the finger that had been pricked and let out a dry laugh. "It needed my blood. Something stabbed my finger when I reached under the wardrobe. What do you suppose that means?"

He gave me a wry look. "My educated guess is you're supposed to read them."

I ignored the jab. "That's a lot of reading."

"I'll take them back to Allure and build something similar in your office. You can read them when you come home."

"Sure thing. I'll get right on that."

Mat's lip twitched. "Come on. Let's close this and get some sleep. Emine and I are heading home first thing in the morning. Your transport leaves at noon."

We closed the secret room, and Mat hugged me tightly like he didn't want to let me go. He rarely hugged me anymore, but when he did, it was always with his whole heart. "I love you, Jen-Jen. Thank you for doing this. I know you didn't want to."

"I love you, too, Mat-Mat." I stepped back. "It turned out okay. I'm glad I came, besides the whole being queen thing."

"Try not to slay any dragons on your way home."

I waved a hand. "Yeah, yeah."

He chuckled, shutting the bedroom door softly behind him.

Chapter 21

As the transport took off, I looked forward to wearing my glamour and returning to our little house. With the shakeup at the Bank of Mahri, I was hopeful I could solve my case soon. Tracy sat on my right, her laptop open. Occasionally, she'd ask me if I would use a specific potion. Bastien sat on her other side, his elbows resting on the armrests. I'd never seen him look so sad. Drake sat on his other side with his eyes closed. Quin and Ara were on my left. Both had their heads back and their eyes focused on the ceiling. Quin tapped the side of my bouncing leg for the tenth time and threw me a chastising look.

I leaned forward and rested my arms on the edge of the enormous observation window, looking for human airplanes rather than continuing to irritate Quin. I caught a glimmer of movement far off in the distance and squinted. Another glimmer further south caught my eye. I couldn't see what they were, but they didn't look like human airplanes. "Can any of you see what that is in the distance?"

All five of my companions leaned forward to look. Bastien shot out of his chair. "We are about to be attacked." He pointed at two griffin guards. "Protect the queen. Tracy, with me."

I scoffed as I stood.

"Everyone move to the lower deck and prepare to evacuate," one griffin ordered.

I scrambled to catch up with Tracy and Bastien, who were already on the other side of the transport. The other leaders loudly protested being herded like cattle but complied, disappearing down the stairs. Half the griffin guards, Drake, Bastien, Tracy, Quin, and I, were the only people left. "How many are there?"

"Six, possibly seven," Bastien ground out. "Go below and take care of the others."

I ignored him, plastering myself to the window. The dragons were drawing closer but were still pretty far away. Like Bastien, I counted six. I heard a 'whoosh' as one of the griffins opened a side hatch on the other side of the craft. Bastien grabbed Tracy, and they disappeared out the door. Quin glanced at me before following. "Wait. Can vampires fly?" I asked no one in particular as the griffin guards followed him out the door.

"Tarquin is unique." Drake's eyebrows drew together. "If I get us close enough, can you use your ruling magic to bring them down?"

I fought to hold back a grin. I always got held back and thought Drake would insist I go below with the others. Apparently, he was different from Bastien and Mat. "I don't know, but I'm willing to try."

He snaked an arm around my waist and jumped out of the transport, shifting into his dragon form so fast I didn't have time to scream. I slammed my eyes shut and concentrated on breathing, my heart pounding out of my chest. I felt talons cradle me and cracked an eye open. With the flick of a talon, I tumbled through the air. I shrieked and might have even peed myself a little before splatting down face-first on Drake's back. "Warn a girl next time!" I sat up and scooted toward a spike and wrapped my arms and legs around it.

The ruling magic wrapped around Drake's giant belly, holding me in place. I released my legs so I could lean over and see where the attackers were. Bastien was already in the fight, weaving in and out of the dragons. Tracy was on his back, throwing an experimental spell she called "weeble-wobble" that made the dragons unable to fly straight. Quin stood on top of a red dragon with a sword in one hand, his claws extended in the other as he pried at its scales. A team of five griffins battled a mint green dragon and a pale yellow dragon, buzzing around them like a swarm of bees. I pointed to a gray dragon that flew apart from the rest. "The gray one is their leader!"

No need to yell. Drake's voice echoed through my head.

"Sorry," I murmured as I clutched the spike.

Drake banked so fast that I almost lost my footing, and we headed straight toward it. *Get ready.*

I once again wondered how he could speak in my mind. No time to ponder it, though, because we were coming up on the gray dragon fast. I changed my natural magic to a knockout spell and tried to coax the ruling magic to help. It ignored me, staying wrapped tightly around Drake. As we banked left, I sent a stream of knock-out magic toward the dragon, aiming for the head. It didn't knock the dragon out, but it did knock out the mage riding on its back. The dragon shook his head a few times and began flying erratically, trying to land. "They have mages on their backs, and my magic is only sort of working," I reported unnecessarily.

Whatever you have wrapped around me is trying to link to my magic. Use that.

"Okay..." I caught a flash of red out of the corner of my eye a millisecond before the much smaller dragon slammed into Drake. He instinctively reared up, and I lost my grip on his spike. I tumbled backward, smashing into another spike, and felt the ruling magic tighten its grip. Red flames came straight at me, and I threw myself down. The red dragon's nail on the chalkboard squeal made me cover my ears. It lunged toward me. "Oh, shit!"

I sent a blast of knockout magic toward it. The red dragon fell away, struggling to maintain flight. I grabbed the spike and climbed to my feet, focusing on the ruling magic wrapped around Drake. It had sunk under his skin to his core, where his magic was stored. I frowned and reeled my inherent magic in, trying to understand what the ruling magic was attempting to do. Suddenly, a torrent of foreign magic filled me, and I stumbled back, falling on my butt. I shook my head, "I think I got it."

Drake roared as Bastien flew past. A couple of dragons chasing him. Tracy stood on his spikeless back, hurling spells, looking like a goddess. I didn't know how to use Drake's magic, so I unwrapped all three of my magics, no longer fighting the ruling magic, and yelled, "Land!" The ruling magic laced itself with the foreign magic and blanketed everyone in the fight. I hoped that Drake's mental magic was more potent than the mind control devices.

Everyone started descending at once, including the griffins and Bastien. "Oops," I muttered.

Drake shook his massive head and followed. *Did you just use my own magic against me?* His voice sounded amused.

"Um. I have no idea."

We landed in a clearing, and everyone turned their attention to me. I held on to Drake's power as I slid off his back. "Shift." I ordered. Everyone shifted at once. Mages riding the dragons ended up sitting on the backs of naked men in the blink of an eye. One tried to blast me, and I ducked. I held up a hand. "Don't use magic!" I turned to Drake, who had also shifted. He raised an eyebrow. "You *did* use my own magic against me. Twice."

"Your idea," I reminded him as I turned back toward the clearing. "All dragons––except Drake and Bastien––and all mages stay. Everyone else, get those mind control devices out of them."

The clearing came alive with activity as everyone scrambled to follow my orders. The ruling magic released Drake, and I sighed in relief. I wrapped my magic back around me, once again disguising it.

"What did you do?"

"Gah!" I jumped at Quin's voice. Even with my new ruling magic boost, he didn't register. "Stop sneaking up on me!"

"One would think that someone so powerful would use their senses more."

He was right. One more thing to work on. I elbowed Drake. "Sorry about the magic thing."

His lip twitched, but he didn't get the chance to say anything because Quin smashed into my back. I braced myself on Drake, who reached out to catch me. Quin's momentum took us all to the ground in a flash of light, and we landed in a tangle of limbs.

I raised my head as the pressure on my back disappeared, scrambled to my feet, and turned in a slow circle. We were no longer in a mountain clearing in the summer sun but a frozen tundra. I shivered and wrapped my arms around myself. Drake and Quin started arguing, but I ignored them. It didn't matter what happened. What mattered was where we were and how to get out. About fifty meters away was a semi-plowed road with a giant mountain range in the background, colorful plumes of magic spouting in every direction. "Mage Mountain," I said.

"A projectile was tossed at Jen. Would you rather I did nothing?" Quin asked.

"I would rather not be attacked by a vampire!" Drake shot back.

"You would be dead if I attacked you, First."

"Not likely."

"Um, guys." They paused the argument and turned their attention to me. "We're in the pocket of Mage Mountain. I get that this sucks, but there must be a reason they sent us here, so we should move. It's always winter here, and we're dressed for summer. Maybe we should concentrate on clothing and shelter instead of arguing."

They continued their argument.

I sighed. "If we can figure out where we are, I can flash us to Brumal, where I own a cabin that no one except me, Mat, and Emine knows about."

They still ignored me, so I fished my glamour earrings out of my pocket and put them in before trudging through the snow toward the road. Mage Mountain was in the mountains of Montana and differed from any other pocket. Instead of a major city center, it contained a collection of small, sparsely populated villages, and the weather ranged from light winter to deep winter. We were lucky because it was light winter season, so the snow wasn't as deep. The pocket was named because the mountain range held strange, colorful magic that shot into the air in rainbow plumes or bubbled up from the earth. No one could wield the magic, but it didn't stop paranormals from trying. Many had lost their lives thinking they'd be the ones who could wield it. It called to me like no other place. I'd never told anyone that and never planned to because it somehow felt too personal.

Teeth chattering, I wrapped my arms tighter around myself as I stood on the road and looked for signs of civilization. I ignored Drake and Quin as they appeared next to me. After a few seconds, I pointed. "Brumal is somewhere over there. If we follow this road and figure out where we are, I can flash us there."

"I can fly us in that direction," Drake said.

"Nope. The magic in Mage Mountain shoots down anyone who flies in this pocket."

"So, we have to walk?"

"Or flash. If he stays on the road, Quin can do his vampire fluid thing."

Quin pointed. "I hear signs of life in that direction."

As we trudged down the road, it started snowing. It wasn't the kind of light, fluffy snow that tickled your eyelashes and feathered the ground, but a slushy, sticky snow that stuck to everything it hit. I picked up my pace to stay warm, grateful that my healing magic was taking care of the frostbite as it formed. Neither Drake nor Quin seemed cold. I was pretty sure my lips were blue. Drake and Quin were ahead of me in a quiet discussion, probably still arguing. I tried to keep up, but they were much taller and less cold than me. As I tripped on a rock, I found myself on my hands and knees, the wet snow penetrating my bones even more. I was so tired I decided I needed to sit for a minute and rest, so I plopped my butt in the wet snow and rested my head on my knees. I couldn't remember why I was there, so I attempted to get up but tripped on my own feet and fell over sideways.

"Jenella! Stay with me."

I heard my name and pried an eye open. "Mmllbpt."

Warmth flooded me, and I wondered what was happening, but I couldn't think clearly enough to come up with anything. After a few minutes, my head cleared, and I could open my eyes. I found myself surrounded by dragon fire.

Quin appeared in my field of vision. "Do you not have the ability to control your temperature?"

"N...n...nope. Healing magic."

He rubbed his forehead. "That would have been nice to know before your episode."

"D...d...didn't think of it."

"Obviously." He turned his attention to Drake. "Shall I go into town and find proper attire, or can you glamour her some clothes?"

Drake lifted me to my feet and wrapped an arm around me. I snuggled into his warmth as he pointed to the trees. "Glamoured clothing won't keep her warm like real clothes will. I'll go over there and shift. My second form can keep her warm while you retrieve clothing."

"I shall return. Do try to stay alive." Quin disappeared.

Drake lifted me in his arms, and I burrowed into his chest and tried to ignore my violent shaking as he trudged into the trees. He set me down, and it was all I could do to keep my knees from buckling. My mouth fell open as he shifted…into a giant furry creature. I blinked a couple of times to make sure I wasn't hallucinating. The beast shook his long, black fur. I realized it was tipped with green, like his scales. I couldn't help the ragged giggle that escaped as he turned his koala bear head toward me. My smile melted when I noticed the razor-sharp teeth. I remember watching a human television show with a long-haired brown elephant as a kid. He looked like a version of that, except for his coloring and the lack of a trunk. And he was much, much bigger. Drake curled up under a tree and lifted his front leg, paw, or whatever. *Come here, Jenella.*

I stumbled toward him and climbed onto his leg. A giant, razor-sharp claw nudged me into his armpit and he brushed fur over me. Warmth engulfed me and I sunk into him. His wonderful wood smoke and spice scent, thick fur, and warmth wrapped around me in a gentle hug. *Thanks, Snuffy.* I sent the thought toward him.

Who's Snuffy?

A human TV character.

You're making fun of me.

No. I loved Snuffy when I was a kid.

Rest, Jenella.

Exhausted and more content than I'd been in a long time, I closed my eyes and snuggled closer.

Mean brown eyes with red and gold flecks peered down at me. "I should kill you and be done, but alas, it would ruin my plans." The man leaned forward, his breath so rancid I gagged. "You are pathetic." Fetid magic slammed into me, cracking a rib, and I screamed.

I came awake all tangled up in something and started punching and kicking, trying to get free.

"What is she doing?" a dry voice broke through my panic, followed by a feral growl.

My brain engaged, and I relaxed. Just a dream. No, it wasn't just a dream, but a memory. One that was as important as it was terrifying. I separated Drake's fur and peered out at Quin, who stood a few meters away, a pile of clothes in his arms. I climbed out of Drake's armpit. "Hey, Quin."

He eyed me briefly before depositing a pile of clothes in my arms. "I got a set of winter wear for each of us. The village is only a couple of kilometers down the road."

I peeled off my soaking wet clothes and scrambled into the warm winter ones. The clothes were thin and soft, made of hair with magically enhanced lining for warmth. Quin brought coats, pants, boots, and gloves for each of us. The clothes had a warming spell, and I let out a relieved sigh. "Thanks, Quin. That's much better."

He ignored me and stalked toward the road. "I heard conversations of unrest, so we should hurry. Can you manage that, or are you too fragile?"

"I am not fragile," I protested.

Drake patted my back. "Let's move out."

He set off at a jog, and I found it easier to keep up without hypothermia. Drake and Quin stayed with me, watching me like a couple of hawks. As we reached the edge of the village, we slowed to a walk. Quin guided us to the sidewalk that ran the length of the main road. The village was small, with a row of businesses on both sides of the main street and steep-roofed cottages built close together behind them. He pointed to a sign that read, "Vier Fontane". "Do you recognize this place?"

"No, but we could ask someone," I said, motioning to a group of robed figures in front of a building.

"Is this a Rübezahl village?" Drake asked.

Rübezahl were mountain people. They used to defend less fortunate humans and were revered as guardians of the mountains. They mostly prefer to keep to themselves these days. Their insular culture was steeped in tradition. They still wore traditional dress and took things like the golden rule seriously. "It looks like it. Do either of you have something I can offer as a gift?"

"Oh yes, I often carry random trinkets to offer Rübezahl," Quin answered.

I ignored him and unclasped my gold necklace. "I'm the least recognizable, so I'll ask." I strode toward a small store. "You guys stay here and try to be nice."

Drake raised an eyebrow. "Are you saying we are not nice?"

"No, I'm just reminding you that the Rübezahl are only hospitable to super nice people." I opened the door to the shop and gingerly stepped through.

The man behind the counter looked up, his eyes narrowing. "What do you want?"

I formed my face into what I hoped was a pleasant smile. "Good afternoon, guardian. I apologize for the unwelcome visit. Could you please let me know our current location in relation to Brumal? I brought a gift for the trouble." I held out the necklace.

He raised an eyebrow. "Are you trying to bribe me?"

I shook my head vigorously. "No. We need help and don't expect it for free." I set the necklace on the counter. "I would offer something more appropriate, but my friends and I are stranded here without our belongings."

He rubbed his chin. "You are being pursued by the bellicose."

My heart skipped a beat. "The bellicose?"

His eyes narrowed. "The rebellious. An organized group designed for no other reason than to overthrow you. We do not like this group, and they are not welcome here. Tell me why you, a First, and the vampire King are in our territory, Your Grace."

My face paled at the realization that he could see through my glamour. "Um. Well, uh.."

"Do not lie."

I held up a finger. "Wasn't going to, but it's a long story."

He crossed his arms.

I told him about the battle and the teleportation device that dropped us there, skipping the part where I got hypothermia. I clarified I didn't know why they dumped us near this village. When I was done, he uncrossed his arms and leaned on the counter. "They wanted us to take care of their problem. They have been active here for the last few weeks, but have steered clear of the Rübezahl villages. We wondered if you were aware."

I shook my head. "We knew they were stirring up trouble, but not that they were active in Mage Mountain. No one has reported disturbances here."

He stared at me unblinking for so long that I had to fight not to fidget. "Very well." He reached behind him, pulled out a piece of paper, and drew on it. "You are here." He pointed to the paper, and I stepped forward. "Brumal is here."

The map was a detailed hand drawing of the entire pocket of Mage Mountain. I leaned forward to see it better. "This is amazing."

He inclined his head. "You can follow this road, but do not deviate from it and do not split up. Most of my people are peaceful, but you are not the downtrodden, so we do not have the desire to protect you."

I slid the necklace toward him. "Thank you, guardian. And please let me know if these...bellicose cause your people any problems."

I stepped out of the shop and flipped my hood up, motioning Drake and Quin to follow. When they fell in beside me, I picked up the pace. The gray-robed figures filled the street and stood as still as statues, glaring at us as we went by, but didn't pursue. When we reached the end of the village, they turned as one and went about their business.

When we were far enough away, I pointed south. "Brumal is that way on the other side of the pocket."

"Can you flash there?" Drake asked, scanning the forest.

I had no idea. I'd never flashed that far without the help of flashing circles, and it would take a lot of energy to flash myself and two extra people that distance. "Yes, but the guardian told me to stay on the road. He called the pursuers bellicose. Does that ring a bell with either of you?"

They both stopped in their tracks. I continued walking. "I'll take that as a yes."

"Are you sure he used the word bellicose?" Quin asked.

"Yes. He said it was a rebellion designed to overthrow the crown. He knew who we were. Said the bellicose have been causing problems in Mage Mountain." I glanced at Quin. "That didn't come up in your investigation?"

"If you mean the case that you keep trying to poach, then no. Very few consider Mage Mountain a hospitable pocket and, therefore, don't pay it much attention."

"A perfect place to set up a rebellion."

Quin grunted in agreement. "If they knew who we were, why did they let us pass?"

"The guardian didn't say, and I didn't ask. He made it clear that we needed to stay on the road, though." I pointed down the road. "When we get around that bend, I'll flash us out of here."

Chapter 22

We landed in front of the cabin in Brumal, and I guided us through the wards and put my hand on the access panel. A quick prick to check my blood and the door opened. The cabin wasn't big. Downstairs was an open concept, with pine floors, high ceilings, and log beams running across them. Multicolored rugs adorned the floor. The back of the room had a farmhouse-style kitchen with quartz countertops. In front of the island was a wooden table with six chairs. The solid wooden stairs that led up to the four bedrooms, each with their own bath, were on the left and had a powder room under them.

Drake started a fire in the fireplace, and I took the stairs up to the master bedroom, shedding my new winter clothes. A brownie took care of the place most of the time, so it was dust-free, and everything worked. I put on some of my own clothes and headed to the kitchen. The magichef was empty and off. My visits to that place were limited to about once or twice per year. I had the delusion that I could make it my own home when I was younger. I was twenty when I realized that would never happen.

"I'm going into town to see if I can find a phone," I announced.

Quin was nowhere to be seen. Drake nodded once as he opened the magichef and peered inside. So I bundled up and headed out.

The sun was near the horizon as I stepped out the door. The cabin sat outside the town at the foot of the mountain. I grinned as I watched colorful magic shoot from it in giant plumes and small puffs. Every strand was a different color. The colors never blended before they dissipated. There were a thousand tones, some I'd never seen anywhere except that pocket. In the center was what looked like a rainbow waterfall shooting from one crevice to another. A puff blew out twenty feet above my head, and I watched it swirl around a tree before disappearing. Nothing was more beautiful than that magic of the mountain.

Shouts from the town drew me out of my euphoria, and my head snapped toward them. I could see people running, some fighting, and others on rooftops with bows, arrows, and guns. "Down!" someone shouted from across the street.

I hit the ground just as a giant snowball flew by and hit a group of people in black snowsuits, flattening them. Someone grabbed the back of my coat and yanked me up. "Which side are you on?"

"I'm just going to the store!" I shouted over the growing crowds of people fighting.

The woman yanked me between two buildings and pushed me up against the wall. "So you're on our side."

She was a medium-powered mage that I'd seen in town before. I noted the smattering of freckles across her nose before focusing on her big brown eyes. "Yeah. I have a cabin here. What's going on?"

She rolled her eyes. "Some idiots thought they would take over the town and control the mountain. Happens every few years."

I'd heard the stories, but not that they went so far as to take over the towns around the mountain. It didn't surprise me that some were arrogant enough to believe they could control the magic. Trying to take control of a town frequented by mountain guardians and sasquatch was just plain stupid. "What can I do to help?"

"Do you fight?"

"I'm no warrior, but I can fight when necessary."

"Great. Stay close and try to disable as many as possible." She took off.

I ran after her, dodging stray magic blasts and throwing some back. It was easy to tell what side people were on. The townspeople wore regular clothes, and the invaders wore dark snowsuits with scarves and goggles covering their faces. I caught up with the local mage. "Doesn't get more cartoon villain than those snowsuits."

She laughed. "No shit. These guys aren't even that powerful."

They weren't, but there were a lot of them. I watched one create a small ice sculpture and toss it at the head of a man in a red hat. Another threw spells at the snow, turning it into ice. Dumb since the locals all wore spelled ice grips on their shoes. Most of the bad guys didn't seem to have their hearts in the fight and were only making a minimal effort. They knew controlling Mage Mountain was impossible.

An arm came around my neck, and I kicked the guy in the shin and blasted him with the tiniest thread of shredding magic. He hit the ground, screaming. The ruling magic pushed at its restraints. I wrapped it tighter as I ran across the street, throwing sleeping magic into a crowd.

I darted down an alley and stopped. Three men in jeans guarded a door. I didn't know whose side they were on, so I held off attacking them. One pointed at me, and two shifted into chimeras. The other threw a spell. I ducked around a corner as the spell hit. I flashed behind the witch, kicked the side of his knee, and blasted a chimera with sleeping magic. The other chimera's snake head struck at me, and I hit it with raw magic. He slammed into the wall. I took a blow to the head at the same time someone hit me from behind, and I landed on my face. The chimera dug a knee into my back.

"Get this bitch, Jack."

I hated that name. It was too close to the name of the sadistic brother that once made my life hell. The ruling magic vibrated so hard that I had difficulty keeping it from unraveling. A claw pierced my shoulder, and fetid breath tickled the back of my neck. I tuned my inherent magic to sleeping magic and jammed my hand toward a paw. He moved it at the last second and lunged toward my neck. I let the ruling magic go. The chimera hit the wall with a yelp. I crouched, ready to fight.

The entire town fell silent. I fixed my hat and peeked around the corner. "Oops," I said at the multiple bodies littering the town. The ruling magic snapped out further than I intended. I reeled it back in and brushed off my pants. I tiptoed toward the door, unsure how long the sleeping magic would last. The building used to be a feed store, but it was closed the last couple of times I came here. "What were they guarding?" I crept up to the door and tried to listen through it, but I didn't hear anything. I turned the knob, careful not to jostle my pierced shoulder. The door was unlocked, so I slipped inside and quietly shut it behind me.

The front of the store was boarded up, so it was dark except for a bare lightbulb in the center. A newly built cinder-block wall about five feet tall partitioned the front and back. I tiptoed to the edge and peeked around the corner. Rows and rows of supplies filled the building. Everything from weapons to potion ingredients to home goods and clothing.

I peeked into an office. Four unconscious guys slumped at a table. They'd been loading bullets into guns when my sleeping magic hit. I sensed the same magic we thought was mind-control coming from them.

I gathered a couple of laptops and shoved them and their chargers into a bag, along with papers that were scattered across a desk. Then, I moved on to a filing cabinet. It mainly was old financial information for a legitimate business. I flipped through the files and was about to shut the drawer when I noticed a newer file jammed into the center. I pulled it out and flipped it open. It was older than I thought. The pages were handwritten with a ballpoint pen. I flipped through them, seeing the word "hybrid" on a few of them. I shoved that in the bag, too.

The outside door burst open, and boots thudded at the entrance to the building. I grabbed the bag, bolted to the far corner, wedged behind a shelf, and wrapped my magic tighter. Enforcers streamed in and fanned out, clearing the building before turning their attention to the unconscious men. One headed in my direction and stopped at my hiding spot. My heart raced, and I tried to slow it and keep my breathing as quiet as possible.

The man, a shifter, sniffed a couple of times and scanned the shelves, his eyes skipping right over my spot before moving away to help the others. I let out the breath I'd been holding as they gathered the men and started to leave. One of them stopped by a box of clothes and bedding. "What do you suppose they had going on here, Colonel?"

A woman broke off from the others and joined him. "Nothing good. This place reeks of that mind-control magic. Mark it, and let's move on."

They marked the door with a large "X" and shut it with a click.

I waited a few minutes and left the building. I remembered the empty magichef and flashed to the grocery store. Once I had grabbed four fabric bags, I stopped. I should have asked Drake what to get because I didn't have a clue about how to go grocery shopping. I shrugged, deciding it couldn't be that hard. Without a plan, I gathered vegetables, fruits, and meats in bags, purchased a prepaid phone, and proceeded to the checkout. Everyone in the village was asleep, including the employees. Guilt over stealing threatened to overtake me as I flashed the groceries back to the cabin. Drake lounged on the couch, a bottle of water in his hand. There was a giant plate of meat in front of him. I set the groceries on the counter and rubbed my face. Drake had culinary magic. I didn't even need to get groceries with him here.

"What happened to you?" he asked.

My eyes rolled as I pulled the heavy backpack off my shoulders and set it on the table. "I may have got caught up in a rebellion and put the entire town to sleep. They were using an abandoned store as a warehouse, and I took a bunch of information." I paused. "Don't tell Mat."

Quin sat at the kitchen island with a phone in his hand. I guess I didn't need to get a phone, either. He set it down. "I'm not sharing the payment for this case with you."

"Really, Quin? All of that, and you're worried about me poaching your case?"

"Yes." He rifled through the papers I pulled out of the backpack.

"I'm not poaching your case. I accidentally found information and took it. No need to mention I was involved at all."

Drake slid into a chair beside me and plugged in a laptop. He looked as sad as Bastien did on the transport. I opened my mouth to ask but realized my concern was the last thing an ancient First needed. I eyed the groceries and moved toward the magichef to try and figure out how to put them away. "Does anyone need anything?"

Neither of them answered. They were both engrossed in the information I stole.

"Quin, do you want something to eat?"

"No. I have contacted Bastien, Mat, Ara, and Tracy to let them know we are alive. Any other notifications needed?"

"No." I pondered the magichef. Drake had already restocked it, but I pulled the groceries out and tried to decide where to put them. I figured it couldn't be too difficult. I crammed a few vegetables in when Drake came in and leaned against the counter, watching. He reached past me, rearranged things, and pointed to labels I hadn't noticed. Amusement danced in his eyes. "I'll take care of this."

"Sure. Not that I needed to bother." I sucked at basic life skills.

I dragged my butt upstairs and tore off my torn and bloody clothes, and washed up. I threw on a pair of leggings, an oversized long-sleeve t-shirt, and thick socks. When I returned to the kitchen, Drake pulled a couple of sandwiches out of the magichef and set them on the kitchen table. Quin was nowhere in sight.

"Did you find anything in that laptop?" I asked as I eyed the sandwiches.

He tapped his fingers on the table. "Not yet. I hoped to find out where my aunt..." he waved a dismissive hand.

I cleared my throat. "Is that why you and Bastien are so sad? Because the queen is missing?" I held up a hand before he could protest. "Anyone with half a brain can see something's off about her absence, so don't lie or brush me off."

"She is not at her horde. It may have been compromised. We have looked everywhere but still don't know where she went."

"Do you think these bellicose idiots have her?"

"It's one theory. I can't understand how they would have gotten to her, though. Most of the dragons we've found mind-controlled are weak in both magic and might. The impact would be much more evident if the queen was willingly helping them."

My gaze landed on the papers I stole. "I'm sorry. I can't imagine how painful that must be for you and Bastien."

Drake rubbed his hands over his face. "I was twenty-five when they chose me to come to this realm. I hadn't even developed my second form at the time. The dragons who ruled wanted a multidrakelandarnarian to come here. There were only three of us, and the other two were mated. Both my aunt and mother were queens in different provinces. The rulers, including my mother, chose me. The day we went through the portal, my mother didn't even show. She thought it was a cruel joke that her heir was a male and abandoned me as a hatchling, so my aunt, her twin, raised me as one of her own. I think I told you that."

"Yes."

"Deva showed up like she always did, along with three hundred of her most loyal followers, and sat on the outskirts during the ceremony. I remember thinking how lucky I was to find my purpose so young as

I stepped through that portal to join the other Firsts." Drake paused, a reminiscent smile lighting his face. "I was so naïve. We were all very young and thought of it as a grand adventure. We began trekking through the desert we'd been dumped in before they closed the portal. There was a loud roar, and three hundred dragons, led by my aunt, flew through the portal. We watched in horror as they blew it up."

My eyes were as big as saucers. "I've read similar accounts in history books, but don't think I ever believed it."

"Deva loved me like a son and believed that family should stick together. She was livid that the other rulers insisted on sending me away. She gathered the family and followed. The other Firsts were not happy. They shunned me and later forbade me from creating my own magical species using the excuse that I already had one. I didn't care. I didn't want to create my own species and was content staying with my family. Playing with my young cousins was such a joy. Eventually, the other dragons began to resent me for being stranded here, and they would have shunned me, too, if not for my aunt."

"Wait. Bastien played as a kid?" I couldn't imagine the grump playing and laughing.

Drake chuckled. "As you know, being an heir is not easy. He was once very playful. Funny, even. His responsibilities and the expectations of being a rare male heir jaded him."

I shook my head over dramatically. "I don't believe you." Another thought struck me. "You said the third born of a third clutch is always a multidrakelandarnarian, but Bastien isn't."

My heart sank when the sparkle left Drake's eyes. "He is the third born of the queen's only clutch. He is also the sole survivor. One of the other Firsts decided to wipe out the queen and her family. He got her mate and two kids, but not her or Bastien. She could not have more children without her mate, so the heir's magic passed to Bastien."

My eyes stung with tears. "That's awful."

"It was a long time ago, and no, your grandmother wasn't responsible. She was a good and fair leader. Lissa didn't treat me differently than any other First. She even told me I could make my own magical race. I considered her a friend."

I found the Firsts fascinating. "What about Jonas?"

"Jonas has always kept to himself. He is and forever will be more concerned about the welfare of shifters than politics. My point is I love my aunt and would do anything for her. I am frustrated that I haven't reestablished myself enough to do more to find her."

"We'll find her." It was out of my mouth before my brain engaged. I knew I shouldn't offer since it was Quin's case, but the feeling of the moment and the utter devastation on Drake's face were too much for me not to try to do something. "I'll work with Quin, and we'll get her home safely."

"You would do this for us? Even though we have never contributed much to the coalition?"

"Sure. And the dragons are part of the coalition. By staying neutral, you *have* contributed, considering you are strong enough to take it over..." I stopped when the realization hit me, my eyes going wide. "The dragons are strong enough to take over the coalition." I slapped a hand on Drake's arm. "That's what they're trying to do, these bellicose."

Drake raised an eyebrow. "You're just now figuring that out?"

"No. Yes. No. I figured out they can't. The mind control magic isn't strong enough. That's why they only picked low-level supernaturals as targets. I need to talk to Quin." I patted his arm as I hopped off the stool and headed for the coat rack.

Quin was on the roof, leaning against the chimney. He had a sword in one hand and a cloth in the other as he cleaned the blade. He didn't bother to blend into the shadows. I flashed up and grabbed the chimney to steady myself. "I figured something out."

Quin didn't look up from his task. "Of course you did."

I told him about my revelation, then paused. "There's something else. I recognized the magic they're using for mind control, or at least part of it."

His cleaning stopped, and the sword disappeared. "Tell me."

"It's the same magic Jaques had."

"And you know this how?"

My stomach flipped, and I cleared my throat, "Becauseheusedittotortureme."

Quin's expression didn't change. "I see. And have you told your brother about the type of magic?"

"When I was stuffed in Drake's armpit, trying to get warm, I figured it out. I have dreams and...well...there you go."

Noticing the unusual amount of activity, I examined the town as I waited for him to respond. There were a lot of Enforcers running around. A black transport vehicle blocked the main intersection, and others patrolled the streets. Several tall sasquatches carried unconscious people, loading them in the vehicles. They seemed to be separating them by the type of clothes or maybe by who had mind control implants. I motioned to the town. "We need to leave tonight."

"That sounds like a marvelous idea." His tone suggested otherwise.

My shoulders slumped. "Are you always sarcastic?"

"No. Sometimes I'm more sarcastic. It's useful when dealing with idiots."

"I bet." I went back to watching the activity, ignoring that he called me an idiot.

Quin's eyes darted to me before landing back on the town. "We need to figure out a mode of transportation."

"We as in us, or we as in me?"

"As in you. You are still my apprentice."

"Nothing in the apprentice rules makes me obligated to do that. In case you haven't noticed, I'm inept when handling life's little details. After all, I have already gone above and beyond by providing free food and shelter.

Not to mention all the information I've passed on without attempting to steal your case. Unless you're saying you need the help of an idiot apprentice. If so, I'll be glad to find us a transport."

"Manipulation is unbecoming of a detective." Quin's creepy magic grew more intense, making the hair on my arms stand up.

"Says the vampire."

Chapter 23

DRAKE SAT AT THE table, concentrating on a laptop, when we let ourselves in the front door. "What are you two up to?"

I removed my coat and boots. "Can you use your glamour skills so we can take a transport back to Allure?" If we could all use Drake's glamour skills, we could sneak past the Enforcers and to the castle unnoticed. I wished I could change mine. I hated that so many people knew my identity because it made me feel like I was being trapped in a cage, the door closing a millimeter with each person who knew. Unfortunately, too many people also knew what Detective Hendrix looked like.

"I can glamour myself, but not Tarquin. Even multidrakelandarnarian magic does not work on vampires."

"I'm sure Quin can hide himself. Do you need a watch or something for your glamour?"

"I don't need a trinket to glamour myself, but it does take a lot of energy."

He had dark circles under his eyes. I reached for my phone out of habit and realized I couldn't make transport reservations without it. The prepaid phone was in a bag on the counter, so I dug it out. "We should all get some sleep and take the first transport out in the morning if there is one." Transports didn't run to Mage Mountain daily. "What is the significance of the Bellicose?"

Drake frowned. "The Bellicose is an ancient secret society. I don't know much about the modern organization, but they began when the first queen formed the coalition. They were the opposition. We crushed them. There are rumors that they were responsible for the death of the second queen and her mate. That might be why Mat never told you about them."

I sucked in a breath at the nonchalant way he talked about my parents' deaths. I understood he hated my mother and thought she put him to sleep, but that was a little harsh. On top of that, I was getting sick of being the last to know everything. Mat and Helen used the excuse of my safety to keep me ignorant, and the gap in my knowledge pissed me off. "So, these guys killed our parents, pursued us relentlessly for nearly a year, and no one ever did anything about them? Not even Mat?"

Drake blinked. "Mat killed a great many of them, from what I'm told. Is he not nicknamed the bloody prince?" His lips twitched at my flat stare. "I'm sure others tried, but they move in secrecy, so there's no telling who their members are."

I suddenly had an overwhelming need to do something. The ruling magic vibrated violently, and I leaned my head back and took a couple of deep breaths. I knew by the attack on our transport that they were after me. "Can all dragons see through my glamour?"

"No. Not even I can see through it well."

My muscles relaxed a little. It wasn't the first time I wondered if my identity would hold. At the rate people found out about it, I doubted I'd have freedom for very long. Which meant I needed to figure this out while I had anonymity and the freedom to move around. "What is their end goal? I get it's a rebellion against me taking the throne, but what's their plan after they take it?"

"From what I remember, they are interested in power. When the coalition began, they wanted to set paranormals up as gods and enslave humans. I don't know about the ones who currently exist. Mathias would, though."

I was five years away from being forced to be a full queen. It made sense that they wanted to cut me down before I established myself. It was also why Mat insisted that I figure out my magic as fast as possible. He probably knew about the bellicose long before that dragon crashed into the ward in Allure.

The mind control was new, though. I was sure of it. I bet that they were using it to grow their organization and keep us occupied. It gave them time to slip their spies into our ranks. I couldn't let that happen. I needed to get back to Allure and figure this out. Mat was probably already doing that and didn't bother to tell me, as usual. The memory of finding the diaries inside the wall crossed my mind, and I decided to prioritize studying them. If I was going to figure out how to beat these guys, I needed to know how my grandmother did it.

The only transport leaving for Allure was scheduled for dawn. Reaching Allure from Brumal only took about twenty minutes. Quin begrudgingly set up the new phone, and I managed to make reservations.

We slipped onto the transport after being scanned for mind control magic by Enforcers. I don't know how Drake created an ID spell for himself, and I didn't ask. Drake separated himself from me as we stepped on the transport. He disguised himself as a deer shifter with long blonde hair and a thin body. Normally, I would have laughed at the contrast from his bulky form, but I was too tired. I leaned back and closed my eyes the entire way home.

We filed off the transport and headed to the flashing circle just outside. Drake blended into the crowd and stayed behind me. I hadn't seen Quin since we left the cabin, but for once, I had my senses engaged, so I knew he was close by. As I stepped into the flashing circle, Drake casually approached and asked for a ride. I slapped a hand on his arm and flashed us to the hidden family circle at the castle.

I took out my glamour earrings and turned to check on Drake, who had already morphed back into himself.

Helen and George met us at the door. Two pairs of cold eyes swept over Drake. "What happened to you, Jenella?" Helen asked as Quin swept through the door.

Mat entered the kitchen and stopped short, scanning everyone. Tracy darted around him. "What the heck happened? I mean, we were taking care of business one minute, and the next, you were gone. I didn't even see you disappear. Some guard I am."

I couldn't help but grin. "A mage threw some kind of portal device at me. Quin tried to intercept, and it took us all."

"Why would they send you to Mage Mountain?" she asked.

"We don't know, but we think they were trying to get the Rübezahl to take me out. The portal dumped us near one of their villages. What are you doing here? I thought you'd be at the house."

Tracy hitched a thumb over her shoulder. "Mat wanted me to stay here because it's more secure."

My head snapped to Mat. "You decided you needed to guard my guard?"

"Yes. She is the only guard you've accepted since Bastien stepped down. I do not want anything to happen to her."

I didn't roll my eyes, though I wanted to. My attention turned to George and Helen, who were peppering Drake with questions.

"Why did you jump into battle?" Mat growled.

I lifted my chin. "That I needed to protect the people on the transport." I raised a hand when he started to argue. "Even with my magic issues, I am still one of the most powerful supernaturals. I wasn't going to send my friends out there to fight while I cowered in some ejection pod. I did the right thing, and you know it."

His jaw clenched. "Friends…"

"Alright, maybe not friends, but you know what I mean." I kept forgetting that they weren't my friends.

"You are a queen, not a warrior. You need to think about the coalition before you sacrifice yourself so easily. The right thing to do would have been to stay safe."

Drake threw his head back and laughed.

"Do you have something to say, First?"

"Jenella took down four mages, six dragons, successfully negotiated with the Rübezahl, and stopped a rebellion. Those are the actions of both a warrior and a queen. On top of that, she had me and Tarquin at her side, so she was hardly alone and vulnerable." He leaned forward. "Your little sister may not be who you want her to be, but she is extraordinary."

My mouth dropped open. No one ever stood up to Mat except me and Emine. I cleared my throat, "Um––"

Quin cut me off. "Jen stumbled through it, but the outcome was satisfactory. She will make a great warrior queen should she pull her head out of her ass."

I rubbed my face with both hands, ignoring Tracy's chuckle. "I get that you're worried about my safety, Mat. And Quin is right. I do need to think through things more before I act. But I can't just sit on the sidelines and watch people be killed because I think I'm too important to help."

"Then you need to learn." Mat didn't quite yell, but it was close.

Helen put a hand on Mat's arm. "When canning, it is important to ensure that the pressure cooker is tightly sealed to create a stable environment for sterilization. It is equally important to slowly allow the pressure out at the proper time. If not, the batch could go bad. Bacteria can grow, or the pot will explode."

Mat blinked. "I don't see what that has to do with Jenella's safety."

Helen's eyes turned hard. "Jenella has been in a properly sealed pressure cooker her whole life, and you waited too long to crack the seal. When you did, you sent her out into the world rather than allowing her to slowly integrate. You cannot blame anyone but yourself that she is spoiled from being in the pressure cooker too long and has exploded into life."

"So now I'm a canned good?"

Helen patted my cheek. "Of course not, love. But you are spoiled and fighting for your independence decisively." She turned to Mat. "Now that she is out of the pot, Jenella will not be more careful because you demand it. She needs to learn these things for herself."

Mat's eyebrows drew together. "And the whole coalition could pay the price if we lose her."

I fought back tears, my fatigue suddenly bone deep. "Right. Because the institution is more important than people's lives or the mages fighting for Brumal in Mage Mountain." I shook my head, "I am not suicidal and don't plan on getting myself killed. But that doesn't mean I'm going to sit back and let these Bellicose idiots mind control people."

"There are other ways to deal with them," Mat said.

I waved a hand. "I'm sure there are, but that's not how it played out, and I'm too tired to go over the what-ifs right now. It's time for me to get some sleep." I headed toward the elevator to the family quarters. Turning to Drake and Quin, I said, "Sorry you had to witness this ongoing family spat."

I headed to my suite, Tracy on my heels. "Are you really okay?"

"I am. We got lucky that they dumped us in a place I recognized. I'll tell you all about it later, I promise."

She eyed me for a few seconds. "Okay. Get some sleep, and then we'll go home. I mean, the castle is nice, but I don't know how you put up with being locked down all those years. It's driving me stir-crazy, and it's only been a day."

I grinned. "I didn't know any different." And it beat being hunted down and slaughtered, but I didn't say that because it would justify Mat's decisions. I slipped into my apartment and flopped down on the bed, asleep before I even pulled the covers up. I dreamed of flying over a dense forest on the back of a green and black dragon.

After my nap, I checked in with Verity, who handed me a schedule, telling me I was expected to attend hearings later in the week. I was still grumpy as Tracy, and I put on our glamour and headed toward our house. As we went through the front gate, I waved at the raccoon shifter next door who sat on her porch watching over her many children, tearing something apart in the front yard.

After settling in, I went to the office and stacked some of my grandmother's diaries on the desk. I checked my messages, ignoring the three from Mat. Emine had sent me a list of theft victims from the Bank of Mahri. It didn't take me long to realize there was only one victim from each supernatural race, none as rich and powerful as Jedediah. I sat back and considered that. My current theory was that the bellicose used the money to fund their operation. If that were the reason, why would they only take money from one wealthy person and several middle-class people instead of targeting the rich and powerful? I wondered if I'd ever solve my case. I rubbed my eyes and turned back to my grandmother's diaries.

With a finger, I traced her name on the cover of the top one. "Lissa," I muttered. I'd never met her and wondered what she was like. Since my mother's pristine image had been shattered with Drake's information, I wasn't sure I could trust what I'd been taught about my grandmother. I opened the diary and began to read.

It took me forever to read ancient Mahri. After the first few entries, I realized the diaries weren't my grandmother's personal thoughts but more of a chronological account of events beginning with a meeting of the Firsts where they hashed out the formation of the coalition. I was so immersed in it, I had to drag my gritty eyes away when Tracy came in. "What's up?"

"You were going to fill me in on what happened when you disappeared."

I marked my page and closed the diary. "What did you want to know?"

She wiggled her eyebrows. "Spill everything, including why the First defended you."

I told her everything, waited for her to stop laughing at me for being stuck in Drake's armpit to get warm, and watched her face grow grim through the rest. "So, the mountain guardians think this Bellicose group is active and renamed themselves the Sentinels?"

"Yes. Not only that, neither Drake nor Quin was surprised. That means Mat probably already knew and didn't tell me."

"I mean, Drake and Quin are ancients, so they're not surprised by much. Plus, don't you think Mat would tell you something that big?"

"Not if he thought he was protecting me."

"But he *did* tell you about a rebellion. He just didn't name them. I mean, it's not like he's maliciously holding back information. I think you need to have a serious talk with him."

I let out a long breath. Tracy was right, but I didn't want to discuss it, so I changed the subject. "What's up with Bastien?"

She frowned. "What do you mean?"

"The queen is missing, and he's sad. He needs you. I get that you hide your match because of the stigma surrounding mixed-magic couples. But he needs you right now."

She sighed. "We've been mated and hiding it for ten years. In all that time, he's needed my help exactly zero times. He won't even talk to me about it."

Bastien and Tracy were the only people in my life who were always truthful with me, and the thought that he didn't rely on her made me a little sad. "That's not okay."

"Yeah." She held up her hands. "He loves his mother more than me, I think. Maybe. It's hard to tell with him. Did you know that when you first suggested I take this job, I thought you would treat me like crap? I was going to refuse. Bastien talked me into it to keep me close and protect me, but he won't let me do the same for him. He also won't announce our status because he's afraid the witches will kill me."

"The witches seem to like shunning people over death, though after what you told me about your grandmother, he might have a point. Wait. Why would I treat you like crap?" I remembered how I ditched, ignored, pranked, and snarked at my previous guards. I held up a hand. "Never mind. I was pretty terrible to some guards. In my defense, Mat kept giving me people who were void of personality and weak enough that I'd end up guarding them if anything happened."

Her brilliant smile shone through the glamour. "That's what I told Bastien. My theory was that you respected him because he was powerful and confident. I mean, it made sense. And that was before I saw the strength it takes you to wrangle that ruling magic. I bet it lashed out at every opportunity."

"I liked Bastien because he's the only person who is always honest with me. Or he was until you and Quin came along. The ruling magic wasn't as strong back then, but that was part of it. With your power level and your personality, you have nothing to worry about."

Her eyebrows drew together. "My personality?"

"Meaning you have one. One of the first guards Mat hired after Bastien left was so terrified of me that the 'Your Graces' drove me nuts. I had to decree that she wasn't allowed to call me that. She couldn't handle it and quit. Another one said maybe two words to me the entire time, so I'd make a game out of trying to get him to talk. They were good people, but I hated every minute I spent with them. Bastien would have kicked my ass if I'd even thought to try some of that stuff with him. Not that I would have."

Tracy grinned. "I've heard the stories about jump scares."

"Every chance I got. It's probably why Quin does it to me."

"What about the fake door that led to the pool?"

"Not my proudest moment. That lady almost drowned. Who knew that guerilla shifters can't swim?"

She shook her head. "I spent the first few weeks looking around every corner, expecting something. When you blew up the magichef, I thought it was a prank."

I sighed. "You don't have to worry. It was more of a message to Mat than anything else, and I've been done with all that for a while now. Part of growing up, I guess. Besides, I actually like you, so...."

She nodded. "Bastien said you were a bit of a hellion and a trouble magnet, which you are, but you're not as bad as all that."

"Gee, thanks. Now, let's get back to why Bastien won't let you support him." I wiggled my eyebrows.

We were interrupted when the wards in the back of the house pinged. She'd spelled the back alley to cloak our visitors so Mat and Bastien could come and go without our neighbors noticing. Not that Bastien needed the spell. Dragons could cloak themselves from other paranormals.

Tracy jumped out of the chair and went to greet them. I leaned back and stretched, thinking about all the times I was awful to my guards and wondering if I could help Tracy and Bastien. I quit being an ass after the near drowning. Helen asked me if that was the person I wanted to be, and I decided that it wasn't. I ignored the guards after that. But I'd never treat Tracy like that because I respected her. Maybe I should remind Bastien that respect is a two-way street.

Tracy poked her head into the room. "Drake and Bastien are here."

I already knew who it was, but hoped to stay in my office. "Want to spell your face neon green and tell Bastien I pranked you?"

She snorted. "We totally should do that one day."

Chapter 24

Drake and Bastien sat at the table, coffee in their hands. I nudged Drake's shoulder as I sat. "I thought you were going to get some rest."

Sad green eyes focused on me. "We have a lot of work to do."

"Doesn't mean you don't need sleep."

Bastien nodded. "I tried to tell him that, but he won't listen. You have come a long way from that scrappy little girl who got the best of the shifter kids."

High praise coming from Bastien. "Thanks. Why are you guys here?"

Bastien's eyes flicked to Tracy before focusing on me. I decided it meant he wanted to check on her. "My mother is missing. We've looked everywhere. I can feel her bond, but can't get to her." He ran a hand through his black hair. "They might be using her magic as the source of mind control."

I sighed. "Those devices aren't laced with your mom's magic."

Drake put his hand on mine. "Tell us about that magic. You recognize it, and it bothers you."

It did, but only because of the type of magic I sensed. "I can't tell you much about it until I talk to Mat." It was the safest answer. No reason to get everyone stirred up. I'd already told Quin, and that was enough.

The front wards pinged, and Tracy got up and went to the door. I heard the voice of our raccoon shifter neighbor, Penelope, and got up to peer out the window.

I frowned, realizing something was off. Not only was Penelope talking too fast, but the rest of the neighborhood was quiet. Tracy thanked her and shut the door. "Jen, do you think you can flash us to the castle?"

"Yes. Why?"

She peeked through the blinds. "Penelope said three chimeras were snooping around, and a dragon broke her wards and landed in her yard. I mean, it scared her enough that she said her family is in hiding and thought we should hide, too."

"It's a trap," Bastien said.

Tracy nodded. "Yeah. They're trying to lure Jen outside the wards. Do you think they know who Jen really is?"

I flinched. "I doubt it. If they did, they'd send more than one dragon and a couple of chimeras. Especially if they knew Drake and Bas were here."

"Agreed." Bastien rubbed his chin. "You two flash from the yard to the flashing circle and get to the castle. Drake and I will handle this."

Tracy started weaving a spell as she strode toward the back door. "I'm going to send a spy spell to scope out the neighborhood and make sure the flashing circle is safe. It might be best if we stay inside our wards. Either that or blow our cover and let Bas and Drake get us out of here."

"No need to use a spy spell." I used my new ruling magic senses. "There's five chimeras scattered up and down our street. One is at the circle. I couldn't sense the cloaked dragon. Does your camouflage magic keep you from being sensed by other paranormals, Bas?"

Bas shrugged. "Some dragons have cloaking magic where they can completely disappear, but not all."

Tracy peeked out the window. "I should go out there and see what they want."

"Absolutely not," Bastien protested.

"Tracy's right. If that dragon is mind-controlled, which is likely, he won't hesitate to do what he's compelled to do by whoever is pulling his strings, including hurt kids." I paced, thinking. "The question is, are they even here for us? They're at Penelope's house. I think the Bellicose has been recruiting low to mid-level paranormals. This neighborhood is full of them."

"True..." Tracy said. "And everyone is hiding, which means they know what's going on."

"Yeah. Or at least they sense that something's not right." I turned to Drake. "We need to see if the dragon knows anything. Can you get through with your mental magic?"

Drake shook his head. "He's got the same singular thought process as the dragon who cracked the ward. I think it's the same guy. He's looking for Detective Hendrix and thought the raccoon house was yours. The chimeras are as singular-minded and ready to ambush you."

Bastien put a hand on Tracy's shoulder. "So, they're all mind-controlled."

Drake eyed Bastien's hand. "Yes."

I picked up my phone. "Should we stay here or do something about it? I'm going to text Emine." That done, I headed to my office, locking the diaries in a spelled safe. I grabbed a set of daggers that Mat gave six-year-old me to defend myself. I rubbed the family crest on the handle and brushed the memory away as I strapped them on my hips.

When I returned to the kitchen, Tracy and Bastien stood in the corner, quietly arguing. Drake leaned against the wall as he calmly observed them.

"What did we decide?"

Tracy hefted her pack of potions. "We're going to wait for the Enforcers. Bas will deal with the dragon."

Something hit the wards hard. Tracy and I both grabbed our heads. Another hit came, along with a magic surge. The wards held, but our ears were still ringing. I staggered to the back door and peered out the window. A turquoise dragon stood in the back alley, his neck stretched, examining the wards. The front and side wards pinged with several more hits, followed by an onslaught of magic.

"The wards will hold," Tracy said.

Bastien shoved me out of the way. "That might be true, but we can't risk it. Drake and I are limited inside the house, and we need to bring that dragon in to answer for his crimes."

"We'll go out the front. You two go out the back and distract that dragon until we take care of the chimeras," Drake said as they slipped out the front door.

As we entered the backyard, the dragon drew back his head and blew a stream of fire at us. It bounced off our wards and hit a nearby tree. Tracy threw a spell and put it out. "What do you want?"

I felt a tingle in my head, and the ruling magic lashed out at the dragon. He shook his head. Then he went nuts, pounding his weight and magic against the wards. I rubbed my temples. "What did he say?"

"That he is here to collect the detective, meaning you." The wards crashed, and the dragon charged. Tracy pulled a potion out of her bag and threw it at him. "Bas! What the hell do you think you're doing?"

"Bas took down our wards?"

"Yep. Get the hell out of here, Jen!"

I had to duck, bob, and weave as the dragon flapped his wings while he tried to get his balance. I sensed the mind control magic in his right leg and headed in that direction. "He's under mind control. Right leg."

"Get down!" Tracy's spell hit the dragon, and he wobbled. I flashed behind him when he drew back his head to blow more fire. Tracy threw a potion, causing his dragon fire to turn to bubbles. I flashed back under him.

The mind control device was embedded under his scales and ran from the slight bend in his leg to just above his massive toe. "Interesting," I muttered as I thought about my options. The mind control device had grown to match his dragon size. I didn't know an object could grow with a shift, but it made sense. So did the magic. The dragon moved his leg, and I tried to move with him, falling on my knees. I hopped to my feet just as his giant spiked tail swung toward me. It clipped me as I dove out of the way. I didn't dare scream as sharp pains shot across my side.

I hit his belly with shredding magic, trying to think of other magic that might work. I jumped to his knee and jammed both daggers above the mind-control device. One lodged between two scales, but the other didn't stick and fell to the ground. A loud roar that I recognized as Bastien's overpowered the dragon's shriek. The dragon shook his leg with me still holding onto the dagger. I lost my grip and flew toward his giant penis. "Eeekkk!" I squealed as I flashed myself back to the ground, rolling twice before settling into a crouch.

"Jen!" Drake ran under the dragon, naked and in human form.

Outside, spells flew, Bastien roared again, and the dragon shifted his weight, causing the giant penis to swing toward Drake. My eyes grew wide. "Watch out for the giant dong!"

Three things happened at once. Drake turned to look. I lunged to flash him away, and the dragon moved again, causing the penis to move faster. It hit Drake at the same time as I did, and we both bounced off a giant claw and landed in a heap of twisted limbs. I flashed us out. "Are you okay, Drake?"

Drake chuckled as he untangled himself from me and helped me up. "Absolutely."

I threw us back to the ground as a potion bottle flew by, landing on the dragon's foot, turning it green. "Sorry," Tracy yelled.

Drake grabbed my arm. "Do you think you can connect with my magic again?"

"I don't know how I even did that," I said as I darted under the dragon.

I found my dagger still hanging from the dragon's leg and was about to flash up to it when Drake lifted me. "Get the dagger and let's go."

I grabbed the handle with both hands and pushed, shredding magic through it. The ruling magic shoved my inherent magic aside and pierced through the dragon scale with such force both the knife and I slid down the leg at an alarming pace. I would have face-planted if Drake hadn't wrapped his arm around my waist, catching me. I yanked my dagger back and began trying to pry the mind control device out of his leg, ignoring the dragon's squeals of pain and Drake's insistence that we get out of there.

The dragon stretched his giant neck between its front legs and drew in a breath. Panic overtook me, and I couldn't think. Drake burst into his dragon form. The turquoise dragon lifted off the ground and tumbled through the air. Bastien batted him, and he came back down like a missile.

I got flung across the yard and rolled, landing in a heap on the back porch just in time to see Bastien land on the dragon. My dagger and the mind control device were flung across the backyard in one direction as Bastien and the turquoise dragon rolled in the other, crashing through a stone fence. Drake's massive head leaned over the much smaller dragon, his huge, sharp teeth showing. The turquoise dragon melted into his human form and curled into a ball.

I lay on the grass, trying to catch my breath. "I think we got it."

Drake shifted and marched over to me. "That was reckless. Bastien and I could have handled one wayward dragon if you had only got out of the way."

"Yeah, I saw that." I spotted Tracy lying unconscious on the other side of the yard. I rushed over and dropped to my knees. "It'll be okay, Tracy. Hang in there," I murmured as I took her hand. I was relieved when the only major injury I found was a concussion. I healed her and scanned the yard.

Bastien and Drake stood over the cowering man in deep discussion. A pile of chimeras lay on the side of the house. I sighed in relief. Tracy stirred, and her eyes popped open. She jumped to her feet, shook her head, and focused on me. "We got him?"

"Yeah." I pointed to the still giant mind control device by the fence. Bastien said something to the cowering man that I didn't catch and pulled him to his feet. I swept a piece of hair out of my face. "We need to figure this out before it destroys the coalition."

"Yeah," Tracy said absently as Bastien and Drake frog-marched the guy toward us.

Drake's eyes swept over me. "Are you okay, detective?"

"I'm fine. Thanks for the assist." I turned my attention to the dragon. "What did you want with me?"

The dragon shook his head. "I don't know. I was compelled to come here and get you by any means necessary."

"Who compelled you?"

"I don't know." He pointed to his head. "It's foggy."

"We will secure him with the others. I didn't ruin your wards. I took them down temporarily." Bastien's eyes never left Tracy.

Tracy stomped toward the mind control device and picked up my dagger. "You could have ruined our house. And don't think our prior discussion is over."

Bastien sighed as Enforcers streamed into the yard. He and Drake talked to the lead Enforcer, then shifted in unison. Bastien clutched the dragon, still in human form, with one talon as they flew off. It took Tracy another fifteen minutes to reset the wards. I answered questions and watched the Enforcers drag the pile of chimeras away. When they left, I showered and collapsed on my bed, the events of the endless day playing over in my mind.

Chapter 25

MORE DETERMINED THAN EVER, I pored over the information I'd gathered from my case and read my grandmother's diaries the next day. Tracy spent that time messing with our wards. She was pissed that Bastien was able to take them down and attacked the problem like a dog with a bone.

Quin showed up in our kitchen on the second day. I stumbled to the kitchen to get coffee like I did every day, only to find him sitting at the kitchen island drinking coffee and scanning his phone. "Hey, Quin," I mumbled as I headed to the magichef.

"Have you solved your case yet?"

He knew the answer, so I grabbed my mug and sat beside him. "I have an appointment with Emine today to get the information they got from the Bank of Mahri. I'm close to figuring it out. Did you solve yours yet?"

The look he gave me would have made most people pee their pants. "I am not the apprentice."

"Want to go with me and see what the Enforcers got from the dragon that ran the Bank of Mahri?"

"Yes."

I continued drinking my coffee. No way I'd go see Emine without coffee. I drained it and put the mug in the magiwash. "I'll go get ready."

The Enforcers' division was two blocks from Dragon Headquarters in a three-story glass building. Since Enforcers were interspecies police, they employed people of every magic type. People called the building The Cauldron because it was a giant melting pot. While most supernatural factions had their own laws, the Enforcers handled interspecies crimes and enforced only coalition laws. Over the years, they morphed into a kind of police force. Even though they represented the crown and Emine headed the agency, I'd never been inside the cauldron.

Tracy and I trailed behind Quin as we climbed the stairs. She scanned the area. "Do you feel that?"

A tingle went up my spine, and I shivered. "Someone's watching us."

Quin waved a hand. "No one is going to attack us here. We'll deal with that later."

The lobby of the building was typical, with magic scanning stations manned by guards. We approached a guard who watched Quin, identifying him as the biggest threat. He ignored Tracy and me as we presented our credentials and laid our hands on the magic scanner. We moved to a waiting area that smelled like ozone and coffee. It wasn't too long before a woman with brown hair swept into a severe bun called my name. We took an elevator to the third floor, and she led us to the back of the office area.

Emine emerged, waving us in. "Come on in, Je——um, detective." She nodded to Quin. "Consort."

We filed into the room, and she shut the door with a loud click. "What's with the entourage? You causing trouble again?"

"No," I said as I sat. "Wait. Why would you think I'm causing trouble?"

She sat at the head of the table and pointed at Quin. "Why else would the head babysitter be here?"

I frowned. "Quin is my mentor, not my babysitter."

"Sure thing." She rummaged through some papers.

I eyed Quin, but he ignored me, pulling out his phone and tapping on the screen. It wouldn't surprise me if Mat hired him to guard me. My stomach sank at the thought. That meant Quin didn't choose me as his apprentice at all. I shook off the depressing thought. "What did you find out about the money?"

She pushed a file in front of me. "Not much besides what I sent you. The odd part is that it looks like all the victims were from different supernatural factions."

I opened the file and read through the report. At first, I thought the Bellicose were using the money to fund their operation, but it didn't look like it. "I noticed that. Did you find out where the money was transferred?"

"See, that's the weird thing. We can't get into other people's accounts, and the former bank manager isn't talking. Luckily, the Mer King came ashore and told the local Enforcers that a strange deposit in his account matched the amount stolen from one of his mermaids."

"So, they stole money from a mermaid and deposited it into her king's account?"

"Duh. That's what I just said. Or are you just restating the obvious?"

"Why would they do that?"

Emine tapped the report. "That's the several million-dollar question. Why would someone steal from a poor person and give it to a wealthy king?" Her eyes told me I should know the answer.

"To cause mistrust," Quin answered when I didn't. "The Bellicose have traditionally been masters at causing hate and discontent in an attempt to destroy the coalition."

"Exactly," Emine said. "And I think they've been doing it for a while."

I thought of the hybrids and remembered the file I'd pilfered from Mage Mountain. I held up a hand, dug through my bag, and pulled it out. The file was old. The papers hadn't been spelled to preserve them, so they were yellowed. They dated back almost thirty years. The memo suggested their followers hang out in bars and restaurants to spread the message, among other propaganda strategies. I read through it and handed that page to Quin. "They used a propaganda campaign to get people to turn against the hybrids."

"Let me see that." Emine wiggled her fingers, and I handed over the file. She scanned it, her eyes getting big. "Holy shit! Where did you get this?"

"I found it in a dusty filing cabinet near Mage Mountain," I answered. "I'd forgotten about it until just now."

Emine sat back and rubbed her eyes. "You realize what year that was, don't you?"

I did. It was the year my parents were killed. Mat and I spent the year fleeing for our lives. "It doesn't mean anything. They've been doing stuff like this for hundreds of years."

"If you say so." Emine went back to reading through the files and pulled out a paper. "Says their leader, the king, eliminated the fake royals. Who do you suppose that is?" She wiggled her eyebrows.

The crown's weight settled on my shoulders, and I broke out in a cold sweat. "Okay, so say this is all about getting rid of us. What's the end goal? Why target the dragons? Why only steal money from one person per faction?"

"What part of 'causing mistrust' do you not understand?" Quin asked. "Each action is designed to make the public not trust their leaders. The dragons are the most powerful supernaturals. If you can control them, you control the coalition. It does not matter what their end goal is. If they can succeed in dividing us and controlling the dragons, they win."

I blinked. I'd never heard Quin talk that much at one time. "Okay." My mind started turning. "So the question isn't what they're doing, but what do we do to stop it."

"Ding ding ding. Give the girl a cookie," Emine said. "But that's not your problem. It's the queen's." An evil grin spread across her face.

"Right." I turned my attention back to Quin. "Can you check to see if Ara has received a deposit from Jedediah?"

"Oh yes, I will gladly solve your case for you."

I raised an eyebrow.

He sighed. "We will see her when we are done here, and you can ask my love yourself."

We talked it over a few more minutes and left the cauldron, heading toward the central flashing circle on the square. The back of my neck began tingling as soon as we stepped out of the building. Quin caught my unease and latched on to my arm, moving me forward. Tracy walked on my other side, her eyes alert. "I don't like this. I mean, we still haven't figured out why that dragon came to our neighborhood looking for you."

Quin stopped in his tracks, almost pulling my arm out of the socket. "What dragon?"

I filled him in while Tracy continued to scan for threats. When I was done, he picked up the pace. "We need to move."

We raced to the flashing circle and landed at the one near House Umbra, the mansion where Quin and Ara lived. Quin flashed with us, which he never did. His concern made me nervous. He escorted us through the gate before disappearing. I shrugged off the chills running up my spine that warned me I was in a predator's den.

A vampire with a pixie cut and brown eyes opened the door. "How did you get in here?"

"They're with me." I didn't jump at Quin's sudden reappearance, but my heart skipped a beat. I was getting better at sensing him, though I clearly needed to keep practicing.

He led us down a few winding hallways, and we stopped in front of a set of double doors that opened by themselves. Ara sat at an antique desk, her head back and eyes closed, "Come in, my love." She opened her eyes. "Hello, Jenella, Tracy. Please, come in."

I glanced around the office. Unlike most offices, there were no conference tables or sitting areas. The walls were bare and painted pale gray. There were no paintings or decorations. The tile floors were bare of any rugs.

There weren't even windows in the room. I shifted uneasily as the door closed behind us. "Hello, Mistress Ara. Sorry to barge in on you like this."

Quin strode around the desk and kissed her cheek. "Hello, my love. How is your day going?"

A sly smile crept across her face. "It has been rather trying. We had a rogue incident." She waved a hand when he opened his mouth. "It has been handled. Now, what can I do for you two lovely ladies?"

I got straight to the point. "We were wondering if you would check to see if there was a large transfer to one of your bank accounts from Jedediah on May third."

"Why?"

"We think the Bellicose is transferring funds from supernaturals to their leaders to create mistrust."

"I will have my people take a look only if you stay for lunch." She leaned forward and smiled. "I've made pot roast. I do so enjoy cooking."

Tracy and I exchanged a look, and I nodded. "We'd be honored to have lunch with you."

Ara's magic was different than other vampires, even Quin's. Where his magic gave me the creeps, hers made my skin crawl. The ruling magic sensed she was lonely. I knew all about being surrounded by people, yet feeling completely alone. If I could ease even a little of that by eating her pot roast, I'd show up for lunch every day.

Conversation throughout lunch was effortless. We sat in a massive kitchen littered with human appliances and talked about cooking. We laughed about my mishap with the magichef as we ate the most delicious pot roast I'd ever had. When we were done, the same vampire that answered the door slipped in and handed Ara a piece of paper. "Thank you, Elsie." Ara read the paper and handed it to me. Her magic amped up, causing Tracy to shiver. "It seems there was a deposit. Unfortunately, my accounting team didn't catch the discrepancy."

By the tone of her voice, I didn't want to ask what she would do to punish the accountants. I didn't want to know anything about vampire discipline. "Thank you. I truly appreciate the help."

She inclined her head. "In an official capacity, what do you plan to do with this information?"

She meant as queen. "I have some ideas, but need to talk to Mat about them before I do anything."

"But you plan to do something." It wasn't a question.

"I do."

Ara stood. "Good. I must get back to work now. Do let me know if there's more I can do to help."

We stood as vampires swarmed in and began clearing the table. "Thank you for the information, the lunch, and the company, Ara. It was one of the best meals I've ever had."

She beamed. "Of course. You stop by anytime, dear."

Quin escorted Tracy and me out of the castle gates and disappeared again. So many vampire eyes were on us that I had to reel in my senses to keep from being overwhelmed. As we rounded the corner, heading toward the flashing circle, the prickling on the back of my neck began again. I sent my senses out, but they didn't pick up on anything. "Do you think it's the vampires watching us or someone else?"

Tracy scanned the circle area. Since it was in an affluent district where everyone had their own flashing circle, there wasn't anyone around. "I don't know, but I don't like it. Did you need to go see the queen?"

Her words were code for we needed to get to the castle for safety reasons. I saw a shadow move on the other side of the road, the ruling magic telling me it was a chimera. I scanned the sky, checking for dragons. "Yes."

The attack came the second we stepped into the flashing circle. A giant paw flashed in front of my face. I blasted raw, inherent magic so fast that the creature rolled to the other side of the circle. Another smashed me in the back, and I sprawled on my face. A sharp pain shot through my shoulder. The ruling magic didn't like that and blasted it off me before my brain could engage. Tracy yanked me to my feet and slapped a shield around us. We moved to the circle's center and stood back-to-back, ready to fight when the creatures circled us. The ruling magic pulsed, and I struggled to wrap it around me tighter. More chimeras burst into the circle and bounced off Tracy's shield. We were surrounded. Trapped. I readied shredding magic, wishing I'd thought to bring my daggers.

"No need to fear us, detective. We will not hurt you," came a familiar voice.

I whipped around, facing the director of the PISD. "What do you want, Director?"

He slithered around in front of me, causing the other four chimeras to move out of his way. He lowered his giant lion's head. A goat head peeked over his shoulder and bleated, smoke billowing from its nose. "It's not about what I want, detective. It's about what paranormals need."

I dragged my eyes away from the goat and focused on the lion. "And I suppose you have all the answers," I muttered. "I fail to see what that has to do with me."

Both heads grinned. "You are the key to our goals, detective. The king is quite pleased you've been cunning enough to thwart our recruiting efforts, but grows impatient."

"As far as I know, no one has tried to recruit me for anything. And since when do chimeras have a king?" I knew he wasn't talking about chimeras, but I decided it was in my best interest to play dumb.

He threw both heads back and laughed. The lion's laugh sounded like the bark of a big dog, and the goat was like a hyena. "I am not talking about false leaders, but the one true king. He wishes to bond with you to legitimize his claim to the throne."

My stomach sank. "Why me?"

"Because you are a mage of Ahl, which means you have royal blood. Very few of them left these days, and none are as weak as you." He leaned forward. "We eliminated most of the old royal family, but they insist on pretending they still hold power. Our king is close to taking care of that problem. Matching with you will give him a claim to the throne."

I felt Tracy complete the complicated spell she'd been working on. I wanted answers, so I pushed forward. "The problem is, I don't understand a word you just said. The legitimate queen has taken the throne. There is no king."

He leaned forward. "The bloody prince and his sister will be eliminated by the end of the week. Now, come along. We have a bonding ceremony to attend."

He reached for me like I was going to say, 'Sure, I'd be glad to overthrow the coalition and put a mind-controlling freak in power.' Tracy unleashed her spell. Three of the chimeras crashed through the illusion at the edge of the circle. Tracy's spell spread and hit the illusion spell. Unfortunately, it also took out our protective barrier. It broke with a loud *crack*.

I charged forward and hit the fire-breathing goat's head with knock-out magic, causing it to lilt to the side. It didn't affect the lion or the serpent, though. The Director slashed with his paw, and I ducked, throwing shredding magic at it. His serpent tail coiled around me so fast I didn't have time to think. I hit it with shredding magic, too. It let me go, but its head struck, sinking into my shoulder. I skidded out of the circle on my ass and landed in a shrub on my back. The Director wasted no time. He pounced on me and roared. I tried to throw shredding magic down his throat, but couldn't lift my arm. I sent healing magic to expel the venom, but it was too late. The Director had already attached magic nulling cuffs on my wrists. The last thought I had before I went under was, 'Where did he get Enforcer cuffs?'

Chapter 26

THE RULING MAGIC WOKE me up. I wasn't sure how long I'd been out, but I didn't think it was very long. I kept my breathing even, my eyes closed, and I sensed my surroundings. There were several weak paranormals surrounding me in a circular shape. In the center was a bright, glowing light of dragon magic. I could sense several other dragons not far off, along with a few chimeras and something very dark. I opened my eyes to the tiniest slit. Swallowing back bile, I found myself in a jail cell so similar to the cage I had been kept in as a kid. I shot up and looked closer. A steel toilet sat in the corner with a tiny sink next to it. The cell was small but tall enough that I could stand up. The cot I sat on was hard and uncomfortable. I felt a powerful urge to gag because of the stench of mold and unwashed bodies. I turned my head and gasped.

I was in a round stadium with cells lining the upper level. Most of them were full of gaunt paranormals of all different types. In the center was a tattered bronze dragon. "Devarkalara," I whispered. She had a spelled metal collar around her neck, secured with several chains bolted to the stone floor. Her limbs had a similar cuff with chains, as did her tail. A tear slid down my cheek. If the Dragon Queen couldn't get away from these people, I doubted I could.

I leaned back on my cot to think, rubbing my glamour earrings, a fire lighting inside me. I was sick of being kidnapped. And I sure as hell wasn't going to stay in a cage any longer than I had to. I remembered Tracy saying that I'm a grown-ass woman who couldn't be caged. A small smile spread across my face. I couldn't escape if they knew who I was, but they didn't. They thought I was a low-level mage of Ahl, not the queen with a huge helping of ruling magic. This meant they didn't have the same kind of restraints on me they had on the Dragon Queen. I could use that to my advantage. I could set the others free and get the hell out of there. My gaze fixed on the Dragon Queen. I wasn't sure if I could set her free, but I was willing to try.

A door clanged in the distance, and I positioned myself exactly as I'd been when I woke up and faked sleep. Footsteps pounded down the corridor. I felt the foul magic before they reached my cell, and I struggled to keep my breathing and heartbeat even. I concentrated harder.

"You see, sire? She is weak but has royal blood," the Director's smug voice rang through the stadium.

"Oh, yes. The king will be pleased." The foul magic poked at me, causing a stab of pain to rattle my bones. I concentrated on blocking it out. "Too bad she's so ugly. How long before we can present her?"

"My venom takes several hours to wear off. Perhaps this evening or tomorrow."

The magic withdrew. "Very well. I shall tell the king to expect us tomorrow night. Clean her up and make her presentable."

"Yes Sire." The footsteps retreated.

After waiting several minutes, I opened my eyes. I didn't have much time, so I needed to act fast. I slunk to the cage door and put my hand on the spell. My shoulders relaxed a little when I realized it was the same spell that held Verity and me in the cage on the dragon's back.

I ducked back to my cot when I caught movement at the center of the ring. I peeked around the edge. The bronze dragon's intelligent eyes bore into me. I couldn't tell if the queen was mind-controlled and didn't want to take the chance. I pushed my hair out of my face and tried to bite back the panic. If she was mind-controlled and I broke the spell on the bars, I doubted I'd make it out before she got to me. I peeked again, and a realization struck. There was no way she'd be chained if they had control of her. I chanced it and gave her a small wave.

Relief flooded me when she lowered her head and looked the other way. I put my hand back on the spell and started reversing it.

If you break that spell, they will know. Your safest course of action is to stay put and hope for rescue. A woman's voice boomed through my head.

The ruling magic didn't react, so I leaned forward to get a better look at her. "Hey, Devarkalara. Nope. Not an option," I whispered.

Then you will put us all in great danger. And call me Deva. Even in my head, her voice held resignation.

I squared my shoulders. "We're already in great danger. I don't know about you, but I'm not going down without a fight."

Laughter boomed through my head. *I have been fighting for months, love. I am the sole thing standing between paranormals and their doom.*

"They can't mind control you. I wondered."

They cannot. But they can siphon my magic and use my dragons to manipulate me. Tell me, how do you plan to get us out of here, Jenella?

My heart skipped a beat. "You know who I am."

Don't worry, love. Your secret is safe with me. I can sense the ruling magic in you. However, I wonder how you accessed my nephew's glamour magic.

"He gave it to me."

There was a long pause before she continued. *Our captors are weak in magic but strong in conviction. They won't know it's you until you show them.*

"Great." I kept working on the spell. "Can you break loose?"

I cannot. The restraints drain my magic and energy.

I stopped and examined her restraints. I couldn't feel them from my cage, but I bet they used the same spell as the Enforcer cuffs used. Magic that my mother created. She made sure that the cuffs couldn't hold her, and, as a result, they couldn't hold me. The only spell reversal she ever taught me was how to remove those cuffs. "And if I break the spell?"

I can break the chains, but my magic is drained. They are funneling it to the demon to use on the dragons.

I froze. Although I recognized the foul magic, I didn't realize it was demon magic. I threw the slew of thoughts out of my head. I needed to concentrate on the task at hand. "Are you sure you have enough strength to help?"

I'm not at my best. Get me free, and I will do what I can.

Instead of breaking the spell containing me fast, like I did when Verity and I were kidnapped, I unwove it by reversing it piece by piece. It took me a few minutes, but I cut through. The unraveling swept around the arena in a *"whoosh,"* and I hopped to my feet. I flashed to the neck of the Dragon Queen. Like Drake, she had spikes, so I wrapped my arm around one and touched the collar. Other mages realized they were free and started flashing paranormals out of the cells, making too much noise. I glanced up at them and concentrated hard on breaking the spell. Like the cracked ward in Allure, it began sucking the ruling magic out of me. I didn't resist. I only hoped I had enough energy to get out of there once I was done. It didn't matter how much magic a mage had. If they didn't have energy, they were useless. And using magic always took energy. I hoped I had enough to get out of there. It wouldn't have been a problem if my magic had mixed because the ruling magic would feed me energy. It couldn't, with my magic separated like it was.

I broke the spell and moved to her legs. I still had the one on her tail left when the door at the center of the arena crashed open, and the Director strode through, along with a group of chimeras and dragons in human form. "Shit," I muttered as I flashed to the last restraint. The Dragon

Queen reared up and sent out a mental pulse that I felt down to my bones. I tumbled away from her restraint and flashed back and slapped my hand on it. White hot pain shot down my back just as I reversed it.

I shrieked as I spun, sending shredding magic straight down the chimera's throat. He reared back, and I rolled into a crouch just as another chimera hit me from the side. We rolled across the ground, and I hit her with knock-out magic and hopped out of the way as she fell.

The Dragon Queen yanked the chains free, and I had to duck as one came at my head. She reared back and swallowed a chimera whole. She stomped across the stadium, obliterating the others with her fire before melting into her human form and passing out. I stood there like an idiot, staring at her as the freed paranormals filed out the door. The dragons lay unconscious, probably from her mental pulse. I couldn't leave the Dragon Queen, but I didn't know if I had the strength to carry her. She stirred, and I knelt beside her. "Can you walk?"

"I don't believe so, no." Her regal voice was ragged, and she smelled like she hadn't hadn't bathed in months.

I braced myself and lifted her onto my back, using my inherent magic to give me a boost. I trudged toward the exit. It was too slow, so I used more inherent magic to go faster. When I made it out the door, a long hallway went left. I flashed to the end. I blinked as spots danced across my eyes. "Which way?" I wondered aloud.

"Left. Right at the end, then past the guards, and we're free." Her voice was barely a whisper. I flashed past several running paranormals as they limped their way out. I hated leaving them, but Mat was right that I couldn't save everyone. No way was I leaving the Dragon Queen behind.

We came to the entrance, and bright sunlight blinded me. I blinked when I saw two dragon guards ripped to shreds at the entrance. The scent of vegetation washed over me, along with stifling humidity. "Hospa?"

"Yes," the Dragon Queen answered. I didn't realize she was still awake. I pictured the Enforcer's office and flashed to the front entrance, falling on my knees and gasping for air. The queen hit the ground with a 'thud.' The front doors flew open, and several pairs of feet surrounded us.

"Hang on, Detective. We'll get you some help. You've got to hold on."

I recognized Colonel Ballard's voice and slumped to the ground. The adrenaline drained, and I began to shake violently. My healing magic was working, but I was out of energy, so healing would be slow. I had huge gashes down my back and sides, bruises, and I had lost a lot of blood. "C-call B-Bastien and M-m-m-mat. Prince Mathias. It's a d-d-demon."

"We got you. Healer's on the way." Colonel Ballard picked me up bridal style and set me on a bench in the waiting room. I recognized the detectives who questioned us after my last kidnapping standing by the entrance. My shaking would not go away. A man rushed through the doors. A mid-level healing mage. "Q-Q-Queen first," I told him when he kneeled in front of me.

"My partner is taking care of her. I'm going to check your injuries and give your healing a boost."

A few minutes later, the pain subsided. The injuries weren't healing as fast as normal, but were on their way. I needed food and sleep so my energy and blood could be restored, but at least I wouldn't bleed to death.

Colonel Ballard sat beside me, rubbing his chin. "What kind of shit show did you dump on my doorstep this time, Detective?"

I closed my eyes. "I don't even know where to start, Colonel. It's important I talk to the Regent."

"Yes. Mat, you called him."

"Yep."

"And you called the dragon prince by his first name. Just what the hell kind of connections do you have?"

"Deep ones. I'm a mage of Ahl, Colonel. The royal family are my relatives. Bastien is who the Dragon Queen requested."

"I see." He didn't sound convinced. Probably because it was a partial lie. I didn't have the energy to care.

Colonel Ballard checked me into the Red Brick Inn, and I staggered to my room on the third floor. I stripped out of my torn and bloody clothes and threw them away. I cleaned up and slid into bed naked.

When I woke up, I checked my healing injuries, took a shower, and put on a hotel robe. I checked in with Colonel Ballard using the hotel phone. He said that Mat and Bastien would be there in an hour. I ordered a change of clothes from a shop down the street and called Jedediah. He answered with his usual arrogance, and I told him what happened to his money and let him know it would be refunded soon. I suggested he talk to his mother.

He grunted. "I am disappointed that there is no one to kill. I would like to find all the Bellicose responsible. Do you want the job?"

I wouldn't take another case for Jedediah for all the gold in the world. "Not wise, considering Quin is assigned that case."

"I see. You got my money back, so your final payment will be transferred today. Do try to work faster in the future."

I disconnected the call and sat back, deciding to choose better cases in the future. The main reason I chose to be a detective was to meet regular supernaturals, and so far, I'd only met a handful. I needed to look for cases where I could help regular people and stay away from the Jedediahs of the world.

As I reached out to the leprechaun leadership about Thaddeus's stolen money, an idea started forming in my head. An idea that could solve a few of our problems.

Chapter 27

I STRODE INTO THE conference room and headed straight to Verity. I ditched my glamour in the alley on the side of the Enforcer's office in Hospa. Despite receiving a few weary looks, no one stopped me as I made my way to where everyone was meeting. "Contact Travis Lyka at PISD. I'm appointing him Director."

Verity eyed me from head to toe. "You sure you don't want to do that yourself?"

"No. Travis is no longer my friend. I'm appointing him because he's too worried about public appearances to join a rebellious cult and try to kill me or force a bond."

She blinked. "Um. Sure."

"Thanks. You're the best." She inclined her head and left the room.

Colonel Ballard and the vampire Enforcer stood and bowed as I approached the table, "Your Grace. Would you like something to drink?"

"No, thank you." I took a seat next to Mat.

"Colonel Ballard, please give us the room for a few minutes," Mat said as he eyed me.

The Enforcers almost knocked each other over as they rushed out of the office.

"Are you okay?" Mat asked as soon as the door shut.

"I am now." I turned to Emine. "Colonel Ballard and his entire office saved our lives."

"Sure thing." She frowned. "Although he says Detective Hendrix is responsible for both."

"Funny. There were several other paranormals they hadn't mind controlled yet, but I had to leave them behind. I had to choose between getting Deva out and finding help or bleeding to death trying to save them." I rubbed my eyes. "They were using Deva to control the dragons. She said they couldn't mind control her but used magic nulling cuffs to siphon her magic."

"She told you that?" Bastien asked.

"Yes. She was chained in her dragon form and couldn't break free. I had to break the spells. I almost didn't have enough energy to flash us here. The Enforcers had to get me a healer."

Mat flinched.

"Where was this?" Bastien growled.

"In a cave system designed to house dragons."

"Watch your mother closely. Once she is well enough to give us more information, we'll worry about the Bellicose and the remaining dragons," Mat said.

I wanted to go in immediately, but I let it go because I wasn't in any shape to do anything useful. "What happened to you when they took me, Tracy?"

Tracy's face turned hard. "We'd already taken out most of the chimeras. Quin and Ara swooped in and took care of the rest. Quin and I were both pissed and got into a huge fight. I mean, I get that I'm supposed to protect you, but it happened in Quin's territory. And that was a lot of chimeras for one guard."

"The Director and his remaining chimeras are dead," I said without remorse. I wondered what that said about me but dismissed it. It wasn't something to worry about just then. "I took the Director out myself. Deva ate the rest." I ignored Drake's nod of approval. "If you'll excuse us, I'd like to talk to Mat alone."

"Don't go far," Mat said.

"We won't." Bastien led Tracy, Drake, and Emine out of the room, shutting the door behind them and activating the privacy spell.

Mat leaned back. "What's this about, Jenella?"

I held up a finger, gathering my thoughts. "Okay. Let's ignore the fact that you have a whole lot of information about the Bellicose and circumstances around our parents' deaths that you kept from me." When he tried to interrupt, I cut him off. "You might want to stay quiet and listen to me right now because the ruling magic really wants to lash out at you."

"Okay."

"Until the ruling magic calms down, we'll ignore the fact that keeping that information from me and ordering others to do the same almost got me killed. Twice. Odd, since you're always so concerned with my safety."

"It doesn't sound like we're ignoring that fact."

"We are for now, but we'll talk about it later. I have an idea of how to counter some of the damage the Bellicose has done to the coalition. Also, I've appointed Travis as Director of PISD."

Mat inclined his head, so I continued. "While working my case, I thought the Bellicose were stealing money to fund their operation. Emine discovered they were depositing it in the bank accounts of the various leaders. It's not the first time they've done things like that to cause mistrust and divide the coalition. In the past, they've been successful." I tapped the file that Emine left behind. I got up and paced while he flipped through it.

His face grew grim. "I did not know this."

"Welcome to the darkroom. May you enjoy it more than I do." He opened his mouth to say something, and I waved my hand. "I'm going to take the list of theft victims and send a note to their leaders about the money transfers. I'm also going to use excerpts from that file as evidence to show that they were coerced to treat hybrids so terribly. To help smooth things over, I'll offer each victim one thousand dollars for their trouble."

"I don't have a problem with you setting the record straight and winning people to our side."

"You understand what I'm saying. I'm going to use their own tactics against them."

"How?"

"By setting the record straight on the hybrids. Send people out to start rumors about them based on enough truth that it alienates them from society." I pointed to the file in his hand. "I'm using that as a step-by-step model."

Mat leaned back. "Using propaganda to push your agenda no matter the intentions is a bad idea."

"Even if I'm telling the truth?"

"Yes. It's a slippery slope. If it works this time, it will be an easier decision next time. Before you know it, you'll use it as your go-to tactic. I do not recommend starting down that path."

"Okay. Then how do you propose we take care of them? Because I refuse to sit back and do nothing while they chip away at the coalition using these very effective tactics." I sighed. "You should have seen the Dragon Queen, Mat. And all those other paranormals. We can't allow them to continue abusing our people."

"I'm not denying it's effective, but you cannot solve a complex problem with a simple solution. The Bellicose has been around for a long time. They can withstand a little propaganda campaign. We need to think long term and develop a more complex solution."

"People are throwing children out of the pockets. They're kidnapping paranormals and putting them in cages. They chained the damn Dragon Queen and used her magic against us! We need to stop sitting around with our thumbs up our asses and do something. I won't sit back and let people be tortured while we talk it in circles."

"It's politics. Circles are what we do."

"It didn't use to be that way. Our grandmother took care of business. She crushed these guys once, and we need to take up that mantle. We can't let this go on." I stabbed a finger at the folder. "It starts with this. I'll alert the leaders of the attempted mistrust and include information about the plot to alienate the hybrids. If that's successful, we'll discuss the rumor-spreading portion."

"Fair enough, but I warn you to use caution and think hard about that decision." He ran a hand through his hair. "Are you really okay, Jen?"

I lowered myself into a chair. "Not even close. I'm both terrified and pissed. My back hurts, and I could sleep for days. I killed people yesterday and have no remorse, which makes me question my mental health. But none of that is important right now." I took a deep breath. "What's important is stopping the Bellicose before they become so powerful that we can't. Now, let's talk about how paranormals are being controlled by magic similar to Jaques's."

Mat's eyes filled with sadness and guilt. "I hoped you wouldn't remember Jaques's magic."

"People don't forget the cause of their trauma. They might lock it away, compartmentalize it, or even deny it exists, but something always triggers it. In this case, it was the feel of Jaques's magic torturing me while I was locked in a cage." I couldn't keep the tremor out of my voice.

Mat's jaw clenched. "I'm sorry you had to go through that. It's why I've encouraged you to deal with your emotions. Instead, you ignored them."

I didn't want to talk about my trauma, so I changed the subject. "What have you not told me about the dragons, particularly the source of this mind control?"

"Only that we thought they were based here in Hospa. Colonel Ballard was monitoring the situation until you landed on his doorstep. He suspected they kept Deva there. We were planning to attack in the next few days."

"Then let's do it. There are a lot of paranormals in those caves, and we need to go in and get them."

"Not we. That task will be delegated to the Enforcers and the dragons."

I shook my head. "Nope. We need to make a statement that this sort of thing will not be tolerated under my rule."

"I understand that you're angry and frustrated, but we don't need to be there. It's a dragon problem, and Bastien wants revenge for what they did to Deva."

"I disagree. It's a coalition problem. They're not just screwing with dragons, but paranormals of all types, and they're not worried about the consequences." I leaned forward. "They've forgotten who we are, Mat. What you are capable of. We need to give them a reminder."

His eyes glowed. "What are you thinking?"

"I'm glad you asked."

Mat and I hashed out the details of our plan, and I left him to strategize while I headed toward the rental house that Colonel Ballard procured for Deva, a silent Tracy by my side. Drake opened the door before I could ping the wards, and we stepped into the small house. She lounged on a plush sofa, casually reading a book with a blanket I knew she didn't need draped over her lap. I sat in a chair across from her. "I don't have much time, so I won't beat around the bush. Do the bellicose still have you in their grips?"

Deva closed her book before turning her attention to me. "It is true that they tried to get in my head. However, they were unsuccessful. Even the demon did not understand how dragon magic works."

"So, there's no compulsion at all?"

"I have no urge to harm you or direct my dragons to do anything. I can't say that was the case when you first found me, although my nephew's mark on you helped remedy those thoughts."

My eyes snapped to Drake. "Explain. Please."

His lip twitched. "You wear my glamour and have accessed my magic, Jenella. My essence saved your life."

I eyed Deva. "How strong was the pain and the urge to give in?"

She grinned, her sharp teeth peeking out. "I am a very old dragon, love. I must fight the urge to hunt constantly. Resisting thoughts is second nature. Fighting the urges the Bellicose planted was no worse than fighting the urge to chase a supernatural that runs from me on the streets."

I let out a relieved breath, hoping that was true because my plan hinged on her cooperation. "Thank you."

She inclined her head. "I'm glad they weren't powerful enough to control me, or it would have been a different outcome. One I doubt many would survive."

I brushed a curl out of my eyes. "Would you consider helping us shut down their operation and free the rest of the paranormals?"

I held my breath as emotions danced across her face. First was surprise, then anger, before it settled on determination. "I would like nothing more than to free my people and exact revenge."

Not what I was going for, but I'd take it. I turned my attention to Drake. "And you?"

His eyes bore into me. "I will do whatever you want."

I explained a small part of the plan. When I finished, Tracy and I slipped our glamour back on and left.

We were a block away from the Inn before Tracy spoke. "I'm sorry."

My eyebrows drew together. "Sorry for what?"

"For letting you get taken. I couldn't maintain the shield and throw that spell at the same time, and it was a mistake."

"Don't be sorry. If I hadn't been kidnapped, Deva would still be in that disgusting cave, and I wouldn't have learned that demons were involved. Mat would have kept me in the dark indefinitely."

"Still. I didn't do my job. I don't know if I *can* do my job."

"You're not getting rid of me that easy. We need each other. Shit happens, and we'll handle it as it does. Blame Quin if it eases your guilt. It was in his territory, after all."

She chuckled. "You're in your element when you slip on the crown. I know you don't want to hear that, but you are. It's weird to see you so confident."

"You get to see the real me more often than anyone other than Mat and the griffins. I'm the least confident person I know. Most of the time, I pretend. I don't ever remember being in my element in any situation."

I returned to the inn after the third long day of strategy meetings. Planning an invasion was fascinating, but drained me. I hoped I never had to help plan a large invasion because my head was spinning. It didn't take long to realize I was the most naïve person there, so I stayed silent and listened, giving my consent or veto to the different ideas only when needed. Tracy and Verity followed me into my room as Verity reviewed my schedule for the next day. Tracy peeled off and went to peer out the windows facing the street, and I headed to the magichef to get some coffee.

"Why was I not included in your plan?"

"Gah!" I jumped, spilling coffee on my hand. "Holy hell, Quin. What are you doing here?"

Verity frowned. "Do vampires have cloaking magic or something? I always know who's around, but didn't sense you."

Quin's mouth formed into one of the scariest grins I'd ever seen. It sent chills up my spine. "It is one of my special talents."

I waved a dismissive hand. "Of which, he has many. Trust me, you don't want to go down that rabbit hole."

"Back to my question. Why are the vampires not included in your plan?"

"I didn't know you wanted to be included. Why would you?"

"Did you forget that five chimeras invaded our territory and took my apprentice? Or that I was transported against my will to the frozen pocket? No? Then I will remind you it is my case."

"Okay." I opened my laptop and turned it on. "Be at the Enforcer's building at seven tomorrow morning."

His mouth froze in the "going to argue" position. I chuckled when he snapped it shut and regrouped. "You have no problem with me being part of this?"

"No. I can't promise Mat or Bastien won't have a problem with it, but I'm happy to add another powerful person to the team."

"Very well. I shall inform my love that we have been invited." He disappeared.

I stared at the space Quin had just occupied. "Did I just invite the vampire faction to help with the dragon problem?"

"I think so." Verity shook her head. "That is the strangest man I've ever seen. And I've seen a lot of strange since meeting you."

"He's...eccentric, but I like him because he tells me the truth. I find his jump-scares and sarcasm entertaining."

"Don't be fooled by his weirdness. I mean, Quin is super dangerous, but he's as loyal as they come and will defend people he claims as his to the death. And he's decided Jen and I are his. We're safe with him," Tracy said.

Verity shrugged a shoulder. "Whatever floats your boat. Personally, I'm gonna keep an eye on him."

Chapter 28

IT'S FUNNY HOW THE perception of freedom can change. When I was a kid, I thought freedom was getting away from Jaques and the cage. When I grew up, I thought it was getting out of my protective bubble. But those freedoms were nothing compared to how free it felt to fly on the back of a dragon, or in my case, a Multidrakelandarnarian First. The wind ruffled my tightly bound hair, and I breathed in the humid air with a smile so big that my cheeks hurt. "Flying is amazing."

I'm glad you like it. Amusement laced Drake's voice.

"It's great when we're not being attacked."

His laughter boomed through my head as he descended toward the jungle.

Bastien provided us with a secret place to amass our troops, which was close to the dragon stronghold in Hospa. We spent an entire day moving people from the transport station to a vast cave with a fresh spring and several bathrooms. I flashed a bunch of times and was exhausted, so I hitched a ride on Drake's back after grabbing a quick meal and showering.

Drake veered toward a solid cliff side, retracted his wings, shot through the spell, and landed inside the cave. I flashed to the ground just as he touched down. He shifted and dragged me to the side so Bastien could land. My eyes swept over our army. We had about fifty Enforcers, twenty dragons, thirty castle guards, six griffins, and fifteen vampires, including Ara and Quin. The battle leaders were seated at a table at the far end of the enormous cave.

"What was this place originally?" I asked Bastien as we marched toward the assembled leaders.

"This is where I used to keep my horde. I moved it about five years ago because it was too close to the Hospa dragon lair."

"And no one knows about it?"

"No. The wards ensure it's well hidden. An advantage of mating with a powerful witch."

We reached the makeshift table where Mat and Quin argued about strategy. I took a seat beside Ara, who sat with an elbow on the table, her chin resting on her hand. "It might be time for you to step in, dear, or I fear we will be here for days," she said as soon as my butt hit the chair.

Colonel Ballard waved a hand from his spot beside Emine at the other end of the table. "Thank you for coming to help, Your Grace."

I gave him a slight nod. "Are the people responsible still in that cave?"

"As far as we can tell. They have about fifteen dragons still under their control that do regular patrols, though more than that left right after the queen was rescued. The magic coming out of the lair is still tangible. One of my sergeants said it feels evil."

"It is twisted and evil. Dragons are not so easily influenced. Me, least of all. This magic is different and hard to resist. Be very careful around it," Deva warned.

Mat quit arguing with Quin, his face stonier than usual. "Jenella and Tracy will stay with the First and the Dragon Prince. Tracy has provided spells that work against dragons, and Jenella has ruling magic. They will use it to bring the dragons down. The castle guard will remove the mind control devices as soon as they bring them to the ground."

"The Enforcers will go into the caves with vampire backup and take out their leadership," Emine added, uncharacteristically serious.

I wanted to pace to think better because I was sure we were missing something. I glanced at Quin, who stood against the cave wall deathly still, his hands clasped behind his back. "What are we missing, Quin?"

"A lot," he answered. "This plan is too simple, considering we don't know what we're up against."

Colonel Ballard frowned. "And what do you suggest we do?"

"I suggest we come up with a better plan. This one does not use our strengths or account for our weaknesses. It is the plan of a brand-new queen who does not know what she is doing."

I scanned the cave, eyeing the separate factions, setting up tents and gathering in clusters of their own kind. "You're right. We're trying to solve a complicated problem with a simple solution, which you told me doesn't work, Mat."

Mat's jaw clenched. "What do you propose?" It was his way of saying, 'Are you going to listen to the vampire?'

I met his eyes. "I don't know. While I'm not a very good strategist yet, I've had this awful feeling that we're missing something big. Quin's right that we can be far more resourceful. I'm not sure a loud, traditional invasion in the mid-morning sun is the right choice, even if the demon is weak during the day."

Everyone began talking at once.

"Quiet!" I threw out a bit of ruling magic with the order, and the table grew silent, all heads turning to me. "Let's review our current strategy, note our strengths and weaknesses, and revise it where necessary. Don't be afraid to share unpopular opinions and, for fate's sake, don't argue. We don't have the time, and I don't have the patience."

Mat leaned forward. "We planned this for three days. Now you want to throw out those plans?"

"No. But the plan didn't account for having several powerful vampires. If there's one thing I've learned from the attempts on my life, it is that the more adaptable we are, the better our chances. I want to make sure our plan is the best before we send people into a battle to get hurt or killed."

"You have a right to be nervous about your first battle, but death is a part of war," Mat said.

"I am aware," I replied and changed the subject. "I think our biggest advantage is our magical diversity. We can use that."

"Our biggest advantage is you." Deva leaned back and crossed her arms. "I heard you can access Drake's magic. Can you do the same with others?"

"No. I planned on trying to access Drake's again, though. I circumvented the mind control once that way, so I might be able to do it again."

Emine didn't try to hide her crazy smile. "No shit? How big of a scale can you do that on?"

"I don't know."

"Good. We'll use that." Colonel Ballard tapped the table. "I propose we create teams of five or six people that can go unnoticed for as long as possible. Our witches and mages can put up shields to create mini-safe zones around the teams. Also, let's not forget that vampires are immune to magic and hella fast. We can use them to confuse the dragons with hit-and-run attacks."

Mat rubbed his chin. "The problem I see with that strategy is that these people have never worked together before, and we don't have time to become a team."

"We also need to remember that most of our mages and witches are mid-level in power and will run out of energy fast if they have to hold barriers. I mean, I could have them to create protection charms, but we still have the same problem with our magic users being drained," Tracy added.

"Instead of barriers, I can try to take back my dragons. If that doesn't work, I can send a fear signal. It will weaken their outer defenses and allow our people to sneak in," Deva said.

"Chaos." Emine tapped her chin. "I say we create as much chaos as we can."

"Chaos is good," Tracy said. "If Deva can bring the dragons down or confuse them, and on top of that, we use whatever Drake and Jenella have going on, the rest can remove the devices. I say we form teams based on personality and skill. Some create maximum chaos as a diversion. Others can focus on hitting weak points and removing those mind control devices."

"Controlled chaos," Ara drawled, "I do like that idea. We should also form a powerful hit team to take out their demon amongst the chaos." Her eyes scanned the people at the table. "I suggest Quin, Deva, Mat, and me, as we are the deadliest."

Mat leaned back and folded his arms. "I don't like chaos because it muddles the battlefield. Too many things can go wrong. Including a total communication breakdown and casualties from friendly fire." He held up a hand before anyone could protest. "However, I can see how it could give us an advantage in this situation. Colonel Ballard can lead the ground teams while Jenella runs the teams in the air. Emine will oversee a few teams charged with creating chaos. We can designate those we think can handle chaos, including the vampires. Other than the chaos, that allows us to stick to the original plan to use the terrain to our advantage. Tracy, can you create a potion or charm to protect the lead teams from mind-control magic?"

She shook her head. "No. I would have if you hadn't tried to keep the information about the magic from Jenella, but since I haven't had time to study it, I'd need time. I can give you some potions that might help."

I fought not to smile at her backhanded way of defending me.

"We value anything you can contribute." Mat rolled out the map across the table. "Form the teams, and I will assign them attack zones. Emine and

Colonel Ballard can ensure each team has a member who is adaptable and experienced in charge. Jenella and Bastien can organize the dragons. If we are going to have four powerful leaders on the assassination team, we need to decide how to work together with minimum conflict."

I once again stood on Drake's back, one hand on a spike, my sense of freedom gone. I tried to keep my stomach from heaving by taking deep breaths and focusing on the scenery. The jungle below was beautiful through my magic sight. Different colors laced the foliage. An occasional black lake or bubbling stream flowed through it, the white rapids glowing in the moonlight. During the day, everything in Hospa was lush and green. At night, it was all shadows with a slight green tinge. I decided I wasn't a fan of jungles at night.

Are you ready, Jenella? Drake asked in my mind.

"Let's do this," I answered, sounding more confident than I felt. My earlier resolve hadn't faded, but I'd never been to battle or fought a war, so I assumed being nervous was normal.

I felt better about this plan, but not by much. I swallowed the bile that rose as we drew closer. "Can you see in the dark?"

Yes. Drake banked left with a whoosh and dove low. *I am going to stay low. Do not let go because I might have to move fast if we're spotted.*

I wondered how to contribute more, as several explosions sounded around the area. "Let me know when you plan to pop up, and I'll unwrap my magic to add to the chaos."

Are you sure you want to do that, Jenella?

My resolve solidified. "It's time we reminded them who we are."

Drake didn't answer, but I felt his satisfaction at that statement through the ruling magic that connected us. He dove under the tree line and blew a stream of fire at a wyrm dragon slithering through the trees toward one of our teams. I leaned over and let Drake's foreign magic flood into me. I directed the wyrm to shift. He dropped like a rock, and our team swarmed him as we flew away.

In the distance, explosions echoed across the valley, giving the illusion that we had a much larger force than we did. "Emine is good at chaos."

An enormous magic wave swept over the jungle from the south, quieting the natural creatures. Goosebumps popped up on my arms. Deva sending her signal to the mind-controlled dragons. Drake slowed almost to a stop and shook his enormous head before continuing. I looked for Tracy and Bastien but couldn't see them. Bastien's black form blended into the night. The other dragons on our team hadn't shifted, but instead stayed with the teams on the ground as their shields. Deva sent another wave of magic across the jungle. This time, coming from the east. Mat must have flashed her to a different location. Drake slowed, but it didn't affect him as much as the first signal did.

The cliff wall in front of us exploded as dragons poured out. *Get down!* Drake's voice boomed in my head. I wasted no time. I plopped onto my butt and ducked behind the spike. He banked left and shot into the sky, causing my stomach to flip. He tucked his wings and dove toward the dragons so fast I felt the skin on my face flap. *Get ready.* His wings snapped out, and we leveled out.

I climbed to my feet and wrapped an arm around the spike. The dragons from the cave circled around a clearing, bumping into each other and wobbling in the air. Drake zipped by three of them in a mid-air battle with each other, and I let his magic flow through me, noting that it was easier and less foreign each time I did it. I held a hand toward the battle and whispered, "Sleep." They fell to the ground, including the one on our side. "Are they going to be okay?"

Dragons are tough. They'll be fine, Drake said as he dove toward five dragons still hovering over a clearing.

I directed the sleep command toward them. Instead of responding, all five turned and barreled toward Drake, plowing into us. He roared and reared back so fast I didn't have time to brace myself and would have tumbled off if it weren't for the ruling magic that spun around the spike, holding me in place. I tightened my grip and tried to clear my head. The ruling magic picked that time to unravel itself and start putting the beat down on everyone in the area.

I watched in horror as a yellow dragon was flung into the dense jungle like a bowling ball. A maroon dragon got slammed repeatedly into the ground. A gale-force wind roared across the valley, spinning the dragons in the air in circles. I tried to reel it back in with everything I had. I could feel the intentions, but couldn't control it. Sweat dripped down my face with the concentration, but it wouldn't obey me. "Oh shit, oh shit, oh shit. Drake, I'm going to try something."

This is not part of the plan, Jenella. What are you doing? I caught a hint of amusement.

"This is not my fault! The stupid ruling magic just does whatever it wants sometimes." I pulled on Drake's mind magic and slammed a sleep command into the out-of-control torrent of ruling magic.

All the dragons in the area dropped like rocks.

Well, that's one way to do it, Drake mused.

With a sigh of relief, I sat down and hugged a spike but didn't bother reeling the ruling magic back in. "Sorry about that. It's a problem. I did say I'd let my magic loose."

I'd say it's more than a problem but now is not the time. We need to get to the caves.

"Jen! What the heck was that? Did that magic go haywire again?" came Tracy's voice next to me.

I tipped my head in her direction. "Something like that. You guys okay?"

"Yeah. I mean, we almost got caught up in that mess, but Bastien got us out of there." She patted his back.

I met her weary eyes. "Good. Let's wake our sleepers and head to the cave." Deva said there were fifteen missing dragons, and we put twelve of them to sleep. I woke the ones on our team that got caught up in my magic, pretending I meant to knock them out. Our teams streamed into the area to remove the mental magic and secure them.

The caves were too small for Drake to fit in while in his dragon form, so he took human form while Bastien and Tracy flew ahead. I frowned at the sheer number of dead at the entrance of the cave. They still wore the mind control wristbands. Mat said that supernaturals wearing a wristband were voluntarily part of the bellicose, so I guess he didn't think they deserved mercy. We didn't know for sure why even the volunteers were mind-controlled. Mat theorized it might be a way to track them and ensure no one betrayed the organization. It made sense in an evil genius kind of way. We planned to mark the ones who wore them so we could separate the two groups, not kill them. "Do you think they just came in here and started killing everyone?"

"Probably." Drake noticed my shiver. "This is what war looks like."

"Yeah." I didn't like what war looked like. It made me sick to my stomach. I knew it wouldn't be the last time I had to witness something like that, but I hoped it wasn't often.

Drake pointed to the left at a pair of ornate double doors that lay mangled on the floor, and we wove around them and slipped inside. I directed him to the arena I'd escaped from. He grabbed my hand and led me down the hall at a brisk pace, following the trail of bodies.

Bastien and Tracy stood, peering into a room. "What's up?" I whispered as we approached.

Tracy pointed to an unconscious dragon in human form, his neon green hair a tangled, bloody mess. "They left the dragons alive, but not anyone else."

"That's what happens when a group of powerful predators are left to their own devices," Bastien said.

"Sure." I didn't want to argue about how wrong it was to assume one magical type's life was more valuable than others. "Which way did they go?"

"Just follow the bodies." Bastien strode down the hall.

The further we went, the fewer bodies we found. As we approached the arena, we flattened our backs against the wall, and I leaned over to peer in. Mat, Ara, Quin, and Deva were nowhere to be seen. A man...no, a demon, I decided, addressed a crowd of supernaturals. "Today is my lucky day. I get my lovely Dragon Queen back, a powerful vampire and the bloody prince." The small crowd gathered around the stadium cheered. "Bring them to me. In addition, two weeks of serving the king will be rewarded to the one who brings me the fake queen."

"That's the same demon that wanted me to match with his king." I clenched my hands to hide the shaking.

Drake peered around me and pointed back down the hall. When we got far enough away, we slid into a sitting room, and he closed the door. "We need to find our team. Does anyone know how to counteract demon magic?"

Tracy opened her mouth, closed it, and opened it again. "I don't know anything about demons."

"They cannot be killed, only banished," Bastien said.

"The question is, how do we banish it? It is different for every type of demon." Drake raised an eyebrow.

I rubbed my temples, trying to clear the sheer terror that wanted to overtake me. Damn childhood trauma. I didn't know how Jaques got demon magic, but this magic felt identical to his. At that moment, I realized my fear didn't matter. As much as I hated being queen, we needed to save the people who were here against their will, along with the coalition, or we'd all be in serious trouble. "Does all demon magic feel the same?"

Everyone stopped talking at once and focused on me. "What do you know about demon magic?" Bastien asked.

"Have you seen this type of magic before?" Drake asked at the same time.

I cleared my throat and squared my shoulders. "It's identical to Jaques's magic."

"Are you sure?" Bastien's eyes glowed. "You were very young when he died."

"I'm sure." A person didn't forget something like that. I started pacing. "Okay, let's think this through. I know Mat recognizes the magic because we sort of talked about it before deciding to do this." I swallowed my rising hysteria. "And not even demon magic works on Quin and Ara. That means they have a plan and are fine. We just need to find them and help."

A golf clap sounded from the corner, and we all jumped. "Outstanding deductions, detective," Quin said as he stepped forward. "Wrong, but good."

"Quin! What happened? I mean, where's the rest of your team?" Tracy bounced from foot to foot.

"I was not with them. My role was to scout ahead and eliminate threats. They are being held in a secure room."

Bastien crossed his arms. "And you decided to do nothing instead of getting them out. Give me the location."

Quin crossed his arms, too. "You are very rude."

I held up a hand. "Bastien's right. Can we skip the argument and get to the part where we find a solution?"

"You are right that their magic does not work on Ara. She may be playing along. Mathias does not seem distressed, as his heart rate and breathing are even." Quin tapped his ear. "But I assure you, they did not plan to get captured."

I perched on a chair and closed my eyes, trying to remember how I fought against Jaques's magic as a kid. Some of my memories were so awful that I'd locked them away. For example, I couldn't remember what Mat did to kill him. I held out my hand, trying to remember what type of magic I'd used to stop his magic from entering my body and causing pain that felt like my innards were boiling. If that memory was even real.

"What is that, Jen?" Tracy asked.

I cracked an eye open and saw a ball of putrid brown magic sitting in my palm. I poked it with a finger and gasped at the sudden jolt of memories. "This is the magic I used against Jaques. I think. Maybe. My memories aren't exactly reliable."

She leaned forward and examined it. "That's extremely complicated."

Drake poked at it. "How much of that can you create?"

"I don't know. As I said, my memories are sketchy. I don't know if Mat knows about this or if it was even that effective."

"It's better than nothing," Bastien growled. "We cannot let this demon retake my mother."

Drake leaned down so his face was level with mine. "Will you be able to do this?"

"Yeah." My voice wobbled, so I added. "Mat is the only family I have left." I hoped I sounded more believable.

Quin's eyebrow rose. "Yes, you sound very convincing." He waved a hand dismissively. "Come. I know a back way in."

Chapter 29

QUIN LED US DOWN a wide hallway to a row of heavily fortified doors. Demon magic prickled my skin as we inched our way toward a magically fortified steel door. I could sense Mat, Ara, and Deva inside the last one. The others held dragons. A lot of dragons of all power levels. When Quin stopped in front of the door, I pointed to the doors and raised an eyebrow. He shook his head. "Why do you think the Dragon Queen came this way?"

Bastien and Drake stared at the door. I fell silent and waited for them to finish their mind conversation with Deva. Bastien broke out of the conversation first. "The women and children are in these cells. Mat is working on the magic holding the door."

I put my hand on the door and examined the spell. It was the same spell they used to hold the cages. "I can break it."

Bastien shook his head. "Mat said for you to leave."

"Of course he did." I plucked at a thread and reversed the spell, and it began to unweave. I felt Mat's magic. He wasn't subtle, but that wasn't his style. If he kept going, he'd alert everyone to what he was doing. The ruling magic grabbed ahold of his magic and guided it through the unweaving process. When he started unweaving on his own, I withdrew. "I showed him how to release the spell without making much noise."

The three of them spilled out into the hallway a minute later. Mat's glowing eyes focused on me. "Leave, Jenella. They are offering a prize for you."

"Oh, it's a little too late for that," came an arrogant voice at the end of the hall. "Seize them and bring them to the arena."

Ten weak demons skittered out from around the powerful demon. They had long, triangular bodies and several eyes. Their spindly legs ended in a single rounded claw that clicked on the stone floor as they moved. One sent out a net of magic. We all ducked. It hit the wall and burst into a pile of bugs. Drake and Mat shoved me behind them at the same time. Drake burst into his snuffy form, and Mat dodged underneath him, katanas out. Mat sliced one demon to pieces while Drake bit another in half.

One got through, and I threw my anti-Jaques magic at it. It melted into a pile of dust. Tracy put a hand on my arm and threw a similar, though much weaker, spell at another. The demon melted to the floor, and I finished it.

Quin and Ara morphed into monsters with long claws on their hands and feet, and they became blurs as they darted around Drake's massive form, leaving a trail of demon goo in their wake. Bastien and Deva stepped in front of Tracy and me, guarding us from the fight.

I tried to shove Bastien out of the way, but he was much bigger and stronger than me, so it was like trying to move a boulder.

More demons poured into the hallway, shrieking and grunting. Drake stopped fighting and went on a rampage, trampling them. Quin and Ara moved so fast I couldn't see them, leaving pieces of demons in their wake. Bastien shoved me against the wall. That's when I felt it.

A single thread of magic linked the spells holding the doors closed. Dumb, considering if that if one thread broke, the entire spell would fall apart. I tuned my magic to the reverse spell and poured the magic into the link. I didn't try to be subtle.

With a loud *"boom,"* the doors clanked open, and filthy, gaunt dragons in human form filed out. The stench of body odor and excrement added to the sulfur smell of demon, and I gagged.

Deva's fists clenched, and she sent a wave of magic through the cave. The dragons turned as one and ran toward the entrance, smashing demons. When they disappeared around the corner, I realized the four of us were the only people left in the hallway.

Bastien shoved me. "Drake said to get to the arena."

I ran with Tracy by my side. Bastien and Deva trailed behind us. The arena was in total chaos. Still in his snuffy form, Drake bounded around the seating area, chasing demons and glassy-eyed paranormals. His mind magic smacked me in the face, and my heart kicked up a beat. The instinct to run was overwhelming. I shook it off and focused on the stage where Quin and Ara faced off with the human-looking demon. Mat worked on getting a pair of magic nulling cuffs off.

Ara's face broke into an evil smile. "I must inquire why you think you can take over and lead the coalition."

The demon flicked a hand. "The coalition needs a powerful leader. Everyone knows the child queen is not strong in magic or personality. My king is powerful and has a clear vision."

"I see. And what does your *king* plan to do?"

"You are in no position to ask questions, vampire!" Brown spittle flipped from his lips as his human façade slipped. He pointed at Mat. "He is bait. You are nothing more than a cute little piece of ass."

Quin hissed.

The demon's head snapped toward us. "Well, well, well. What have we here?" He pointed a finger, and his putrid magic exploded toward us.

Bastien burst into dragon form and charged. The ruling magic snapped out like a whip around us. I took advantage of that, held up my hand, and blasted the putrid magic away, following the stream back to the demon.

The demon went tumbling across the stage at the backlash. I hopped over bodies and charged toward the stage. Tracy stayed on my heels, throwing spells at anyone from the crowd that got too close. Halfway to the stage, I saw Mat's cuffs snap. His katanas appeared with the same anti-demon magic I used flowing through them.

He sliced someone's throat and stabbed someone else through the heart at the same time before charging the demon. Ara morphed into her gangly creature shape, which consisted mainly of claws and fangs, and followed him, tearing through everyone in her path.

A similar version of Quin zipped around Tracy and me as we fought through the crowd. A giant roar rang through the cavern as Drake stomped through, his mind magic still projecting fear. Just as we reached the stage, an explosion went off near the door. The blast threw me forward, and I landed on my hands and knees. Clawed hands jerked me to my feet. "Keep moving." Quin's voice sounded solid––a true feat considering four long, sharp fangs hung out of his mouth.

I hopped up on the stage and blasted the demon from behind as he fought Mat, who looked like an avenging angel with his glowing golden eyes and magic katanas. I tried to get the ruling magic to go crazy, but I'd used a lot of energy and was almost drained. It needed to recharge somehow.

The demon spotted me. "There you are."

It flicked Mat aside like he was batting a fly. My heart raced as he started toward me. Quin moved to block, and the demon swatted him aside like a gnat. The demon backhanded me across the face before I could react. I hit the ground with a *thump*, and it pounced on me, his hands around my throat, and poured demon magic into me.

Thousands of burning needles pricked my body, making my eyes water. I blocked out the pain and dug deep, transforming every ounce of all three pools of my magic into anti-Jaques magic. I didn't let it loose, though.

Mat yelled something, but I ignored him. My magic roared inside as the demon's magic poured into me. I had to focus hard to keep mine from exploding.

The demon smirked. "You are weak and worthless."

I turned my head to avoid the stench of his breath. Emine stood off to the side, a massive gun in her hands, shooting into the crowd, causing my ears to ring. The demon gripped me tighter. My ears popped from a spell that I thought might have been Tracy's. I should have felt relief, but I knew she wasn't enough. No one was. No one but me, and even that was questionable. I kept building my magic.

Spots formed in my vision. My eyes wanted to close. I was so damn tired. I gathered every drop of energy I had. "Get out of my realm."

I focused on the demon and let the magic I'd been building explode.

My anti-demon magic barreled into him, piercing his hide. The boiling pain disappeared. The demon screamed in anger as we were blown in opposite directions. I got launched off the floor and rocketed face-first toward the stone seats surrounding the stage. A million things rushed through my mind. Everything from how disappointed Mat would be that we lost the throne to how death would finally set me free. I closed my eyes, ready to die. My face smashed into fluff. I sneezed and cracked an eye open. The fuzz was green and black. "You have opposing thumbs?" Drake didn't answer, and I began struggling. "Let me go, Drake!"

I got jostled around and placed gently on a stone floor. I swayed a little and reached for a rock to balance myself. We were at the top of the stadium by the door. The demon looked pale and weak on the stage as Mat, Ara, Quin, and Deva circled him. Off to the side, Tracy stood beside a heavily armed Emine, spell ready. All over the cavern, Enforcers, vampires, and castle guards restrained people. I turned my attention back to the stage just in time to see Ara and Quin lunge, claws digging into the demon. I flinched when Ara dug her claws into his chest and removed his heart. It looked like Quin was just shredding whatever he could get ahold of. I fought not to heave. With a slice of a glowing sword, Mat beheaded him, and they all stepped back as Deva breathed a stream of white fire. The demon turned to ash.

"Is it gone?"

Drake had shifted to his human form and threw an arm around me. "I don't know."

Mat's eyes drifted from the ashes to me, still glowing from the fight. "Uh oh."

I flinched when he stalked toward me. "What was that?"

I ignored his question. "Is it gone?"

"Banished, yes. How did you weaken him?"

I expected Mat to be angry at me for letting the demon touch me, but his calm, cold voice and reasonable tone were much worse. I rubbed my sore neck. "Defending myself against that type of magic is something I've had experience with."

"How did you know it was the same type of magic? Demons are masters of deception."

I wrapped my arms around myself. "He used it on me."

"Irrelevant."

"That doesn't even make sense...."

"We had it under control! You did not need to put yourself in danger."

"Yes, being cuffed and kneeling before a demon screams control."

"It was part of our plan."

"I know. And you still needed a diversion to pull it off. I'm not stupid. Jaques's magic was recognizable to me from all the times he tortured me with it while I was caged. I recognized it on the mind control devices. I recognized it when it had me by the throat! It worked out, and it's banished, so I don't see what the problem is."

Mat pointed to the door. "You were supposed to be outside!"

"Safely tucked away at the kiddie table while the adults took care of things."

He leaned in close. "You still have severe magic problems. What if it misfired at the exact moment the demon touched you?"

"It didn't."

"But it could have."

"That's not how––"

"You never know what the ruling magic will do. You rely on the fact that it will protect you and have no control over it. You allow it to randomly lash out with no intention or control."

"––it works. No, it doesn't. Mostly. Look, I'm trying."

"Try harder."

That pissed me off. "I'm not a child! I haven't been for over ten years. Stop treating me like one. I helped banish the demon because the people must know I'm willing to step in. I used my anti-Jaques magic because I knew it would work. As far as fixing my magic, even with the impediment, I'm stronger than everyone here, except Deva and maybe Drake. And I have access to Drake's magic. So, I'm not exactly helpless."

"No, you are not helpless. But you are young, impulsive, and reckless. I'm asking that you stop and think before you act and stay alive long enough *to* grow up." He dismissed a privacy spell I didn't realize he'd set and flashed back to the stage, leaving me fighting tears.

"Did he not just hear me say I've been an adult for years? What's with this grow-up bullshit?"

A warm hand landed on my shoulder. "You scared him. Are you okay?"

I wanted to bawl. I wanted to turn around and burrow into Drake's chest. The realization struck that Mat would never see me as anything other than a child. I knew it was normal for people who took on the parental role, but this was different. It felt like he didn't respect me. That hurt worse than anything. Even worse, I couldn't show how much that hurt in front of all those people. I swallowed my emotions, squared my shoulders, and headed to the door. "It's going to take some time for the Enforcers to get this mess cleaned up, and I don't need to stay here. I'll be outside checking on the freed dragons."

I thought Drake might say something. Instead, he followed me out the door. "I let Bastien know that I'd guard you. He and Tracy will catch up to us in a while."

We stayed in Hospa for two days. Mat didn't say anything else about my safety as we healed people. He said nothing during the debrief meetings or when we helped Deva gather wayward dragons. Tears sprung to my eyes whenever I thought about his words, so I stayed busy. The last night, I finally thought about what he said and, through tears, decided that he was right. I *was* young and impulsive. I had never made my own decisions. He'd never let me. So, it made sense that some decisions weren't perfect or safe, but I was learning. I hardly recognized that naive girl who yearned to be a detective. It would take time and a lot more experience for me to *not* be young and impulsive. I only hoped I didn't alienate Mat in the process. Those thoughts ran through my mind all the way back to Allure.

"Jen?" Tracy's voice tore me out of my thoughts.

I sat at my desk at the castle, waiting for the follow-up meeting to start. "Yes?"

"Thaddeus is here with the catering. Verity said to tell you she's sending him in."

"Okay." I'd asked Helen to hire Thaddeus and his leprechauns to cater some meetings at the castle. I didn't think she would go for it because she was very proud of her food. She agreed because she thought building good public relations was essential to establishing myself. Though I suspected she hoped some of Thaddeus's luck would rub off on me. I didn't think it was possible. Griffins tended to be a little superstitious, so I didn't argue.

Thaddeus and two other leprechauns rushed in with their arms full of trays. Verity directed them to the enormous conference table. The food smelled delicious.

Thaddeus bowed. "Your Grace. Thank you for using my deli. We will take care of you."

"Your deli came highly recommended. I'm sure it will be great. And don't worry about formalities."

"She hates formalities," Verity offered. "But she loves great food. This smells amazing."

Thaddeus's smile stretched from ear to ear as he set up the food. I admired his carefree attitude. I recovered his money from the leprechaun leaders and started my anti-Bellicose campaign that Mat called propaganda. He wasn't happy about my decision. Mat didn't seem to approve of anything I did.

Deva pranced through the door just as they were finishing setting up the food. Drake wasn't with her, and I was both disappointed and relieved. It embarrassed me that he witnessed such raw emotion in the cave. She sauntered to my desk and perched on a chair across from me. "Hey, Deva."

"Hello, Jenella. How have you been?"

"I'm great. How are you?"

"I am recovered from my ordeal. Thank you for asking." She watched Verity lead Thaddeus and his team through the office. "I do so like that deli. The homemade chips are delicious, and the meat is fresh."

"I'm glad. He was one of the theft victims, so I like supporting his business."

She turned her attention to me. "Those are the kinds of things a true leader does. Why have you been avoiding me?"

I fought not to flinch and almost pulled it off. "I apologize. I've been busy."

"Not just me, but you've been avoiding everyone."

"Yes."

Her eyes danced with humor. "So, it was intentional."

"Yes."

"And why is that?"

"I have my reasons."

Deva leaned back and tapped the arm of her chair. "I suppose I don't blame you for running away from your responsibilities. If I had that option, I'd do the same."

"I didn't intend to run from responsibility. Although, you do make a good point."

"In my long life, I have found that it is futile to practice avoidance, no matter the reason. For example, I am here because I wish to stop the bellicose and owe you my life. I would like to discuss that debt."

"You owe her nothing," Quin interjected as he appeared out of nowhere. I sensed him that time, so I didn't jump.

Deva focused on Quin. "The dragon way is a life for a life. Traditional dragon culture would demand I pledge my life to her."

My eyes widened as I thought through the political implications of her statement. She and the dragons would serve the crown if I agreed she owed me. It wouldn't go over well with the leadership council. "Nope. No one owes anyone anything. Uh...thank you, though."

Deva's lip twitched. "Very well. I also wanted to speak privately about the dragons' plight and my nephew's uncharacteristic obsession with you."

"There is no obsession. Drake simply wants to find a purpose in his new life. I wanted to solve my case and save the coalition. Working together made sense." It was a total lie. I liked Drake and hoped he felt the same way, but that didn't mean it was an obsession.

"I see." She didn't sound convinced.

Ara and a gaggle of vampires came through the door, causing Quin to head that way and giving me the perfect opportunity to change the subject. "We should get ready for the meeting."

Deva shot me a knowing smile but didn't comment. She winked as Bastien and Drake came through the door, though.

I moved to the head of the table, Deva on my right with Bastien, Tracy, and Drake. Ara, Quin, and Emine sat on my left. Mat took the chair at the other end. I inclined my head, keeping my face intentionally blank.

His eyes scanned the room. "Everyone who is not sitting at this table needs to leave." Verity, the gaggle of vampires, and three palace guards filed out of the room. "We have secured the supernaturals who conspired against the crown. We secured the dragons who were part of it at Deva's lair. The rest are secured at the Enforcer building until we know which ones were there voluntarily and which ones were mind-controlled. We are here to discuss putting safeguards in place to prevent something like this from happening again."

Deva leaned back. "I believe the queen has already enacted some measures."

"I want to do something more substantial than Jenella's little propaganda campaign." His tone was equivalent to a dad agreeing to let a child have ice cream. It pissed me off, but I said nothing.

Ara leaned forward, suddenly interested. "You don't agree with this decision?"

"It doesn't matter what I think about it. What matters is that Jenella establishes herself as a strong ruler."

Bastien pointed at Mat. "You don't like it. It pisses you off that it's been so effective." He leaned forward. "The question is, why?"

"Wait. Jenella made a decision and actually enacted it?" Emine interjected. "How come you didn't tell me, Mat? What did she do?" She bit into a chip.

"I used the file that had details about how the Bellicose alienated the hybrids to prove their involvement. It was dated just before our parents were killed, for those who haven't seen it. I sent it to the coalition leaders along with a note that inferred they were helping the Bellicose by rejecting hybrids."

Quin set his phone down. "It was an unusually brilliant move by Jen."

Ara patted his arm. "And it's been effective. She also compensated the leadership and the victims for their trouble. I've heard positive feedback from several leaders."

"Some are even reconsidering their stances on hybrids," Bastien added.

Mat cleared his throat. "Aside from that, we need to enact a strategy that establishes defenses against demon mind control."

The meeting moved on to a brainstorming session, with Tracy offering to work on some potions based on the magic I used to defeat the demon. Drake offered to work with me to figure out how I used his magic and help build on that. I listened, only interjecting when necessary. Although I was glad that exposing the Bellicose worked, I didn't want to get roped into staying full time at the castle and sacrifice my freedom. At the end of the meeting, I leaned forward. "What about the dragon who cracked the ward?"

Deva's face turned hard. "I was forced to help with that. I made sure the order carried a safeguard that he didn't fully break the ward, only crack it."

"And where is that dragon now?" I asked.

"He is contained in the dragon lair with the others."

I tapped the table. "And that's where the bank manager is, too?" I waited for Deva's nod. "How do you plan to punish them?"

Mat shifted in his seat. "Since they were coerced, we plan to let them sit in jail for a while as punishment."

I inclined my head. The punishment was fair, since they weren't acting of their own volition. "And the other paranormals from the cave?"

"They're being sorted," Emine answered.

"Put out the word about that symbol I found. If anyone sees it, they should report it."

Mat's face turned to stone. "I doubt that will be effective."

I tried to keep my face neutral but couldn't stop an eye from twitching. "Everything we do to prevent this from happening again will help. Has anyone figured out who this so-called king is?"

Mat cleared his throat. "Quin has agreed to find the one they call their king."

When the meeting was over, I removed myself and a sandwich from the table. I sat at my desk as everyone lingered, chatting and eating.

Unfortunately, Deva followed me and waved a hand, enabling a privacy spell. "I don't know what kind of power struggle you and your brother are having, but I do know the woman before me is not the same woman who risked her life to rescue a Dragon Queen she barely knows. Regardless of what Tarquin thinks, I owe you, so I swear that any conversation between us will stay between us."

I jumped as the magical contract settled over me.

"Now, tell me why you've been avoiding everyone."

I rubbed my eyes. "There are a lot of reasons. I've been avoiding Mat because we need to have a hard conversation that I don't want to have. Because she's crazy, I've been avoiding Emine. I've been avoiding Drake because he saw inside me and glimpsed emotions I keep heavily guarded. I've been avoiding you because I'm not sure how the demon magic has affected you. Before I put myself at risk, I wanted to let you work that out. I'm not ready to get trapped in this office for the rest of my life, and Mat and I are always in a power struggle, so don't worry about it."

"That was a candid answer." She stared at a blank spot on my desk. "The demon has no control over me, nor did he ever, which is why they had me in chains. It wasn't from lack of trying. You rescued me before they could do too much damage. I cannot speak for my nephew, but I know him well enough to assure you he is very careful with the emotions of people he cares about. And I do believe you fit in that category." She leaned forward. "This brings us to the real problem. What makes you so afraid to talk to the one person in this world who has always loved you?"

I glanced at Mat, standing with Bastien and Drake by the door. "Mat and I have very different ideas on how I should rule. I don't know who is right. My whole life has revolved around preparing for the role, but I still need to learn so much." I shook my head. "It's a fight I'm not ready to have." It was a half-truth. Mat hurt me with his lack of confidence in both my campaign and the little lecture he gave me after we took out the demon.

"Ah. I see. You are avoiding conflict."

"For now."

She stood and dissipated her privacy magic. "Then I will leave you to it. Just know I am available if you need someone to talk to outside your little bubble."

I watched her practically drag Bastien out of the room. Drake gave me a long, thoughtful look before following. Mat pushed everyone else out before shutting the door and turning to me. "What was that about?"

"It was about none of your business."

He sat and ran a hand through his hair. "You're pissed at me."

"I don't think 'pissed' is an accurate word for my feelings toward you right now."

"I understand you don't like my opposition to your little plan, nor do you like that I want you to consider your safety in all situations. But I don't see why you are so upset that you would avoid me."

I leaned back as if slapped. "Let's start with how condescending you sound."

"I'm not being condescending."

"My *little plan*?"

"Perhaps I could have used better wording."

"Perhaps you could respect that I made my first proper decision as queen, which was effective. Perhaps you could support me in front of other leaders, even if you think I'm wrong. Perhaps you could refrain from devaluing me because *my little plan* isn't something you would do. In case you haven't noticed, *my little plan* is working. It's giving my rule support that would have taken years had I not done anything." I'll admit I used air quotes several times to make a point. It wasn't my proudest moment.

Mat's face grew stern. "You used propaganda against my objections. I will not compromise my integrity as easily as you do."

"I did not compromise my integrity. And telling the truth is not propaganda."

"Sometimes it's not what you say, but how you say it. You even used monetary bribes, which sets a dangerous precedent."

"I compensated some supernaturals for trouble that could have been avoided if we were better at this whole ruling thing."

"Then get better! I cannot hold this throne with you making hit-and-run style decisions and leaving me to deal with the fallout! Either you rule, or you let me be regent, but you can't just swing in, make decisions, and go back to pretending to be a detective while I clean up the mess!"

"Mess? It seems I saved you a lot of time and effort with that decision. And sure, I'll step back and let you be regent." I motioned around my office. "I don't want this bullshit title, and you know it. It's all yours. Good luck getting the coalition leaders to follow you and your integrity." I slammed my food into the trash, no longer hungry. "Should I abdicate now, or do you want a ceremony?"

"I don't want your throne, and you know it." Mat's voice was low and rough.

"Could have fooled me, considering *my little plan* is such a tremendous blow to your integrity that you needed to publicly condescend it."

He stared at me for a long minute. "I apologize for that. I should have held my tongue, and it won't happen again. But I would appreciate you listening to me in the future."

I held up a finger. "I'll consider what you say just like I did this time. Listening to you is not the same as doing what you say. Let me remind you I'm not a child anymore and haven't been for a long time. I appreciate your guidance and protection, and your opinion is always welcome, but I need to be able to spread my wings if I'm going to fly. That includes making some decisions you disagree with. I'd also appreciate it if you belittle and devalue me in private next time instead of in front of other leaders."

He rubbed his face. "Belittling you was not my intention. I'm as angry at you as you are at me. I didn't think."

"Right. So, it's okay if *you* make rash decisions, but I get crushed for mine. Which brings me to your little safety speech after we defeated the demons."

"I shouldn't have said some of those things."

I closed my eyes, exhausted. "You said what you really thought. It's my fault that I didn't know how little you respected me until you made it clear."

"Is that what you think?" The sheer hurt in Mat's voice almost ripped my heart out.

"It's the truth based on what you've shown me. I don't blame you. It's not like I've been a model of maturity. I just...always thought you'd have my back when I took the throne. It hurts to realize you don't. That you think so little of me."

The pain in his eyes told me I'd gone too far, but I didn't have it in me to take it back because it was my truth. He cleared his throat. "That hurts to hear you say. I love you and have thought of you as my own child since the day I pulled you out of that dungeon. I only want what's best for you."

"I know."

"It's not that I don't respect you. You're an adult, yes, but still very young. I want to protect you, even from yourself."

"You can't."

"I'm beginning to realize that." He sighed. "I'm sorry for undermining you at the meeting. It won't happen again. I'm also sorry for treating you terribly while trying to protect you. I only wanted you to be safe."

"And I'm sorry for being so young and impulsive and not listening to you as much as I should. I'm not sorry about doing something about the bellicose or for doing everything within my power to stop that demon."

Mat inclined his head. "Fair enough."

I moved around the desk and hugged him with my whole heart. "I love you. Thank you for everything you've done for me. I will try to do better."

"For the record, I will always be on your side. But I will not stay silent when I think you are needlessly endangering yourself or making a poor decision."

"Fair enough."

Chapter 30

I PRACTICALLY SKIPPED DOWN the street as Tracy and I headed toward our raccoon shifter neighbor's house. I'd never been invited to a neighborhood party before. She carried two huge platters of food we bought from Thaddeus, and I had a box of shiny toys for the kids.

Tracy shifted one of the trays. "Jen, you need to do something to contain your excitement. I mean, this is what normal people do."

"Exactly."

She grinned. "I cannot believe you sometimes. One minute, you're like a child meeting the world for the first time, and the next minute, you're crushing demons and deploying propaganda campaigns. It makes no sense."

"It makes perfect sense to me. I'm required to crush demons and make hard decisions. It's part of the job. I didn't have a childhood. And I only have a short time to live before I become one of those human fairytale princesses locked in a castle. I plan to relish every minute of joy and freedom I can get."

"See, I don't get that. You won't be locked in a castle unless you choose to be."

"Have you met Mat?"

She chuckled. "I don't think he wants to lock you up."

"Could've fooled me. I think he will spend the next couple of years plotting just that."

"I disagree. He will spend the next few years proudly watching you transform into a strong, independent, kick-ass woman. I mean, you have Quin and me to help make that happen."

"I hope you're right."

We stopped at the wards and waited for our neighbor to let us in. One kid raced to the wards and yanked us through. "Mom's in the back. Gotta go."

We made our way around the house. Several neighbors were already there, talking and laughing. A portable magichef sat on her back porch, along with a table of food other neighbors brought. Tracy headed that way while I headed toward Penelope and handed her the toys. "We brought these for your kids."

The raccoon shifter's eyes went wide. "Oh, my. Thank you so much." She dug through the box. "This is very kind of you. Kids! New toys!" She handed them to one of her many kids and turned back to me. "So, aside from the dragon and chimera attack, how are you liking the neighborhood?"

"I love it here. It's a great neighborhood."

She nodded. "It really is. Have you met any of the other neighbors?"

"No, we've been busy and haven't had time."

"I did notice you're gone quite a bit. Come. I'll introduce you around."

My smile grew so big my cheeks hurt.

My delusion of freedom was crushed by the third neighbor she introduced me to. They were all palace guards and their families. I forced a smile and made small talk with everyone, but I was so disappointed that I had a hard time hiding it.

After making the rounds, I grabbed some food and headed toward Tracy, who sat alone. Her eyebrows drew together. "What happened to all that enthusiasm?"

"Mat ruined it, as usual." I glanced around the yard. "Half of these people are palace guards. The other half are their families."

Tracy's eyes darted around. "So?"

"I'm still in a cage. It's just bigger and disguised better."

"I don't think that's true," Tracy whispered back. "It's more that your brother is obsessed and can't help himself. I mean, it doesn't seem to even be about you at this point."

"Doesn't matter. When is it polite to leave one of these things?"

I trudged down the street toward home a couple of hours later, Tracy at my side. I hated my life. Hated being lied to, fooled, and protected. Yeah, I was feeling sorry for myself. So what?

"You need to let this go." Tracy's voice interrupted my pity party.

"I know."

"No, you don't. Have you seen the dragons flying overhead at regular intervals?"

I glanced up at the sky, my eyes drifting to the roof across the street from our house. I *had* noticed that dragons regularly patrolled this neighborhood since we took down the demon. "Is that Bastien's way of protecting you?"

"Yeah. Mat's not the only one who's overprotective. At least they give us enough space, ya know? It could be much worse."

I sighed. "You're right. I just can't help feeling like…like…I don't know, betrayed? Penned in? It sucks that I had this delusion that I was going to be free. Maybe meet some real people. Not a single person in this neighborhood, other than the raccoon shifters, are regular people."

"I'm pretty sure she's a plant, too, since raccoon shifters are excellent spies. But there's nothing wrong with getting to know the palace guards and their families. They're regular paranormals, for the most part."

"I suppose."

Tracy snorted. "Besides, it doesn't matter. It's not like we're going to be here much, anyway. Let the guys have their fantasy that they're protecting us and ignore it. Trust me when I say it's the best way to handle things like this."

I followed Tracy through our wards, a little less sad as I considered her words. I smacked right into her back when she came to a sudden stop and peered around her shoulder to see why she stopped.

Quin sat on the front steps wearing dark sunglasses and one of his usual pristine suits. "Hey, Quin," Tracy said as we approached. "What brings you here?"

Quin stood. "Have fun at your little shindig?"

"Not really. What do you want?" I asked.

"I want an apprentice that answers my texts, but that is not reality, so here I am, wasting my time waiting for you while you party."

"Uh-huh. And you're here because...?"

"I've got a lead on the one the Bellicose calls king. It will take me away for a short time. It appears the demon you destroyed is not the only one."

"Damn. I hoped they only had one demon."

"Just because you live in a state of denial does not mean everyone else does. Your brother insists I solve this case as fast as possible. He fears their attacks will only ramp up."

I ran a hand through my hair. "I thought we had more time."

"Of course you did." Quin's tone couldn't have been drier.

"Where do you think this king is, and what are his plans?"

Quin's lip twitched. "Since you cannot help yourself from poaching my cases, the regent requested I keep certain information from you. I am looking into a disruption among the shifters."

I sighed. "I don't want to poach your case, so that's fine. From now on, I'll stick with smaller, less complicated cases. What's wrong with the shifters?"

Quin blinked. "It is my case, detective. Do try to choose cases wisely and remember our agreement." He disappeared.

Tracy and I melted onto the sofa as soon as we entered the house. "Are you sure you want to pull back from big cases, Jen?"

"Yeah. I think it's for the best. My goal isn't to be a successful detective. I only want to know what makes people tick so I can rule better when I reenter captivity."

She snorted. "What are you going to do about Drake?"

"There's nothing to do about Drake."

"Coulda fooled me. Wanna watch a movie?"

"Yeah."

Chapter 31

Drake leaned against the chimney in his human form. He'd used his best cloaking magic, but she still looked his way. Not even her grandmother, Lissa, could find him when he was cloaked. But then, he didn't have a bond with Lissa. Jenella didn't realize that she'd chosen him. Rather, that uncontrollable magic of hers did. He rejected it twice, but it was persistent, and he accepted it the third time.

He couldn't decide if it was the smartest thing he'd ever done or the dumbest. Probably the latter, considering that Jenella would see their bond as a shackle. She had her end of the bond locked down so tight that he couldn't even monitor her wellbeing. Dragon bonds were powerful and came with an unavoidable compulsion. Mate bonds even more so, no matter how weak. Because of that compulsion, he'd been reduced to sitting on a roof and watching over her. It was humiliating. It was another thing that would anger her when she learned about it.

Bastien, also cloaked, circled twice, and landed on the roof of the house next door. He knew his cousin was looking for him for the last two weeks. Drake also knew Bastien couldn't see through his cloaking magic unless he allowed it. Drake rubbed his face and decided to allow it. He included his cousin in his cloaking. *What do you want, cousin?*

You need to tell her.

I don't believe I asked your opinion.

She deserves to know. And you are too noble and powerful to be reduced to a lovesick stalker.

He heard the humor in Bastien's voice, though they both knew the situation wasn't funny. *The one thing Jenella wants most in life is freedom. I cannot set her free from her obligations, so this is the best I can do.*

Bastien lowered his huge black head. *I disagree. She values the truth as much as freedom.*

Perhaps. She will not be happy when she learns about the bond.

She still needs to know the truth.

She needs time to know I won't trap her.

What you are doing now is not healthy for either of you. You need to tell her.

Drake glanced back at Jenella's house. She wasn't going anywhere, and he had his fill of advice from his cousin. He re-cloaked himself, shifted into his dragon form, and launched into the air.

He made a loophole in Jenella's house and castle wards to let himself in when he added his magic. At first, it was to spy on her to ensure she didn't follow in her mother's footsteps and become a tyrant. Now that he understood her better, he wasn't worried about that. Instead, he used them to ensure she was safe and to spy on Mathias. Jenella's brother knew more about the Bellicose than he'd told anyone, including Jenella. It didn't sit right that the Regent was hiding so much from her, not that he had any room to talk.

With a sigh, Drake dipped down toward the castle of Ahl and shifted back to his human form. He slipped through the ward and made his way past the castle guards and toward Mathias's office. Mathias exited his office and strode to the waiting area to greet Tarquin. Drake slipped into the office, moved to the far corner, and sat behind a plant.

"I do not know if she'll stay out of it. Jen is unpredictable and does as she pleases. She indicated that she would take safer cases. That is all I know." Tarquin's voice held a ring of pride when he talked about Jenella.

"Good." Mathias sat behind his desk and rubbed his face. "Make sure you warn her regularly about poaching your cases. It bothers her that she got involved and may act as a deterrent. If she does take a dangerous case, you need to take it from her. She doesn't know what she's doing."

Tarquin's shoulders tensed at that statement. "You are wrong. Jen is brave and thinks things through more than you know. It is her confidence that is lacking, or perhaps your confidence in her. I cannot decide which."

"She said the same thing." Mathias ran a hand through his hair. "I can't do anything right by her these days. My insistence that she stay safe has pushed her in the other direction. Now she is acting like a rebellious teenager."

"Jen is young and asserting herself, but is hardly rebellious. I remember a certain prince that was worse," Tarquin said. "Perhaps she is better protected than you think. The First is watching over her."

Rage flashed through Mathias's eyes. "What does he want with Jen?"

"I am not the foremost authority on Drake the First. I simply know his essence is all over her neighborhood."

Drake's fists clenched and unclenched. He knew Tarquin was perceptive but didn't know he could read essence. He forced himself to relax. It wasn't like either Mathias or Tarquin could do anything about it. Drake was far too powerful. It wouldn't stop Mathias from trying, though. And that would hurt Jenella, which was unacceptable. She'd been hurt enough in her life.

Mathias rubbed his chin. "He likes Jen. I'll touch base with Deva to ensure he is an extra layer of protection and not a threat. What have you found out about the Bellicose King?"

"There was a laboratory in the human world where they worked on their spells. I destroyed it. I do not have Jen's skill set to put entire towns to sleep and steal documents, but I sent you what I got from there. Tracy would be a good consultant should you want to uncover the spells' intentions."

A smile grew on Drake's face at Tarquin's reminder of Jenella and Tracy's power. Mathias didn't feel the sheer burning power that Jenella kept tucked away. He didn't realize just how powerful Jenella was. No, he thought her magic was broken. He'd even convinced her that there was something wrong. It wasn't broken. Drake could feel the giant pool of it inside of her. No, she simply needed it to fuse, which it would when the time was right.

"I am unsure Tracy is the right person to call," Mathias said, drawing Drake's attention back to the conversation.

"Oh yes. Let's hire an inferior witch when we have the most powerful one on call. After all, keeping Jen ignorant has worked out so well for you."

"She needs to focus on fixing her magic."

"I do not care. I am simply pointing out your mistake so you can learn from it."

Mathias shook his head. "I'll talk to Tracy."

"I believe the one they refer to as a king is a puppet for someone much more ruthless and powerful." Tarquin's fangs extended. "I believe your mother is the puppet master."

Drake almost jumped to his feet. Jenella said her parents had died. She *believed* her parents were dead. If the second queen was still alive, he could get his revenge. The urge to hunt sang through his soul. He closed his eyes and took a deep breath.

"How big a threat is she?" Mathias didn't even flinch, which told Drake he knew she was alive.

"To Jenella? Not much. She is...diminished. To the coalition?" Tarquin shrugged a shoulder. "I will find her and this king if you wish."

When the two broke up the meeting, Drake slipped out of the castle and took to the air. He gave in to the call to hunt and headed toward the human world.

The End (for now).

Before you go...

For authors, reviews mean everything. Please take time to post a review on Amazon.

Want to read about Jen's next adventure? Bug Magic (The Paranormals of Ahl Book 2) is available on Amazon.

Sign up for my newsletter at www.mlconklin.com to stay up to date on upcoming releases.

With that out of the way, I'd like to thank everyone who helped me with this book. The editors, proofreaders, beta readers, ARC readers, and cover designers at getcovers.com were all wonderful to work with and helped Jen fly. I'd also like to thank my family because they are amazing.

A special shoutout to my cats, Callie and Gracie, for keeping my laptop warm and improving the story with long strings of letters and numbers when I took a break without closing the file. And my dog, Zorro, for insisting that I take those breaks to let him in and out.

Finally, thank you, the brave reader who took a chance on a new author and battled your way to the end of the book.

Cheers.
ML Conklin